Praise for C.J. Darlington

"We at the Christian Writers Guild couldn't be prouder of our First Novel Contest winner. This one engages your senses and reaches your heart."

JERRY B. JENKINS, novelist and owner, Christian Writers Guild

"Great job! You kept me turning the pages."

FRANCINE RIVERS, *New York Times* best-selling author

"C.J. is a wonderful, talented writer . . . extraordinary. . . ."

BODIE THOENE, award-winning author of the A.D. Chronicles

"Thanks for taking on the all-too-familiar subjects of guilt, rejection, and loss in a story line that offers hope and healing through forgiveness!"

JENNIFER O'NEILL, actress, author, speaker

"*Bound by Guilt* is a beautifully told story with complicated characters who linger long after the last page is turned. C.J. Darlington is one of those writers who get better with every book. After reading this heartfelt novel, I'm more eager than ever to see what she writes next."

SIBELLA GIORELLO, Christy Award–winning author of *The Stones Cry Out*

"C.J. Darlington's *Bound by Guilt* is a fresh tale of broken lives, the longing for completion, the hard binding of guilt . . . and the power of forgiveness. Every reader will find a part of his or her own life within these covers."

TOSCA LEE, author of *Demon: A Memoir*

BOUND *by* GUILT

BOUND

by

GUILT

——— ❧ ———

C.J. DARLINGTON

TYNDALE HOUSE PUBLISHERS, INC.
CAROL STREAM, ILLINOIS

Visit Tyndale's exciting Web site at www.tyndale.com.

Visit C.J. Darlington's Web site at www.cjdarlington.com.

TYNDALE and Tyndale's quill logo are registered trademarks of Tyndale House Publishers, Inc.

Bound by Guilt

Designed by Jennifer Ghionzoli

Edited by Kathryn S. Olson

Scripture taken from the Holy Bible, *New International Version,*® *NIV.*® Copyright © 1973, 1978, 1984 by Biblica, Inc.™ Used by permission of Zondervan. All rights reserved worldwide. www.zondervan.com.

This novel is a work of fiction. Names, characters, places, and incidents either are the product of the author's imagination or are used fictitiously. Any resemblance to actual events, locales, organizations, or persons living or dead is entirely coincidental and beyond the intent of either the author or the publisher.

Library of Congress Cataloging-in-Publication Data

Darlington, C. J.
  Bound by guilt / C.J. Darlington.
    p. cm.
  ISBN 978-1-4143-4012-8 (pbk.)
  1. Foster children—Fiction.   2. Theft—Fiction. I. Title.
  PS3604.A747B68 2011
  813'.6—dc22
                                                   2010040226

Printed in the United States of America

17 16 15 14 13 12 11
7 6 5 4 3 2 1

For Tracy

My sister, best friend, and biggest fan.

Your genuine interest and constant support mean the world.

Acknowledgments

First and foremost, thank You, God, for allowing me to share another story with readers. Help me to never forget that all good things come from You. May my words bring You honor.

Mom—you're an awesome first editor! There's no way I could have written this book without your help. We make a great team, and I'm so thankful you've come alongside me in this exciting journey. I really had to do my research when I wrote the bad mother figures in this book because I certainly couldn't draw from personal experience!

Papa—one of my fondest memories writing *Bound by Guilt* is when you read my rough draft out loud around that Idaho campfire and helped me brainstorm the ending. I'm blessed to have you on my team! Thanks for being a fantastic first reader.

Tracy—for always lending a listening ear. Your enthusiasm and tireless promotion spur me on, and your loyalty is something I never want to take for granted. Love you, Sis!

Jan Stob—it's such a blessing to have the best in the business as my editor. Thanks so much for your encouragement and support. And thanks for brainstorming until you came up with the perfect book title.

Kathy Olson—your keen editorial insights have made this book stronger. Thanks for going the extra mile to work with me on making this manuscript the best it can be. What an honor to have the chance to work with you.

Babette Rea—for answering all my numerous questions, coming up with fantastic ideas, and helping me spread the word to the masses!

Stephanie Broene, Karen Watson, Vicky Lynch, Jennifer Ghionzoli, Christy Wong, and the other fabulous people at Team Tyndale—you guys rock! I'm excited to do this again with you.

James Scott Bell—for giving so freely of your time to answer my questions and offer much-needed wisdom. I look to your books for how to do it right.

Sibella Giorello—your kindness has picked me up on the days when the words wouldn't flow. Thank you for your transparency and honesty. I look forward to reading anything that comes from your pen.

Jerry B. Jenkins—I wouldn't even be on this journey if it weren't for your generosity. You model the humility I aspire to possess. Thank you for nurturing the writing gifts of so many.

Pam & Frank Lione (writing as F. P. Lione)—for reading this manuscript (at the gym, no less!) for police procedure accuracy. Any mistakes are mine.

Diana Prusik, Candace Calvert, Marti Pieper, Jennifer Erin Valent, and Jan Watson—for wonderful inspiration, cheering words, and advice when I needed it most!

1

"DON'T YOU EVER FEEL GUILTY?" Roxi Gold cracked open her icy can of Dr Pepper and took a long sip.

Diego fell into the seat across from her at the RV's dinette table, opening his own can. Fizz erupted over its side. He licked it away and took a big gulp. "Not like we're hurting anybody."

"No, we're just stealing thousand-dollar books."

Diego eyed her. "You getting cold feet?"

She bent the silver tab of her soda can back and forth until it broke off in her fingers. A warm breeze blew through the window screen and filled her nose with the scent of dry pine needles. Could that be it? She just didn't have the guts?

"Any idea how lucky you are?" Diego leaned back, lacing his fingers behind his head. "Nothing but the wind at our back, the open road before us . . ."

Roxi managed a smile. He was right. For the past three weeks she'd been traveling with her seventeen-year-old second cousin and his mom, Irene. The thirty-foot RV was like an apartment on wheels. She'd been to places other people only saw on the Internet, experiencing things she'd never forget. Not all of them were earth-shattering, Grand Canyon moments, either. In Flagstaff, Arizona, she'd seen her first bald eagle perched high in a rustic pine, majestic and totally unreal. She even rode in an Amish buggy in Lancaster, Pennsylvania.

"This is our life," Diego said, raking his hands through his black hair. "And it sure beats standing in line at a book sale for three days like we used to."

"Doesn't it ever bother you?"

He chugged down more soda, then belched. "Nope."

"What if we get caught?"

"Come on, Rox."

"They'd send me back to juvie."

Diego leaned forward, both hands holding his drink. "Listen, we're okay. We're not gonna be caught. Ma's careful."

She downed half of her Dr Pepper in one shot just to keep herself from blabbing. She didn't want Diego to know how she really felt.

"Why the change?" he asked. "I thought you were into this."

"I am; it's just . . . I don't know."

"Well, you better get a hold of yourself before Ma comes back."

Roxi blew air out of her mouth in frustration. Why couldn't she be more like Diego? Hungry for adventure. Strong under pressure. More than anything she didn't want to disappoint Irene. Because of her, Roxi had seen half the country this summer. How many sixteen-year-olds could say that?

"I've got a surprise for you," Diego said.

"You're making dinner?"

"Surprise, not shock." He pulled a slip of paper from the back pocket of his Levis, handing it to her with a grin. "I was gonna wait till your birthday, but I think you need it now."

"Wow. I've always wanted a piece of paper."

"Just read it."

Roxi unfolded the sheet. *Marie Greeley. 1264 Poplar Lane. Amarillo, TX.* She looked at Diego. "Is this supposed to mean something?"

He got serious. "Remember when we were talking about your mom? how you wished you knew where she was?"

Marie. That was Mom's name.

"I did some searching online, and I think I found her."

"But her last name . . . ?"

"Looks like she married a guy named Tom Greeley."

Roxi's mouth went dry. She hadn't heard from her mother in eight years, and she wasn't sure she wanted to now. Mom was married? Roxi didn't even know who her bio dad was, and now she had a stepfather?

She got up from the table and rested her back against the fridge a few feet away. The RV was designed to utilize every inch. Even the table where Diego still sat folded down to become her bed at night.

"She ditched me. Why would I care where she is?"

"Because she's your mom."

"Like that meant anything to her."

"Hey, people do dumb stuff." Diego crumpled his empty can with one hand and pitched it into the plastic trash bag they kept rubber-banded to a cabinet knob.

Roxi crossed her arms. "Not even a phone call?"

"You don't have to do anything with it now, Rox." He slid out from behind the table and opened the microwave, pulling out a bag of chips. With space at a premium, they used it more for storage than for cooking. And Irene never used it. She swore microwaves were bad for their health and mutated food.

Roxi stuffed the paper into her back pocket. Sometimes Diego could be annoyingly macho and cocky, but other times he surprised her. Like now. She'd tried to dig up this information herself a few years ago and found nothing.

"Thanks," Roxi said.

Ripping open the chips, Diego held them out to her, but she shook her head. She definitely wasn't hungry anymore. "I'm taking a walk."

"Ma should be back soon."

Which meant Irene would want to talk to both of them about tomorrow's plans, something Roxi didn't want to think about. She'd get some fresh air. Maybe things would look better after that.

She swung open the RV's door, bounded down the three metal stairs, and slammed the door behind her. This was one of the nicer campgrounds. No screaming kids or low-life slobs leering at her from their lounge chairs. The Fall River was within walking distance. Up here in Rocky Mountain National Park, late August was usually the height of tourist season, but for some reason, today there weren't many other campers. Just a few full-time RVers with satellite dishes mounted on $200,000 rigs. The place would probably be packed over the weekend.

She headed for the river and sat at the water's edge, knees to her chest. Living with Irene and Diego was better than any of the foster homes she'd been placed in over the years. The last one had two other guys her age living in the house. One afternoon she'd come home from school to find they were the only ones home, as usual, since both parents worked. The moment she walked into the kitchen and saw their faces, she knew what they planned to do to her. That split second of intuition saved her. She dropped her backpack right there and ran away. Never went back. Three days later the cops picked her up for shoplifting from a grocery store, and she'd spent a month in juvie. Finally her caseworker placed her in a group home. Only after she got beat up for the third time did they manage to find a relative willing to take her in. Irene Tonelli was her mom's cousin, and Roxi thought living with the Tonellis was the best thing that ever could've happened to her. Diego wasn't like those other guys, and she finally felt like she belonged somewhere.

Roxi heard the trill of a broad-tailed hummingbird's wings, then caught sight of the bird diving toward the rushing stream. All her life she'd prayed for a family. She used to imagine she'd wake up one morning and find everything had been a dream, and she really did have a mom and dad who loved her. Straightening her legs, she stared at the deep blue sky visible through the treetops. But no, this was her life. She shouldn't complain. Irene needed her to be a team player.

Swallowing back her emotions, she unbuttoned the cuff of her left sleeve and slowly rolled it up. With each flip of the fabric, more of her scar came into view. From wrist to elbow, a thick purple line wormed across her arm. She'd been eight when the glass had etched her with this eternal reminder of the night she lost Mom.

The night that changed her life forever.

2

People always stared when Abby Dawson walked into Starbucks, but she was used to it. Something about a cop in uniform compelled people to gawk.

She ordered her usual grande red eye, coffee with a shot of espresso for an extra kick, added three Splendas, then took it back to the patrol car. Now was as good a time as any to call Kat. After that scare last week when Kat had collapsed in the middle of the school cafeteria, Abby just needed to hear her daughter's voice.

Besides, a girl turned sixteen only once in her life. Abby had mailed a card and a crisp hundred-dollar bill. Maybe this time Kat would actually get it. Last year Michael had returned her card unopened.

Abby pulled out her cell phone and held down speed dial 2.

"Hello?"

Abby tensed at the sound of Sarah's voice. It was no surprise

Michael had fallen for her. Petite, blonde, cute. Everything Abby wasn't. Did Kat call her Mom?

"Hi, Sarah. It's Abby. Is Kat there?"

"She's got some friends over."

Abby softened her voice. "I just want to talk for a few minutes." She hesitated, then forced herself to add, "If that's okay."

"I can't make her talk to you."

"Can you just tell her it's me?"

A pause. Sarah sighed. "Hold on."

The phone clunked on something hard. Abby heard footsteps, then Sarah's voice yelling, "Your mother's on the phone!"

Would Kat pick up? She hadn't last time.

"Mom?"

Abby's insides melted at the sound of Kat's voice. "Happy birthday, sweetie."

She wanted to add "How are you feeling?" but didn't. The doctors had concluded nothing was wrong with Kat and chalked it up to stress at school. Of course that didn't stop Abby from worrying. Was her daughter eating enough?

"Guess what? Dad bought me a car."

Good old Michael. "Really? What kind?"

"A red Jeep. It's sweet."

And what had Abby given her? A lousy hundred bucks. Somehow she had a feeling "it's the thought that counts" would be lost on a teenager. Everything in her wanted to bad-mouth Michael and win Kat over, to somehow woo her daughter into the relationship Abby wished they had. But she held back. That would put Kat in the middle, something Abby vowed never to do.

"Where are you?" Kat asked.

As if on cue, Abby's radio squawked to life. The dispatcher broadcast a 10-57, a hit and run, on the other side of the city. She quickly turned down the volume. Kat used to have nightmares about her getting killed in the line of duty, so she'd tried to downplay her job over the years.

"Outside Starbucks right now."

And where was Kat? An hour and a half away in Michael and Sarah's mansion on a hill overlooking Utah Lake, probably wishing Abby would just leave her alone. Last week when Kat collapsed, Abby hadn't been called until they'd already released her. She hadn't gotten to be with her daughter or kiss her forehead and tell her everything would be okay. She hadn't been able to be her mother at all.

"Mom, I've gotta go."

Abby pictured Kat glancing across the room at Sarah, who was probably monitoring every word on the other phone like she'd done before.

"Okay, honey." She thought she heard a door slam in the background. Maybe Michael was home early. "I love—"

"Bye."

Abby stared at the phone. *Call ended.*

She let out a long breath. It was so easy to blame Michael. He'd fought tooth and nail for sole custody six years ago. Not because he wanted Kat more, but because he wanted to hurt *her*. And thanks to his Provo law partners, he'd gotten his way. For some foul, crazy reason, her daughter was being raised by another woman.

❧

Irene pulled the minivan into the parking lot of Dawson's Book Barn, and Roxi got a clear view of the barn-turned-used-bookstore. Plaster was chipped around its windows. A mound of split wood was stacked on the porch, and a cart of books sat by the door. Probably bargain stock they were trying to move quickly.

She undid her seat belt as the van came to a stop. According to their Web site, it was one of only a few stone barns listed in Colorado's register of historical properties, and for that alone it was a landmark. Built in 1903 and four stories tall, over 300,000 volumes called it home.

Irene twisted around in the driver's seat. "You guys ready?"

Roxi nodded and got out, not waiting to hear Diego's response. He was in his element and would no doubt be raring to go. Like she should be. But the apprehension was working through her stomach again, just like yesterday. This was no place for it. She had a job to do—one that required her full concentration. All it would take to be caught was one slip of the tongue or a clumsy move.

Mother and son joined her at the store's entrance, Diego giving her an encouraging pat on the shoulder. Then it was showtime, and the familiar thrill of danger took over. If she could just feed off that, she'd be okay. After this they could go back home to Cheyenne, and she could prepare herself for school starting next week.

The first thing Roxi noticed was the mountain of books on a huge table in the middle of the room. She thought she saw Collier's complete set of O. Henry's works and a stack of dust-jacketed Nancy Drews just asking to topple. It struck her how silent the room was, like a library, except for the rhythmic ticking of a clock somewhere nearby. The faint odor of wood smoke drifted to her nose, mixing with the old-book smell of yellowed leaves and dry leather.

A woman stood up from a laptop computer perched on the corner of the table. She was dressed casually, like many of the book dealers Roxi had met this year, in jeans and a sweatshirt.

"Oh, hello," the clerk said to Irene with a cheerful smile. "Glad you decided to come back."

The day before, Irene had visited the store alone to scope things out and plan their modus operandi. With a store this size, she liked to get the lay of the land.

Irene smiled back at the clerk. "I knew these guys would love it here."

"Can I help you find anything?"

"Actually, yeah," Diego said, giving Roxi's arm a playful punch. "Sis here's doing some research for a school paper. Science stuff."

Roxi returned his punch as if she really were his sister. "And Bro's dying for another Stephen King."

The woman left her computer and came toward them. "Fiction's in the first room on your left. It's all alphabetized. But science is up on the fourth floor."

Roxi made a practiced confused face. "Could you show me?"

"Sure." The clerk gestured for Roxi to follow her down the low-ceilinged hallway that led to the rest of the store. "It's a hike, but we've got a good selection up there."

Actually, science was the furthest section from downstairs as possible. Which was exactly why Irene had told them to ask for it. They took turns with the diverter role, but Roxi got it more than Diego, and today they'd decided she would be the one to distract the clerk. Stores like this usually didn't have many employees, and no one ever questioned their innocent family facade. If she could keep a clerk busy long enough, Irene and Diego would have enough time to take a valuable book or two. Just one could pay for their trip if they turned it around quickly. A lot of stores kept their most expensive titles under lock and key, but often a few rarities would be displayed within the customer's reach. That's what they banked on, and it's why Irene had visited this place yesterday. They needed to know what to go for. It was the best way they could be in and out before someone noticed any books were missing. Irene's purse was large enough to conceal a standard-size hardcover book, and Diego's backpack could hold several more.

The clerk led Roxi up a short flight of stairs.

"So how long have you been working here?" Roxi asked. Small talk was always a good time eater.

"Six years."

"Like it?"

"You bet. My name's Christy, by the way. Watch your head." Christy pointed toward the low doorframe at the top of the stairs, where a painted sign declared *Duck or Grouse*. She was probably in her thirties and growing out a blonde dye job by the looks of her dark roots.

Clomping up two more flights, Roxi followed Christy through room after book-lined room. All the floors were made of uneven wooden planks, some with knotholes big enough to catch a view of the floor below. So far she'd given Irene and Diego about a minute. She could only hope some other employee downstairs hadn't shown up offering his services to them. That would throw a wrench into everything.

Christy finally reached the fourth floor. She brought Roxi to a corner of the first room, where a wall of shelves was labeled Science & Nature.

"Here you go," Christy said. "Looking for anything specific?"

Roxi hesitated. If she said "no" or "I'll just browse," that would free Christy to return to the entrance room.

"What's your paper about?"

She hadn't rehearsed anything with Diego, and him spouting off like that about a science paper had caught her off guard.

"Einstein."

"Here's a nice biography." Christy pulled out a four-hundred-plus-page book titled simply *Einstein: A Life* by Denis Brian. She blew the dust from the top page edges with a *poof* and handed it to Roxi.

"Have you read it?" Roxi asked.

"No, but I've heard it's good."

Roxi paged through the thick book hoping to drag this out. She waved her hand toward the rest of the shelves. "These in any sort of order?"

"They should be, but sometimes things get mixed up." Christy ran her fingers across the spines of the nearest titles. "It's general science along here."

Roxi spotted two copies of *Cosmos* by Carl Sagan—that thing was everywhere—and at least three copies of *A Brief History of Time* by Stephen Hawking. Both too heady for her.

"Things get more technical this way," Christy said, following the shelf to Roxi's right. "Different theories and stuff. Here's Einstein's book on the theory of relativity." She plucked a light blue dust-jacketed book from the shelf. "Is this more what you're looking for?"

"Uh, maybe. Yeah."

Christy handed her that book too, smiling, which made Roxi's insides twist with guilt. This lady believed she was just a teen girl doing research.

"Well, I'll leave you to your browsing. I'll be downstairs if you need any more help."

Roxi's pulse kicked up a notch. She couldn't let the clerk go back too soon, but if she stopped her, wouldn't that look suspicious? She glanced at her watch, a cheap plastic thing she'd picked up at a thrift store a couple of weeks ago with Diego. Four minutes. That was enough, right?

Christy's footsteps faded. And then it was quiet except for the hum of the fluorescent lights. Leaning her forehead against the spines of some old green McGraw-Hill textbooks with titles like *Organic Chemistry* and *An Introduction to Physics*, Roxi closed her eyes. *Please be enough time.*

She needed to move. But instead she stayed where she was. Hitting stores like this used to be a huge thrill. When Irene had finally trusted her enough to let her in on their secret business, it seemed like the chance of a lifetime. With their ability to travel in the RV towing the minivan, they could sell books wholesale to another store states away or even list them online themselves with the laptop. But lately it was all becoming more than she could handle. She hated the way guilt crept up on her like this.

Returning the Einstein books to the shelf, she quickly started downstairs. At least this was their last stop. After this they could go home for a while. She lost a good minute winding her way back to the entrance room, and when she finally burst into it, she was out of breath and wondering where in the world Irene and Diego were. For one moment Roxi let herself enjoy the store's ambiance. The potbellied stove in the corner, the rainbow of book spines crowding every shelf, the ticking of the antique clock she now saw sitting above the front door. If things were different, if *she* were different, every book in a store like this could be a potential treasure. As it was, every one was a target.

"Done so soon?"

Roxi jumped at the voice, then saw clerk Christy, a pencil between her teeth, reaching for a book in the front window display. Should she look for Irene and Diego? Maybe they were waiting for her in the van.

Think fast.

"Didn't find much."

Christy slipped the pencil behind her ear, walked over to the counter, and picked up a business card. "Give me a call if you ever have a specific title I can look for. We get new stuff almost every day."

Roxi joined the clerk at the counter and managed a weak smile. She took the business card and glanced at the display case beside the register. Customers could see right down into it as they paid for their purchases. She stared at a copy of *The Great Gatsby* with its weird blue cover depicting eyes and a mouth hovering over an amusement park.

"Is that a first edition?" she asked, tapping the glass above the *Gatsby*.

"Sure is. Wanna see it?" Christy pulled a set of keys from a drawer under the cash register. They jingled as she unlocked the case's sliding back panel.

Even though chatting with this clerk wasn't in the plans, Roxi nodded. It still fascinated her what books were considered rare.

Christy reached in and removed the *Gatsby*. Its dust jacket was protected in a clear Brodart protective cover, and Christy cradled the book like it could break in her hands. She held it out to Roxi.

When she hesitated, Christy smiled. "It's okay. What's a book good for if you can't touch it?"

Roxi finally took it, turning it around in her hands.

"Look at the back flap of the dust jacket."

The Brodart crinkled as Roxi carefully opened the book.

"In 1925, when this was first printed," Christy said, "Jay Gatsby's name was accidentally spelled with a lowercase *j* on the back flap of the dust jacket." Christy pointed at the error. "See it there? Not many of those original jackets survived. I'd never seen one before, myself. We bought this copy from a collector who'd kept it safely packed away for years. It has a few flaws. I know it doesn't look like much, but you're holding a treasure right there."

She was about to ask how much it was worth when she heard Irene's and Diego's voices in the hallway. Roxi quickly handed the *Gatsby* back, and Christy returned it to the case.

When Irene and Diego walked into the room, Irene came up behind Roxi and squeezed her shoulder three times. The signal to get out.

"Ready to go, dear?" Irene asked. She only called her "dear" when they were around other people. Roxi managed a nod.

Christy rang up Diego's purchases—more horror titles to add to his collection by the look of the covers. Stephen King really was his favorite author, and they always tried to buy something at the stores to further strengthen their cover. If Roxi had been concentrating at all, she would've brought that Einstein book down.

"Have a nice day," Christy said.

And then the three of them walked out. Just like that. No one suspecting anything. Another store a little lighter, and more money in Irene's pocket.

Only when they were in the van again did Roxi ask how they did.

Diego groaned. "Lousy. I got one book." He pulled it out of his backpack and showed it to her. *Farmer Giles of Ham* by J. R. R. Tolkien. "It's a first American edition, the jacket isn't price-clipped, and it's in decent shape. But still. We're talking fifty bucks wholesale. If we're lucky. And I spent ten."

"That's it?"

"There was barely time to grab that," Irene said, eyeing Roxi in the rearview mirror.

Roxi sank a little into her seat. "What happened?"

"You were supposed to give us more time."

"I tried, but I couldn't think of anything to say. I thought it would make me look suspicious asking questions."

"She had no reason to suspect you."

Roxi stared at the scuffed toes of her roper boots, then looked up again. She had to act more confident. She wanted to pull her weight in this family and make Irene proud of her.

Diego threw back a sympathetic look. "Better luck next time, eh?"

"I'm sorry, Irene. I'll do better. I promise."

Irene kept driving, and Roxi's throat tightened. Couldn't she do anything right?

The older woman drove the van out onto the road. "I'm starting to wonder if bringing you along was a good idea."

"I'm really sorry."

"Ma, cut her a break. Our luck'll be better next time."

Irene glanced in the rearview mirror again. This time Roxi didn't meet her eyes.

"Luck has nothing to do with this. We've lost two days, and what do we have to show for it? A fifty-dollar book."

"So let's go back," Diego said.

"We might have to."

Roxi straightened in her seat. "But you said that was a bad idea. If they find a book missing and put two and two—"

Diego swung around in the passenger seat, warning her with his eyes to shut up. "Ma knows what she's doing."

"You had four minutes!"

"Rox—"

"If she'd done *her* job, we'd have more than one lousy book."

Diego slowly turned around and stared out the windshield, and the silence in the car spread like a dense fog. Roxi glanced at the side of Irene's face, already regretting her stupid words. She'd never talked back like that before.

Irene's freckle-spritzed hands gripped the steering wheel harder than necessary, but she said nothing. In fact, no one said anything else the whole ride back to the campground.

3

"WHAT'S TAKING HER SO LONG?"

From the RV's window, Roxi craned to see down the road. An hour had passed since Irene left for one of her walks. She took them for exercise and thinking time, whenever the weather and their schedule cooperated. But she usually wasn't gone longer than twenty minutes.

"Who knows?" Diego said, flipping a page of *Firestarter* by Stephen King. He lay reading on his back in the bed above the front seats. He called it his "loft," and more than once he'd dropped a pillow on her head in the middle of the night.

"She's mad at me."

Diego snorted, his eyes still glued to his book. "She'll get over it. Did you know there were only 725 copies in the first printing of *Firestarter*, and King signed them all?"

Roxi undid her ponytail and let her dark brunette hair fall to her shoulders. "Wasn't there some limited print run too?"

"Yeah, the asbestos edition. It was bound in this aluminum-coated asbestos cloth. And there were just twenty-six of them made. Can you imagine how much they're worth? I'd love to get my hands on one of them."

Roxi leaned back into the sofa. She'd tried so hard to please Irene these past few months, and sometimes she actually had. Like at that store in Ohio where she'd managed to nab a rare Tarzan novel they turned the next day for five hundred. Irene had given her a twenty-dollar bonus for that one.

"What am I doing wrong?"

Diego didn't answer, and she wondered if he'd even heard the question. Then slowly he rested the open book on his chest, one arm hanging over the edge of the bed. "Nothing," he said. "But you know how it is. Three weeks packed in this thing like sardines gets to you after a while."

Roxi gathered her hair up again, looping the rubber band around it four times. It would be easy to chalk everything up to travel fatigue, but somehow she knew the real reason. Despite her best efforts to mask her doubts about what they were doing, she obviously hadn't succeeded. Irene knew. And Roxi's hesitation was becoming a risk to their little family business.

"Things'll be better when we get home," Diego said.

She kept thinking she should stay behind at the campground and let Irene and Diego do the stealing. She didn't mind being alone. After all, she'd spent half her life taking care of herself. But as much as she wanted to, she didn't dare suggest it. She didn't want Irene to think she was ungrateful, that she wasn't willing to help.

Sinking into the sofa, she tucked her knees beneath her chin. She had to contribute. Her greatest fear was ending up in the system again, unwanted, shuttled around like a hot potato at a kid's birthday party. It lurked beneath everything she did, and more than anything, it motivated her to make this work. She'd just have to start thinking of creative ways to justify everything in her mind. She could always pretend she was like Robin Hood.

"Okay, maybe there is something." Diego propped himself up on an elbow and looked at her, wagging his finger. "Stop acting so nervous. You gotta just go with the flow. Move with that adrenaline."

"I'll try."

"No, you have to *do*. Otherwise, you will get caught."

She smirked. "That's encouraging."

He flopped onto his back, returning to his book. "You were good, Rox. Potential galore. Get that back."

"I'll be outside." Grabbing a Dr Pepper from the fridge, she planted herself at the picnic table to wait for Irene. She didn't have to wait long. Five minutes later, Irene, dressed in a dark blue exercise suit with white stripes down the legs, arrived back at the campsite.

"Hi," Irene said.

Roxi scooted over on the bench to make room for her.

"This campground is beautiful." Irene sat beside Roxi. "I'm glad we were able to stay up here a few days."

Roxi nodded. She and Diego had lobbied hard to be able to dry camp up here in Estes Park rather than down in Longmont at the campground with hookups where Irene wanted to stay. It meant keeping close tabs on the thirty-gallon water supply and running the generator on a daily basis to keep the RV's two batteries charged, but they thought the view and fresh mountain air were worth the trouble, and Irene finally gave in.

Roxi picked at the splintering wood of the picnic table, not sure what to say. Would Irene make her apologize for what she'd said in the van?

"Our plans have changed," Irene said. "We're hitting the Book Barn again."

All Roxi could do was stare at the table, unable to respond. If she did, it would only give away her worry and fear. Irene would appreciate neither.

"What are you thinking?" Irene's voice was suddenly gentle.

Roxi glanced at Irene's face. The woman's auburn mane was thick and dark—what Roxi wished her own hair was like. A few small age spots mixed with the freckles on her face. But those green eyes could pierce right through Roxi sometimes, making her feel small and vulnerable.

"Talk to me," Irene said.

"I don't feel like talking."

Irene wrapped her arm around Roxi, giving her a sideways hug. "We're family. I want to hear what you're feeling. You know you can talk to me about anything, right?"

"You're not mad at me?"

"Why would I be mad at you?"

"The store today. I really did try."

"I know. You've got to do better, but I'm not mad." Irene pulled her closer, and Roxi rested her head on the woman's shoulder. "I might've seemed like it in the van. I was more frustrated than anything. I'd expected better of you."

"But I—"

"Just keep it from happening again. That's all."

"I don't know if I can. That clerk. She—"

"We don't need to rehash it. What's important is that you learned something."

"Why do we have to go back?"

Irene let her go and stood up from the table. "I've got some ideas I'll share with both of you shortly, but first I need you to be honest with me."

Roxi's gaze wandered to the fire ring, the dead pile of pine needles, the ground-squirrel holes over by that tree. Anything other than Irene. She grabbed her warming Dr Pepper, taking two huge swallows.

"You've been different this trip," Irene said.

So Irene *had* picked it up. What could she say to that?

"I'm concerned about you. Is there something you're not telling me?"

"I'm just tired."

"That's all?"

"Sure."

"No doubts?"

She worded her response carefully. "I won't let you down."

"It only takes one slipup."

Like she didn't know that. Roxi got up, taking her soda with her. "I'll just caffeine up or something."

"There's one more thing."

She rolled her eyes in the best show of teenage annoyance she could muster, hoping Irene would buy it. She wanted Irene to think all her weirdness was just lack of sleep or PMS or something normal like that.

Irene caught her by the arm. "I've sacrificed so much for you and given you everything I have. I don't ask much in return, but we have to be a team."

Roxi slowly nodded.

Smiling, Irene patted her on the back. "There are more details to talk about."

A few minutes later, the three of them sat at the RV dinette table, Irene on one side, Roxi and Diego on the other. Irene nursed a steaming mug of green tea.

"Okay, kids," Irene said, taking a sip, her eyes animated. She often got excited like this when laying out their plans, and she took pride in masterminding the details. Irene didn't do anything spur of the moment. Everything was planned and implemented with precision, which was probably why she took Roxi's doubts so personally.

"This is where it all comes down," Irene said. "We're on the cusp of great things, and it's only going to get better. But I will require a lot from both of you."

Roxi glanced at Diego, and he returned her questioning look.

Irene grinned, leaning forward, her elbows on the table. "Right now we have an opportunity unlike any other. And we have a choice to make. We can keep doing it the way we always have—traveling from store to store and making a little money. Or we can launch into the big leagues."

Diego's forehead wrinkled. "Big leagues?"

"Here's the deal." Irene met both of their eyes, Diego's first, then Roxi's. "When I first visited the Book Barn, I especially took notice of their front case. The one by the register. Did either of you see it?"

"Yeah," Diego said.

"There was a first edition of *The Great Gatsby*."

Roxi decided not to mention the clerk showing it to her and instead focused on keeping her jittery hands steady. Irene was always teaching them what books were worth nabbing, and her brain spun through all the rare books she'd learned about in the past year with Irene and Diego. They'd told her about how one time they scored a copy of the first book ever published about golf. She couldn't remember the title, but it had been published in the 1700s. Irene sold it to some collector she knew for six thousand, and it wasn't even a first printing.

"I got a good look when I asked to see it yesterday," Irene said. "And then with my research last night . . . it's definitely the real deal."

Anxiety twisted Roxi's stomach, a sensation all too familiar. "But what difference does it make? The case was locked."

"That's why I'm talking about the big leagues."

Roxi didn't like the sound of that. At all.

"Not only are we going back to the Book Barn," Irene said. "But we're going back at night."

"What?" It was the only word she could get out.

Irene smiled. "I know it's something we've never done, but that's why it's the big leagues. You've both been working real hard lately, and I know you've been drooling over those new iPods. We might make enough money with this to get one for each of you. Maybe even that digital camera you've been wanting too."

Diego rested his elbows on the table. "You've thought this through?"

"Big risk, big reward."

"But, Ma, breaking and entering?"

It surprised Roxi that Diego was the one questioning her for a change.

"I'm ready for this." Irene folded her hands, studying them both. "The question is, are both of you?"

Diego and Irene spent the next few minutes hashing out the pros and cons, and by the end, Diego was as gung ho as his mother. Then they were both staring at Roxi, waiting for her response. Which made her feel like a caged tiger. No matter how much she wanted to run, she couldn't. Diego had the end of the bench, and she was crunched up against the window.

"You on board, Rox?" Diego elbowed her.

She'd had a hard-enough time justifying the shoplifting in broad daylight. But burglary at night? Somehow that was crossing a line. Except now with Diego in Irene's camp, what could she say? She couldn't let down the only family she'd ever had.

❧

Abby was changing out of her uniform when Officer Stacy Perlman stuck her head in the tiny locker room. It had taken almost ten years for the department to give Abby one, and it had originally been a utility closet. Now she had to share it.

"Hey, Ab."

She nodded in Stacy's direction as she picked up her jeans. They were the only two female officers in their precinct, and Stacy was a twenty-three-year-old rookie who'd somehow gotten it in her head that she and Abby should become best buds.

"The lieutenant wants to talk to you."

Abby paused halfway through a pant leg. She knew what this was about but decided not to let on to Stacy. "He say why?"

"No, but he's not in a good mood."

Abby thanked her and finished changing. For the past eighteen years she'd worked her butt off to prove herself here. She'd finally earned some respect, a level playing field. But then Stacy came waltzing in expecting the guys to open doors for her and flirting with them every chance she got. It certainly didn't earn her points in Abby's book, and she had a feeling Stacy was finally picking that up. At forty-two, Abby was old enough to be Stacy's mother, and they had practically nothing in common. When Abby was in high school, she'd always been the tall girl with the big feet who never really fit in. Stacy was probably the cheerleader on the arm of the star quarterback. And while Abby had grown a mind and a brash tongue in the years since, the only things Stacy seemed to have grown were protruding from her chest. Why she ever signed up to be a cop Abby would never know. She could just hope some maturity snuck up on the girl before she had to make any snap decisions with a loaded gun.

A minute later Abby knocked on Lieutenant O'Connor's wooden

door with the frosted glass, wishing she could've had this meeting in her uniform. It might've given her the boost of confidence she needed to face a grilling from her superior.

O'Connor barked for her to enter. She walked in and closed the door behind her. O'Connor set down his pen and crossed his arms. He was six feet five and had the build of a linebacker, a blessing and a curse for a cop—a blessing because he could whip any guy who challenged him; a curse because lots of guys wanted to challenge the big cop to prove something. He was coming up on his twenty-fifth year, and rumor had it he might make captain soon.

"You wanted to see me?"

O'Connor rested his elbows on the desk and cracked his knuckles. "She filed a complaint."

Abby took a deep breath and decided honesty was the best approach. "I didn't know who she was."

"Oh, well, that changes everything."

"That's not what—"

"Dawson, there is no excuse you can give me that will change the fact that you sprained the wrist of the mayor's wife. She's got the doctor's report to prove it."

"Yes, sir."

O'Connor leaned back in his roll-away chair and picked up his pen again. "You're lucky she blew a .13; otherwise, you and I both know what would be happening right now."

Abby shifted her feet, glancing at the floor. If they didn't have the Breathalyzer and blood tests to prove the woman really was drunk, the department would've been smeared in the papers by now and Abby would probably be facing immediate dismissal.

It had happened last Friday night. She'd just gotten the call from Michael telling her Kat had been in the hospital overnight after collapsing at school, and all Abby's hurt and anger from the past had resurfaced. She hadn't even gotten a chance to visit Kat while she was there. Once again she was being denied the chance to be a mother to her, and she still had five hours to go on her shift.

She'd pulled the Lincoln over for weaving through two lanes, and just as she suspected, the woman behind the wheel was clearly intoxicated. When she'd started mouthing off, Abby had cuffed her more roughly than necessary.

"I can apologize to her," she said.

"You will." O'Connor twirled the pen between his fingers. "After your suspension."

She'd guessed as much would happen, but O'Connor's verdict still felt like a punch.

"Without pay. Two weeks. Starting tomorrow."

"I understand, sir," she said.

"I hope you do, Dawson." He met her eyes. "I really do."

Only when she was back outside in her silver four-door Acura did the reality of what just happened sink in. Not only had she failed as a wife and mother, but now she was failing as a cop, too.

4

CHRISTY WILLIAMS WAS SURE no one had sold *Farmer Giles of Ham* today. It was five minutes before closing, and she'd just noticed the book by J. R. R. Tolkien was missing. A first edition, they'd priced it at a hundred fifty. She'd displayed it on a special stand right beside the register. Initially she thought she must have carelessly taken it off the stand and left it on the counter. Since she kept the front check-out desk messier than it should've been, she could've easily piled something on top of the book. Sometimes she had to dig through anything from coffee-stained mugs to last week's mail to find what she needed.

She quickly began rooting through the mess. It had to be somewhere. She would've remembered selling it.

Someone cleared his throat, and Christy glanced up to see a guy in a bright tie and business suit that probably cost him what she made in a month. In her rush to find the missing book, she hadn't even seen him walk up.

He set two military biographies in front of the register. One on Patton, the other on Napoleon. "I'd like to buy these, if it's not too much trouble," he said.

Christy held back a snarky response and rang him up. He would be the last customer of the day. She followed the guy to the door and locked it behind him. As soon as he was gone, she went back to the counter. She checked the ledger they kept by the register to keep track of books they sold in the store that needed to be removed from their online inventory, but it wasn't there either. She expanded her search to the rest of the room, a twinge of panic flitting through her mind.

She was searching through the stacks on the new acquisitions table when the store manager, Hunter Dawson, stepped into the room. He wore his favorite uniform—jeans, chamois shirt, and hiking boots.

"I checked the rooms," Hunter said. "All empty."

Ever since they'd accidentally locked an elderly woman inside a few months ago, they made it a point to check each floor. Sometimes patrons could become so absorbed in the books they lost track and didn't know it was past closing time.

She scanned the spines of the last stack. Still no Tolkien.

"Looking for something?"

Christy sighed. "I can't find a book I had displayed by the register."

"Which one?"

She told him, and he looked off into space. He could often remember titles the store sold, and to whom, years after the fact.

"Haven't seen that one," he said. "Sure we didn't sell it?"

"Positive. Ted's off today, and I gave Sue permission to leave early.

I'll ask them tomorrow, but . . ." She shook her head, reluctant to give up her search. "I'm concerned someone took it."

Hunter's eyebrow rose.

"I mean, I've looked everywhere." Christy came and stood beside Hunter. She knew he trusted her now, but only a year and a half ago they'd had several other books stolen. She'd been the prime suspect. It finally came out that a longtime employee, her ex-boyfriend, had been stealing from the store for years, but she still didn't want any book disappearing on her watch ever again.

Hunter pulled her close. Not only was he the owner's son and her boss, but he was now her fiancé. They'd been engaged for almost a month.

"It'll probably show up tomorrow," Hunter said, smelling her hair.

"I hope so."

She gathered up her coat and purse, and because of the missing book, she pocketed the keys to the rare book case. They trusted their four other employees, but she wasn't taking any chances.

Hunter walked her outside to her Honda. The air was cooling quickly, summer's last hurrah barely hanging on at sunset. Even though it often got up into the nineties in the day, with the low humidity, the nights were cool enough to need a jacket.

Christy listened to a cricket or two serenading the night with scratchy melodies. Sometimes she and Hunter dragged out chairs just to sit together and watch the evening arrive. It was a great way to unwind and daydream about their future together. The past few times they'd even heard a pair of owls hooting to each other from the treetops.

"I talked to Pop," Hunter said.

Christy tried to read his expression. "I thought you were waiting until next week."

"It came up."

"What'd he say?"

They'd brainstormed a lot lately. As the owner's son, Hunter had been involved in the Barn his whole life, and he was always looking for new ways to improve things. Not that Robert Dawson allowed much change. That was the problem. She and Hunter wanted to move forward with the times, but the elder Dawson was stuck in his ways.

Hunter hesitated.

"He didn't go for it, did he?"

"Not exactly."

Christy almost cursed but quickly caught herself. Ever since she'd turned her life around, cursing didn't seem right anymore. "Did you tell him our whole idea?"

She was the one who'd suggested they partner with a local coffee shop and add an espresso bar to the store. She'd thrown the idea out just for fun, but Hunter loved it, and soon he was calculating the costs. Still, they both knew their biggest hurdle wasn't money but Hunter's father.

"He accused me of selling out." Hunter shook his head. "Said I was destroying the Barn's integrity with my ideas."

"Doesn't he see that if we don't do something, we won't survive?"

It used to be easy to acquire used books for their inventory. But anymore, folks bypassed selling their books to stores and sold their "treasures" on eBay. The only reason the Barn had survived this long was because of the online department. Now over half their business came from Internet sales. A coffee shop would be just the thing to draw customers in again.

Hunter pulled her into a hug. "We'll come up with something else."

She rested against him for a moment. Hunter always saw the best in people, no matter what they did to him. What he ever saw in her was still a mystery.

"I wish I could offer you more," Hunter said.

She tilted her head up to look into his eyes. "Than what? Letting me share in your dreams?"

"It's just . . . three rooms have been fine for me, and I don't mind using the employee kitchen, but for both of us?"

Christy smiled. Hunter had lived in the tiny apartment attached to the bookstore for years. His father and stepmother called the farmhouse behind the store home.

"You think I care about that?" she said.

"We could build on . . . or move the offices."

"Hunter—" she found his hand and held it in both of hers— "I didn't say yes to your apartment. I said yes to you."

He kissed the top of her head. "I'm finally starting that copy of *Endurance* you gave me."

She'd picked up the book by Alfred Lansing at a sale last month knowing Hunter would enjoy it. It was one of the more vivid accounts of Ernest Shackleton's fateful antarctic voyage.

"Perfect weather for it," she said. "It's going down into the fifties tonight."

"Mm. Beautiful." Hunter squeezed her shoulder. "But it doesn't hold a candle to you."

She felt herself blush.

A few minutes later they said good night, and Christy headed home. She didn't deserve a guy like Hunter. Not in a million years.

5

In the darkness of the van, Roxi leaned her cheek against the cool glass of the passenger window. They'd been parked for hours on a side street a hundred yards from the bookstore, watching and waiting. No lights. Engine off. All she wanted was to can this insane idea, get back to the campground, and curl up in her warm bed. There'd be other stores. They could do better in them.

Pushing away from the window, she poured herself another small cup of coffee from the metal thermos she'd brought for herself and Diego. Irene drank only filtered water and green tea. Roxi would have to find a bathroom soon if she kept this up, but right now it was important to stay alert. She wasn't disappointing Irene again.

In the driver's seat next to Roxi, Irene raised binoculars to her eyes, watching the store. Hitting this place tonight meant doing it while the manager, a guy who lived in the apartment attached to the store, was home. And the lights were still on in what they guessed was his bedroom window.

That's what worried her the most. And it was why Irene was taking no chances. That light had to be out for at least an hour, maybe more, to ensure the guy was asleep.

"Just chill." Diego's voice came from behind her, where he lay sprawled on the bench seat. "And give me some of that coffee."

Roxi handed him the thermos. "What if he hears us?"

Irene lowered the binoculars. "It's definitely our biggest risk. But it's one we have to take."

"We're good, Rox," Diego said.

If he had any apprehension, he was doing a good job masking it. Why couldn't she be more like that? Back in the beginning she had been, when everything was new and exciting. It was a game to be clever and rebellious, and making sure her new family liked her was first priority. She'd jumped in with both feet. Problem was, she hadn't known how deep the water was.

Irene pointed at the window, and Roxi's arms turned to jelly.

The light was out.

"Now the clock starts," Irene said.

But how would they know when the guy was asleep? And was it really possible the store didn't have an alarm? Irene was convinced it didn't and that they just kept their rare books locked up in cases.

It was a full hour of tense blackness before Irene looked at the window one last time and gave the go-ahead. Roxi wiggled her fingers into gloves, then clenched her fists and felt the soft leather grow taut around her knuckles. She no longer needed coffee to stay alert.

Irene caught her by the arm. "You all right?"

All she could do was nod and try to smile.

"I need you to focus. Remember what we talked about?"

"Yeah."

36

"Then let's do this."

At Irene's whispered command, they slid from the van. All three of them were dressed entirely in black, even down to their socks. They each carried a flashlight and a large cloth bag for the books. Diego also had a backpack with tools for their entry, including a crowbar they hoped not to need.

Huddled beside the van, they had a clear view of the Barn and its yard light. A few pines between them and the structure could offer cover, but for the most part they'd be sprinting in the open, like a SWAT team, clearly visible.

"Relax." Diego patted her back.

She forced herself to take a deep cleansing breath, but her nerves were just about shot from waiting.

Irene silently gestured for her and Diego to huddle closer before checking the door and window one last time through her binoculars. "In and out in three minutes," she whispered. "If an alarm sounds at any time, we run. All right?"

Diego pulled his backpack over his shoulders. "Got it."

Roxi couldn't see either of their shadowy faces, but she could imagine their expressions. Irene would be sporting that intense mask of determination she always wore before hitting a store. Diego would be trying to match it, but he never could erase that boyish excitement from his eyes.

She was glad for the darkness. They wouldn't be able to see her face either.

Roxi gripped her flashlight. Her stomach felt like one of those balloons the man at the carnival would twist into different animal shapes. Blood pulsed through her fingers as a burst of wind blew past her ears. She was in deep, and there was no turning back. Everything in her screamed to run away. Right now. Without thinking or questioning. Just run. But then what? She had nowhere to go.

Roxi closed her eyes, then quickly opened them again. Nowhere to go. She had to remember that.

"This is it, kids. Get ready," Irene whispered.

Diego nodded several times like a horse at the starting gate. "Here we go, baby."

Somewhere a dog started yapping, and Roxi hoped it wasn't because it had heard them. Then in slow motion the moment came. Irene pointed to go, and their boots hit the dirt, running across the clearing and floating on tiptoes over the gravel of the parking lot, where tendrils of bluish light illuminated them.

No time to think. Go! Get out from under the floodlight.

They made it to the door in under ten seconds. Diego immediately dropped to one knee, and while Roxi held her flashlight on the lock, he pried at it with his screwdriver.

The countdown had begun.

⁂

The keys to the rare book case were missing.

Roxi dove for the drawer where she'd seen the clerk stash them, but she found nothing but bookmarks, business cards, a checkbook ledger, and pencils.

"They're not here."

Diego was instantly by her side, his voice a raspy whisper. "Shut up."

He ripped out his screwdriver. She held her light on the lock, and metal scraped metal as he jimmied the sliding panel.

Her pulse screaming in her ears, Roxi glanced up at the silhouette of Irene. The older woman's flashlight bounced from shelf to shelf as she deftly swiped volumes from all over the room. They would be valuable too, but if this was going to pay off, they had to access the case.

Diego swore.

Roxi squeezed her flashlight to keep her hand steady.

With a snap the lock finally gave, and Roxi set her light on top of the case so it shone down inside. She crouched beside Diego, hooking books before her knees hit the floor.

A sparkle of gilt lettering. Purple cloth. A whiff of dried leather. It was all a blur. She had no idea what they were taking, and it really didn't matter. They were all valuable or they wouldn't be in this case. Once this was over, they could finally go home. These books would pay the bills for months if Irene found the right buyers quick enough. Maybe they could take a break and live a normal life again.

Sixty seconds. They'd been in a full minute, and they still weren't done. *Move!* She wasn't gonna be the reason this thing bombed.

Her bag was full. Diego grabbed the last book in the case.

"Over here." Irene waved her flashlight from across the room.

Roxi whispered as loud as she dared, "We've got enough. Let's go."

Diego didn't move either. "You said just this case."

"Just hurry and get over here."

Ninety seconds.

No time to argue. Both of them reluctantly moved toward Irene, to a second wardrobelike case with double glass doors. She and Irene aimed their lights on the case for Diego as he went through another wrestling match with the lock. But this time the wood quickly splintered, and the doors flew open.

"Keep your light on it," Irene said.

Their bags were already burgeoning. How were they going to—?

The entire room lit up. Roxi was disoriented, but in a split second she realized someone other than them had turned on the lights.

6

ALL THREE OF THEM SPUN AROUND, squinting at the brightness. A man dressed in plaid pajama bottoms stood in the doorway, his hand still on the light switch.

The manager.

Roxi froze, not wanting to move without Irene's direction. She clutched her miserable flashlight, glancing from the manager to Irene to Diego, then back to Irene. Had he called the cops? Would they be arrested? Should they run? Would they make it to the van?

There was a strange moment of silence, like all their brains short-circuited, unable to compute what they were seeing. Then, before Roxi could do anything to stop him, Diego reached into his coat and pulled out a silver handgun, aiming for the manager's chest.

"Diego!" She grabbed for his arm.

He shoved her away and stepped closer to the manager. "Get the lights, Rox. There's another switch by the front door."

Her voice held every ounce of horror she felt. "What are you *doing*?"

Irene ran for the switch, and the room went black again.

"Don't move." Diego shone his flashlight into the guy's eyes, the gun still trained on his chest.

"This won't work," the manager said.

"Shut up."

"Please put the gun away," Roxi pleaded. She swung her flashlight toward Irene, who was cinching up the bags like a madwoman.

"Hurry," Diego threw over his shoulder.

"You won't get away with this," the manager said, taking a step closer to Diego.

Diego straightened his gun arm. "Stay right there!"

"The cops are on their way."

Sweat trickled down Roxi's cheek. Could that be true? *No. Please, no.*

"Grab your bag, Roxi," Irene said. "Now."

But her legs wouldn't move. And her eyes couldn't leave the gun she hadn't even known Diego was packing.

The manager took another step.

Diego backed up. "Stop. I mean it."

"You don't want to do this."

Roxi felt Irene's presence move beside her; then the older woman's form was standing right behind her son. Irene raised her own flashlight beam to the guy's face. "You heard him. Do what he says."

The manager stopped.

"Get on . . . the floor." Diego's voice was breaking.

The manager hesitated, his eyes darting to the front doorway like he was expecting someone to enter at any moment.

Silence. All Roxi could hear was the ticking of that antique clock she'd seen the first time they came in here.

A sharp *whap* came from behind them.

The noise made Roxi jump, and instinctively Diego swung toward the sound. In that split second, as Roxi realized it was a book falling out of the case behind them, the manager lunged at Diego, grabbing his gun hand. The force sent Diego flying into Irene, and she tumbled to the floor with her flashlight.

Roxi aimed her flashlight at the tangle of Diego and the manager, her arm shaking. The manager's hands crushed down on Diego's.

"Stop it!" Roxi shrieked.

Diego struggled, but the manager was stronger. He was slowly turning the gun away from himself—and toward Diego.

"No!"

Irene clambered to her feet, rushing to help her son.

Fire spewed from the gun's barrel, the shot thundering through the store.

The manager let go.

Diego stumbled backward, gasping, still gripping the gun.

Shining her light on the manager, Roxi sucked in her breath. He clutched at his chest, where blood was inching across his T-shirt, quickly spreading past the width of his hand. Opening his mouth in a gasp, he looked like he was about to speak, then clamped his jaw shut. His body swayed, ready to fall.

Diego cursed—over and over.

Something inside Roxi screamed, but the words never made it to her lips. This was where she should wake up, sit bolt upright in the bed, and realize the whole thing was a dream. A terrible, horrible nightmare.

The manager's knees buckled underneath him, and without thinking, Roxi rushed to his side. She hung on to his arm, desperate to keep him from crashing to the floor. All his body weight landed on her shoulder. She stumbled, and he slid to the floor anyway, dragging her down too.

He choked out a gurgling cough, blood bubbling from the corner of his mouth.

She knelt beside him. "I'm sorry. I'm so sorry."

He slowly lifted his head and looked right at her with fading, pleading eyes.

"Roxi." Irene's distant voice came to her through a thick fog.

It wasn't real. She had to wake up.

"Get away from him." Irene wrenched her to her feet.

"We have to do something!"

Irene stared down at the manager. "We can't." She grabbed Roxi's arm. "We have to get out."

Roxi shook her head, unable to avert her eyes from the bleeding man on the floor. *Please don't let him die.*

Irene pulled her toward the bags.

Diego already had two over his shoulders. "I've got hers."

"Come on!"

They sprinted for the back door. Ran all the way to the van. Irene dove into the driver's seat. Diego pushed Roxi inside, then jumped into the middle bench seat beside her. The van lurched forward before he slid the door closed.

Roxi shook uncontrollably. She couldn't think. Could barely breathe. "He's gonna die."

"We don't know that," Diego said, low and deep.

She grabbed Irene's leather purse from the floor, frantically rifling through its contents. Cell phone. She had to find the cell phone. Her fingers grazed the smooth plastic, and she whipped it out.

"What are you—?" Diego snatched it out of her hand so fast she flinched. "Give me that. What do you think you're doing?"

"We can't just leave him! I have to call 911."

"Are you crazy?"

She almost punched him. "He's dying!"

The van's tire jumped the curb, throwing Roxi against the front seat. Irene spun the steering wheel, and then they were out on the road. "If we call the police, it'll put us on their radar."

"Don't you get it?" She was yelling now. "Your son just shot a man!"

Diego touched her arm. "Rox, please don't. I—"

She did hit him then—shoved him away like he'd shoved her in the store. "Get your hand off me."

His face was barely illuminated by the dashboard lights, but she thought she saw him close his eyes. "I didn't mean to," he said. Turning toward her, he begged her to believe him. "Honest, I didn't. It was an accident. I was only trying to scare him."

Bringing her knees to her chest, Roxi rested her head on them. The way she used to so long ago as an innocent little girl. Only now she'd never be innocent again.

7

ABBY EASED HER CAR up to the Starbucks squawk box.

"Morning, Abby. Usual?"

She recognized the voice of her favorite barista but kept forgetting the girl could see her. "You got it, Trish. And let's add a piece of lemon pound cake to boot."

"Diet be darned?"

"What diet?"

She got the total and drove up to the window, handing over her Visa with a dollar tip. A minute later, she was in her usual parking space in the corner. She removed the coffee's white plastic lid and breathed in the rich, almost-cocoa aroma. She loved the dark French roast with that extra shot of espresso. Nothing like a good red eye to keep her on top of her game.

Abby rolled down her window and nibbled on the pound cake.

Except today there was no game. It was simply routine that had woken her this morning at six and gotten her in the shower and out the door by seven.

She ripped open three Splenda packets from the stash in her glove compartment, dumped them all in at once, mixed it with the wooden stirrer, then carefully took a sip of the scalding coffee. What dent had she ever made in the world of crime? For every perp she locked up, two more took his place. People weren't any safer. She wasn't changing the world like she and every other rookie had dreamed of doing when they graduated from the academy. She'd seen more NC-17 scum and perversion than anyone should ever have to see, and somewhere along the way she'd become jaded.

And this job was the reason Michael got custody. The court-appointed psychologist had concluded her occupation was too high risk and her schedule unreliable. A girl Kat's age needed stability. Michael and Sarah could give that to her. She'd always felt the former defense attorney judge had unduly sided with Michael, the rising star of his firm.

The day the decision came down six years ago, Abby almost quit. If being a cop cost her Kat, it wasn't worth it. But by then it was too late, and every passing year had erased a little more of her drive to be the best cop she could be. Now it was just a job—and a dangerous one at that.

Abby broke off a huge piece of pound cake and popped it into her mouth. Only one other time had she been close to suspension, and for the same reason as this time. Right after she lost Kat, her rage at the system had become almost uncontrollable, and she'd been a little rougher than necessary during some arrests. One perp complained, and a warning from her supervisor finally woke her up.

Her cell phone shrieked from the passenger seat, an acid guitar lick one of the guys had downloaded without her permission as a joke, and Abby just about jumped out of her skin. She really needed to change it to something softer.

Scooping up the phone, she checked the number.

Dad.

Great. They weren't exactly on the best terms these days, but at least they were talking. And that was actually progress.

Abby flipped the cell open. "Hi, Dad."

"A-Abby." Her father cleared his throat. "I don't know . . . how to tell you this."

Her fingers tightened around her coffee cup. His tone triggered her imagination, and for some reason her first thought was cancer. Never one for exercising or eating right on his own, the only reason Dad did anything healthy was thanks to his wife, Lynn. Even she couldn't talk him into a lot. He'd never give up his pipe or his Tastykakes.

"What's wrong?"

"It's . . ."

Dad's voice caught like he was crying. That was scarier than if he'd come right out with bad news. When had she ever heard her father cry?

"I'm sorry," Dad said.

He wouldn't be crying for himself, would he? Could Lynn be sick?

"It's Hunter."

Abby's stomach twisted. If something was wrong with her brother, why wasn't Hunter calling himself? Was he in the hospital?

"He . . . died last night."

"What?"

"I found him. In the store." Dad released a long, jerky breath. "He'd been shot in the chest."

All at once Abby understood why people froze at times like this.

Her brain refused to accept what Dad said. *Overload. Does not compute.* She'd just talked to Hunter. He'd been all excited about his and Christy's idea of opening an espresso bar in the store.

She'd heard it wrong. That had to be it.

She leaned forward, and drops of scalding coffee dribbled onto her leg. She set the cup in the drink holder.

"I thought he'd overslept. If I'd only—"

"Shot?"

"I didn't hear anything. Nothing!"

And here she was, hundreds of miles away, her only connection some electronic waves floating through the air. Outside her car, life went on. Humanity streamed into Starbucks for their morning caffeine fixes like . . . flies to a carcass.

Abby covered her eyes with her hand.

"They think it was a robbery gone bad."

Dad's wooden voice echoed in her ear, but she barely heard it. She'd answered hundreds of calls wearing her badge, seen people killed over stupid, petty things. Over someone giving them the finger in traffic, over a lousy pack of cigarettes. Why would anyone kill Hunter, a man who'd give you the shirt off his back?

Abby struggled for words. "What happened?"

"Why couldn't I have woken up? Maybe then he'd be . . . I could've done something."

"Dad." She fought back her own emotion, but it was a losing battle. "I'll be there as soon as I can."

❦

Diego and Irene took turns driving the RV, and all day the miles stretched between them and the bookstore. They couldn't go home now. Instead, they'd fled south down I-25. At six they finally stopped for dinner at a Flying J truck stop in Albuquerque. Normally they didn't eat out much but instead kept the freezer stocked with easy meals like pizza or lasagna. It was Irene's idea to treat them tonight to Country Market restaurant. Good old comfort food, she called it.

Roxi felt like a robot on low battery as she got out of the RV. Her movements were slow and stiff, her mind numb. Her body yearned to recharge, but her brain refused to allow it. Like anything could comfort her now. With each hour the truth sank in harder—a lead anchor to her soul.

She was an accomplice to a murder.

This morning they'd driven by the bookstore on their way out. Didn't matter that she thought it was crazy and just asking to get caught. Irene and Diego did it anyway. And all it took was one glance to confirm the worst. The squad cars, the coroner's van . . . He was dead. There was no denying it now. They'd killed a man.

In an instant, the manager's expression projected onto her mind's eye, his ashen face begging for the help she wouldn't give him.

Roxi blinked the image away and forced herself to walk into the restaurant behind mother and son. People always assumed she was Irene's daughter, even though her frame was smaller and her hair the wrong color. She had never corrected them. She would now.

Inside, Diego ordered a steak and fries, but Irene and Roxi chose the buffet. They went up together. At the island, Irene handed her a warm plate. She'd been nice to her all day.

"Try to eat something."

Roxi could barely stand the food smells wafting up from the stainless steel trays.

"The chicken looks good," Irene said.

Eyeing the fried wings, Roxi felt her stomach churn. She'd tried to eat this morning but only managed a handful of Wheat Thins. Across from her, Irene caught her eye and gave her an encouraging smile. "Your favorite," she mouthed, pointing to the macaroni and cheese.

But Roxi shook her head. She'd take a dollop of mashed potatoes and maybe a roll. Those would be gentle on her stomach, right?

Back at the table, she sat on the end of the bench next to Irene.

Diego sat across from them, drumming his fingers on the table and waiting for his order. He hadn't shaved, and his mussed hair was quickly growing greasy on the sides. "Do we have time for this?"

"It's okay," Irene said. "We have to eat."

"I say keep driving."

"I'm too tired, and so are you."

He whispered, "The farther away we get, the better."

"We're far enough for tonight."

Roxi saw Diego's jaw muscle tighten into a bulging cord.

"We all need sleep," Irene said.

Crossing his arms, Diego pushed his shoulders against the backrest. "What if they're onto us?"

Irene squeezed the bridge of her nose.

"We could've left evidence, we—"

"Do you want to discuss this in the middle of a restaurant?"

For a moment Roxi saw real fear in Diego's bloodshot eyes, and she wondered where he'd put the gun. She'd known he had one. Some sort of Glock. He showed it to her once at home. But she'd never dreamed he brought it along on this trip. Why hadn't he told her? She might've been able to talk him out of it.

"None of us are going anywhere tonight," Irene said.

Roxi felt heat slipping up her neck. If only she'd given them more time during the first visit, none of this would be happening. She was to blame for that man's death. And every few hours she experienced all over again the panicked realization that this was not a nightmare.

"The fact is," Irene said to Diego, lowering her voice, "you made a stupid mistake back there."

"It was an accident. Honest, I—"

"But we still have to deal with it. Son, look at me." Irene pressed the palm of her hand against her chest, leaning forward. "I'm your mother. I don't want you to go to jail. I'll do anything to keep that from happening."

A stupid mistake? That's all this was to them? Roxi ripped off a piece of the roll. She saw the man's face again. Blood dripping from the corner of his mouth, pooling on the wood floor. The gurgling breaths . . .

She shoved the bread into her mouth.

Diego glanced at Roxi. "What do you think?"

What did she think? That she wanted to wake up. That she never wanted to see Irene or Diego again. That she was just a pawn, and that neither of them had ever cared about her in the first place.

"I don't wanna think," she said.

Diego finally uncrossed his arms and finished off his ice water. "We should get rid of the books."

The waitress came with his steak and fries, which shut them all up. He dove right in, sawing at the meat with his knife. Bloodred juices oozed out.

Roxi looked away from the plate, taking a bite of mashed potatoes. But the glob sat on her tongue like a wad of cotton refusing to go down.

"I'm not liking this either," Irene said, starting in on her fried wings. "But we have to find a way to move on with our lives."

"What if they find us, Ma? What if we left DNA in there or something?"

Irene gnawed on a wing for a moment, then dropped the picked-clean bone to her plate. "If we lay low and keep from making any more stupid moves—" she eyed Diego—"we'll be okay."

The man's face flashed again inside Roxi's head. In slow motion she watched a replay of Diego and the man struggling, heard the deafening gunshot, saw the shock in the man's eyes, watched the blood drip between his shaking fingers. Why couldn't she have stopped Diego? smacked the gun out of his hand or—?

Roxi jumped when Irene touched her shoulder.

"Hey, it's all right," Irene said.

At another time, the older woman's soft voice might've comforted her. She would lean into Irene and hear her whisper that it would all be okay, that she really did love her. But now she recoiled from the woman. She'd just witnessed her son murder a man, and all she could talk about was moving on?

Roxi pulled away. "That's all this is to you? A stupid mistake?"

Silently Irene stared at Roxi for a moment. Her eyes were bloodshot too, and the creases at the corners of her mouth deeper than Roxi remembered them.

"Honey, that's not true. I care about—"

"A man's dead because of what we did, and all you can talk about is moving on with your life." Tears were building in her eyes, and she could barely hold them back. "I can't move on."

"Shh. Keep your voice down." Irene rubbed her shoulder. "As much as we want to change what happened, we can't. It's done."

Roxi shook her head, staring at her now-cold dinner. "I can't play this game anymore. Look where it's gotten us."

"You're just tired."

"That's not it, Irene. What we're doing is wrong."

Irene's expression didn't change, but she removed her hand from Roxi's shoulder. It was a small gesture, but it hurt more than if Irene had slapped her. As long as she did what Irene asked of her like a good little girl, all would be well. But if she questioned, Irene withdrew.

"I thought I could count on you," Irene said.

"I . . . You can. I'm . . ." Somehow she still wanted Irene to be proud of her, to love her. Roxi squeezed her head with her hands. She couldn't handle this.

"What about our talk yesterday?" Irene asked.

Roxi swung around to face her. "And you don't think things have changed just a little?" She could feel her pulse rising, her limbs getting shaky, the knot in her stomach clenching tighter.

"Please don't make a scene."

"I can't do this." The panic was taking over. "I just wanna go home."

"Shhh, honey. It's okay."

"No it's not!" She jumped up from the table so quickly, the silverware rattled. Before they could stop her, she was running for the back of the restaurant. Spotting the restroom sign, she bolted for it. She shoved open the door, fell to her knees in the first stall, and threw up in the toilet.

8

ABBY CRADLED THE FRAMED PHOTOGRAPH in her lap. A sandy-haired boy and dark-haired girl leaned their heads close for the shot. They didn't look much alike, but their blood tied them together forever. Brother and sister. They sat side by side in a booth at the sixties-themed Charlie's Diner, laughing and making faces for the camera. Just two kids goofing around. She remembered how much fun it had been popping nickels in the tabletop jukebox playing songs like "Blue Suede Shoes" and "Wake Up Little Susie."

Sitting cross-legged on the edge of her bed, Abby closed her eyes, transported back in time twenty-six years to Hunter's eleventh birthday. She, a new driver wanting to burn some rubber, treated her little bro to a movie and ice cream sundaes. They'd asked the waitress to snap this picture.

Abby stared at it. Their appearances hadn't changed much over the years. True, Hunter's hair had darkened to a deep brown, and Abby started coloring hers closer to black. Relatives still said she bore a striking resemblance to her mother, and Hunter favored Dad. Which was ironic, really. Hunter couldn't have been more different from Dad if he tried.

She traced the photo's frame with her finger. After Mom died, their father was never the same. He spent more time at the country club than at home, and even when he *was* home, he was either working in the Barn or locked in his study. He was never mean or abusive or anything like that; he just wasn't there. The cleaning lady spent more time with them than Dad ever did. Abby wondered if he avoided them because they reminded him too much of Mom.

Sliding off the bed, she went to her open closet and felt for the touch keys of her handgun case. She punched the combination, and the case door flipped open. The cool frame of her Beretta 9mm filled her hand. She slipped out the semiautomatic and held it in her palm. Hunter had died from a bullet to the chest. Did it hit his heart and kill him fast, or did he drown in his own blood, gasping for air?

She'd never forget the time she'd been the first on scene at a drive-by shooting. The victim, a twelve-year-old kid, had been minding his own business walking home from school when some gang members drove up, rolled down their window, and shot him three times in the chest. He was still alive when she arrived, and she watched him cough and struggle for each of his last breaths, gripping her hand so hard, his fingernails left dents in her gloves. He was gone by the time the paramedics arrived.

Abby's fingers tightened around the grip, and she wiped her eyes with the back of her hand. Every day she put her life on the line to protect the innocent, and she'd faced armed criminals more than once. Yet here she was. Alive and breathing while her brother, the shy bookworm, lay in a morgue.

She set the Beretta on the bed next to the photograph while she stuffed two suitcases, not knowing how long she'd be gone. She packed mostly jeans and sweatshirts. But just in case, she threw in her nicer pantsuit and a pair of dressy shoes. She'd need them for the funeral anyway. From her dresser drawer she brought over two plastic cartridge boxes and buried them at the bottom of the first suitcase. Sheathing the Beretta in her shoulder holster, she slipped it on over her shirt.

Once finished, she lugged the suitcases out to her car. She threw them in and slammed the trunk so hard, the car shuddered. Any faith she might've had left in mankind—or God—died last night with Hunter. No one had been there to protect her brother, who'd probably never held a gun in his life.

Abby ran back up the steps into the cavern of her lonely house and set the alarm. She'd leave the lights off. Nothing screamed "No one's home" more than a porch light left burning through the night.

Sliding into her car, she listened to the faint electronic beeps as the security system prepared to arm in two minutes. She knew how police worked. Short staffed, overworked, underpaid. Sure, there'd be an investigation. The perp might already be caught by the time she got there.

Or not.

It happened all too often. The detectives followed every lead only to reach dead ends, and the case would turn cold fast, unsolved and forgotten. The killer would get away. She couldn't let that injustice happen to her brother.

Abby shifted the car into drive and slid sunglasses over her puffy eyes, glad for the bulk of the Beretta on her ribs. Someone had killed her brother. Whoever it was, wherever they were, she would find them.

❧

In the darkness, the Coors and Budweiser signs of the White Horse bar were like the beacons of a lighthouse to Christy. *"Come on in. It's safe harbor here."*

Sitting in front of the building inside her idling car, she could see herself walking in, ordering, then waiting in her favorite booth in the corner as she calmed herself with a pack of Winstons. She could taste that first burning sip of a martini gliding down her throat promising to take care of her. Just like old times.

Christy twirled the still-unfamiliar engagement ring on her finger. The one man in her life who'd loved her just as she was, Hunter understood her like no one ever had. His kindness and devotion . . . they'd reminded her of God's love, which she'd only recently discovered. Unconditional. Constant—despite her screwups.

But where was God when that gunman pulled the trigger? Where was He when Hunter lay hurting, dying alone?

She turned off the engine. Would one drink really hurt? She never had to come back after tonight. It could end right here. One drink would be a salve to this raw wound she didn't know how to deal with.

Choking back a sob, Christy dropped her keys into her purse. How could she go on without Hunter? His life was her life. His dreams had become her dreams. She couldn't imagine next week or next year without him.

"I can't do it," she whispered.

She opened the door and stepped into the night. Muted toe-tapping country music met her ears, usual for this place. A pickup swooped into the parking lot and came to a grinding stop two spaces from her. A guy with a John Deere cap got out and marched up to the bar's door. He tipped his hat at Christy, then disappeared into the darkness.

She followed him to the door, peering through the cloudy window. There was Suzie, the middle-aged bartender who called everyone "hon," taking the guy's order.

One drink. That's all she was talking about here. Nothing in the Bible said an occasional drink every now and then was wrong. Even

Jesus shared wine with His disciples. Christy rested her hand on the dented doorknob. Then she thought of May. Her younger sister had been one of the reasons she'd worked so hard to stay sober the past year and a half. She too had believed in her, and Christy knew what May would say: "You don't need this, Chris. It won't bring him back."

She turned the handle. But May didn't have to know, and it's not like she was out buying a whole bottle of vodka or something. That *would* be going too far. After tonight she could go right back to her new, clean life.

When she walked through the door, the old sights and smells hit her like a blast of wind. Wispy cigarette smoke. Yeasty beer. A little sweat. Gritty floorboards under her clogs. And the familiar, seducing darkness closing in from every direction.

Something in Christy shrank back from the darkness.

"Hey, doll. Come sit by me. Let me buy you a drink." The guy with the John Deere hat grinned at her from his barstool, patting the empty one next to him. Handsome in a rugged sort of way with thick graying hair growing over his ears and a day's worth of stubble dotting his face, his friendly smile drew her to the counter. She could forget everything. Just for tonight. Only a couple of hours. That's it.

She slowly pulled herself up onto the stool and smiled back.

Suzie set a foamy beer in front of the guy, then turned to Christy. "Hi, hon. Haven't seen you in a while. What can I get ya?"

"Martini, two olives," she said, knowing Suzie recognized her from the countless times she'd taken her order over the years.

Mr. John Deere rested his grease-stained hand on her arm. "You look wiped."

"You have no idea."

His hand moved around to her back. "I'm a mechanic. Fixing broken things is my specialty. You broke tonight?"

The heaviness of his hand caused her to pull away. She looked up at him as Suzie set the martini in front of her. "You don't even know my name," Christy said.

"Bet it's something sweet." He slid her martini closer to her. "Take a sip, doll. It'll make everything better."

Christy caressed the glass with her fingers. She'd spent half her life in bars like this one, trying to drown away the guilt and pain of a disappointed life. Where had it always gotten her? In a deeper hole. Emptier still.

A woman laughed too loudly somewhere behind her. That had been her so many times. Drunk as a pig and not even knowing it.

"We can go someplace if you want," the guy said.

She'd been here before too, and she hadn't asked the guys their names either. Christy pushed the martini away. *Please give me strength, Lord.*

When it was all said and done, the emptiness always remained. Through all those years, God had been waiting for her, hadn't He? Even after the mess she'd made of her life, He'd accepted her with open arms. Baggage and all. His love had healed her. Could she trust Him to heal her again of the unbearable sorrow that enveloped her very soul?

Christy stood, taking in the bar with its shiny glasses, blaring TVs in each corner, and gleaming bottles one last time. "No thanks," she said to the guy, and with every ounce of strength in her bones, she turned away and retreated out the door.

Locking herself in her car, she rested her head on the steering wheel and wept.

❧

Roxi covered her eyes with her arm, trying to look like she was sleeping. A faint snore came from Diego's bed over the front seats. He could really saw wood sometimes, and she'd learned to tune it out. Now she tuned it in, monitoring his every deep and rhythmic breath. He'd been at it for an hour. It was Irene she had to worry about now.

She strained to hear sounds from the back bedroom, where Irene slept. It used to comfort her that the older woman was a light sleeper—Irene would hear anyone trying to break in. Now it was troubling. Would Irene hear *her*? She'd often complained about her and Diego's restless sleeping up front. Just turning over in bed could rock the RV, and Irene would feel it.

Gingerly, Roxi pushed herself up to a sitting position in her bed. After losing it in the restaurant, she'd come out here in the RV to wait for Irene and Diego. When she'd finally calmed down enough to string two thoughts together, she knew what she had to do.

She reached down to the space between her bed and the floor where she'd stashed her backpack. This was all it was gonna be. Her and a backpack. She'd worn shorts and a T-shirt to bed so all she had to do was grab the pack, her boots, jeans, and a jacket. She slowly eased her weight onto her bare feet, the sum of her possessions clutched to her chest. The door. How was she going to open it without making noise?

Diego groaned, and she froze. *Don't wake up. Please don't wake up.*

She twisted her neck to watch his black silhouette on the bed. If he'd seen her, he would've said something. Pulse surging, she padded to the door. She could be out in two more steps, but first she had to turn that dead bolt.

Her fingers touched the cool metal. *Steady, girl. Breathe.* If Diego woke up, she knew he'd talk her out of this.

It was going to click. She couldn't do anything about that. She could only hope the chugging generator of the neighboring Bounder RV would be enough white noise to keep him asleep. Maybe if she turned it quickly . . . Roxi glanced behind herself one last time at Diego's still form. He'd been the only friend she'd ever really had.

Like a brother almost. Sometimes when she hung out with him, she actually felt like she had a real family. What would he think when he woke up to her empty bed? She took a deep breath, her fingers tightening around the lock. She couldn't think about it. All she knew was she couldn't go on like this anymore.

The lock clicked.

She cracked the door, and air laced with exhaust fumes hit her face. Light streamed in, right onto Diego's bed. What was she waiting for, him to open his eyes?

Two feet to the ground. If she jumped, that would rock the RV. Instead, Roxi stooped to a crouch and eased out onto her right leg. A piece of gravel jammed into her heel.

Now. She eased out the rest of the way and pushed the door just enough for it to stay closed.

Then she was running. In her shorts and bare feet—clothes, boots, and pack cradled in her arms. She ran past the Bounder, across the grassy strip, then through the semis in the truck parking area behind the restaurant.

She didn't look back.

9

ABBY IDLED HER CAR in front of the Barn. Except for a little more plaster chipping around the windows, the store hadn't changed much in the five years since she'd been here last. She half expected Hunter to saunter out the door and pull her into the bear hug only a brother can give. When she started to think about him dying in there, her throat closed up and she could barely breathe.

It was just an old stone barn. Yet it had stolen so much from her. First her father's affection, now her brother's life. Was she ready to confront the memories this place held? Taking a deep breath, Abby turned down the lane leading to her childhood home behind the bookstore.

Her tires crunched in the gravel, and she rubbed at the tight kinks in her neck. She'd driven for eight hours straight and was running on coffee fumes. How would she do this? The walls between her and Dad were as firm as concrete—steel-reinforced concrete. He'd made his choice to be an absentee father when Mom died, and she'd never forgiven him for it.

She parked beside Dad's white Ford Expedition. She would act like she belonged. Like it hadn't been years since she'd set foot in this place.

At her second knock the front door opened, and she was face-to-face with Dad's wife, Lynn. She was only ten years older than Abby. Toned and lean, she looked like she lived at the gym. Yet today her cheeks sported pink splotches. Between her long fingers she clutched a ragged tissue.

"Sorry I didn't call first," Abby said.

Lynn opened the door wide. "I'm so glad you came."

She hesitated. "Where's Dad?"

"He hasn't left his study."

Abby stepped into the foyer, and Lynn hugged her. Not a quick perfunctory hug like she expected, but an emotional embrace that surprised Abby. She returned the hug but was the first to pull away. She'd never really connected with her stepmother. Dad had married Lynn after Abby moved away, and they'd only casually visited the handful of times she'd been back.

"How is he?" Abby asked.

"I wish you'd talk to him. He . . ." Lynn touched her hand to her mouth, blinking fast. "He's taking it very hard."

Abby nodded. Leaving Lynn in the foyer, she slowly walked down the hall toward Dad's study. For a split second she was a little girl again. Back then if his door was closed, it meant one thing: Do Not Enter. She paused outside the door, and the grown-up Abby wondered what kind of man she would find inside. Father or not, Dad was almost a stranger to her. He had been for as long as she could remember.

There was no answer to her knock, but she opened the door anyway. "Dad?"

At first she thought Lynn was mistaken and the room was empty, but then she saw Dad's posh leather chair scooted up to the window. Wisps of pipe smoke met her nose, and the chair uttered a creak, its back still to her. All she could see was the top of her father's white head.

Abby crossed the threshold. The room seemed so much smaller than she remembered it. As a kid she'd found it huge and foreboding, its dark wood panels holding the room in shadows. Now it was just a room—with a desk, entertainment center, and fireplace. If the fire had been lit, it might've been cozy, the type of room where a father and daughter could chat about school or boys or anything, really.

Dad still didn't turn around.

She picked up the only picture on her father's desk, the one where Dad stood proudly with his first golfing trophy, shaking hands with Tiger Woods as the country club owner looked on. Abby set it down before she spoke again.

"I came as soon as I could."

Slowly the chair swiveled toward her, and she realized Dad had been staring at the Barn through the window. Without a word, he rested his pipe on the sill and in three steps was holding her, pressing her face into his shoulder.

"Oh, Abby."

She didn't resist. Her father needed this, and she would give it to him. They'd both been dealt an unthinkable blow. Hunter was her little brother, but he was Dad's son.

When he finally let her go, his eyes were brimming. He fell back into his chair, but she remained standing. Leaning against the edge of his desk, she resisted the urge to defensively cross her arms.

"I guess they've finished in there." Abby tilted her head in the direction of the bookstore. It would've taken several hours to gather evidence, take pictures, and catalog it all.

"The . . . cleanup company was the last to go."

She held her eyes shut at the words, then slowly opened them again. A gunshot wound, or GSW, to the chest could produce a lot of blood if it hit an artery or the heart. Walking to the window, she stared at the part of the Barn visible through the gaps in the pine trees. *Oh, Hunter. What happened?*

Abby turned to face Dad again.

He was just sitting there, his body limp, tears flowing down through the white stubble of his beard. "The last words I said to him . . . The last thing I ever did with my son was have an argument."

When had Dad ever cried in front of her?

"I think the detective suspects me," he said.

Which was procedure. Everyone was a suspect until alibis could be established and evidence weighed. "I know," she said. "I got a call too."

"No, he really does."

"They just have to rule us all out."

Dad wiped his eyes with his sleeve. "I had to tell them about the argument."

She wondered what they'd argued about. "I wouldn't worry."

"I don't have an alibi."

"What?"

"Lynn was gone all night visiting a friend."

She couldn't help rolling her eyes. Great. The cops would have a heyday with this. The domineering father argues with the passive son and in the heat of the moment murders him, frantically staging it to look like a robbery. It wouldn't have been the first time they'd seen that.

"I don't know which is worse. Hunter dying or them accusing *me* of killing him."

Abby ran her fingers through her hair. This was not what she needed. If the police focused their initial energies on Dad, it would bring the search to a grinding halt. At least long enough for the real killer to get away. No, Dad hadn't been the father she wanted or needed. And he hadn't treated Hunter right either. But he *didn't* murder him. Couldn't the detective see that?

"What else are they looking into?"

Dad sighed. "I don't know."

They wouldn't have told him much if he was a suspect. She pulled up a chair and sat across from him, elbows on her knees. "I know you don't want to remember. But please do it for me. It's the only way we're going to find whoever did this."

"It won't bring him back."

"What about the alarm? Was it on?"

He looked off into space. "There is no alarm."

"You've gotta be kidding me. With all those—"

"Hunter . . . he wanted one. I never thought it was necessary."

One more thing in a long list of improvements Hunter had wanted to make but Dad had squelched. She decided not to address that issue. "Was there sign of a forced entry?"

"Do we have to do this?"

She wanted to shake him and yell, "Yes, we do!" but instead took a deep breath and tried a different approach. "The books, then," she said. "What titles were taken?"

"I don't know."

"Dad, please—"

"I don't know!" He catapulted himself out of the chair and returned to the window, resting his hand on the mullions. "Hunter ran that place. He had the vision, the dreams. All I did was discourage him at every turn."

She let the silence hover between them, then said softly, "At least you admit it now."

The moment those words left her mouth, she regretted them. In an instant Dad's walls shot up, and it was back to the way it always was between them. Abby stared at the rug. Even at a time like this, they couldn't come together.

"You'll have to ask Christy about the books," Dad whispered. Conversation over.

❧

Diego opened his eyes. He'd been swimming in and out of sleep for the past hour—ever since that stupid computerized voice started announcing the available showers over the Flying J loudspeakers. He rolled onto his stomach in slow motion, his arm hanging over the edge of the bed.

"You awake, Rox?"

He gazed down at her empty bed, then flipped onto his back again. Probably in the bathroom. He checked his watch and muttered a curse for sleeping in so late. They should've been on the road hours ago.

But when Roxi didn't appear after ten minutes, his fuse shortened. She had to pick now to take forever? He remembered when Ma first brought up the idea of her living with them, and he'd been dead set against it. For years it'd been just him and Ma, and he wasn't looking to share anything, including his mother, with anyone. Especially with a girl. But Ma got her way, and he'd surprised himself by actually growing to like having Roxi around. It was like having an instant kid sister to pester.

He pulled on his Levis while still on his back, then eased down to the floor. Quietly he slid aside the door that divided the kitchen/living space from the bathroom and back bedroom. Ma still had the curtain separating her bed from the rest of the RV closed.

He tapped on the bathroom door. "Hurry up, Rox."

70

She didn't answer, and he tapped again. Nothing.

He wasn't up for this. He started to jiggle the knob to freak Roxi out, but when he did, the door opened, unlocked. The bathroom was empty.

A feeling of panic rose up in his throat like bile, but he stuffed it, like every other feeling he'd had these past twenty-four hours. Stupid girl. Now was *not* the time to wander around. He retreated to the kitchen. Slipping on the T-shirt he'd worn yesterday, he reached to unlock the side door. Only it was already unlocked and, worse than that, barely shut. Man, Roxi was gonna hear it when he found her.

Outside, the sun was high in the sky, but the air still held a slight chill. He slammed the RV door shut behind himself. That'd wake Ma for sure, but he didn't care. It was time to get going. It hadn't been his idea to hole up in this place. He still thought they should've driven through the night.

It took ten minutes to search the entire Flying J store and restaurant, but he didn't find Roxi. Standing outside on the sidewalk, he ran both hands through his hair as the thoughts zipped through his brain. She wouldn't just pick up and leave, right? That would be dumb. Could something have happened to her?

He paced up and down the sidewalk, clenching his hands in his pockets. *Calm down, man. She's just out for a walk. Getting fresh air. Collecting her thoughts. Or she could be sitting at the kitchen table right now with a cup of coffee back in the RV.*

He ran across the parking lot. He had to be sure. Some of the truckers in these places were real creeps.

"Where have you been?" Ma stood at the stove, her back to him, as he climbed in through the RV's passenger door.

He dove for the crawl space under Roxi's bed, where she usually kept her backpack. It was missing too.

It took effort to keep his voice steady. "You seen Rox?"

"Isn't she with you?"

Oh, man.

Ma turned around. "What's the matter?"

"She's gone, that's what!"

"What are you talking about?"

"I searched everywhere, and I can't find her."

"That's ridiculous. She has to be somewhere."

He took a deep breath. "The door was unlocked, and her backpack's not here."

The teakettle on the stove hissed, a precursor to its whistle, but Ma didn't move to silence it. Diego saw something change in his mother's face, as if a light flicked on in her mind the way it already had in his.

They should've seen this coming.

Steam shot from the teakettle's spout, sending the whistle into a screeching frenzy. Ma turned off the stove and moved the kettle to the back burner. She leaned against the counter, rubbing her eyes.

"We have to find her," Diego said.

"She could be anywhere." Ma shook her head.

"If only we knew when she . . . How far could she go?"

Ma went to the sofa and slowly sat down, gesturing for him to do the same. But he couldn't just sit at a time like this! Roxi was out there alone, and they had to do something about it.

"Sit."

He finally obeyed, more out of complete frustration than actual compliance. Leaning his elbows on his knees, he groaned out loud. "How can this be happening?"

That's when he thought to check Roxi's clothes. He jumped up and rushed to the back bedroom. There wasn't much storage space up front for clothes, so Ma and Roxi usually kept theirs back here somewhere.

"Where's she keep hers?" he yelled over his shoulder.

Ma didn't answer, so he threw open both of the closets and stood on the bed to access the alcoves above it. He rifled through Roxi's side—Gap jeans, several tie-dyed shirts, and her extra pair of sneakers. How could he know what was missing? Was there any chance she was still around here somewhere?

"Diego." Ma stood behind him at the foot of the bed. "We have to face it. She's left us."

"Something could've happened to her! Should we call the cops?"

She gave him a look of disbelief.

He brushed past her without meeting her eyes. He didn't mention he'd wanted to turn himself in last night after waking up in a cold sweat. In his nightmare he'd watched that guy take the bullet again in slow motion.

Diego perched on the edge of the sofa. A simple phone call was all it would take to rid himself of at least part of the guilt.

Ma sat down beside him. "This might be for the best."

"What if some guy got her?"

"The only thing that's happened is she went soft on us."

He threw himself back into the sofa.

"There's nothing we can do anyway."

Which was all too true. Roxi didn't have a cell phone, and even if she did, he doubted she'd take it along. He knew Roxi's point was to escape this whole crappy mess.

"Look at me, honey."

He turned toward his mother and for a moment wished he were a boy again, back when his biggest concern was what to have for dinner. He shook his head. No, he was a man now, and he had to keep his cool here. Ma was counting on him.

"You're my own flesh and blood," she said. "Roxi isn't."

He stared at his mother. "You never did care about her, did you?"

"She needed a home, and I gave her everything I could."

"She cared about *you*."

Ma squeezed his arm. "We're gonna get through this. I promise."

He managed a smile for Ma's sake, but as soon as she stood up to pour them tea, he wiped it from his face. Part of him hated Roxi Gold for bailing on them like this. The other part envied her.

❧

Roxi leaned against a wall at the Alvarado Transportation Center, pulling out her wallet and counting the bills. Two twenties, a ten, and a five. That wasn't going far, especially if she bought a Greyhound ticket.

Rooting through her backpack, she checked the contents again. There hadn't been time to grab much. An extra pair of jeans, a sweatshirt she'd picked up in Minnesota with a wolf graphic on the front, a long underwear shirt, one of Diego's knit pullovers, every pair of underwear she owned, three pairs of socks, and two hoodies. She was wearing her jean jacket. But the most important items were packed beneath the clothes.

She removed the first of the books she'd wrapped in a plastic grocery bag. *The Lion, the Witch and the Wardrobe* by C. S. Lewis. This was the book that started the whole Narnia craze, wasn't it? She'd never read it, but Irene said it was a classic. That's why she'd taken it. But to look at the plain, light blue boards, it was hard to believe it was valuable. She opened the book. The store had written in pencil "first UK edition, first printing" on the flyleaf. The publisher was listed as Geoffrey Bles, London, 1950.

She read the first lines:

Once there were four children whose names were Peter,
Susan, Edmund, and Lucy. This story is about something
that happened to them when they were sent away from
London during the war because of the air raids.

She flipped through a couple pages, read a few more lines, then closed the book. It would be better not to put any stress on the binding since this wasn't just any old copy. Even though there was some darkening to the boards and a bit of fraying to the spine ends, first editions had to be worth something. She'd sell this one first.

When she took out the second book, her stomach twisted. *The Great Gatsby.* The one that clerk had showed her. It had to be worth a lot.

Returning both books to the backpack, Roxi took in the huge center with its red-tiled roof. This place was apparently a hub for Amtrak, Greyhound, and a commuter train and bus line. It took up a whole city block, and she took a little comfort in all the people milling around. Irene and Diego must've realized she was missing by now. Would they look for her?

Roxi got up and slung her backpack over her shoulders. When Diego gave her Mom's address, she'd almost ripped it to shreds right then and there. She'd finally convinced herself she didn't need her mother.

Everything was different now.

10

ABBY COULDN'T STAY in the house any longer. She'd tried to take a nap but only ended up staring at the ceiling. She got Christy's address from Lynn, and by one o'clock she was parked behind the building that housed Big Owl Gallery on the first floor and Christy Williams's apartment on the second. It was a decent enough area of Longmont. Coffee shops, art galleries, and boutiques filled the storefronts, with the occasional law office and insurance agency sprinkled among them.

She hesitated at the bottom of the treated lumber stairs leading up to the apartment. Though she'd never met Christy in person, she felt like she had. Hunter talked about her constantly, and apparently she made the world go round.

Abby let herself smile. She'd suspected early on Hunter thought of the woman as more than an employee just by the way his voice changed when he talked about her. She'd watched their relationship grow into something more over the last year. So when Hunter called her a month ago asking for advice on the best way to propose to a girl, she'd been more than thrilled for her little brother. He'd opted for her suggestion of a candlelight dinner, and apparently it worked. Christy said yes and they were to be married next spring.

Abby climbed the steps, pausing outside 2A. She should've called.

She knocked three times and waited. Within seconds the lock clicked, and the door opened. She instantly recognized Christy from the pictures Hunter had e-mailed her. She was seven years younger than Abby, but in some ways she looked older. As if life had been tough on her. From what Hunter had told her, Abby knew it had been.

"Christy?"

The woman nodded, her brow wrinkling slightly as if she was trying to place who Abby was. Christy wore no makeup today, and her eyes were unmistakably puffy from crying.

"I'm Hunter's sister, Abby."

Christy's face instantly softened.

"It was rude of me not to call. I . . . I can come back later."

Opening the door wide, Christy gestured her inside. "No, no. Please come in."

As she did, her cop instincts cataloged the room at a glance. It was one of those open floor plan–type apartments with no walls separating the kitchen, living room, and dining room. A short hall to the right would lead to the bathroom and bedroom. She was acutely aware of the stack of linen wedding invitations on the table beside the door.

"I knew you looked familiar. Hunter talked so much about you," Christy said, closing and locking the door.

"And he thought you hung the moon."

Christy gave her a slight smile. An uncomfortable moment passed as they each apparently wondered whether to hug or shake hands.

"Look at us," Christy finally said, wiping her eyes with her fingertips. "Staring at each other like strangers when we were almost family."

Compassion welled up in Abby, and she pulled Christy into a gentle hug. "Hunter loved you very much, and that's good enough for me."

Christy wept into her shoulder, and Abby tried to be a comfort by patting her back. She never had been good at this sort of thing, and she was having trouble keeping her own tears at bay.

"I'm sorry," Christy muttered, pulling away. "Can I get you something to eat or drink?"

"A cup of coffee would be great."

Five minutes later they were sitting on the sofa nursing mugs. Christy drank hers black; Abby added the sugar equivalent of her three Splenda packets. She leaned back, closing her eyes. Fatigue was overpowering her again. Not even coffee—and Christy had made it strong—was doing much for her at this point.

"You just get in?" Christy asked.

"Drove most of the night."

"You're welcome to crash here if you'd like."

She considered that for a moment. The idea of returning to the house wasn't appealing, especially after her words with Dad. But she was going to have to face him again sometime.

"Thanks, but I'll be needing to get back."

"How are they doing?"

Abby knew what she meant, and all she could do was sigh. "They actually suspect Dad, if you can believe it."

"You're kidding."

"Lynn wasn't home, and he doesn't have an alibi."

Christy tilted her head. "But there's no way he—"

"I know. They'll figure out soon enough he's innocent. But in the meantime, someone is getting away with murder."

Tucking her legs up onto the sofa, Christy sat Indian-style with the coffee mug nestled in her lap. "He texted me right before he went to bed, but my phone was off. I didn't get it till the morning. He said he loved me, but I . . . I never texted him back."

"He knew you loved him."

Christy wiped her eyes. "Why did he go downstairs? Why?"

"He must've heard something. You know how creaky those floors are."

"What's hardest for me is picturing him in there . . . alone. I keep asking myself if he called for help, if he suffered."

There was no need to share with Christy that he probably did suffer. Depending on where the bullet hit, he might have struggled for every one of his last breaths, slowly drowning as his lungs filled with blood.

"I'm going to find whoever did this," Abby said.

Christy's dark eyebrows rose.

"But I need your help."

"Me?"

She set her cup on the end table, turning to face Christy. "I used to work at the Barn too, as a teenager. But it's been a long time since I've had my hand in the book business. You know books."

"A lot are missing."

"Did you notice anything out of the ordinary that day?"

Christy stood, slowly pacing the floor. "We had a book stolen during business hours. Right under my nose apparently."

"The same day?"

"I noticed it was gone when we were closing up. It could've been misplaced, but I'm pretty sure it wasn't. I couldn't find it anywhere."

"Has anything like that ever happened before?"

"Just when Vince worked there. I guess you know about that."

Abby nodded.

"He'd been stealing from the store for years," Christy said.

"Didn't surprise me."

Vince DuBois had been a longtime employee of the store. He'd also been Abby's boyfriend years ago and the reason she left the area. Maybe she'd talk about it with Christy sometime, because apparently Vince had been up to his old abusive ways with her, too. She knew Christy had dated him before Hunter, and when she finally left him after one too many violent episodes a year and a half ago, he'd tried to kill her. Last Abby checked, he was doing a dime for attempted murder.

"That's the only other incident," Christy said.

"Have the police talked with you?"

Christy walked over to the kitchen section of the room and refilled her coffee mug. "I was the one who went through the store to give them an approximate value of what's missing. It's over fifty grand and probably closer to sixty."

Abby whistled.

"Some of our best stock."

"I can't believe there wasn't an alarm."

"We've never had one."

"Because of Dad."

Christy leaned against the kitchen counter. "Things *were* better between him and Hunter the last few months."

"I bet."

Christy looked her right in the eyes, and Abby was surprised at the gentleness of her gaze. It felt as though Christy were seeing inside her soul. She wasn't sure if she liked the feeling, and she wondered how much Hunter had told his fiancée about her.

"They argued earlier that night," Abby said.

Christy returned to the sofa and sat beside her. "I can only imagine what your father's going through, Abby. He found him."

Abby took a deep breath and picked up her now-cooling coffee mug just to give her hands something to hold. "Those books are going to turn up sometime, and right now they're all we've got to go on."

"But you're a cop. Won't the police talk to you?"

Correction: A suspended *cop.*

"They already have," Abby said. "And they don't have much. But if you and I work on this together, we might get somewhere."

Christy didn't answer.

"I just need a list of the books that were taken."

"I can give you the list, but don't you think we both might be a little too close to this?"

"That's the whole point. We care more than anybody. To the cops, Hunter's a case number. Think about it. What if this person's never caught? How would that make you feel?"

Christy glanced at her hands, and Abby thought she saw them tremble.

"Every day I'll wonder," Abby said. "Every person I meet, I'll think, 'Are you the one?'"

"What if you do find him?" Christy asked softly. "What then?"

"I'm not letting myself think that far ahead," Abby lied. Last night she imagined staring straight into the killer's hard, ugly eyes, cursing him to his face. Whoever he was, he was gonna rot in jail if Abby had anything to say about it.

"I can't picture what it would be like to see the person who . . . who took his life." Christy got a faraway look in her eyes. "What type of human being would do that?"

Abby shook her head. "You'd be surprised."

"I guess you've seen it all."

"Anyone's capable of murder. Even people like you and me."

Christy took a sip from her mug. She started to say something, then stopped herself.

"What?"

"Never mind."

Abby felt a kinship she hadn't expected with the woman. After all, they both loved Hunter. "What were you gonna say?"

"Have you . . . you know, ever had to—"

"Shoot someone?"

Christy seemed embarrassed.

"It's okay." Hunter had apparently picked a sensitive one like himself. "And the answer is no, I haven't. I almost did once, though. This guy was pointing a gun right at me, and he refused to drop it. I mean, I was seconds away from emptying my Glock into him."

"Wow."

"Yeah. Not a good feeling."

"What happened?"

"He finally dropped it. And my backup arrived just in time. But I remember when it was all over, I couldn't stop shaking. It haunted me for a long time."

They both fell silent, and Abby wondered if Hunter's murderer felt any remorse. Some of these guys didn't. To them, killing a man was like killing a bug.

Abby clenched her jaw. "I *hate* whoever did this, Christy. Hunter didn't deserve to die. He had a whole life ahead of him. With you. And his dreams? They're as dead as he is because Dad's never gonna follow through with them." She rubbed her eyes, then let her arms flop to her sides, her shoulders sagging. "And I'm just so tired and angry I can't even think straight."

Christy got up and went to the kitchen counter, picking up a set of keys. She pointed at the door. "Why don't I follow you back to the

Barn. If you're up for it, I'll get you that list of books today. I've got it on the computer over there. Then you can get some rest."

Abby peeled herself off the sofa with a groan. "Sounds like a plan."

11

ROXI SPENT ALL BUT HER LAST FIVE BUCKS on the Greyhound bus ticket. When they finally pulled into the run-down Amarillo station, she was stiff and dehydrated. So far no one had questioned a teen girl riding the bus alone, and she desperately hoped it would stay that way.

She'd been on automatic pilot and had been able to avoid thinking about much of anything. But now that she was in Amarillo, she had a harder time keeping the memories at bay.

Was she crazy to come here, like a little kid, looking for her mommy? Mom had abandoned her. Left her to fend for herself in a cruel, dark world. Not one card. Never a phone call. In one instant she had become motherless—and not because of some freak accident or deadly disease beyond Mom's control. That she might've been able to deal with. No, the reality was worse than if Mom had died.

She moved inside with a group of touring senior citizens. Her first stop was the bathroom. She closed herself in a stall and started to change into a clean shirt. She hadn't known Mom was an addict. She thought all moms kept glass pipes in their kitchen drawers. It took bullies at school slamming her into a wall and calling Mom "a using whore" to get it through to her. How they'd found out, she didn't know, but they were right. At least about the drugs part. She was pretty sure Mom never sold herself, though the boyfriends changed on a monthly—sometimes weekly—basis.

She'd been eight years old the night her life changed forever. She remembered it like it was yesterday, hopping up the stairs to the second-floor apartment she and Mom shared, counting each step as she went. She had liked doing that. Reminded her of playing hopscotch with the girls at school. That night, excitement bubbled in her tummy with each hop.

Bursting into the apartment, she threw her books on the floor. "Mom?"

All week she'd looked forward to that night. Mom had said she would rent a movie, and they were going to make caramel popcorn and suck on SweeTarts, Roxi's favorite candy. But the best part was Roxi wouldn't have to share Mom with any of her dumb boyfriends. Tonight it would be just the two of them.

But her mother wasn't home. Roxi guessed she had gotten stuck in traffic, or maybe . . . Roxi giggled. Maybe she'd run out to surprise her with pizza or Big Macs. That would be even better than popcorn and SweeTarts. Roxi just wished she weren't so hungry right now.

She hadn't eaten lunch at school. Mom forgot to pack it. Roxi figured she was probably so busy planning tonight that it slipped her mind. A little snack would be okay. Roxi wouldn't have any trouble scarfing down their treats once Mom got home.

Unfortunately, there wasn't much to choose from. There was

almost a week to go before Mom was paid, and that always meant slim pickings for meals and definitely for snacks. Roxi held the fridge open trying to decide. Looked like it would be a mustard sandwich and applesauce. Not that she minded that. She'd grown to like the taste of the squooshy white bread when the mustard soaked into it. That's what she ate whenever Mom was too tired to make dinner. Sometimes for breakfast too if Mom slept in.

Roxi dropped the mustard and bread on the counter. Only when she went back for the applesauce did she see Mom's note on the fridge:

> *One of the waitresses called in sick.*
> *I had to go to work.*
> *Sorry, sweetheart. I'll make it up to you.*

Roxi shook her head now to clear the unpleasant memories as she slipped into her clean shirt in the bus station bathroom. She remembered ripping the note off the fridge and having a good cry that night, then eating those stupid mustard sandwiches alone in front of the TV watching *Simpsons* reruns. She hadn't known then what she knew now. Mom hadn't been called in to work at all.

Roxi stopped at the vending machines on her way out of the station and bought a bottle of Aquafina and a bag of Doritos. She downed the water, then refilled the bottle at the water fountain.

She absentmindedly rubbed the scar on her arm, hidden by the long sleeves she always wore. Even after all this time, it was still tender sometimes. She guessed some nerves had been severed because her fingers still occasionally tingled. It was her memento of that awful night. She supposed it was only fitting that both her body and her heart had been scarred at the same time.

She'd watched TV much later than Mom would have let her stay up, if Mom had been there. When she couldn't keep her eyes open any longer, she climbed into bed and lay there in the dark, glad no one could see the tears trickling down her cheeks. She should have known it had been too good to be true. She shouldn't have gotten her hopes up.

She tried to go to sleep and forget her disappointment, but the blinking signs from the bar across the street wouldn't let her. And Mom wasn't there to close the blinds. She'd have to get up and do it herself.

Dragging a chair from the kitchen, she pushed it up against the window and climbed onto it, reaching and stretching for the blind. It was one of those plastic kinds that rolled up, and her fingers almost had it.

Just a little bit farther.

Come on, streeeeetch. One finger grazed the curtain.

She lifted her other hand and reached with it too, even as the chair wobbled.

Another teensy-weensy inch. That's it.

Roxi stretched higher, the chair wobbled some more, and then suddenly, it slipped out from under her.

She screamed and fell forward into the window.

Glass shattered.

"Mommy!"

Her body was falling, falling.

She slammed into the ground. For a second, everything was still, and she was too stunned to move. Then shocks of pain zapped through her arm, head, legs. She tried to sit up and screamed when she saw the blood spurting from a gash in her arm.

When a neighbor finally heard her screams and came running, his flashlight revealed just how seriously she was hurt. Roxi remembered freaking at the sight of the slice in her arm, so deep she could see to the bone.

The neighbor tried to comfort her until the paramedics arrived, but by that time she'd become inconsolable. She wanted her mommy, but her mommy didn't come. She'd been too busy getting high at a party with her new boyfriend.

Since there were no relatives willing to take in an eight-year-old, the state had taken custody of her and almost put Mom in jail for negligence because of her injuries. The only way Mom got out of it was to check into rehab.

Roxi pulled out her water bottle and sipped it as she walked. She didn't know why she wanted to find her mother now. Was it stupid to wonder if Mom could somehow still love her, even after all that had happened? Or was she just setting herself up to be hurt all over again?

She kicked at a loose stone and watched it fly into the dry, over-grown grass beyond the sidewalk. What if Mom hadn't had a choice? Maybe that was part of the agreement with the cops. Maybe she'd been forbidden to have any contact with her daughter, and all this time Mom was missing her little girl.

A glimmer of hope sparked inside Roxi. Maybe Mom had been trying to find her all these years but hadn't been able to.

At the intersection, she stopped to check the map she'd picked up at the bus station, glancing up and down the street. She just had to keep following this road until it hit Amarillo Boulevard. She was glad Diego had taught her how to read a map, because it would take a little snaking around to get there, but Mom's development was only a couple miles from here.

A car engine revved behind her, and Roxi swung around to see a yellow Corvette speeding her way. Instead of accelerating past her, this one slowed, then stopped right beside her.

She crossed the street and kept walking, but the Corvette fol-lowed, keeping pace with her steps. Its passenger window crept down, and a guy in his twenties with a goatee leaned toward her. "Need a ride?"

The offer caught her off guard. Her feet ached, and her shoulders were sore from the backpack straps' rubbing. But there was something about this guy's eyes that creeped her out. She had a feeling he was looking for more than she ever wanted to give.

"Nah. I'm cool."

"Sure?" The guy grinned.

"Yeah, I'm sure."

"Your loss, babe."

He zoomed off, the car's tires squealing around the next corner. She listened as the sound faded into the distance, then quickened her steps. The sooner she got out of this area, the better.

12

"THIS IS WHAT I GAVE THE POLICE." Christy gathered a stack of pages from the laser printer tray and handed them to Abby.

Flipping through them, Abby recognized some of the titles as valuable classics, but she never would've guessed the rest were worth much. Even back when she had been involved in this store and knew a few things about books, it seemed strange to her that someone would pay five hundred bucks for a beat-up first-edition copy of Jack Kerouac's *On the Road*. Maybe she just took books for granted. They'd always been around, and they always would be.

"How many?" Abby asked, stapling the pages together.

They were in the Barn's back storeroom at a small computer workstation. The room was also some sort of packing area, as bubble wrap rolls and stacks of unfolded brown boxes filled the corners.

The rest of the space was filled with boxes on wooden pallets packed with uncataloged books.

"All we know for sure," Christy said, swiveling around in her office chair, "is there were twenty-three rare books in the front case. We had those cataloged, and they're first on that list."

Abby read the top entry:

The Big Sleep by Raymond Chandler. E. P. Dutton. 1939.
    First edition. VG/G
    Chandler's first novel. An exceptional copy with the rare dust jacket.
    Some chipping to dust jacket edges and some light sun fading to dust jacket spine.
    Inventory #: 002459
    $6,950.00

She knew *VG/G* stood for the title's condition. *VG* would mean "very good," the actual book's condition. The *G* would refer to the dust jacket. Most antiquarian bookstores went by a standard grading system where "Fine" was the highest grade and strangely, "Good" was on the low end of the scale, closer to "Fair" and "Poor" than anything truly good. A good condition dust jacket could even have tears and soiling, which never made any sense to Abby.

"We know more books than that were taken," Christy continued. "But it's next to impossible to know which exactly since they weren't all cataloged. We had to guess on their values. You want to see the room for yourself?"

Abby wasn't sure she did. To stand in the spot where her brother actually died . . . She briefly met Christy's eyes. The woman was looking less like a wounded victim the more time they spent together. Like she was gaining strength even as Abby was losing it.

"It's okay if you don't want to." Christy stood.

"No, I need to see it."

"We'll make it quick."

As she followed Christy through the doorway, the smell of the front room was the first thing that hit Abby—stale woodsmoke, leather, and old paper. The smells of her childhood. When she was a little girl before Hunter was born, she remembered building castles out of books in here. She still had a dreamlike memory of sitting inside one of her walled forts with Mom's face smiling down at her. She couldn't have been older than three or four.

Glancing around the room, she realized nothing much had changed. The potbellied wood stove still crouched in the corner, cold and awaiting Hunter's skilled hand to bring it to life. Even as a boy he had been the one to start it up in the morning and make sure the fire burned low enough to leave unattended in the evenings.

"I haven't been in here for years," Abby said to herself as much as to Christy. "When Hunter and I got together, we usually met half-way, or he drove out to me."

Christy stared into the empty case by the register. "I set up this display myself," she said. "I can't believe they're all gone. I never imagined I'd hold in my hands a first edition *Great Gatsby* like that."

"Was that the rarest one?"

"Hands down. With the first state dust jacket, we priced it at forty grand. And the dust jacket is what made it valuable. You can't just go out and buy a replacement."

Christy spoke with the same reverence Hunter always had for his books. She lifted her eyes to the shelves behind the counter. "See those gaps? They weren't there before. Whoever it was picked from all over the place."

Abby slowly walked around the room. The used book world had always been extremely competitive, but with the dawn of the Internet age, every Joe Schmo with a computer could now sell books online. And the more sellers, the less books to go around. Hunter had told her stories about dealers actually getting into fistfights at used book sales over a find. It was craziness to anyone on the outside, but she knew one book could sometimes determine whether a dealer put gas in his car or paid the rent. In a moment of passion she could imagine a book dealer killing over books.

"Could another dealer have done this?" Abby asked.

Christy shrugged. "They were definitely after the books, weren't they? The money in the register isn't even missing."

"Really?"

"Still there. Two hundred dollars. Exactly like I left it."

"Which explains why they suspect Dad. If someone was staging a robbery, they might forget to act like a criminal." Abby held up the book list still in her hand. "First step is placing wants at all the used book Web sites. If these titles show up anywhere, I'll hear about it."

"We marked all the books, you know."

Abby stopped in her tracks. "Marked?"

"On the last page we penciled a small *D*. At least in the ones that were in here." Christy rested her hand on the case's glass. "And in most books priced over a hundred. That way we'd know if anyone tried to pull the old switcheroo game and buy a rare book in pristine condition and later return their beat-up copy for a refund."

"People do that?"

"It's happened."

"But wouldn't someone know to look for the mark?"

"Not usually. Different dealers have different marks and in different places. Some don't use them at all."

Abby walked around the room again, taking everything in. That would be a big help. But what about in here? Could there be any clues the police missed? She knew they would've dusted for prints and searched for fibers and footprints.

She stared at the floor with its rough-hewn wooden slats. Why *had* Hunter come down here? Had he heard something? Her gaze came to rest on the floorboards near the arched stone doorway leading to the adjoining room. The wood in this spot was lighter and cleaner than the rest. It dawned on Abby why. These boards had been scrubbed.

Bile rose in her throat, and the strength drained from her limbs. Christy was still talking about something, but Abby didn't hear her. The room was suddenly shrinking, its walls pressing in on her like a huge vise. In that moment she saw Hunter's death in Technicolor. She turned her face away.

"Abby?"

They'd scrubbed blood off these boards.

"Are you okay?"

Abby couldn't help what she did next. She ran. Past Christy, past the counter, through the storeroom, and outside to her car. Cold saliva built in her mouth, and she almost threw up. Gasping for fresh air, she clutched the Acura's mirror to steady herself. She sucked in breaths, making stupid, pathetic sounds. That's where he'd died, wasn't it? Right there on the floor. Alone. Scared. Hurting. Why couldn't he have stayed upstairs? Why hadn't Dad heard something? As a girl, she'd tried so hard to protect her little brother, but she hadn't been able to save him from this.

She didn't know how long she stayed there crying at the car. But as she gradually felt herself coming back to reality, she realized Christy was standing beside her. She probably had no idea, and Abby couldn't possibly tell her what she suspected. It would devastate her. At a loss for what to say, Abby climbed up onto the hood of her car and lay on it with her back against the windshield.

To her surprise, Christy climbed onto the hood beside her. They both lay on the warm metal, a light breeze blowing over them. Neither spoke. Abby closed her eyes, just trying to breathe normally. Hunter had loved this woman greatly. Not some silly puppy love either, but the way love should be. Deep and giving. The way Abby and Michael should've loved each other.

Christy was the first to break the silence. "So how long have you been a cop?"

Another sore subject. But Christy had no way of knowing that, and Abby didn't intend to tell her. Not yet at least.

"Eighteen years this December."

"When you were little, did you say, 'When I grow up, I want to be a policewoman'?"

Abby threaded her fingers together and rested them on her chest. "Believe it or not, it never even entered my mind until I moved away." She let a moment of calm pass between them. "You do know why I left, right?"

"I think so," Christy said softly.

"I figured Hunter told you. Vince was abusive even back then, only I didn't find out until a few months into our relationship. By then Dad had hired him here. The only way to escape was to leave the state entirely. I ended up in Utah."

Christy crossed her arms, staring straight ahead for a moment. "We have a lot in common, then."

"I guess we do." Abby smiled at her.

"So you just decided one day you wanted to be a cop?"

"Almost. I got a job at a little café, and one of our faithful patrons was this lady officer. She must've been my age now at the time. She exuded this confidence, and I realized I wanted that so badly. I'd let people beat me down, and I was tired of it. Seeing another woman doing something meaningful with her life clinched it. Funny thing was, I never even talked to her about it. Just jumped right in and signed myself up at the academy."

"And the rest is history."

"Sorta. I was young and stupid, thinking I could change the world. It took me years to realize just how naive that kind of attitude was."

"I can only imagine."

Abby decided to tell her more. "I was twenty-five when I met Michael, my ex-husband. He's a lawyer, and I was in court testifying against this drug dealer. Guess who was defending him."

Christy laughed. "Really?"

"He ripped me up on the stand too. So later I'm out in the hall, and this same hotshot lawyer walks up behind me and asks me out."

"He was defending a drug dealer and you went out with him?"

Abby couldn't help but laugh herself. "Didn't I say I was young and stupid? He asked me to marry him after we dated four months, and rather than tell either of our families, we eloped."

"You're kidding. Hunter never told me that."

"I can't say it's the best decision I ever made," Abby said. "I think I hurt my dad a lot by not having him there to walk me down the aisle. Our relationship never had been that great. That was just the last nail in the coffin, I guess."

They watched the sun set in silence for a minute or two, and Abby was surprised how comfortable she felt with Christy. They'd only just met, and here she was sharing stuff she didn't normally talk about with anyone. It was like they'd known each other for years. Maybe this was what it would've been like to have a sister.

"What about *your* family?" Abby asked.

Christy hesitated for a second, and Abby wondered if she'd asked the wrong question.

"I didn't have a close relationship with my parents," Christy said. "They both died in a car accident coming home for my eighteenth birthday. It's kind of a long story, but right after that I skipped town, leaving my younger sister to be cared for by our great-aunt. I never said good-bye, and it's one of my biggest regrets. My sister and I lost fifteen years together because of my selfishness."

"But you're in contact now?"

Christy nodded. "Right about the time I left Vince, we found each other again. May lives a couple hours from here in Elk Valley. She'd be here now, actually, if I hadn't told her I needed the time alone. You'll see her at the funeral."

Abby groaned. "I can't even think about the funeral right now."

"Will your daughter be there?"

A pang hit Abby at the mention of Kat. "I haven't told her yet."

"I was hoping someday I'd get to meet her."

"I wasn't a very good mother, Christy. Or wife, either. When Kat was ten, I found out Michael was having an affair. Then he sprang the divorce papers on me. I tried to fight it, but it didn't matter. He got sole custody of our girl, married the other woman, and now they're one big happy family in a mansion on a hill."

"I'm sorry." Christy looked like she really was.

"Every day I wonder if she's okay. If she ever thinks about me."

"You don't just forget your mom."

"You might if you had a stepmother like Sarah. She dotes on Kat like you wouldn't believe, doing everything she can to make Kat forget me. Doesn't help that she's cute, petite, and blonde—everything I'm not."

"But you still get to see Kat, right?"

The sun was dropping below the trees now, a sinking orange ball of fire. Abby tried to keep bitterness from seeping into her words. "Back in the beginning, Michael made an effort to include me. You know, I was at the birthday parties and all that. But now that she's older, they leave it up to her." Abby kept her eyes on the sunset. "And she doesn't want to see me."

"She's sixteen."

"Growing up too fast."

"Kids these days are so much busier than we ever were."

It's possible that's all it was. Kat was a teenager living a fast-paced life. Between friends, volleyball, and dance, the girl could hardly be expected to keep in touch. It was easier to pick one woman to call Mom and let the other fade into the background.

"Did I put my job before my family? I don't know. It was important to me, but I would've given it up in a heartbeat if I'd known Kat was suffering." Abby tapped the back of her head against the windshield. "Did I bring the work home with me? Probably. Maybe that's why Michael found someone else."

"Or it could be none of the above and you're beating yourself up over stuff you can't change."

She shrugged.

"It takes two to tango," Christy said.

"Yeah, but someone has to start the dance, and I have a feeling that was me, not Michael."

They sat together on the hood of the car until the sun dropped below the horizon and darkness crept across the parking lot. When Abby finally slid off the car, Christy did the same. They said good night and Christy drove away in her Honda.

Abby watched the car's taillights disappear down the road, then slowly trudged up the shadowy driveway to the farmhouse. She stuffed her hands in her pockets, the book list tucked under her arm.

13

1564 POPLAR LANE.

Roxi stared at the small ranch house from across the street, her heart a fluttering bird in her rib cage. Would Mom take one look at her, throw her arms around her, and beg for the chance to start over? Would this house, with the minivan parked at the curb and the amped-up black pickup in the driveway, be her new home?

Hunger sliced through Roxi's stomach, and she licked her parched lips. It had been almost two days since she'd eaten much of anything, not counting the Flying J restaurant meal she'd lost in the bathroom toilet. The Doritos today only made her hungrier. And thirsty. Mom used to cook a mean batch of tacos. Would her mother make something for her to eat tonight?

Roxi finally got the nerve to cross the street. She looked okay, right? Her pants weren't too dusty, and her jean jacket wasn't terribly frayed. What about her hair? She tried to work out the tangles with her fingers. She hadn't thought to bring a mirror or a comb.

Lights were on in the front windows, and she saw the flashing blue glow of a TV, but the curtains obscured anything else. What if Diego got the wrong woman and this Marie Greeley wasn't her mom at all? She wished she had a picture of Mom to jog her memory. Every time she tried to remember the details of her face, she saw Irene's. Roxi was pretty sure Mom used to have auburn hair too, like Irene, but Mom's was curlier. She remembered pulling on it as a toddler and feeling the curls straighten between her fingers.

Squaring her shoulders, Roxi walked past the truck, her boots tapping on the driveway macadam even as the nervous bird in her chest rustled its wings. After so many years of wondering, she was here. On her mother's doorstep. Would Mom recognize her? Did she have the guts to knock?

She reached for the doorbell with an arm made of Silly Putty. Canned TV laughter seeped through the door, and she thought she heard a man's voice talking. Was that a commercial or Mom's new husband? A fresh wave of nervousness washed over her. What would it be like to have a dad?

Her fingers hovered over the doorbell. How about a mom?

Roxi pulled her hand away and rubbed the back of her neck. Would they hear the bell over the TV? Dropping her backpack to the ground, she scooted it aside with her foot. Even if she did just get off the bus, she didn't want to look desperate.

Come on. Just go for it.

She finally pressed the doorbell. Long and hard. Then waited. For a second she didn't hear anything different. The TV blared on. A car zoomed down the street behind her.

Wait.

She strained to discern the tapping sound that seemed to be coming toward her. Were those footsteps?

Oh, man. This was a stupid—

The door swung open, and her heart skipped a beat.

It was Mom. She looked Roxi up and down with no recognition.

"What are you selling today?"

Roxi swallowed hard, all words ripped from her tongue. Mom's hair was blonde now and cut stylishly short, but it was still her. Small gold hoop earrings dangled from her earlobes, and she wore heavy makeup.

"If you're from the school, I'm sorry, but we already bought the candles."

Roxi prodded herself to breathe.

"I'm kind of busy," Mom said. "You aren't selling something?"

She knew she was staring and probably looking like an idiot, but Roxi couldn't help it. To stand face-to-face with the woman she'd longed for all these years was almost too much for her to comprehend. She was surprised to discover she'd grown taller than her mother.

"You don't know who I am, do you?" Which was understandable. She was no longer an eight-year-old kid. She couldn't possibly expect Mom to recognize her.

"Well, considering you haven't—"

"I'm Roxi."

Mom's mouth stayed open, but no more words came.

"Your daughter."

A statue, Mom didn't even blink.

Roxi fiddled with a button on her jean jacket, buttoning it, then unbuttoning it, buttoning, then unbuttoning. Was Mom happy to see her? She couldn't read her face. Mom looked jarred more than anything else.

"Say something, Mom."

Her mother glanced behind herself, then lowered her voice. "Why are you here?"

Roxi forced a smile. "Why am I here?"

"Aren't they taking care of you?"

She lowered her eyes to her scuffed boots. "I came to see you."

"Marie?" a male voice called from inside the house.

Mom squeezed the bridge of her nose with a manicured thumb and forefinger. Her gold bracelets clinked together. "I wish you hadn't," she whispered.

Roxi searched her mother's face for something, anything, to indicate she didn't mean that. She was just shocked and not thinking clearly, blurting out the first words that rushed into her head. Roxi smiled again, hoping to break the ice. Of course Mom didn't mean it. It was just a shock. If only Roxi had called ahead, she could've avoided this unnecessary confusion.

"Marie! Who's at the door?"

"Mom, I—"

Her mother yelled over her shoulder, "Just someone selling magazines."

The man cursed. "We don't need any more magazines!"

"Wait here," Mom said to Roxi. "I'll be right back."

"Is that your husband?"

Mom retreated into the house, closing the door. And Roxi was left alone again. She shifted her weight uneasily on the cement stoop. It wasn't supposed to be this way. Had she been too abrupt? But she realized there *was* no other way to say it. If only there'd been some way to prepare her mother.

Of course, maybe Mom was getting that Tom guy so they could both welcome her into their home. He didn't sound very friendly, but some people really hated solicitors. She heard footsteps again, and her spirits rose. This sort of thing was bound to happen at an unexpected meeting like this. It would take them both some adjustment to get used to each other again.

But when Mom returned, she was alone and now wearing a red leather jacket. A matching purse hung from her shoulder, and she clutched a set of keys. Mom gestured toward the minivan at the curb. "Let's take a drive. We can talk."

Roxi scooped up her backpack. She wondered why they couldn't just go inside, but she definitely wasn't complaining. She'd relish this ride alone with her mother, because Mom was right. They did need to talk.

"Where are we going?"

Mom turned around. "Please just follow me."

It didn't really matter. Roxi would be happy if all they did was circle the block. At least they'd finally be together.

They were almost at the van when Roxi heard the front door click behind her. She swung around to see a barefoot girl in pigtails fly across the lawn toward Mom.

"Mommy! Mommy!"

Mommy?

The girl couldn't have been older than five, and she threw herself at Mom's legs, wrapping both arms around them. Quickly kneeling, Mom gently rested her hands on the girl's shoulders. "Didn't I tell you to go to bed?"

"But you said you'd tuck me in!"

"Daddy'll do it."

"No, he won't. He's watching TV."

Roxi could barely wrap her mind around what she was seeing. All at once reality smacked her in the face. Unable to move, she watched her mother lean close to her . . . daughter.

"Honey, I need to run to the store. You get in bed by yourself, and before you fall asleep, I'll be back. Okay?"

The girl pointed at Roxi. "Who's that?"

Marie Greeley didn't look up. "She's just selling magazines." Then she kissed the girl on the forehead, turned her around, and hustled her into the house. Taking swift strides back to the minivan, she nudged Roxi toward the passenger door as if nothing had happened. "It's unlocked."

But something had happened. Mechanically, Roxi climbed in. Slumping into the seat, she didn't bother fastening her seat belt. The adrenaline rush, the excitement—gone, as if she'd crashed from some crazy sugar high. Mom had another kid. One she apparently was having no trouble loving or taking care of.

"Is she yours?" she asked softly, just to be sure.

A pause. "Yes."

"What's her name?"

Mom drove the van into the street. "Erin."

"Is that guy your husband?"

"Yes."

"Do they know about me?"

Mom stared straight ahead, silent and gripping the steering wheel with both hands.

"You mean you didn't tell your own husband you had a daughter?"

"It's not that simple."

"Oh, I can see that."

With tired eyes, Mom glanced at her. "You're almost eighteen, Roxi. An adult. I want you to understand this like an adult."

"I'm sixteen, and what if I don't want to be an adult? What if I just need a mom? Ever thought about that?"

"That's something I can't be for you anymore."

"You're *Erin's* mom."

They stopped at a light, and Mom sighed. "I knew the state would take care of you. I didn't leave you on the streets. And after I got out of rehab, I needed to forget my old life and build myself a new, clean one."

"Forget about me, you mean."

"I never forgot about you."

"Then why didn't you look for me?"

Mom's lips pursed.

"You could've found me."

"But you needed a better life than what I'd given you. Just look at what happened. You probably still bear the scars of my mistakes. You'll realize someday it was the best thing for you."

Roxi didn't answer, thinking of the scar under her sleeve. Did Mom have any idea how badly she'd been cut?

"They did watch out for you, right? You have a new family now?"

"Like you care." Roxi kept her eyes glued to the road. "You don't have a clue what I've been through."

"Did someone hurt you?" Her mother managed a concerned tone.

Only you, Mom. "It doesn't matter now, does it?"

"Please don't make this harder than it already is."

"*I'm* making it harder?"

"You have to realize this will never work. Too much has changed."

"We could try." Roxi swiveled around in her seat. "I promise I won't be any trouble."

Mom was already shaking her head. "You don't understand."

"You wouldn't even know I was around. I'd just melt into the background. I could clean the house, cook dinner, do the laundry, anything."

"Roxi, please."

"Whatever you wanted."

Her mother stopped at an intersection. "Let me explain something."

"But why wouldn't—?"

"Just listen to me for one minute."

Roxi shut up, hoping she didn't sound like some rebellious teenager ready to argue. But even as she tried to listen, panic bubbled up inside her. She'd banked everything on this working.

"I have a new life," Mom said with a nod of her head to emphasize the point. "I can't risk losing Tom . . . or Erin. I already lost you."

"But I'm here now."

"We both need to move on. You need to live your own life. Without me."

Roxi could only stare at her mother.

"Do you understand?"

She faced the window, not wanting Mom to see the tears building in her eyes.

All these years she'd given Mom the benefit of the doubt. Even when she'd been angry, she'd still hoped to find her someday because somewhere deep inside she'd believed Mom still loved her, that it had all been a mistake. The drugs had clouded her judgment, and she never knew how much Roxi had suffered.

"Tom wouldn't . . . ," Mom said.

But it was all becoming clear. Her own mother didn't want her. Not eight years ago and not now.

"I'm sure you have a family missing you. Why don't you tell me what they're like?" Mom checked her mirrors.

In that moment Roxi felt something snap inside her. The hope she'd managed to keep alive for so long died like that man in the bookstore. And no matter what was said or what was done from here on out, there would be no bringing it back to life.

"Didn't someone adopt you?" Mom asked.

Roxi turned toward her mother. "How can you even ask me that?"

"Because I—"

"That would've been perfect, wouldn't it? Pawn me off on someone else so you could go live your 'new life.'"

Mom was silent for a moment as she maneuvered the van onto Amarillo Boulevard. It was a jab and Roxi knew it, but she was beyond caring.

"They wouldn't have let me have you back," Mom said. "They had child services on me well before . . . your accident. I was a lousy mother back then. Don't think I don't know that."

"So that's it, huh? We both just go on like nothing ever happened."

Mom shook her head. "That's not what I'm saying."

"No one adopted me, Mom. No one even came close."

Her mother's face was a mask, but Roxi saw her blink. She itched to lash out and force her mom to explain what could've possibly been in her head to abandon her only daughter in the hospital, leaving her to be raised by a cold, unfeeling state that was more concerned about bureaucracy than giving her a real home. Did she even *think* about what it was like to be eight years old and wonder where your mother was?

Instead Roxi went mute. It didn't matter what Mom answered. It wouldn't change anything. Her mother was still the same selfish woman who'd cared more about her next fix than her own flesh and blood.

"Where will you go?" Mom asked, her voice almost a whisper.

Roxi laughed, but not because anything was funny. "You're something, you know that?"

"I do care if you're—"

"You didn't care the night you left me alone in that apartment to party with your boyfriend, and you don't care now. Just don't upset your perfect little life."

"I never said what I did was right. I—"

"Just forget it, Mom." She jerked her backpack onto her lap as they neared the next intersection. "Or maybe I should call you Marie."

Up ahead she watched the light turn red, and the van slowed. They were almost in the heart of Amarillo again. Where just a few short hours ago Roxi had stepped off that bus with a head full of dreams.

"This hasn't been easy for me, either," Mom said.

Even before the van came to a complete stop, Roxi fumbled for the door handle.

Mom slammed on the brakes. "What are you doing?"

Somewhere behind them a horn blared. Roxi threw open the door and jumped out of the van. "Go on back to your new life, Mom. I'm sure Erin'll be wondering where you are."

"Roxi, wait!"

For one dumb second she actually hesitated. Mom riffled through her purse. She pulled out several bills and, leaning across the seat, held them out to her. "Here. Take this."

Roxi slapped Marie Greeley's hand away and slammed the door. "I don't want your stupid money!"

Then she was running. From the van, from her mother, from Amarillo. Even as tears ran down her face.

14

When Abby got back to the farmhouse, Dad met her at the door. He managed a smile, and she returned it.

"Hungry?" Dad asked, closing the door behind her.

"A little." She surreptitiously folded the book list behind her and stuffed it into her back pocket. She wasn't ready to tell Dad about her little investigation.

"The neighbors dropped off some casseroles. I think one of them's tuna."

It had been her favorite as a kid. She was surprised Dad remembered.

Abby followed him into the kitchen, trying on a good game face. Dad was looking better, but his shoulders still sagged in a defeated posture as he scrounged in the cabinets. A fruit basket and half a dozen foil-covered dishes sat on the kitchen's island. Abby lifted the foil on the nearest, sniffing at it. Condensation had collected on the foil's under-side and dripped into the concoction. Probably macaroni and cheese.

Dad found plates and brought them over to the island. "Lynn said you were visiting Christy?"

"Yeah."

"How's she doing?"

"Okay."

He removed foil from a different dish, sniffed it like she had, then slid it toward her. "Tuna."

"Here. I'll serve." She scooped out a plateful for Dad, less for herself.

He dragged a stool to the island and sat across from her, taking a bite of the lukewarm noodles and sauce. "Not as good as Lynn's."

Abby tasted some herself. "Or Mom's."

They ate in silence for a minute, and she tried to relax and pretend she was sharing a meal with a fellow officer back at the station. The conversation would come naturally then. If Dad were just another cop, they'd have common ground, a way to relate.

"How's your game doing?" she asked, referring to Dad's golfing hobby. She knew it would be a safe subject. He'd been into the sport for as long as she could remember, and he was good at it. Back before she left, he often spent weekends at the country club when she'd wished he were home.

"All right."

Abby dabbed her mouth with a napkin. There were some guys at work who could hold a conversation with anyone about anything, and it served them well on the beat. Not her. She got the information she needed and moved on, which sometimes gave people the wrong impression. One sergeant had even nicknamed her Crabby Abby.

She felt pressure to fill the silence with her father, but she didn't know what to say. There *was* no common ground.

"I'll be going down to the station tomorrow," Dad said.

"They're questioning you again?"

"I offered to go."

"You really should get a lawyer."

"Since I'm not guilty, I don't need one."

"That's not how it works anymore." She set down her fork. "It's the smart thing to do, even when you're innocent."

"Ab, I know how you feel about it."

"But you're not getting one."

"I said I don't think I need one."

She laughed, trying to keep things light. "Dad, give me some credit. I've been a cop for eighteen years. And I was married to a lawyer. I think I might know something."

"I promise I'll be careful."

She shook her head. Why couldn't he just trust her? Police had all kinds of tricks for obtaining a confession. There were no laws that said you couldn't lie to a witness. Badger an innocent person long enough, and many would confess just to end it.

Abby pushed the food around the plate with her fork, suddenly not so hungry. Okay. If Dad wanted to play this way, who was she to stand in his way? She wondered what Christy had meant when she said things had gotten better between Dad and Hunter, because Abby sure wasn't seeing any change in her father. The man sitting in front of her was the same as he'd always been. It was his way or the highway. Which was fine most of the time. His business sense had gotten him and the Barn where they were today. But why couldn't he, just every once in a while, acknowledge that one of his kids might know something he didn't?

She took a halfhearted bite and glanced at her father's face. Was she expecting too much from him?

"There's something I wanted to talk to you about," Dad said.

"Okay."

Dad scooped another chunk of tuna casserole onto his plate. He wasn't meeting her eyes, which knotted her stomach.

"What is it?"

He rested his elbows on the island. "I want to sell the Barn."

She almost choked. "*Sell* the Barn?"

"It's for the best."

"Whoa." Abby raised both hands, palms facing Dad. "Rewind. What are you *talking* about?"

"It's really pretty simple."

"But that's a major decision. We should wait and let things calm down."

"I've already made up my mind."

Abby sat back in her seat, stunned.

Her father looked down at his plate, then pushed it away. "Every time I walk inside that building, I'll think of him. I'll see him lying there on the floor." He looked at her, his eyes full of pain. "Do you have any idea what it was like, finding my own son's body?"

She reached across the table and placed her hand over her father's. No, she didn't know what it was like. She couldn't even *think* about if it were Kat. For a second, she caught a glimpse of Dad's anguish, and she wished she could wipe his mind of the horror he'd seen.

"Please wait. For Hunter. Think of what he'd want."

Dad slipped his hand out from under hers.

"The Book Barn was his dream," she said. "We can't just sell it off."

"With all due respect, Abby, this isn't a 'we' decision." Her father got up and took his plate over to the silver trash can. He stepped on the lid-opening pedal and dumped his leftovers.

She rubbed her eyes. Not this again. She didn't know if she could deal with another confrontation between them. But this was her brother's dream they were talking about, and Abby wasn't going to sit back and watch Dad dash it to pieces. Not when Hunter wasn't here to defend himself.

"I spoke with Hunter right before he died," she said to her father's back.

Silence. Dad set his plate in the sink.

"Do you know what we talked about?"

Dad responded softly, his hands on the sink, head hung low. "I have no idea."

"His dreams. What he wanted to do with the store. You should've heard his excitement. He wanted to add an espresso bar and draw in the community. Make the store more of a destination."

Her father stiffened at her words, and she wasn't sure why.

"That store," Dad said, "is what killed him."

She joined him at the sink, touching his arm. "The store didn't kill him."

"I can't possibly open it again. Not after what happened."

"We could find someone to run it in his honor, someone who knows the business, who'd carry on Hunter's vision. You could do as little or as much as you wanted."

Dad moved away from her again, pulling a glass out of the cupboard. "I'm going to sell it. I just wanted you to know."

She blinked. Had he heard anything she said? "I'd really like to be part of a decision like that."

"That's funny coming from you, Ab. I didn't think you wanted anything to do with the store. You're the one who picked up and left us." He pulled a can of beer from the fridge, cracked it open, and started pouring it into his glass. "I wasn't part of that decision."

"You still don't know why I left, do you?"

Dad pursed his lips. "Let's not do this."

"Do what? Be honest with each other?"

"Argue."

She crossed her arms, unwilling to let the subject drop. "Why is it always an argument if someone disagrees with you?"

Her father sighed, glass in one hand, can in the other. "You know, I almost didn't tell you this tonight because I knew this would happen. But I thought, 'No. She's not a kid. She deserves to know.'"

Abby could guess what would happen if she took this conversation any further. She'd be yelling, and Dad would retreat even further into the shell he'd formed around himself.

Reaching past him, she grabbed a Diet Coke from the fridge. "Fine. Thanks for the announcement."

"Please understand."

She didn't answer him and headed upstairs to the guest room. Locking the door behind herself, she leaned against it and closed her eyes.

❧

"Climb on up, missy."

The trucker looked like Mr. T, complete with Mohawk. Roxi pulled herself up into the 18-wheeler's cab, slammed the heavy truck door, and they were off. It was almost dark, and she just about melted into the vinyl seat from exhaustion.

The trucker held out a baseball glove–size hand. "I'm Gordon, but my friends call me Gordy."

She didn't shake it but just leaned against the door and gave him a halfhearted wave.

"What's a kid like you hitchhiking for?"

"I need a ride."

"That's not real smart."

"Did I ask you?" She pulled her feet up onto the seat and hugged her knees. She knew it was stupid. But she only had five bucks. That's it. Not enough for a bus ticket, hotel, or restaurant. She hadn't slept last night. She hadn't eaten today. What else could she do?

Gordon lifted a hand off the wheel in resignation. "Just be glad it's me pickin' you up and not some perv. Where you going?"

As far from Amarillo as she could. "Where you headed?"

"Got a delivery up in Elk Valley, Colorado."

"Then that's where I'm going, if you'll take me that far."

"Running away?"

Roxi didn't meet his eyes. "No."

That shut him up for a few miles, and she was left with her jumbled, frantic thoughts. It would be completely dark soon. And she was alone with a strange man. What if he really was a pervert and was taking her to some run-down motel? She glanced at him. His biceps were as thick as her thighs. She wouldn't have a chance.

"Hungry?"

She shook her head.

Gordon smiled, and she thought she caught the glint of a gold tooth. "Come on."

"Come on what?"

"You're not a very good liar." He pointed at the glove compartment. "Some Snickers bars in there. Help yourself."

She decided not to argue and popped open the compartment. Inside she found three candy bars next to a bundle of maps and some napkins. On top of the maps was a creased paperback copy of *Try Dying* by some guy named James Scott Bell. Next to them was a black leather book. She couldn't resist slipping it out far enough to read the title.

Holy Bible. Stamped in gilt.

"You read this?"

"Every night."

Tearing open the Snickers wrapper, Roxi took a huge bite. The sweetness of the caramel and the crunch of the nuts was a feast for her tongue and growling stomach.

"Good?"

"Mm-hmm."

"Have another if you want."

Her fingers brushed the Bible as she pulled out the second bar. "Man, you don't seem like the type."

"To be reading a Bible?"

"Yeah."

"Missy, there's stuff in there for every type, including yours."

Roxi bit into the Snickers. She'd never read a Bible before. Hadn't even owned one. If Mom had ever taken her to church, she couldn't remember it.

Gordon thought for a minute. "My favorite's Psalm 32. Wanna hear it?"

She didn't really but shrugged anyway. At least if he kept talking religion, he seemed safe enough.

"Goes like this," Gordon said. "'Then I acknowledged my sin to you and did not cover up my iniquity. I said, "I will confess my transgressions to the Lord"—and you forgave the guilt of my sin.'"

She stuffed the last of the first bar into her mouth and ripped open the second. Didn't make much sense, but she got the "guilt of my sin" part.

"I used to be a pretty mean guy," Gordon said. "Spent the best years of my life in the joint, actually."

Her skin went cold. Not only was she alone at night on a deserted highway with a strange man, but he was an ex-con, too. The truck bounced along an overpass, and she slid a little closer to the door. What could she possibly do? Jumping out of a zooming truck was not an option.

"But the guy who came out of prison wasn't the same guy who

went in." Gordon glanced at her, giving her a look of genuine concern she didn't expect. He shook his head. "I used to hate God. But I came to find out He loved me anyway. Cool, huh?"

"Sure."

The truck gently rocked over the bumps in the road, and Roxi found it harder and harder to keep her eyes open. But she couldn't fall asleep now. Not when she knew zero about this Gordon guy. All his talk could be part of the act. Lure girls in with his jailhouse conversion story just to get their defenses down.

"Got any family?"

Despite her best efforts, Roxi still choked up at the question. Was Mom tucking Erin in bed right now? She answered Gordon softly. "No."

"Aw, come on. Everyone's got family somewhere."

Roxi rolled her eyes. "Listen, I'm just bummin' a ride, 'kay? I don't need the third degree here."

"Okay, okay." Gordon ran his finger and thumb across his lips in a zipping motion. "You got it, missy. I'll shut up."

15

Diego stepped out of the RV, glad to be alone. Ma was on the computer researching some books, and he had a few minutes to himself. They were staying in a campground near Santa Fe.

He walked a few paces from the RV and stared at the moon. Where was Roxi right now? Was she safe? Brotherly instincts he didn't even know he had kept cropping up, and he couldn't stop worrying about her.

He closed his eyes and breathed in deeply through his nose. What kind of man was he? How could he have *done* what he did? Somehow he'd managed to keep that guy's face out of his thoughts during the day, but at night, like now, it was a different story.

Glancing back at the RV, he pictured Ma at the dinette table hunched over the laptop, a steaming cup of green tea in hand, her depressing Celtic music quietly playing over the sound system. They'd had two arguments already today over stupid things like which camp-ground to stay at and which route to take. Ma's fuse was definitely short, but his was even shorter. It didn't help that he'd gotten only two hours of sleep last night.

Diego ripped out his keys and unlocked the largest bay under the RV. It ran the width of the vehicle and could fit plenty of gear. Back when he and Ma used to go camping just for fun, before Roxi, he could stuff all kinds of junk in here. Sleeping bags, chairs, coolers. Man, those were the days. Back when summer was fun. Now all they used the bay for was books.

He eyed the boxes inside. They kept all the books in plastic file containers after learning the hard way that the bay wasn't waterproof. He pulled the lid off the closest container. Right on top was that first edition of *Farmer Giles of Ham* by J. R. R. Tolkien that he'd swiped their first trip to Dawson's Book Barn. Illustrated by Pauline Baynes, the same gal who'd illustrated the first editions of C. S. Lewis's Narnia series, it was Tolkien's second novel, written after *The Hobbit* but before his Rings trilogy. A hundred-fifty-retail kind of title. Which meant he'd be lucky to get forty or fifty for it. Still, he'd set it aside. Checking out the other boxes, he cherry-picked titles he knew weren't so rare they'd be missed but would still sell for something.

Soon he had a small stack. Peeling off his flannel shirt, he wrapped it around the books and carried them to the van, where he safely stashed them under the backseat.

Ma would never notice.

❧

Roxi jerked awake, fear flying through her body. She wasn't supposed to sleep. It took her a second to realize the truck was stopped, and she was alone in it. Frantically she peered out the windows. Where was she?

A gas pump.

Grabbing her backpack, she flung open the door and jumped the couple feet to the ground. And where was Gordon?

"Over here, missy."

His voice came from the other side of the truck, and she found him pumping fuel into the silver tank behind the driver's door.

"Where are we? How long was I asleep?"

"Outskirts of Elk Valley, and I'd say a good two hours."

Stupid. She didn't even remember closing her eyes. "Have you been here before? Is it a big town?"

"Not that big." Gordon replaced the diesel nozzle and screwed the cap back on his tank. "But it'll have everything you need."

"Does it have a bookstore?" She tried to sound casual.

He gave her a funny look. "A bookstore?"

"One that sells used books."

"Well, I don't know that. Maybe."

She turned to leave. "Thanks for the ride."

"Wait just a sec." Gordon jumped up into the cab and returned with that black Bible in his hands. He held it out to her, the last Snickers bar on top. "Food for the body and for the soul."

"That's okay; I—"

He stretched it out farther. "Psalm 32. Check it out sometime. Easy to remember: 3-2-1."

When she finally took it, he smiled. "You know, I never got your name."

She told him, and Gordon reached out his hand. This time she shook it.

"I'll be prayin' for you, Roxi. Oh, and . . ." He pulled out his wallet, stuffing some bills into her jean jacket pocket before she could protest. He patted her shoulder. "Keep safe."

A minute later, Roxi watched his truck lumber out of the station, and she followed his taillights down the road until they disappeared altogether. Only then did she pull out the bills. Two twenties.

"Thanks," she whispered, relief flooding her that she wouldn't have to sleep on the street. Roxi walked into the gas station to ask for directions to the nearest motel.

❧

Abby slowly eased into the parking space next to Christy's Honda. She cut the engine and rested both hands on the steering wheel, staring up at Christy's apartment. The lights were off. This was an inconsiderate thing to do. It was after midnight.

She pulled out her cell phone and pressed the speed dial she'd assigned to Christy. She waited. Ring one, two, three, four . . . Just as she pulled the phone away from her head to hang up, she heard Christy's voice pick up with a hello she would've expected to be groggier.

"Uh, hi, Christy. It's Abby."

Pause. "What's goin' on?"

"I hope I didn't wake you. I know it's late, but . . ." Abby sighed. Christy didn't need to be dragged into her troubles. She had enough of her own. She should just come up with some excuse for calling at this hour and get off as quickly as she could.

"Is something wrong?"

"No, no." Abby was ready to back out at the last minute if she picked up anything close to inconvenience on Christy's end.

"Abby?"

"I was just wondering . . . could I come over there?"

"What happened? Are you okay?"

Might as well be honest. She'd already told Christy things she hadn't shared with anyone but Hunter and Michael. "Dad and I . . . It's . . . I can't stand being in that house anymore. I tried the hotel, but it's full, and I just don't—"

"Of course you can come over."

"I really hate to impose, but I didn't know where else to—"

"Abby, you're not imposing. I'd be happy for the company. Tonight's been rough for me, too."

"You sure?"

"I'll make up the sofa as soon as we get off."

Abby felt herself relax. "Thanks."

"What's your ETA?"

She hesitated. "I'm parked outside your apartment."

That seemed to take a second to register. She heard a noise like Christy was setting a mug of coffee or tea on a counter. "You are?"

"I'd have slept in my car if you hadn't picked up."

"Well, come on up, then."

A minute later Abby knocked on Christy's door. The dead bolt clicked and Christy opened it wearing a green terry cloth bathrobe.

"Tell me I didn't wake you."

Christy shook her head. "I couldn't sleep."

Hefting her suitcase, Abby stepped inside the apartment for the second time today. If Christy were anyone else, she'd be feeling uncomfortable right about now. But instead, Abby felt at ease. It was a far cry from the tension in her father's home.

"Listen, normally I wouldn't ask this of you, but basically I'm about to lose it with Dad. I feel like I'm smothering over there. If I didn't get out of the house . . ."

"What happened?" Christy locked the door.

"He wants to sell the store."

A look of disbelief colored Christy's features. "What?"

"Yeah. My thoughts exactly."

"Seriously?"

Abby set down her suitcase and sank into Christy's sofa, holding her head in her hands. What a relief to be here. She was so exhausted it hurt, but she hadn't been able to sleep. After midnight she gave up trying. She'd remembered how Christy offered to let her crash here, and she'd hoped the offer still stood. Even if it was almost one in the morning.

"I tried suggesting he wait until things calm down. But he wouldn't listen to a word I said."

"He's not gonna open it again?"

"I don't know."

Christy looked like she was having trouble digesting the words.

"I'd start looking for a new job if I were you," Abby said.

Christy stood speechless for a moment, then headed toward the bathroom. She returned with cradling sheets, blankets, and a pillow.

"I really appreciate this," Abby said.

"I'll rest easier knowing you're out here anyway." She started unfolding the sheets. "It's been a long night."

Abby reached to help her with the blankets, wondering if she really was imposing and Christy was just being nice. After all, what else could she say? "Go spend the night in your car"? Once the bed was made, Abby unzipped her suitcase, digging out a T-shirt and some sweatpants, her favorite sleepwear.

"We'll both rest now," Christy said.

Abby smiled, realizing she really was welcome here. "That would be nice."

16

"DIEGO TONELLI, please come to the service desk."

The announcement came over the PA system of Pages Past bookstore in Santa Fe. Diego shelved the paperback copy of Stephen King's *Cujo* he wasn't really reading and made his way over. It was one of those bookstores that sold recent books at half the retail price. Mostly general consumer stuff like best-seller fiction, coffee table books, and the latest health fad handbooks, all no older than ten years. The air even smelled of new paper and ink like a Barnes & Noble. But even at a store like this, there was usually a section for collectible rarities like he'd brought, and they listed them online, too. When Ma was out on her walk, he'd checked out this place and knew several thousand of their books appeared on AbeBooks.com and Amazon.

He wiped his palms on the front of his jeans, hating his nervousness. *Come on, man. Get with it. You do this all the time.* But this time

Ma thought he was out buying groceries, and he needed to be back to the campground in an hour.

The woman with graying hair pulled into a ponytail slammed her cash register drawer as he approached. Brother. Just what he needed. A cranky clerk.

"I'm Diego Tonelli."

She barely made eye contact. "I can offer you seventy for all twelve."

He shot her a you've-gotta-be-kidding-me look. "But that's good stock!"

"I'm sorry. It's the best we can do."

He spotted his books on a side counter behind the woman. Without thinking, he rushed around her and pulled off *Farmer Giles of Ham* and waved it at the clerk. "This book alone's worth one-fifty!"

She rested her hands on her hips, turning around. "If you'd rather not sell them, that's fine."

"You think I'm stupid?"

"Excuse me?"

He was sick of people like her trying to rip him off because he looked like a kid.

"I'm not stupid." Diego held the Tolkien inches from the clerk's face. "Bet you didn't even know this was a first edition." He flipped to the title page and tapped it with his finger. "See right here? Houghton Mifflin Company. It's got all the points."

Houghton never marked their firsts with the words *first edition*, but instead the date on the title page had to match the one on the copyright page. Elementary stuff any clerk should know.

She smiled at him. "Very good."

"You better believe it's good. Worth more than a measly six bucks."

She produced a business-size checkbook ledger. "I was actually referring to your . . . enthusiasm."

He felt his cheeks suddenly grow warm.

"It's good to see someone your age so passionate about books."

"Make it a hundred."

She paused for all of two seconds. "Eighty-five."

He glanced at the Tolkien in his hands. Some stores would give him a third of retail for a book like this. He could take his business somewhere else if he wanted. Eighty-five wasn't fair.

"Deal?" The clerk's pen was poised over the checkbook.

Then again, it was eighty-five that would be all his.

He returned the book to the stack and walked back around the counter. "Deal."

"I'll need to see your ID."

Diego felt his shoulders tense. "ID?"

"We require it of everyone." The clerk eyed him over her glasses. "It's just policy."

He pulled his wallet from his back pocket, slipping out his driver's license. He stared at it for a second. It was the real thing, complete with his home address. They'd never seen the need for fakes, and he didn't know where to get one anyway.

If he refused to give his ID, that would only make him look guilty. And it's not like these books were super rare. No one probably even realized they were missing. It was the big fish like the *Gatsby* they'd be looking for, if they were looking at all.

The clerk cleared her throat. Diego gave her the license.

❦

Roxi had no reason to get up. She'd slept till eight but lay on her back for an hour longer, staring at the stained ceiling. The walls were so thin in this motel, she'd spent half the night with a pillow over her head trying to drown out her rowdy neighbors.

Eventually her growling stomach got the better of her. She had to do something. Stumbling into the bathroom, she splashed cold water on her face, then eyed the shower. The once-white grout was black with mold, there was hair in the drain, and the rusty showerhead dripped incessantly. Not exactly the Ritz. She'd just make sure she didn't touch the walls.

Fifteen minutes and a tepid shower later, things looked brighter. She changed into clean jeans and did her best to comb out her wet hair with her fingertips. Swiping the toilet paper roll from the bathroom, she took one last glance around the shoddy room, then scooped up her backpack and walked outside.

She drew in a deep breath of the fresh air, trying to keep herself from freaking over her dwindling cash supply. That stupid room took all of the trucker's money, which left her once again with only five bucks. Somehow she had to get some money and fast. The only way she knew was to sell the books.

She asked the motel's front desk guy if she could go through the yellow pages, and after asking for directions, Roxi was on her way to the only bookstore listed—Aaron's Book Exchange. She'd at least get something to keep her floating.

But when she finally found the place on Main Street, her heart dropped at the orange sign hanging in the glass door.

Sorry, We're Closed.

No hours posted either.

Pressing her face against the door, she peered inside. Piles and piles of books were stacked all over the floor and in front of the shelves. Roxi slowly crumpled in the doorway, her back against the door, knees to her chest. She dropped her head in her hands wanting to cry. She should've planned better or brought more money or never left Irene and Diego at all.

She couldn't do anything right, could she? If she hadn't broken that window as a kid, she'd have grown up with her mother. If she'd given Irene and Diego more time in the bookstore the first visit, she'd still be safe with them, barreling down the road in the RV jammin' to the radio and planning their next heist. She could be hanging out with Diego right now eating anything she wanted.

What could she do now? Just like Gordon said, Elk Valley wasn't a huge town. There wouldn't be a homeless shelter or a soup kitchen. She'd passed a Safeway on her walk in, the post office, at least two ski shops, and a place called Walker's Feed Store, but she couldn't exactly walk into one of them and just ask for help. If anyone reported her, she'd end up in juvie for sure.

"Hey, are you okay?"

The voice came from above her, and Roxi jumped, then scrambled to her feet. A fiftyish woman stood right in front of her on the sidewalk, a concerned look on her face.

Roxi yearned to answer her honestly, to say, "No, I'm not okay." But talking to anyone would be stupid. They'd want to know more than she could share.

She hitched her backpack over her shoulders. "Yeah, I'm fine."

"You don't look it."

The woman held a paper cup, the type that held lattes or cappuccinos, and Roxi zeroed in on it to take control of the conversation.

"Where'd you get that?" she asked, nodding at the cup.

The woman hesitated for a second, then finally pointed down the street. "The Perfect Blend. It's right up there. See the blue awning? They make the best coffee this side of the Divide."

"Thanks." Roxi sprinted in the shop's direction.

❧

"What can I get ya?" The gal behind the counter was probably a few years older than Roxi, with short, spiky hair.

"Small coffee, please." Roxi's mouth watered at the bagels and pastries beside the counter in a refrigerated case. How much more could a bagel be?

"House blend?"

"Yeah."

"Room?"

She shook her head. "I like it black. Could I also have a bagel?"

"What kind?"

Her eyes darted to the case again. There weren't many selections left, but they all looked good. "Plain's fine."

Digging in her pocket, she pulled out two dollars and change, hating to part with it. But it would make a better impression if she did. At first she'd only come into this place to get away from that woman. Then she'd seen the Help Wanted sign in the window.

"Here ya go." The gal set a paper cup full of a pungent, dark brew in front of her. "Free refills over there." She gestured to a table against the wall holding three silver carafes, ice water, napkins, stirrers, sugars, and quarts of skim and whole milk on ice.

Roxi cleared her throat. "I, uh . . . saw the sign in the window. You still have an opening?"

The gal rolled her eyes. "Do we ever. But if you're interested, you'll have to talk to the owner. He won't be back for another twenty minutes."

Roxi's hopes rose. "I can wait."

Finding a table in the corner, she first devoured the bagel. Fresh and chewy, she didn't care how much it cost. It was the best bagel she'd ever had.

Her mouth full, Roxi watched the gal behind the counter bustling to make someone's sandwich and smoothie simultaneously. Getting a job here wouldn't fix all her problems, but if she could get an advance payment, maybe she could find a place to stay. Didn't some motels offer discount rates if you stayed longer than a few days? Eventually she'd save enough for an apartment. She might be able to pass for eighteen, and soon she would be. Then the state would have nothing on her.

She slurped her drink. She used to hate coffee, but Diego had taught her to drink it. At first she'd drowned it in milk and sugar. But Diego had a way of bringing out the brave side of her, and eventually she was drinking it black like him.

Roxi stared into the depths of her cup. Who was she kidding? She couldn't just walk into a place like this and expect them to hire her off the street. You needed references, a permanent address. She had neither.

She was standing to leave when a short, pudgy man entered the shop. She guessed he was the owner. Probably in his forties with thinning hair and glasses. He was dressed casually in jeans and a polo shirt that had the store's emblem, two coffee cups leaning against each other, embroidered on the front. Immediately he toured the room, checking with each table and asking customers if things were to their liking.

Yeah. The owner.

By the time he reached her table, she'd finished her coffee and could feel the caffeine buzz lifting her spirits. Maybe this was worth a try.

"How's everything?" The owner smiled, resting his hand on the back of a chair.

"Good." Roxi put on her friendliest face. "I saw your sign in the window, and I'm really interested. The girl behind the counter said you still had an opening?"

"Yes, yes. We certainly do." He pulled the chair out and sat across from her, extending his hand. "I'm Stan Barlowe."

She returned his shake. "Roxi Gold."

"It's just Nell and me ever since Becca quit a week ago, and it's been crazy. Have any experience?"

"I can learn anything."

Stan nodded. "Learning's good. I'd prefer someone who's done this before, but we might be able to make something work. We're kinda desperate at this point. How 'bout I get you an application."

"Application?" A splash of concern flitted across her chest.

"Won't take you long."

Great.

"I'll be right back."

Roxi watched Stan bustle behind the counter, whisper a few words to his worker, then disappear into the back. He reappeared a minute later and brought the application over to her table. "Need a pen?"

She scanned the fields. There it was. References.

"You can use mine." Stan dropped a ballpoint on the table. "If you have any questions, I'll be at the counter. Enjoy your coffee?"

Roxi nodded and picked up the pen. She hated lying. But she didn't have a choice, did she? She had to have this job.

"I'll get you a refill." Stan snatched away her empty cup.

She thanked him and, taking a deep breath, got to work on the application. Okay. The references would have to remain blank. She made up an address using a generic 100 Broad Street in Walsenburg, a nearby town.

Prior jobs? She didn't have any. If she made something up here, he might call her on it. Would it be so bad if this one was her first? Didn't everyone have a first job sometime in their life?

It took her fifteen minutes until she was satisfied with the form. She took it up to the counter, where Stan was busy explaining to a customer how they roasted their own beans and which ones were organic.

Stan flashed her another friendly smile. "Finished?"

"When will I know?" She handed him the form.

He barely glanced at it. "Can you be ready for work tomorrow at 6 a.m.?"

"Tomorrow?"

"Or the end of the week if that's—"

"No, tomorrow's fine." She couldn't resist the grin that crept onto her face.

"Good. Lots to go over. I'll see you then."

Outside, the warmth of the afternoon sun hit Roxi's face. Maybe her luck really had turned. She lifted her eyes to the sky dotted with fluffy white clouds. Because things were looking up.

17

CHRISTY'S BEDROOM DOOR was still closed at ten thirty, and Abby couldn't bring herself to wake her. She quietly made a pot of coffee, taking a mugful and her cell phone out to her car. Sitting in the driver's seat with the door open, she punched in Michael's office number. There was still a bite in the air, but she didn't mind. Fall had always been her favorite season, and it was coming up on them fast.

"Cantrell, Burgess & Long," came the receptionist's syrupy voice.

"Barbara, it's Abby. Could you patch me through to Michael?"

"I'm holding all his calls. He's in a meeting."

Which had a fifty-fifty chance of being true. Michael used to have Barbara give that same excuse when he and Sarah were fooling around. Some meeting.

"It's important."

"He said no calls."

"Make an exception, okay? I need to talk to him."

Barbara sighed loudly. She'd played the go-between for years and was probably sick of it.

Abby heard a click, and Michael's clipped voice spoke in her ear. "What is it?"

She took a deep breath. "I wanted you to know I'm not home. I had to leave unexpectedly to be with my father."

"What's wrong? Is he okay?"

"Michael . . . my brother was murdered."

The line went silent.

"I'm going to be here for a while."

"Murdered?"

"Shot in the chest two days ago. Probably a robbery gone bad at the Barn."

"I'm sorry. Anything I can do?" Michael was talking and eating at the same time. She could hear the food swirling in his mouth.

"I thought Kat might want to come to the funeral."

More silence. "When is it?"

"This Saturday."

"We've had our last beach trip of the year on the lake planned for weeks."

"This is my brother, Michael. Kat's uncle."

"Whom she didn't know."

Abby tried to set her coffee mug in the car's cup holder, but it was too big for it. "She did know him. Remember when he came for Christmas?"

"Ten years ago."

"Let me at least ask her."

"Listen, Ab, I know you want to be a part of her life. That's fine. But I have to think about what's best for my whole family here. Kat *and* Sarah."

"I'm not saying—"

"Sarah's been looking forward to this trip for a long time. It's her birthday gift to Kat."

"Like you didn't give her enough?"

Her ex paused. "What's that supposed to mean?"

"A car? She *just* turned sixteen."

"She won't drive it till she gets her license."

Abby closed her eyes, reining in her sarcasm. "That's not the point."

"What *is* the point?"

She couldn't say what she really thought. That he was spoiling Kat. That he was molding her into a snob. At this rate Kat would never learn how to handle money responsibly.

"She at least needs to know where I am," Abby said.

"I'll tell her. After the trip."

Her eyes flew open. "What if she wants to come?"

"Listen. I don't know how I can make it any simpler. I want Kat to enjoy this vacation. Not be worrying about death and funerals."

"But it's not your decision to make. She's old enough. She can decide for herself."

"After. That's the way it's going to be."

"You have no right to tell me what I can and can't tell my daughter."

"*Our* daughter."

She rubbed her forehead with the heel of her palm. It hadn't been easy over the years, but for Kat's sake she thought it was important she and Michael stay on amicable terms. Conversations like these always threatened her resolve to stay civil. "You know I don't do anything behind your back. I never have."

"Please keep it that way."

"Yet you've never given me credit for any of it. You think this has been easy for me? You ripped Kat out of my life. What do you expect me to do? Forget about her?" She could hear herself getting shrill.

"I'm sorry about your brother, Ab. I really am. But until Kat's an adult, I make the decisions." *And you don't.* The unspoken words hung between them.

"When will you be back?" Michael asked.

"I don't know."

Abby flipped her phone shut without waiting for his reply.

⅋

"Is this everything?" Ma asked.

Diego hoisted himself into the RV without bothering to put down the stairs. Ma had apparently spent the two hours he was gone at the dinette table researching the values of the books they'd lifted from Dawson's Book Barn. She looked up from her laptop, her expression a mixture of frustration, anger, and worry.

"That's it," he said.

"It can't be."

Diego's pulse immediately began knocking in his ears.

She knew. Somehow she knew.

"Four boxes. I brought 'em all in."

Books littered the RV. Ma had even stacked several full leather volumes on his bed. The sight of them almost turned his stomach. Seeing the whole cache laid out like this took him back to that horrible night.

"You're sure?"

He pulled open the fridge, swallowing hard. "Positive."

"I don't believe this," she muttered.

Diego went for a can of Coke. No going back now. He had to keep his cool. "What's the problem?"

"It's gone." Ma was rubbing the bridge of her nose.

He turned his back to her, cracking open his can with fingers he could barely keep from trembling. This was not good. She usually went all weird and quiet when she was mad. Never like this.

"How could she do this to us?"

Diego froze, can halfway to his mouth. *She?* He slowly faced his mother. Her eyes flared, but he realized the anger wasn't aimed at him.

"Wanna clue me in here?" Diego asked.

"She took it."

"Took what?"

"The *Gatsby*. I can't find it anywhere."

Diego set down his Coke. That book was the reason they'd gone to the store in the first place. Come to think of it, he hadn't seen it when he'd done his cherry-picking earlier. Could Roxi really have taken it?

He didn't know how to respond. He couldn't suggest Ma search the boxes again. She might notice other books were missing.

The ones *he* took.

❧

Roxi spent most of the afternoon wandering the streets of Elk Valley trying to figure out the best way to talk Stan into giving her an advance payment tomorrow. Did employers do that sort of thing? If she gave him too much of a sob story, he might start asking questions she couldn't answer. Like where her family was. But if she was too secretive, it would also make him curious.

By three o'clock the bagel and coffee had long worn off, and her stomach started growling again. She planned to spend the last of her money on something for dinner at the Safeway later. If only she wasn't so hungry now.

When she passed the Elk Valley Public Library for the third time,

Roxi stopped in front of it. The cornerstone said the brick structure was built in 1939, and an American flag flapped on a short pole by the door. They'd have a computer in there, wouldn't they? With an Internet connection.

Curiosity's pull was too strong. She walked inside.

At the front desk a man with white hair and reading glasses sat typing at a keyboard. He glanced up as she approached, glasses sliding down his nose. "Can I help you?"

"Do I have to sign in to use the computer?" She pointed to three terminals against the wall. One was being used by a college-age guy. The other two were available.

"Right here," the man said, pushing a clipboard across the desk surface.

Roxi signed *Amber Smith* and went to the terminal farthest from the student. She tucked her backpack under the table and took a deep breath. *Okay. Be brave.* She really needed to know the value of her books.

She double-clicked on the blue Internet Explorer icon and was online in seconds. Surreptitiously she glanced at the student, but he was in his own world taking notes and printing out pages. She could hear the light tapping of keys behind her as the librarian continued whatever he was working on. At least she wouldn't have to worry about anyone interrupting her.

Roxi pulled up the Google search page, then hunted and pecked *Dawson's Book Barn*. She hit Enter before she could think anymore. The results spilled onto the page. The first Web site looked like the store's official home page. She swung the cursor to the link and clicked it.

The page that came up was a simple design with the store logo on the top and a large photo of the bookstore in the center. It looked quaint and inviting.

Her cursor went to the About tab, and two paragraphs of text popped onto the screen beneath the photo:

Built in 1903 and originally used to house dairy cows, "The Barn" has become a cultural icon in Longmont. Opened by owner Robert Dawson almost forty years ago, the store now holds over three hundred thousand volumes and has been featured in countless national magazines and newspapers. "I started the Barn on a whim," Dawson says, "but it quickly became something much more than I ever dreamed possible."

   The Book Barn's inventory has something for just about everyone. From rare book room treasures to childhood favorites, the store caters to collectors and readers alike. "You can't leave empty-handed," Dawson adds with a smile. "We welcome customers from ten to seven daily."

In the Press section of the site, Roxi saw a photo of Hunter Dawson, and nausea flooded her empty stomach. In full color, staring back at her on the computer screen, was the manager. Apparently he was also the owner's son, and it looked like he was standing in the bookstore in front of the counter. Smiling broadly, he was holding the *Gatsby* now sitting in her backpack. Beside him stood a woman, and when Roxi saw her face, she did a double take. It was the clerk who'd taken her up to the science section. She was smiling too, her hand resting proudly on Hunter's arm. The caption beneath the photo read:

Hunter Dawson holding the rare Fitzgerald. Pictured with him is his fiancée, Christy Williams.

Roxi gawked at the picture, clenching her fingers into fists to keep them from shaking. The guilt was never going away, was it? She'd have to carry it inside forever, never knowing which day the cops would come knocking. Wouldn't it be better to just get it over with and turn herself in? At least if she ended up in juvie, she'd have a roof over her head and three meals a day.

Frantically Roxi closed the browser, grabbed her backpack, and raced out of the library.

❧

Finding a place to sleep in the dark was harder than Roxi thought it would be. Elk Valley didn't even have a public park. She ended up behind the Safeway Dumpster using the backpack as her pillow. Even with her jean jacket buttoned to her chin and wearing every shirt she owned underneath it, she couldn't get warm. Up here in high elevations it could get down to the fifties at night, even in the summer.

Roxi rolled onto her side, gravel digging into her hip. She couldn't escape the stench of rancid trash either. She'd spent the last of her money on a loaf of white bread and a jar of peanut butter. With a plastic knife from the salad bar, she'd made and eaten three sandwiches for dinner tonight. At least her hunger pains were gone.

Closing her eyes, Roxi tried to focus on her new job tomorrow. If she could just concentrate on something else, she might be able to keep from losing it. In a couple of hours, she'd be okay. She wouldn't have to sleep on the street tomorrow. Somehow she'd manage to get some cash from Stan.

She must've drifted off to sleep because the next thing Roxi knew, she was even colder, and a car engine rumbled loud and very close by. She lay still and listened.

Headlights.

They spotlighted the weeds beyond her, then disappeared. She tensed. Was someone coming? She scooted toward the Dumpster's edge and peeked out.

The car was driving straight toward her.

Roxi jerked back out of sight. What should she do? If she ran, she'd be seen for sure. But if she stayed put and the angle was right, she might not be seen at all. Daring a second look, she crept to the edge of the Dumpster again, ready to bolt, fingers clutching the strap of her backpack.

The moonlight gave her a clear-enough view of a two-door sedan as it crawled forward, gravel popping under its tires. Why was it here behind the Safeway in the middle of the night? Did they know she was here and had just been waiting for the opportunity to catch her unawares?

Roxi watched the car come to a stop on the edge of the pavement, engine still running, headlights turned away from her. No, that didn't make sense. They'd have come up closer or snuck up if they really wanted to hurt her.

Suddenly the car's passenger door swung open, and the interior lights blinked on. She caught a glimpse of a big man with a cigarette hanging from his lips, but his gaze was focused on something in the car, not on her. What was he doing?

Before she could guess, he flung a dark bundle into the weeds, slammed the door, and zoomed off so fast she smelled the rubber from his tires.

Roxi pulled up onto her knees. Had that bundle made a sound, or was it just the screeching tires? She waited until the fear melted from her body before standing up and venturing out. Maybe she hadn't heard anything at all. It was just a bag of trash the guy was too lazy to throw into a can.

She crept forward, tuning in to every sound. Her boots clicking on the pavement. A lone cricket. The breeze rustling the dry weeds. Nothing more.

Roxi slowly approached the area where the car had stopped and stared into the weeds. Even with the moon she couldn't see much. Just weeds. A beer can. Some shreds of paper. Where was the sack?

Running her fingers through her hair, Roxi looked all around. What if the car came back? She could not be seen, especially by some creepy guy who dumped trash behind the Safeway at one in the morning.

She shrugged, turning back to the Dumpster. He must've thrown it farther than she thought. She'd check it out when it was lighter.

Then she heard it again.

It sounded like a high-pitched whine, like the tires had made. Okay, she hadn't imagined *that*. It almost sounded like . . . Roxi spun toward the weeds. And saw them.

Two glowing eyes.

18

Roxi froze, squinting at the reflecting orbs. She was almost positive it had been a dog's cry. For a second the animal stared back at her, then blinked and disappeared.

"Hey, wait. Don't go."

But any animal's eyes could glow, right? For all she knew the guy could've thrown away a rabid raccoon. She called for it again anyway.

"I won't hurt you," she whispered, strangely not afraid.

Roxi edged away from the weeds. She probably should have been afraid. She really didn't know what she was dealing with, and dogs could bite. Especially if they were scared or hurt.

She decided crouching would seem less intimidating and lowered herself to the pavement, still talking. "It's okay now. You can come out."

A whimper came from the weeds directly in front of her. Could you tell a dog's size by the sound of its whine? If only she had some of that bread and peanut butter here with her; she'd use it to coax the dog out.

"Just let me see you, 'kay?"

The weeds moved, and then a dark form took shape on the edge of the pavement.

She held her breath. It *was* a dog.

"That's it. Come here, buddy."

Not daring to move from her crouching position, she kept talking to the animal. It wasn't just the night making the dog appear black—it really was black. She still couldn't see its face entirely, but it didn't *look* mean. And it wasn't big either. Its head would barely reach her knees. She didn't know enough about dog breeds to guess what it could be, but it kinda reminded her of a small version of the Greyhound bus dog.

The dog sat down, lifted its paw off the ground, and let out another pathetic whimper.

"Oh, boy. Are you hurt?"

She saw the dog's nose twitching, smelling the air, checking her out.

"Can you walk?"

As if it understood, the dog took two tentative steps toward her, nose still raised in a perpetual sniff.

She slowly reached her hand out. Something glistened on the dog's right shoulder. Was that blood?

"What did you possibly do to deserve this?" She started to touch the dog but stopped herself. A wounded animal could snap at any time. So could an abused one. And chances were this one's family hadn't exactly been the Brady Bunch. What had this pup endured that he couldn't tell her? She wanted to kick the man who'd so callously dumped him.

Roxi dropped to her knees, and the dog instantly lowered its head, backed up, and plastered down its small ears.

"Hey, hey. Don't go. We were making progress."

They stared at each other again, only now the dog was clearly shivering. From fear, pain, or cold, she didn't know. Maybe all three.

"You hungry? 'Cause I've got some food in my pack. Right by the Dumpster over there."

Would it run if she stood? Probably. She'd have to try crawling. The dog was thin, and who knew when it ate last. She understood hunger, and if she could do something to keep anyone from feeling that terrible gnawing, she would.

She scooted over to her pack, grabbed it, and was back in front of the dog, who'd stayed put. It might've been her imagination, but it seemed to relax a little. She opened the bread bag, and the dog's ears perked up. When she unscrewed the peanut butter jar, its nose did that sniffing thing again that reminded her of an anteater.

"Not exactly gourmet," she said. "But neither of us can be picky now, can we?"

Roxi slathered the peanut butter on a piece of bread. It did smell good, didn't it? She held it out to the dog, and it couldn't help but step closer. She hoped it would come far enough for her to examine that cut. If it was deep, she didn't know what she'd do. Not like she had money for a vet, and even if she did, that would call way too much attention to her. No address, no parents. Red flags galore.

"Let your stomach do the walking," she said. "You know you want it."

The dog hesitated with each step, head down, tail swooshing from side to side. But it was moving toward her. Only four feet separated them now.

She waved the bread to send more peanut butter aroma into the air. "You gotta come here to get it."

Three feet away the dog stopped, sat down, and stared at the bread. No matter how much she coaxed, it wouldn't move any closer. She gave in and tossed the bread the rest of the distance. He pounced on it, eating it in two gulps. After it was gone, his tongue kept smacking as he tried to lick the peanut butter off the roof of its mouth.

She laughed. "I knew you were hungry."

The dog's head cocked ever so slightly, its ears sticking out to the sides like little wings. She could see his shoulder clearly now in the moonlight. There was definitely blood, but the scrape didn't look too serious. It would need to be cleaned, though. She could use her drinking water and maybe one of her socks as a rag, but that would only happen if the dog let her touch it.

Roxi globbed on the peanut butter, trying not to think about how she'd already used half the jar. "Sure you won't come closer?" She extended her arm again, hoping. No go. The dog moved its eyes from her face to the bread, face to bread.

"You win this time, little guy." She threw the bread, but not as far as before.

Again, it was gone in a flash.

"So, boy, what do people call you?" Roxi licked the knife, then thought to check if the dog really was a boy. She chuckled when she realized it wasn't. "Sorry. Looks like it's just us girls."

Pulling two more bread slices from the bag, she made a sandwich and broke it into fourths. She tossed the first, making sure it was closer to her than the last time. The dog would have to creep nearer with each piece.

"I suppose you're wondering why I'm out here," she said. "I should be warm and cozy in a bed or something, shouldn't I?"

The dog's eyes bored holes into her hand holding the three other pieces.

Roxi was suddenly aware of the cold again—how it seeped through her clothes and brought goose bumps to her skin. "Yeah, I should be. So should you. Things don't always work out the way we want, do they? Guess you know all about that."

She threw the second sandwich piece, and the dog took a step forward, grabbed the food, and waited for more.

Roxi smiled. It was working.

"We're kinda in the same boat here," she said. "No one wants me, either."

It felt good to talk to someone. She hadn't been able to share her real feelings with anyone in a long time. And now that the dog was closer, Roxi tried to examine the rest of her to make sure she wasn't hurt in any other way. She was favoring that scraped leg, but the other three seemed fine.

Roxi held out the third sandwich piece, not giving in this time. "I'll need to clean that, you know. So you're gonna have to come closer."

The dog stood up from her sitting position, letting out a quiet whine.

"You've gotta trust me, girl."

Roxi set the food down in front of her, purposely tempting the dog. If she was going to help her, she'd have to earn her trust. The dog was understandably wary of humans. How could she break through? Food was all Roxi had to offer.

She nudged the food closer but still kept it out of the dog's reach. "Listen, I'm the same way. But you have to realize you can't make it by yourself. It's cold out here, and you've got next to nothing for a coat, babe. How do you expect to eat? You can't march into the grocery store like I can."

Lying down again, the dog crawled toward the food slowly and carefully. When she reached it, she grabbed the sandwich with her tongue, as if to stay as far away as she could, and swallowed it whole. Then she stared at Roxi for more.

"I've got this last piece here," she said, waving it under the dog's nose. "But you have to take it from my hand. Deal?"

She was at arm's length now, and Roxi resisted the urge to try stroking her. It might be too soon. Instead, she extended her hand with the food resting in her palm. The dog leaned forward, straining to grab the tantalizing chunk without coming closer.

"Uh-uh. Your turn to move. I'm not budging."

Roxi held her breath as the dog snaked forward. An inch. Two inches.

"That's it. Good girl."

Gently the dog pulled the bread from her hand, and a wave of satisfaction rolled over her. She'd done it! Roxi made one more peanut butter sandwich, then restashed the leftover food in her pack. What now? She couldn't just leave this dog out here alone. But how in the world was she going to take care of her when she could barely take care of herself? The food would be out by tomorrow, and surely Stan wasn't going to let her bring a dog into the coffee shop.

Roxi took a deep breath and stared at the dog. She wasn't a puppy, but she wasn't an adult either. There really wasn't an option here because Roxi knew she could not abandon this creature like that—Roxi called the guy a crude word.

She scrunched her feet underneath herself and stood. The dog jumped nervously to her feet too, but she didn't run away. Roxi backed up two steps, holding out the sandwich. She didn't know why the pup mattered to her so much. Just a few minutes ago she hadn't even known it existed. "We can get through this together," she said.

Roxi knew she'd need to make the first move—before the dog did.

Turning around without looking back, she walked toward the Dumpster, the sandwich in one hand, her backpack in the other.

"Just follow me, girl," she whispered. "You can do it."

When she reached the Dumpster, she was afraid to turn around. Would the dog still be standing where she'd left it, or would she be gone?

She set down her backpack and made sure to keep her movements even. She glanced at the sandwich in her hand, a lump forming in her throat. *If You're really out there, God, please make this dog trust me. I promise I won't ask for anything else.*

Maybe it was stupid, praying at a time like this. Why bother? Not like God had answered any of her other prayers. If He cared at all, none of this would be happening. She'd have a family. She'd be safe. Someone would love her. It would all be—

The whimper so close made Roxi jump. She turned around and saw the little dog sitting right behind her, eyes glued to the sandwich in her hand.

19

ABBY GOT THE E-MAIL at five thirty in the morning. Sitting at Christy's kitchen table with her laptop and Christy's wireless connection, she'd hoped to spend a mindless hour surfing the Internet and watching the sunrise. That idea shot out the window as she read an e-mail from AbeBooks.com.

She'd placed wants for all the stolen books at the major bookselling sites. Whenever a new book with that title became available online, she'd automatically receive an e-mail letting her know the price, condition, and the bookseller's details. It was a great way to find an obscure book and for her to look for the stolen ones. She'd gotten many e-mail matches already, but all of them had either been reprints or book club editions, not the firsts from the Barn's inventory.

This e-mail was different. A twinge of hope crept through Abby as she reread the description in the want match:

Tolkien, J. R. R. *Farmer Giles of Ham.* Illustrated by Pauline Diana Baynes. Boston: Houghton Mifflin Co., 1950. First edition. 8vo (between 7¾" and 9¾" tall). Hardcover. Good+ condition book / Good+ condition dust jacket. 79 pages. Yellow and blue illustrated dust jacket. Drawings by the same artist who illustrated the Narnia series. With the words "First published in the U.S.A. in 1950" on the copyright page. Date of 1950 on title page. $2.00 price on dust jacket flap. Tight copy with clean interior pages. $150.00.

Abby scrambled for her laptop case and pulled out the stolen books list Christy had given her. Flipping through the pages, she found the Barn's listing and compared it line by line. Of course the wording was different, but the points matched exactly. They were both first editions with dust jackets. How often did this book come on the market? It wasn't the rarest title, but the timing was uncanny. Could it be coincidence?

She scanned the listing again. Pages Past bookstore in Santa Fe had posted the title. Abby leaned back in her chair and glanced at Christy's closed door. She scribbled the bookstore's contact info, downed the rest of her coffee, and went to wake her.

❧

Roxi opened her eyes, instantly awake. After the dog had come to her last night, she'd hand-fed it the last sandwich piece by piece, then lain down facing her. For a few minutes they'd just watched each other. But then, to her amazement, the dog lay down too—curled up in a tight ball against her stomach. Shivering. She'd taken off her jean jacket and draped it over the dog, then spent the night shivering herself.

But now . . . she sat straight up, staring at the flat, empty lump of her jean jacket. Where was the dog? On her feet in an instant, she frantically scanned the lot. The sky's predawn grayness gave her more visibility than last night, but Roxi saw nothing.

No. She couldn't be gone. Roxi had spent the entire night waking every few minutes just to rest her hand on the dog's back and reassure herself she was still there. How could she have slept through her leaving?

"Where are you, girl?"

She ran up and down the lot, searching every nook and cranny. Behind the air conditioner units, around a second Dumpster, all through the weeds where she'd first seen the dog.

Nothing.

She whistled.

Silence.

Whistled again.

A burst of wind blew her hair into her face, but all she heard was a distant car engine. The Safeway would open soon, which meant employees could show up at any time. By then she needed to be out of here, but she couldn't just take off and leave the dog. How would she survive? Her owner dumped her, for crying out loud. She'd need food and shelter and someone to take care of her.

Running around to the front of the store, she spent thirty minutes searching every possible hiding place. By the time she came back around to the Dumpster, she was crying. For one glorious moment last night, she hadn't felt alone.

Roxi scooped up her backpack, unzipped it, and pulled out breakfast. At the sight of the bread and peanut butter, she almost lost it completely, thinking only of the dog. Mechanically she forced herself to make two sandwiches and eat one of them. There would only be enough bread for two more after this and barely enough peanut butter.

Stan needed her at the coffee shop by six. If she stayed here, she might lose her brand-new job. But if she left and the dog came back when she wasn't around . . . Roxi held her eyes shut for a second, then purposefully opened them and made herself get ready to go.

She went to the bathroom in the weeds, then changed into her other pair of jeans as fast as she could to keep from freezing. She used the last of her bottled water to scrub her hands and face, trying not to imagine the dog's scraped shoulder and how she'd planned to use the water to clean it. Brushing her hair with her fingers, she peeled off some of her layers and slipped into her least-dirty hoodie.

When she couldn't wait any longer, Roxi walked the lot one last time calling for the dog every few steps. Still nothing. With a lump in her throat, she gently placed the extra peanut butter sandwich beside the Dumpster.

❦

On the empty streets of Elk Valley, Roxi was sure she stuck out like a goth at a cheerleader party. She knew if she was stopped and questioned by the cops now, they'd see through her story. Even if they didn't find out about her involvement in that guy's death, she was a runaway. That fact alone could send her to juvie until the state found a home to take her in, which probably wouldn't happen. Most foster families wanted cuddly babies or cute toddlers. Not troublemaker teens like her.

A truck drove past her down the street, and Roxi kept her eyes straight ahead. Once she had a job and a place to live, it might be different. No more shuffling around. She could make her own decisions and not have to worry about anyone's approval.

By five forty-five she was waiting outside The Perfect Blend, hands shoved into her pockets, feet stamping to keep warm. Why had she let herself get attached to that dog? Now every time she thought about it, a little part of her heart ached. She should've known the dog would bolt. The poor creature had been neglected and abused. Why *should* the dog trust her?

Stan showed up in a blue polo shirt and ski cap, whistling and jingling his keys. He looked surprised when he saw Roxi standing in the doorway.

She threw on a perky smile, pulling her hands from her pockets. "I'm a little early."

"I wasn't sure if you'd show," Stan said, unlocking the door and holding it open for her. "Come on in and I'll brew you something."

Roxi reveled in the store's warmth, and the delicious pastry and coffee smells made her mouth water. What would be her first duty? Sweeping the floor? Wiping down the tables? Maybe Stan would teach her how to make a latte or a cappuccino.

"What would you like?" Stan gestured toward the wall of coffee selections behind the counter. They were displayed in clear bins so patrons could see the coffee beans. Each bin was labeled with the coffee's name on a gold nameplate. "Take your pick. We roast it all ourselves in the building next door. Got a gazillion loose tea selections, too."

Tea was Irene's department. Sometimes after a successful book run, they'd stop at one of the local coffeehouses and Roxi and Diego would enjoy a good cup of java. But Irene always went for tea. Sometimes black, sometimes red, but usually green.

"House blend was good yesterday," Roxi said.

Stan gave her a thumbs-up. "You got it. One house blend comin' up."

She watched him scoop the beans into the grinder and flip on the screeching machine. He dumped the finished product into an industrial-size coffee filter, and within a minute the brew was dripping and filling the room with an even richer, wet-forest scent.

"Have a seat," Stan said.

"Don't you have to open soon?"

"Yep, but we're good. I get everything but the pastries ready to go at the end of the day. Want a bagel to go with that coffee?"

Did she ever. Roxi nodded. Even after the peanut butter sandwich, she was still hungry.

Stan brought over a cinnamon raisin bagel on a plate with a knife and a pack of Philadelphia cream cheese. "Black, right?"

It felt a little weird for him to be serving her when she was supposed to be working for him, but she wasn't complaining. "Yes, please."

"Most teens who come in here order the sugariest concoctions we've got," Stan said from behind the counter. "What got you started drinking coffee black?"

Roxi took a huge bite of the bagel, then had to chew a few times before she could answer. "I didn't used to." She swallowed the bite down. "A friend taught me. Easier, you know? If you don't have milk, no worries."

Bringing a steaming paper cup to the table, Stan sat down in the chair across from her. He rested his elbows on the table and sighed. For the first time Roxi noticed the dark circles under his eyes behind his glasses.

"Where should I start?" she said. "I can work while I eat."

She started to get up, but Stan stopped her with an upraised hand. "Stay put for a minute."

Roxi slowly lowered herself to the chair, suddenly uneasy. What was going on?

"Why didn't you include any references on your application?"

So that was it. She'd been worried about that yesterday when she filled out the application, and apparently rightfully so. She decided honesty could go a long way here. "Because I don't have any. This is my first job, and I don't have a former employer."

Stan digested that, then sighed again. "I grew up in Walsenburg, Roxi. There is no Broad Street. So do you mind telling me why you put that as your address?"

Mouth full of bagel, she tried to chew but found the bread sticking to the roof of her mouth. She could make something up. Enough new construction happened these days for the road to be one he didn't know about. But somehow she had a feeling Stan wouldn't buy it.

"I'd really like to hire you," Stan said, leaning back in his chair. "You seem like a nice girl. But I need my help to be up-front with me. I don't know why you lied about your address or why you have no references, but—"

"I'm a hard worker. I can pull my weight. If you'll only—"

"I don't doubt that, but I need someone I can trust."

"You *can* trust me. I just . . . I can't explain everything."

Stan studied her for a moment. His eyes were kind, but they were also rock solid. "Honesty is very important to me, Roxi. You can understand that. Some business owners will do anything to get started and maintain a customer base. Not me. It might cost me things in the short term, but in the long term? It's worth it. And I've got to live with my decisions forever."

She picked at the seam of her coffee cup, not looking him in the eyes. "So I'm not getting the job?"

"I'm very sorry."

Roxi felt like a deflated tire and could only sit in the chair and stare at her cup. How could this be happening? She'd banked everything on this job working.

"Maybe I can still help you, though," Stan said. "Where are you staying?"

She almost told him about the Safeway. The need to talk to someone was burning hotter every day, but she stopped herself short. For all she knew, Stan would call the cops. If he couldn't trust her, she definitely couldn't trust him.

Roxi stood.

"I can still help you, if you'll let me."

Scooping up her backpack, she clumsily tried to swing it onto her shoulder and grab her coffee and bagel at the same time. "Yeah, and maybe I don't need a handout."

"No, wait. Don't go just yet."

She stomped toward the door, then turned to face him. "I need a job. If you can't give me that, then we're done here."

Stan jumped up. "Where are your parents? Are they looking for you?"

"Who said that was your business?"

"It's not my business, but I just—"

"Then keep it that way." Hostility was creeping into her voice without her even trying. She didn't need this guy. And she didn't need Mom, a social worker, Irene, or anyone else telling her what to do.

Stan pulled out his keys and walked over to the door she was ready to bash through. "I can't make you stay. But if you'll just calm down, there are a lot of good people in this town, and whatever's going on, we could help you."

Oh, that's just what she needed. She stood there staring him down.

"You've made up your mind, haven't you?"

She went for the door. "Thanks for the coffee and bagel."

"Just remember," Stan said, slowly unlocking the door, "that's a standing offer."

Managing a nod, she left him in the doorway.

20

"I CAN'T BELIEVE you talked me into this." Christy slipped into the passenger seat, threw her small cloth purse in the back, and smiled at Abby. Both of their overnight bags were already stowed in the trunk.

Abby pulled the car away from the apartment, mentally recording their departure time. It would be at least a six-hour drive without stops, and she hoped to keep those to a minimum. They planned to drive all day and make it to the store well before it closed tonight at seven.

"This could be our big break," she said.

"What if it really is one of our books?" Christy fastened her seat belt and started fiddling with the console cup holder. She'd brought along a silver travel cup of coffee decorated with the outline of a cat.

"Some used bookstores require the name and address of anyone they buy books from. If we're lucky, they'll give it to us."

"But I'm sure they won't release it to just anyone."

"Leave that part to me."

"What will you say?"

"Don't worry. I'll take care of it."

"Abby."

She kept her gaze on the road.

"You're not telling me something."

"I'm sure you want to find who did this as much as I do."

"That's not an answer."

Abby chose the shortest route to the freeway. Christy had this way of knowing what she was thinking, and she wasn't giving her the advantage of eye contact. "Trust me. I won't be stupid."

"If you've got something up your sleeve, I'd like to know about it."

"Nothing up my sleeve."

"Promise?"

She lifted both hands from the steering wheel. "I thought you wanted to come!"

"Yeah, because someone has to keep you out of trouble."

Abby managed a smile. "Ha-ha."

"So the plan is . . . ?"

"I'll call the store at nine, get them to hold the book, and then we'll be there before they close."

They rode in silence for a few minutes. Abby's black leather jacket was making her hot, but rather than taking it off, she turned up the AC. She didn't want Christy to see her shoulder holster. Not yet, at least.

"Did you get any sleep last night?" Abby asked.

Christy didn't answer for a moment. "It's better now that you're here."

"I dream about him every night."

"Me too."

"Good dreams?"

"Mostly. But it's always so sad to wake up."

"Mine are more like nightmares." Abby checked her mirrors and the traffic, then merged onto the freeway.

"I've had those too." Christy leaned against the headrest, staring out the window. "Actually, I haven't slept very well at all."

"Maybe you should try taking something."

Christy chuckled. "Uh, no. I can't go there."

Abby gave her a funny look. "Why not?"

"I'm not sure how much Hunter told you about me."

That piqued Abby's curiosity, but she didn't bite. "He said you were smart, beautiful, and loved books."

Christy gave her an embarrassed smile. "He *would* leave out the other stuff."

"Bet he left stuff out about me, too."

Christy took a sip from her coffee, still looking out the window. "Things haven't always been like this for me. Having a good job, living in a nice apartment. I've made so many stupid choices. One of them was turning to a bottle for comfort. The other night was probably one of the worst I've had. I was this close—" Christy held up her index finger and thumb with about a centimeter of space between them—"to throwing in the towel."

"Well, you certainly wouldn't be the only person in America to wind down with a glass or two of chardonnay."

"I'm not talking about a glass of wine here and there."

Abby changed lanes and started to make a joke but then realized Christy was being serious and seeming to struggle with what to say next.

"About a year and a half ago, I was arrested for DUI." Christy's voice went so quiet, Abby could barely hear her. "It was late at night, and I'd been drinking by myself. I should never have gotten behind the wheel, but I did."

Abby did her best to keep her expression even, but she was having trouble picturing Christy in the back of her patrol car.

"I could've killed someone. I'm sure you've seen that happen."

She nodded.

"I'm sober now, but it was that experience, among other things, that brought me to my rock bottom. Actually, it's a long story."

"Well, it's a long ride," Abby said.

Christy spent the next hour telling her how she'd met her sister, May, after fifteen years; how Vince had set fire to her apartment; how she'd finally found refuge at May's ranch only to experience a horrendous riding accident.

"Wow," was all Abby could say. Hunter had definitely left out the details.

"Last night was bad too. If I'd had anything in the apartment, I know I would've fallen off the wagon."

Abby found herself without words. These revelations made her see Christy in a new light, though not in the negative one she was probably expecting. Instead, she felt an even greater respect for the woman.

"I always wondered what Hunter saw in me," Christy said. "He knew about it all, but for some reason, he never gave up on me."

"Perhaps he saw who you could become," Abby said. "Who you are now."

"Maybe." Christy managed a smile. "I mean, he wasn't perfect, but . . ."

"But he saw the best in everyone." Abby nodded as if finalizing the subject. "Not many people do."

"Which always reminds me of God. He didn't give up on me either."

Abby urged the car faster and passed a slow-rolling semi. She wasn't sure what Christy meant by that.

"What's your story, Abby? Spiritually, I mean."

"I guess I'd say I'm a Christian, if that's what you're talking about. Are you?"

"I am now."

"Was Hunter?" Abby surprised herself with that question. She was the one who'd taken Hunter to church when they were little, but that was so many years ago, and she hadn't talked to him or anybody else about that sort of thing in a long time.

"He definitely was," Christy said.

"How do you know?"

Christy thought for a moment. "He had an understanding of God way before I did, though not in the same way some people would expect. He didn't go to church very much. You know how he spent Sundays?"

Abby smiled. "Outside."

"Whenever possible. Even if it was snowing."

"He's been doing that since he was a kid."

"He said to me one time he saw more of God in nature than he'd ever seen inside a church building."

"Now *that* I can relate to."

"Really?"

Abby slipped on a pair of sunglasses. "You spend as much time on the streets as I have, and you see people at their worst. Something's wrong when you can't tell the difference between the pastor and the pimp."

Christy winced.

"Years ago I went to a church," Abby said. "The pastor seemed to have it all. The pretty wife; a clean-cut, obedient kid; nice house; decent car—you name it. He was the type of guy everyone wanted to be like. Living the American dream. And what he preached really did make sense. Had a down-to-earth way I enjoyed."

Christy took a sip from her travel mug. "I'm guessing there's a *but* here."

"Oh, there is. Out of the blue one week he announced from the pulpit he was leaving his wife. I found out later he'd been seeing this other woman for months, hiding it from everyone. He used the church offerings to buy the woman gifts."

"You're kidding."

"It turned me off, big-time. And it wasn't just him. There were people in that church who were complete hypocrites. In the pew on Sunday, sinning on Monday."

"But we all make mistakes. I mean, I oughta know."

"This wasn't just a 'mistake.'"

Christy held her travel mug with both hands, staring down at it. "I don't know very much about God yet. But I do know what my life was like before. Not that everything magically changed. I don't know why I'm still struggling with temptations. I don't know why God didn't keep Hunter from dying. But last night before you came, I talked to my sister on the phone. She helped me understand one thing: God hasn't left me."

"I'm glad you're sure of that," Abby said.

"He hasn't left you, either."

Coming from anyone else, Abby would've tuned the words out entirely. Enough people had tried to shove their religion down her throat. But Christy wasn't doing that. This was the story of her life. Take it or leave it.

She let Christy have the last word.

❧

It was late afternoon when Roxi trudged across the Safeway parking lot. She had stopped by the used bookstore again, but it was still closed. No indication of when it would open, either. Her backpack seemed heavier than ever, her body ached from last night on the pavement, and she was starting to smell herself.

Fighting to keep alert, she slowly made her way around to the back of the store. She couldn't lose her edge now. It would take only one person asking too many questions. She had to stay invisible, but what she yearned for more than anything was a warm bed. And sleep. The lack of it had given her a headache, and even thinking about another night behind the Dumpster made her want to cry. But she couldn't even try to sleep yet. Until the Safeway closed, there was too much chance of an employee finding her, and that wouldn't be for hours. She had to wait.

Where could she possibly go? Her money was gone. Her food almost gone. She could thumb her way to the city, but hitchhiking was like playing Russian roulette. She'd lucked out being picked up by Gordon. How long would it take before the wrong guy offered her a ride? And while she could refill her water bottle in public bathrooms, how many days could she go without food?

All morning she'd managed to keep her underlying panic at bay, but now she was almost at the breaking point. She'd entertained the thought of begging Irene to take her in again. But of all her options—including some she wished she hadn't thought of—Roxi couldn't bring herself to do it. Maybe it was pride, maybe it was anger, maybe it was both, but her fingers wouldn't dial *that* number.

She made it to her Dumpster, rested her back against the rusted green metal, and slid to the ground. Its odor of rancid trash was impossible to escape, but she had nowhere else to go. And come to think of it, this was probably where she belonged. Thrown away and forgotten. Lifting her face to the sky, she let the tears come. Why couldn't one thing go right? Just for once. Was God punishing her for her part in that guy's death?

Her eyes drifted to her backpack, and she remembered the Bible

Gordon gave her. Unzipping the pack, she pulled it out, ready to pitch it in the Dumpster. She didn't need this. God didn't care about her.

But she couldn't quite bring herself to make the toss. Gordon's expression when he'd given it to her was so sincere. *He* believed in God. And he'd given her forty bucks.

Roxi absentmindedly flipped the Bible open, wondering what Gordon would read if he were in a scrape like this. Hadn't he told her to read something? something about a song?

His words came back to her. *"Easy to remember: 3-2-1."*

Thirty-two. Thirty-two what?

She scanned the table of contents, barely able to see it in the dimming light, and stopped at Psalms. That sounded right. Psalm 32. Flipping to the right page, she read the first line of 32 and mumbled the words out loud.

"Blessed is he whose transgressions are forgiven, whose sins are covered.

"Blessed is the man whose sin the Lord does not count against him and in whose spirit is no deceit."

Roxi stopped. A man was dead, and she'd played a part in it. She'd lied and stolen from people who'd never done her wrong. What kind of sins were they talking about here? She started to read on, but then she heard a faint sound that sent her scrambling to her feet.

A bark.

She dropped the Bible, her heart instantly jumping. And then she remembered. The peanut butter sandwich she'd left behind. Where was it? She searched around the Dumpster, but she couldn't even find crumbs. Could a worker have thrown the sandwich out?

Roxi didn't breathe as she listened. *Come on. Bark again. Please.*

Nothing.

She listened for a full minute, but all she heard were normal supermarket sounds. A few car doors slamming. The rattle of a shopping cart in the front parking lot. A car horn's sharp honk as someone locked up with a key remote. Could it just have been the bark of a dog in a passing car?

Roxi crumpled to the pavement, the back of her head knocking into the Dumpster's rusted green side. It was stupid to get her hopes up. She should just forget about the dog. Things would be a lot easier if she didn't have attachments.

But where had that dog gone? She'd racked her brain all day. It would be completely dark soon, and with the dark would come the cold. Roxi picked up the Bible again, trying to send her thoughts in a different direction.

She read another sentence:

When I kept silent, my bones wasted away through my groaning all day long.

Okay, that line she totally got. She never realized how hard it would be not to have anyone to talk to. Sometimes at the campgrounds, she and Diego would sit out talking in lawn chairs until it was too dark to see each other. Usually the conversations would go no deeper than who Diego thought would win the World Series, but the companionship was nice.

Diego was the closest thing to a friend she'd ever had, and now even he was gone. Would she ever see him again? She wasn't sure she wanted to after what he'd done, but she knew he had good in him. Behind that macho attitude he was capable of kindness. Why had he been stupid enough to bring that gun?

Then a frightening thought hit her. What if the police *did* catch up with Diego? Would he go to prison? Even if he didn't mean to kill that guy, he still had. He'd do time, wouldn't he?

And what about her? She was an accomplice to a murder. She

hadn't known about the gun, but she'd been burglarizing the place just as much as Diego or Irene.

Skipping down a few lines, she found the verse Gordon had quoted to her:

> *Then I acknowledged my sin to you and did not cover up my*
> *iniquity. I said, "I will confess my transgressions to the Lord"—*
> *and you forgave the guilt of my sin.*
> *Selah.*

Selah? What did that mean? The odd word appeared three times in this chapter. Roxi closed the Bible, as unclear about the meaning of the verse as when she'd heard it from Gordon. She understood the sin part, but what did *iniquity* and *transgression* mean? And forgiveness— she had a feeling murder wasn't a forgivable sin. More likely it would send someone to hell, if there really was such a place.

Her knees to her chest, she took in her world, and—

A movement on the edge of the lot caught her attention. That was definitely something. She was on her feet again, all other thoughts shoved aside.

Roxi shook her head. This was silly. Every shadow was a dog. But . . .

This shadow moved toward her.

She didn't dare to . . .

No, she wasn't imagining it. Walking toward her, slow and deliberate, was the small Greyhound-like dog. Roxi dropped to her knees, arms outstretched.

She could hardly believe what she saw next.

The dog actually ran toward her in a silly sideways gait, still favoring its leg. And when she made it to Roxi, tail swooshing back and forth, head lowered like last night, Roxi threw all caution to the wind

C.J. DARLINGTON

and reached for the dog. In one smooth motion she pulled the animal to her chest, stroking the dog's velvet fur, fresh tears dripping down her cheeks.

The dog didn't struggle.

"Where *were* you? I didn't think I'd ever see you again," Roxi whispered. The dog wiggled in her arms, but she didn't let go. A long sob escaped her lips, and it was almost like she heard it from a distance and didn't recognize herself.

When she finally loosened her grip on the dog, her tear-streaked face was instantly bathed in a slathering of licks.

Roxi held up both hands, warding off the dog's tongue. "Okay, okay, I'll stop blubbering." She would focus on the dog. It would keep her sane.

Sitting down, the dog cocked her head, her gaze moving toward Roxi's backpack, then to Roxi.

"Oh, so that's it. Stomach's got the better of you, huh? Well, I've got some bad news, girl. I only have two sandwiches left. You know that job I told you about? It fell through. I don't know what I'm— what *we're* going to do."

Reaching for the pack, Roxi slid it closer and brought out the last four pieces of bread and peanut butter. Her stomach growled, but she knew she wouldn't be eating these as originally planned. She'd at least had a bagel and coffee today. What had the dog had?

"The first thing I'm doing is getting you a leash. Then we've gotta come up with a name for you," she said, handing over the first sandwich. "I can't keep calling you 'Dog.'"

She could name her something associated with her color, like Shadow or Midnight. But neither seemed to fit. Scraping the plastic jar with her knife, she extracted every last morsel of peanut butter for the final sandwich. Something had to change. And soon. Now she wouldn't even be eating dinner.

173

"You'll feel fuller if you eat slower." She broke the sandwich in fourths and enjoyed every moment of hand-feeding the dog.

A few minutes later, she got lucky on her first Dumpster dive, finding a four-foot section of string. Roxi promptly tied one end around the dog's neck. "That's to keep you from running away again," she said. "Hope you don't mind."

The dog's still-hungry eyes stared at her backpack.

"I'm real sorry, but that's it." Roxi sat down, tying the other end of the string to her wrist. She brought the pack closer so the dog could see the food really was gone, but that only sent her into a nose-curling sniffing frenzy.

"You can lick the jar, but that's all I've got."

She held the empty jar out, and the dog stuck her long nose straight in, her pink tongue extended to its max, poking and licking every last square inch. She pushed her nose further in, almost knocking Roxi over.

After minutes of licking, the dog finally retracted her nose, still smacking and smacking her lips. Brown peanut butter morsels clung to her whiskers and blotched the top of her nose.

Roxi smiled, realizing how long it had been since she'd felt like laughing.

"Here's the way it's gonna be, girl." She leaned against the Dumpster, and the dog lay down beside her. Roxi stroked her back as she talked. "I'm gonna sleep here tonight. Then in the morning I'll knock on every business door I can find. Someone has to need me, even if I don't have references."

It was the only thing she could do. Even in a town this size there had to be an opening somewhere. She'd do just about anything. Flip burgers. Clean toilets. But wouldn't they all require an application? She wasn't up for calling attention to herself again like she had with Stan by filling one out. If word got out that some sorry-looking girl was searching for work, people would ask questions she wouldn't be able to answer.

"We're not in a good place here," she said, then smiled when the dog rested her long black head on her thigh. "But at least I have you again."

She sat there, thinking and petting the dog. As glad as she was to have her back, a dog did pose a problem. Now she had two mouths to feed, and how was she going to get work with a dog at her side?

Roxi caught sight of Gordon's Bible spread-eagle on the ground, and she stowed it safely in her backpack's front pocket. Maybe there was a bright side, even if it was only a sliver. "What do you think of the name Selah?"

The dog's ears perked up.

"I don't know what it means. I wish I knew your real name, but really, you're starting over too. Might as well have a new name, huh?" Roxi crossed her legs, feeling the temperature dropping. "Maybe you never had a name. Has anyone ever loved you before me?"

Selah licked her hand.

"We've gotta have food," Roxi said. "That's all there is to it. I'm already on empty. I don't know how I'll do any kind of work tomorrow if I don't eat."

Roxi shook her head at the desperate facts, hoping another idea would spring up in her brain. None did. There was only one option.

She'd have to steal again.

❧

Pages Past bookstore occupied the corner storefront of a strip mall. Red neon signs glowed *We Buy Books* and *We Buy CDs* in the front window, and several doorstop-size best sellers were displayed in stacks beneath them.

"Let me do the talking," Abby whispered to Christy, opening the bookstore's front door. A bell jingled as they walked inside to the smell of new books, and Abby headed toward the customer service counter in the middle of the room. Volumes were piled everywhere on the counter with only a narrow tunnel cleared for the computer keyboard and monitor. She'd expected an antiquarian store more like the Barn, but most of the books here were recent. There was only a small section for rare titles.

A female clerk with green highlights in her hair greeted them without a smile. "How can I help you?"

"My name's Abby Dawson. I called earlier to have a book held for me."

"Title?"

"*Farmer Giles of Ham.* By Tolkien."

The girl nodded, turning toward a wall of shelves behind her. The bottom row of titles had pink pieces of paper stuck out their tops with names written on them in black marker. The girl came back with a book whose cover was bright yellow and blue.

"Here you go."

Christy instantly edged closer, and Abby gave the book to her. For a tense moment Christy examined it with Abby watching over her shoulder. When Christy turned to the back page, her expression changed from curious to solemn. With a trembling hand Christy showed the page to Abby, pointing at the small penciled *D*.

It was the Barn's mark. This book had been in the hands of Hunter's murderer.

Abby took a deep breath, then reached into her coat pocket and pulled out her badge. She flashed it at the clerk slowly enough for her to see it was official, fast enough so she wouldn't see it was from a different state. And she made sure to briefly expose her gun. "Miss?"

The girl's eyes widened. So did Christy's.

Abby focused on the girl. "Don't worry. You've done nothing

wrong. I'm part of an investigation that's looking into a ring of book thieves. We have reason to believe someone stole this book from a different store and then sold it to you."

"You're kidding."

"Unfortunately, no." Abby returned her badge to her coat. "Here's what I need from you."

The clerk nodded vigorously even though she hadn't yet asked for anything. A badge and a gun could do wonders.

"We need to know who sold it to you. Do you keep record of that?"

"Yeah, definitely." The girl came to life and spun to her keyboard, tapping and scrolling the mouse wheel, her eyes glued on the monitor.

Abby sent a smile in Christy's direction, but Christy just stared at her.

"Got it right here," the clerk said, grabbing a pen and paper scrap. "Want me to write it down?"

"Please," Abby said.

The clerk scribbled. "Got an address and license number too."

"I'll take everything."

Handing the paper to Abby, the clerk lowered her voice, eyeing the Tolkien. "Is it really stolen?"

Abby nodded. "We think so."

"From where?"

"I'm sorry, but I can't share that."

The girl picked up the book, tilting her shoulders back slightly. "We would never deliberately sell stolen books."

Abby gave her a sympathetic smile. "Unfortunately, we'll have to confiscate this." She tucked the book under her arm, hoping to avoid more unnecessary fingerprints. It would go straight in an evidence bag outside. "You've been a big help. Thanks for your cooperation." She was also hoping the clerk wouldn't call her manager over. No one needed to know she wasn't from the local police, and an astute bookstore owner might check up on her if given the opportunity.

Only when they were outside at the car again did Christy speak. "You mind telling me why you lied to her like that?"

"I didn't lie." Abby unlocked the doors with her key remote. "I *am* part of an investigation."

"You know what I mean."

"We got what we needed, didn't we?"

Christy slipped into the passenger seat, and Abby got in the driver's. "I thought you said you had nothing up your sleeve."

"Everything I said in there was true."

"You didn't tell me you were carrying a gun, either."

"For cryin' out loud. I'm a cop."

Christy stared out the windshield.

"Does it really bother you?"

"If I said yes, would it matter?"

"You have to understand: I'm not gonna go do something stupid."

"You should have told me."

"Why, so you could worry?"

Christy sighed. "I thought we were in this together."

"And what would you have done? Told her your fiancé was murdered and you were going behind the backs of the authorities to find the person who did it? Think they would've given you this?" She handed Christy the piece of paper.

Christy took it but didn't read it. A flash of hurt passed across her face, then quickly dissolved. "What else are you hiding?"

"Nothing."

"'Cause I'd like to know now if you are."

Abby started the car and pulled out onto the road. A police cruiser zoomed past them, lights flashing, and she thought to tell Christy about her suspension. Yeah, right. That would go over real well right now.

"Listen," Abby said, "all I want is to find who did this. I'm willing to risk everything, even my job, for that."

"And that's something Hunter would want you to do?"

"Hunter is the *only* reason I'm doing any of this."

"We don't know who or what we're dealing with. I don't see why we don't take this information and give it to the detective."

"I didn't say I wouldn't."

For the first time Abby saw real distrust on Christy's face, making her regret the jab at how Christy would've handled the situation. Hunter had loved Christy. That meant something.

"You're too close to this," Christy said. "Let someone else handle it."

She shook her head and changed the subject. "Does the name on that paper mean anything to you?"

"Diego Tonelli. No, never heard of him."

Silence filled the car, and Abby guessed they were both wondering the same thing. Could this man be Hunter's murderer?

21

IT WAS COMPLETELY DARK when Roxi finally worked up the nerve to walk into the Safeway. She tried to hide her face with her hair as she passed under the security camera. Those things always unnerved her. Especially the screens where you could see yourself. She was always startled by her own image, and no matter how hard she tried, she could never look herself in the eye. How many cameras were in this place?

She'd stolen from a grocery store only twice before. The first time she did it on a dare from a school bully and walked off with a pack of gum. The second time, right after she ran away from her last foster home, store security caught her in the act. She hadn't eaten for two days, and she'd tried to smuggle a turkey sandwich from the deli in her pocket. They'd somehow seen, and she'd spent a month in detention.

She could not be caught tonight. Selah needed her.

Nervous energy took over, and she cruised the produce department hoping to find some fruit or crackers in one of those tempting freebie displays. But all of them were empty except for one that held a few crushed tortilla chips. She snatched up every stale piece. She hated that it had come down to stealing. But what other choice did she have? This wasn't for thrills. She had to eat. Luckily, the store was crawling with people. She could only hope no one would notice an unobtrusive teenager.

Deep breath. Irene taught her never to show nervousness or look like she was scoping the place. Just walk in, do the job, and walk out.

It was easier said than done. At least with the bookstores she always knew where she was going. Here she was clueless. It felt like everyone, from the woman with the bouncing toddler in her cart to the old fogy with a cane, was checking her out. Did she really look that bad?

She finally found the pet supplies aisle, with its faint smell of rawhide and kibble, and confidently turned in. Blood was pounding in her temples now, intensifying her headache. She had to focus. Get this job done. Selah depended on her. The dog was safely hidden and tied behind the Dumpster, and she'd left a sweatshirt and Diego's knit pullover for a bed. But Roxi wasn't putting much faith in that string. She had to do this fast.

Roxi slowed when she saw the array of collars and leashes hanging from metal display hooks. There were too many choices. Neon colors, cutesy patterns, even one that reflected light. She didn't care about color. It just needed to fit. Selah wasn't a large dog, but she wasn't a puppy either.

It was now or never.

Walking right up to the display, she removed the first collar and leash her fingers touched and walked off with them like she was heading to the checkout. Only when she was out of the aisle did she slowly pull them into a ball and shove them both inside her jean jacket's inner pocket.

Just keep going. Don't look around.

No one stopped her.

She'd already decided what food to take. It had to be something compact yet nourishing. Not like she could steal a loaf of bread without someone noticing. But protein bars would be good for both her and Selah. Just a few. She only needed enough to get through tonight and tomorrow.

It took longer to find the health food aisle than she'd planned, but when she finally did, there were three other patrons browsing. She swallowed the knot in her throat. How could she do this without them noticing?

She couldn't. She'd have to wait.

Pretending to absorb herself in comparing boxed soy milk prices, she watched each shopper out of the corner of her eye. The young guy in baggy khakis and a black T-shirt stretched tight across his muscular chest reached to the top shelf and pulled down a plastic container of whey protein powder. Then he walked right past her. She caught a whiff of cologne.

One down, two to go.

A woman in a flowing peasant skirt and sandals slowly pushed a shopping cart full of vegetables down the aisle, perusing every item she passed.

Roxi slid closer to the protein bar display. In a moment that woman would be gone, which left the hiking boots guy with the beard. He held two supplement bottles side by side, apparently comparing ingredients.

Come on.

She eyed the bars. At least ten choices, but it didn't matter what brand she got at this point. She just needed something to eat. Something small enough to hide.

Bearded guy put one bottle back. He pushed his glasses up his nose and reread the remaining bottle's label.

Roxi could've screamed. Selah was probably pulling on that piece of string . . . or chewing through it.

Finally Beardy placed his precious supplement in the top of his shopping cart, the part where little kids usually sat, feet dangling. Only when his back was to her did Roxi move the final feet to stand in front of the protein bars. Security didn't usually stop someone right in the store. When they caught her before, they'd waited until she was almost out the door. Which meant they could've already seen her take that leash and collar.

Don't go there. Get what you need and get out.

She snatched three bars in one swipe, painfully aware of the crinkling sound the wrapper made as she shoved them into her pocket. Swiping three more, she pushed them into her other pocket. Go! Another handful would tide her over. Her fingers wrapped around two more.

That's when someone grabbed her shoulder.

Roxi jumped, jerked her hand away, and spun around. A woman wearing a black cowboy hat and a blue down vest stood behind her.

"They might not like you doing that," the woman said.

She froze, speechless. Should she pretend she didn't know what the woman was talking about? laugh and throw the bars back?

Before she could decide, the woman reached into Roxi's pockets and pulled out the six protein bars. She held them up with a smile that only deepened the crow's-feet around her eyes. "This isn't a good idea."

The only thing Roxi knew to do was run. And she did. She spun on her heels and raced down the aisle, ignoring the woman's protests.

Out! Get out now! She darted through the dairy section, then slowed to a brisk walk only because running would call attention to herself.

Go, go, go.

She dodged around the woman with the peasant skirt, her boots clicking on the linoleum, surely drawing stares from every direction. *Don't look guilty. You're just grocery shopping and didn't find what you wanted. No big deal.*

Roxi forced herself to breathe and almost slammed into a shopping cart that materialized directly in her path.

"I'm sorry; I didn't—"

She couldn't stop for the guy's apology. She could see the door from here. Just a few more steps, and then it was home free.

Picking up her pace, she made it to the automatic doors only to find they were the entry doors, not the exit. She banged her fist into the glass, frantically glancing behind herself for a glimpse of that lady with the cowboy hat.

There she was, stepping out of the aisle, searching the room. *Please don't see me. Please don't . . .*

The door whooshed open, and Roxi shot from the store as if the devil himself were nipping her heels. She never raced so fast in her life. Past the row of silver shopping carts, around the corner of the building, back to the—

Her foot slid on a patch of gravel, and she tumbled to the pavement. Hard. Instinctively her palms made first contact, shielding her face from the brunt of the fall, but the length of her left forearm scraped asphalt.

Roxi cried out in pain but scrambled again to her feet, holding back tears. *No time to cry. Keep going.* She could see the Dumpster from here. It was now her refuge, her safe harbor.

As soon as she reached it, Selah jumped up, wagging her tail and making little whining sounds.

"We gotta go, girl." Roxi heaved in breaths, wincing. She couldn't even take time to examine her bleeding scrapes. "Now."

Fumbling with the string around the dog's neck, she glanced behind herself. Was someone following her?

She ripped at the knot with her fingernails, but it pulled into a tighter wad. Dropping to her knees, she bit at the lump of string. Selah patiently waited. It finally came unraveled, and Roxi whipped out the new leash and collar.

"Think you can run, girl?"

Selah wagged her tail.

❧

Abby lay flat on her back staring at the textured ceiling of the hotel room. They had both been too tired to drive home tonight. Her cell phone rested on her stomach, and she traced her finger absent-mindedly around its smooth plastic edge. Since Christy was in the shower, Abby had decided to call in a favor with a PI friend named Cesar Martinez. She'd just gotten off the phone with him. She needed to know everything she could about Diego Tonelli. Hopefully Cesar would dig something up.

The water in the bathroom stopped, and Abby contemplated how to broach the subject she'd been mulling ever since they got this guy's address. Should she let Christy in on all of her plans or keep some to herself?

The bathroom door opened, and Christy stepped out in an over-size T-shirt and sweatpants, mopping her head with a towel. They'd spent the whole ride over here debating whether or not this guy could really be the murderer. Was it possible he'd gotten his hands on the book some other way? Maybe he'd bought it off the real killer unknowingly.

Abby threaded her fingers behind her head, the cell phone still resting on her stomach. She'd start with the easy questions. "What do you think about Dad selling the Barn?"

Christy plopped down on the second bed, rummaging in her overnight bag. She pulled out a small, wooden hairbrush. "Think he's serious?"

"Oh, he's serious."

"I guess I can't blame him, but that's the last thing Hunter would want."

"Exactly what I said."

"Maybe if he waited a little bit."

Abby laughed sarcastically. "I suggested that, but do you think he listened to me? Doesn't matter to him what I think."

"What if *you* bought it?"

Abby gave Christy a surprised look. "Me?"

"I guess it's kind of yours already."

"No, the Barn's Dad's. Always has been." She lifted herself up on her elbow. "But what about you? You're the one who knows books. And then you wouldn't have to look for another job."

"I could never afford it."

Christy stood, running the brush through her hair. Two inches of her natural brown hair color was visible at the roots; the rest was still bleached blonde. It struck Abby how different they were. Christy was probably only five-foot-three, maybe four. Abby was almost six feet. Christy had a little meat on her bones; Abby could barely keep her weight on. One of them had been arrested; the other could've done the arresting. And yet here they were. Thrown together by circumstances beyond their control, working together by choice.

"Have you thought about it?" Abby asked.

"No."

"It would almost be like it was staying in the family, then." Abby pulled down her bedspread and slipped under the covers. "You, of all people, would carry on Hunter's vision."

"It's too early to be thinking like this."

"Not for Dad."

"It is for me."

Christy's response was short, and Abby realized she was pushing the issue too soon. Christy might not let it show, but her wound was just as raw as Dad's. Hunter had almost been her husband.

Abby fell back onto the pillow, trying to remember what it had been like when she and Michael fell in love. Theirs was definitely a whirlwind romance. In her twenties, four months had seemed like plenty of time to truly know someone, but now Abby could only shake her head at their naiveté. They hadn't known each other. Not really. At least Christy and Hunter had worked together for the past six years.

When she and Michael got back from their honeymoon in Vancouver, it took all of two weeks before their bubble burst. They sprayed so many hurtful words at each other like shotgun pellets, knowing some would hit where it hurt. Kat's birth had helped them tolerate each other, but only for a little while. They'd taken turns walking the halls of that tiny rental house, rocking Kat back to sleep. But in a few short years, they couldn't stand to be in the same bed together.

Thinking of Kat, Abby couldn't keep tears from forming. Kat had been the one to pay for their selfishness. She closed her eyes. Being a teenager wasn't easy when she was growing up, but it was ten times worse now. Based on the statistics, Kat had probably already had her first drink and been exposed to drugs Abby hadn't even known existed when she was a kid. Who was going to warn her about the dangers of fooling around with that stuff or of driving too fast in that new red Jeep? Would her daughter grow up and make the same mistakes she had?

Christy finished brushing her hair and climbed under her own covers. She rolled onto her side and faced Abby. "If you want to talk about the Barn, we can."

"No . . ." Abby wiped her eyes with her sleeve. "I just keep thinking about Kat. She doesn't even know about Hunter yet."

"I thought you called her."

Abby shook her head. "Michael and Sarah are taking her on some stupid beach trip, and they don't want her to know until after. She's my daughter, and I have absolutely no say in her life."

"At least you had her, and she knows she's wanted," Christy said.

There was deep sadness in Christy's voice and something about the way she said it—like there was more to her words than their initial meaning.

"I didn't realize how much having a child would change me," Abby said.

"Neither did I."

Abby met Christy's eyes.

"Only I didn't have mine," Christy whispered, her voice catching.

Abby now realized what Christy was saying. She wanted to fill the silence, but no words came. And it was probably better that way.

"I'm sorry," Christy said, trying to smile. "But—"

"You don't have to say anything."

"Cherish every moment, Abby. Even if they're few."

She nodded, suddenly feeling guilty for her pity party.

Christy turned off her bedstand lamp. Abby did the same with hers, and the room was plunged into darkness.

After a brief silence, Christy's blankets rustled. "What should we do next?"

"While you were in the shower, I called in a favor with a friend. He'll run a background check on Diego Tonelli. I also left a voice mail with the guy working Hunter's case."

"That's good."

Abby glanced at the other bed, her eyes gradually able to discern shadows. "You know I'm not one to sit around and wait for others to do something I can do myself."

"So I'm learning."

"We have this guy's address. . . ." She paused, waiting for Christy to get her hint.

"Oh, man. You're kidding, right?"

She pulled up on her elbow again. "Cheyenne's only about an hour from Longmont."

"Abby, we can't just go gallivanting up to his front door!"

"What if this sliver of time is all we've got? Every minute counts in an investigation like this. If we hurry, we might find something tying him to Hunter's murder."

"But you're not the investigator."

Abby threw herself back onto her pillow. "Come on, you've got to admit we're doing better than the police are right now."

Silence.

She almost rolled her eyes. Christy was great about a lot of stuff, but it was starting to bug her how safe the woman played things. If you were going to get places in life, you had to take risks. Make snap decisions. Abby had learned in the field that hesitation could cost someone their life.

"All right."

Abby grabbed the light cord and flicked the lamp back on.

Christy squinted. "Turn that thing off."

"I just had to see Miss Play-It-Safe's expression to make sure she was serious."

"Oh, shut up." Christy lobbed her pillow at Abby.

They both laughed.

22

ROXI DIDN'T STOP RUNNING until she and Selah were on the out-skirts of Elk Valley. Sweat dripped down her rib cage under her long-underwear shirt, and Selah was panting. Now the cool evening air would give them both a chill.

She buttoned up her jacket, trying to decide whether they should stop following the road and take to the fields. She didn't like how noticeable she was, but she was scared to veer off without a flash-light. Houses were few and far between, and most weren't even visible from the road. A twisted ankle was not an option out here, and she didn't want to meet a prowling coyote or cougar either, especially with Selah.

Holding up her hands toward the moonlight, she tried to see the damage from her fall. Her palms stung, and so did her forearm. They were sticky, but in this light she couldn't tell how much they were bleeding. The best she could do was keep going and feed off the fear that still laced her veins. She'd find somewhere to clean herself up later. The next town was probably several miles down this road. If she could hang on until then, she'd find somewhere to spend the night and start over tomorrow.

Roxi let her backpack thump to the ground and knelt beside Selah. "Come on, girl. We've gotta do something to keep you from getting the chills."

But there wasn't time to do anything. A car's headlights pierced the darkness, approaching fast. Roxi jumped to her feet and started walking again, keeping Selah on a short leash and determined to look like she knew exactly where she was going. She was just out walking her dog. Then in a wave, she realized her mistake. Of course they'd come looking for her on the road. She was a sitting duck! Frantically she scanned the barbed wire fences parallel to the road, searching for an opening, a driveway, something. But there were no breaks.

Behind her the engine growled, so close she could practically feel the headlights on her back—spotlighting her. This was the end, wasn't it? She slowly turned, resigned to her fate. Running from a cop would only make things worse, and he'd catch her either way.

Roxi shielded her face with her hand, trying to see past the blinding headlight beams. Weren't those too high to belong to a police car? There was no sign of flashing red or blue lights.

Wait a minute.

She strained for a better look. That was a pickup truck. Cops didn't drive pickups. Before she could decide whether she and Selah would get through the barbed wire without damage, the truck pulled up beside her. As the driver leaned over and unrolled the passenger window, Roxi saw the black cowboy hat and the woman's face illuminated by the dashboard lights.

"Hey."

It was her. The lady from the grocery store.

Roxi stepped away from the truck. "Did you follow me?"

"I'm just heading home. I didn't see it was you until I got closer."

Roxi didn't know what to say, so she started walking again, hoping the woman would get the message and keep driving. But instead of driving on, the truck slowly drifted forward until it was beside her, keeping pace with her steps.

"You need a ride?"

"No thanks."

"It's fifteen miles to Walsenburg."

"I said, no thanks." She quickened her pace. The truck kept up.

"Is everything okay?"

"Lady, just leave me alone."

"I didn't tell the store, you know."

She wanted to run. This was not in the plan. She couldn't trust anyone. Not Stan, or even Gordon, and certainly not this strange woman who'd seen her stealing from the Safeway.

Roxi heard another car engine in the distance, and she twisted around to see headlights peeking over the rise in the road. Glancing in her rearview mirror, the woman saw them too. She gunned her engine and pulled the truck forward onto the shoulder. Roxi hesitated. Fifteen miles was a long way. The other car zoomed around them, sending a chilly breeze swirling around her and Selah. It wasn't getting any warmer, either. No telling who might come along after this woman left.

The truck's emergency brake ratcheted, and the driver's door creaked open. Leaving the headlights on, the woman exited the truck and came around to Roxi, her boots crunching in the gravel. She was taller than Roxi by several inches.

Roxi backed away, pulling Selah closer. "What do you want from me?"

That stopped the woman in her tracks. "You think I want something from you?"

"I don't know."

The woman shrugged. "Listen, I see a girl out alone at night, and I get concerned. I don't know where you're going, but—"

"I can take of myself."

The woman gestured toward the fields on both sides of the road. "Hon, there's nothing out here."

"We're fine." Roxi looped Selah's leash around her wrist one more time, careful to avoid her scraped palms. "We've made it this far."

"What happened? Why are you by yourself?"

"That's my business."

"Yeah, I know, but—"

"I want it to stay that way."

The woman stuffed her hands into the pockets of her vest. "All right. I understand. But can I give you a lift somewhere?"

Roxi touched Selah's back. The dog was shivering like a leaf. Maybe if it had just been her, she could refuse help and be okay. But now she had more than herself to worry about. Selah didn't have much of a coat, and even if she bundled her up in a shirt, it probably wouldn't keep her warm enough.

"Where'd you say you're going?"

"I live nearby."

"Can you drop me off in Walsenburg?"

The woman considered, then nodded. "I could do that."

"'Cause that's where I'm going."

Narrowing the space between them, the woman stuck out her hand. "My name's Jan."

"I don't think you want me shaking your hand right now."

"Uh . . . okay."

"They're kinda scraped up. I fell in the parking lot back there."

"Well, let's take a look in the cab." Jan tilted her head toward the truck, then glanced at Selah. "Cute dog."

Roxi took a step toward the truck but drew back again. Was she being foolish? What if Jan took her straight to the police station?

"Throw your pack in the bed if you want," Jan called over her shoulder, already at the driver's door.

She could feel her body succumbing to the exhaustion she'd been fighting all day. The prospect of riding in a warm truck, no matter who was driving, appealed to everything in her. She had to trust this woman and take whatever consequences came.

Roxi made it to the passenger side of the truck, her shoulders drooping, her mind no longer a match for her weary body. The moment she opened the door, Selah jumped inside, greeting Jan with a wagging tail and a licking tongue.

"Well, hello there," Jan said.

Roxi climbed in behind the dog. "Her name's Selah. I'm Roxi."

"Selah?" Jan patted the dog's back. "I like that."

She almost asked if Jan knew what the name meant but decided against it. Better to keep this as impersonal as possible. Dropping her backpack in the floor well, for the first time Roxi saw her hands. The heels of both palms were scraped raw; dried blood mixed with dirt and tiny pieces of gravel.

"Ouch," Jan said.

She'd have to check her arm later. But while the truck's dome light was still on, she took the opportunity to examine Selah's shoulder again. There hadn't been time to clean it earlier, and it didn't look much better than her palms. Blood caked in the dog's fur, and Selah flinched when she touched the skin around the scrape.

Leaning back in her seat, Roxi held her eyes shut for a second. She was marked somehow, wasn't she? No matter how hard she tried or how much she longed for things to change, they never would. She was destined for failure. It would always be like this.

"I saw you yesterday."

Roxi opened her eyes.

"Outside Aaron's bookstore. Remember?" Jan released the emergency brake and pulled the truck out onto the road. "You asked me where I got my coffee."

She tried to see Jan's face better in the darkness. This was the same lady who'd seen her huddled in the doorway?

"Here." Jan took off her hat and flipped on the overhead light again. "The hat makes me look different."

Okay . . . now she recognized her.

"You were kinda in a hurry then, too," Jan said.

Selah curled up on the bench seat between them, resting her head on Roxi's lap. Roxi focused on the dog, stroking her head.

"You just passing through, or do you live around here?"

"Passing through."

"Anyone looking for you?"

Roxi kept her head down. "No."

It wasn't necessarily a lie. She didn't know if Irene and Diego were looking for her or not. And Mom certainly wasn't.

"You're what, sixteen?"

Gordon had said she wasn't a good liar. Roxi could only hope Jan would believe this one. "Eighteen."

"Oh, sorry."

"I get that a lot."

"I did too when I was your age. Trust me. You'll appreciate it in a few years."

"How old are you?"

Jan smiled.

And Roxi quickly backpedaled, forgetting you didn't ask that question to any woman who looked over thirty. "I didn't—"

"Fifty-two. And I don't mind saying so. A woman should be proud to be over fifty," Jan said, driving with one hand while her elbow rested on the door ledge. "Worked long and hard to get here. Might as well enjoy it."

Warm air coddled Roxi, and the truck rocked her. She blinked to keep herself awake. "How long . . . did you say we'd be?"

"Probably make it in twenty minutes. Give or take."

Selah scooched closer to her, and Roxi leaned her head against the door. She closed her eyes again as the heater slowly warmed her feet, her legs, and then her core. The last thing she remembered was the vibrating truck window against her cheek and how odd it was to feel safe.

❧

Selah woke her by licking her face, and Roxi warded off the dog's tongue with her hands. The truck wasn't moving. She sat up with a start, head throbbing.

Jan pulled the keys out of the ignition and switched off the head-lights, the only sound the *tick, tick* of the cooling engine. They were parked beside a house with the porch light blazing and a stack of firewood by the door.

"Where are we? I thought you were dropping me off!"

"You were dozing so soundly," Jan said.

She grabbed her backpack and Selah's leash, wincing as the fabric raked across her palms. "You could've woken me."

"I know."

"Why didn't you?" She went for the door handle, but Jan caught hold of her coat sleeve.

"Hey, hey. Wait a sec."

Roxi wriggled out of the woman's grasp but didn't open the door. She knew Jan was only trying to help, but involving her would complicate things in ways she couldn't handle right now. How could she possibly tell her the truth?

Jan pocketed her keys. "Roxi, it's no secret to me you have nowhere to go. You don't have to tell me why, but you don't have to pretend everything's fine."

Comebacks flitted through her brain, but she couldn't bring any to her tongue. Were her lies that obvious?

"You weren't taking those bars for fun, were you?"

She glanced away. "What difference does it make?"

"A lot, in my book."

Roxi tried to read the woman's shadowy face. Her expression was a mixture of concern and exasperation.

"I was hungry," Roxi finally admitted. "I didn't want to take anything. Really."

"They could've arrested you either way."

"Yeah."

"So I'm glad I stopped you."

Fingering Selah's leash, Roxi stared at the dirty floorboards. "You didn't stop me from taking this collar and leash."

Jan went silent, and Roxi fought to keep herself from crying. What was she *doing*, admitting shoplifting to a complete stranger? A tear slipped down her cheek before she could stop it, but she quickly brushed it away with her sleeve.

"When was the last time you had a home-cooked meal?"

She looked at Jan. The exasperation was gone.

Jan opened her door. "Do you like beef stew? I was going to heat some up for myself. I can easily warm enough for three."

"Anything sounds good right now."

Roxi and Selah slipped out of the truck. A huge barn hulked in the darkness, its yard light shining down on two other trucks, a horse trailer, and a tractor. Farther out was a wooden corral, where she thought she saw the long faces of several horses.

"What is this place?"

Jan pulled three grocery bags from the truck bed. "Lonely River Ranch. Been in my family for three generations. You coming?"

Selah nudged Roxi's arm with her nose, and she remembered how only last night she'd coaxed the dog with a peanut butter sandwich. In the end, food had won out. Apparently dogs and humans weren't all that different.

"Come on, girl," Roxi said.

They followed Jan.

"My husband, Keith, might be in bed already," Jan said over her shoulder. "We get up at five."

They entered the house through the back door, and Roxi found herself in a small kitchen with a thick, round wooden table. Straight ahead through a doorway she saw a TV, couch, and fireplace.

"Let's get your hands cleaned up first," Jan said, dropping her groceries on the floor.

Roxi set her backpack on a chair and knelt in front of Selah. "She's got a scrape too."

"We'll get you both cleaned up, then. I'll just go get our first aid kit and be right back. Make yourself at home. And Selah's welcome to run around."

Jan disappeared, leaving Roxi feeling completely out of place in the strange, quiet house. She didn't belong here. Should she just thank Jan for the ride and take off no matter how much the woman protested?

Unclipping Selah's leash, Roxi quickly ripped off its price tags and stuffed the thing into her backpack. But where could she go? It was late, and they were in the middle of nowhere out here. Her instinct was to run, but she longed to trust someone.

Jan reappeared, motioning for Roxi to follow her to the sink, and she reluctantly obeyed.

"You fell hard," Jan said, eyeing her bloody palms again. "This'll probably hurt, but you don't want any infection."

Nodding, she gritted her teeth at the sting of the running water. Jan dribbled some sort of dark antiseptic—maybe iodine—into the scrapes and gently washed them with a clean dishrag. Her shoulder-length hair was pulled back into a loose ponytail, dark blonde streaked with gray. A few wrinkles fanned out from the corners of her eyes.

"Anywhere else?" Jan dabbed at her palms with a soft paper towel, but Roxi took it from her and finished drying them herself.

"My arm."

"Why don't you slip out of that jacket while I check your dog."

Roxi did as she was told and watched in awe as Selah let Jan clean her shoulder without a growl or even a whine, though she did tremble the entire time.

"She likes you," Roxi said.

"Well, I like her." Jan rubbed Selah's ears. "Had her long?"

She shook her head. "A guy threw her out of a car."

"You're kidding."

"That's how she got banged up."

"And you saw this?"

"Last night."

"What an idiot." Jan stroked Selah's neck. "She's a beautiful girl."

"I've never had a dog before, but I couldn't just leave her."

"Of course not."

Slipping out of her jean jacket, Roxi examined her arm. Some blood had seeped through the weave of her long-underwear shirt, now stuck to the scrape. She peeled the fabric away, wincing as she gingerly pulled up her sleeve. That's when she realized Jan was going to see not only the fresh scrape but her scar, too. Would she stare? ask nosy questions? That's what the kids at school used to do. Or worse, whisper behind her back and spread rumors about how she got it. She'd always tried to make it through spring without wearing short sleeves at school.

Roxi went over to the sink to clean the cut herself, but Jan was beside her before she could protest. She didn't say anything, even when her fingers ran right across the ugly purple line as she placed bandages on the wound.

"Now how about that stew?" Jan patted her shoulder, then went to the fridge and pulled out a Rubbermaid container. "It's leftovers, but I must say, my beef stew is even better the second day."

Roxi slumped into one of the kitchen chairs, resting her forehead on her arms. That catnap in the truck had only reminded her body what it had been missing the past three days—sleep. Roxi forced herself to sit up. She was desperately hoping Jan would ask her to stay the night, but she didn't dare broach the subject herself.

Jan popped the container into the microwave, punched some buttons to get it working, then filled a glass and a bowl with water from the tap. She brought the glass to Roxi and set the bowl in front of Selah. The dog had her tongue in the water almost before Jan could let go.

"I—we really appreciate this," Roxi said. She'd lost the energy to protest, but it was still uncomfortable having someone do things for her.

"Everyone should have the chance to taste my beef stew." Jan laughed.

"Hey, hon?"

A man's voice called from the other side of the house, and Roxi jumped. That would be Jan's husband.

"In the kitchen," Jan answered, pulling the stew from the microwave and dishing it out. The aroma of meat and gravy sent Roxi's stomach gurgling, and Selah licked her chops.

A tall guy appeared in the doorway with bare feet and a head of wet, curly gray hair. "Hi," he said, eyebrows raised in puzzlement.

Selah growled, the fur on her back spiking, and Roxi grabbed her collar.

"This is my husband, Keith," Jan said, bringing the food to the table. "Honey, this is Roxi. She'll be staying with us tonight."

Roxi looked to Jan, but the woman just smiled at her.

Her husband's expression softened. "Nice to meet you," he said to Roxi, then to Jan, "I can't find my wool socks."

"On top of the dryer."

As soon as Keith left, Selah's tense body relaxed slightly. "Settle down, girl," Roxi whispered. Was the dog wary of men because her abuser had been a guy?

"Every now and then I make the mistake of putting his wool socks *in* the dryer." Jan handed Roxi a fork and set a bowl of stew on the floor for Selah. "What comes out doesn't even fit *my* feet."

Selah dove into the food. Steam wafted up from the plates, and Roxi's mouth watered. It seemed like a week since she'd eaten anything herself.

Sitting down across from her, Jan bowed her head. "Lord, thank You for this food. And thanks for bringing Roxi and Selah safely here. We appreciate all the good things You give us. Amen."

Not sure how she was supposed to respond, Roxi didn't say anything and shoveled a forkful of meat into her mouth, quickly chasing it with a bite of potato.

"Good?"

She nodded, barely chewing before swallowing.

Jan let her eat for a few minutes before the questions started again. "So where are you really headed?"

Roxi shrugged, not sure how truthful she should be. Jan *had* opened up her home and fed her. Maybe a little honesty wouldn't hurt. "Don't have anywhere in mind."

"What about your family?"

Another shrug. "They don't care."

Jan didn't press for an elaboration, and Roxi didn't offer one.

"What about you?" Roxi asked.

"Well, it's just me and Keith here."

"No kids?"

"We had a son, but he was killed in an accident five years ago."

She took another bite of stew. "Sorry."

"His truck rolled off a mountain road. He was a year younger than you."

An image of the bookstore manager's plaintive face flashed unbidden in Roxi's mind. Had Jan's son died quickly, or had he suffered for each of his last breaths as the manager had?

Jan looked off into space for a second. "It was tough. But we're managing. The Lord's helped us through it."

"Why didn't God just keep it from happening?"

"I asked myself the same thing."

Roxi decided she was prying and went on eating. And why hadn't God stopped Diego from pulling that trigger?

"I think sometimes it comes down to our decisions too." Jan cut a piece of meat with her knife, and Roxi noticed how strong her hands looked. She didn't wear any jewelry except for a thin gold wedding band.

"Why was Trae up on that road when he knew it wasn't passable? I don't know. Maybe God tried to warn him, but he didn't listen."

Roxi focused on her plate. Had God warned Diego? She had a feeling it would take a neon sign to get through to him.

Later Roxi finished off her second serving of stew and helped Jan clear the table. She could barely keep her eyes open.

"You look like you're about to drop," Jan said. "I'll finish this up. Let me show you to your bed."

A bed. That would feel amazing. She followed Jan up a short flight of stairs.

"Feel free to use the shower." Jan waved toward the bathroom. "I'll get you a fresh set of towels."

"I think I just need some sleep."

Jan brought her to the room at the end of the hall and flicked on the light. The walls were painted blue, and a small desk, baseball-theme lamp, and neatly made bed were the only furniture.

"This was Trae's room," Jan said. "But we use it for guests now. If you need anything, holler. I'll be up for a little bit."

Roxi stared at the bed, tears filling her eyes. She was so tired. So tired. Turning toward Jan, she tried to thank her, but her voice caught in her throat.

"Rest well, sweetheart," Jan said, then closed the door.

Undressing down to her T-shirt and underwear, Roxi left her clothes in a pile by her backpack and slipped under the covers. Selah jumped up beside her. Nudging the blankets with her nose, she looked at Roxi, tail wagging.

With the last of her energy, she lifted the covers for the dog. Selah spun and swirled underneath them, finally dropping and curling up with her head on Roxi's leg. Roxi barely had time to wonder why Jan had called her sweetheart before blissful sleep washed over her exhausted body.

❧

Jan climbed under the covers, trying not to disturb Keith. But the bed sank and the springs squeaked. Keith rolled onto his back, and they lay side by side in the darkness of their bedroom.

"Who is she?" Keith whispered.

"I caught her lifting protein bars in the Safeway."

"And brought her home?"

Jan found her husband's hand and squeezed it. "She ran out of the store, and I never expected to see her again. But I couldn't get her out of my mind."

Keith sighed. "You shouldn't do things like this."

"I finished shopping, loaded the truck, and drove away. On my way home I saw her walking along the highway. I couldn't just let her hitchhike out there."

Keith reached over and patted her thigh. "Always the mother hen."

"I had to pull over."

He got up on his elbow, his face a shadow. "Is she a runaway?"

"She wouldn't tell me, but I think she might be."

Keith lay back down.

"What was I supposed to do?"

"I don't know, but we could be asking for trouble. Why was she stealing from the store in the first place?"

"She told me she was eighteen." Jan tugged the covers up to her chin. "But I have a feeling she's younger than that."

"Maybe it's all an act to rob us out of house and home."

"She didn't pick *me* up. And her hunger wasn't an act."

"So she'll eat us out of house and home, then."

Jan chuckled, resting her hand on her husband's arm. "Maybe I am too much of a mother hen."

"We just need to be careful; that's all."

"I know."

"And what's with that dog growling at me like that? Most dogs love me."

"It was abused. Someone threw it out of a car."

Keith got quiet, his breathing slower. "What are you planning to do?"

She crossed her arms over her chest. "I keep wondering what could possibly have driven a kid to travel alone at night with no place to go."

"Did you ask her?"

"She's not talking much. I ask about her family, and she says, 'They don't care.' I ask where she's going, she says she doesn't know."

"Well, maybe she'll talk more in the morning."

"Yeah."

An hour later Keith was snoring, but Jan was still awake, staring at the ceiling. Perhaps she had been foolish. She knew nothing about this girl. Where did she come from? What was she trying to escape from? They didn't have anything really valuable in the house. Just some old dishes and silver from Keith's mother. But there'd be something you could steal and sell for quick cash if you knew what to look for.

Jan rolled onto her side. And the scar on her arm—no small scratch. Something bad had happened to that girl, and Jan wished she knew what it was. The wounded look in Roxi's eyes stayed with her long into the night.

23

When Roxi woke up, she had no idea where she was. Then slowly she remembered. The Safeway. Jan and Keith. Their ranch. Their dead son's bedroom.

She relaxed and closed her eyes again, reveling in the bed's warmth and comfort. She couldn't remember the last time she'd slept in something so soft. Her bed in the RV was tolerable, but it was more like sleeping on a couch. And even her mattress at Irene and Diego's house had a few unruly springs that would sometimes wake her up in the middle of the night.

Roxi reached under the covers and rested her hand on Selah's back. The dog woke at her touch, wagging her tail and slithering up to the opening. They spent a few lazy minutes lying there together, slowly waking. Things could sure change in twenty-four hours. They weren't shivering behind some rusty Dumpster wondering where breakfast would come from.

Gently rubbing Selah's ears, Roxi closed her eyes again and let herself play with that fantasy she used to have about waking up and discovering her life had just been a bad dream. That she really did have a family who loved her and cared what happened to her. She tuned everything out and concentrated hard. Jan and Keith were her parents, this ranch her home. . . .

It almost worked.

Roxi opened her eyes again. She glanced at her watch and let out a long sigh. It was nearly eleven. So much for fantasies.

She groggily pulled down the covers. What she needed was a plan. Peeling off her T-shirt, she redressed in her jeans from last night and checked her scrapes. They didn't hurt quite as badly, but they were still tender. She dug around in her backpack for a clean shirt, but there wasn't one. She'd worn everything at least once. If it hadn't been for Jan, she'd still be out there somewhere, hungry and cold. And she was probably going to be again.

"I don't know what to do," Roxi said to Selah, who was still curled up in a ball on the bed. "Even if they let me stay, they're gonna ask questions. What then?"

Selah thumped her tail.

She threw her pack on the bed, plopping down beside it. "I should just thank them for everything and leave." As the words left her mouth, she knew that would be the hardest choice of all. There was something about Jan and Keith. Last night with Jan, she'd felt something she hadn't felt in . . . maybe she'd never felt it.

Safe. Like someone was looking out for her.

Which was stupid, really. The second they found out who she was, it would be over. Then she thought about the kind way Jan had looked at her in the truck and how she'd washed the cut on her arm without even mentioning her scar.

"So what do I do?" Roxi ran her hands through her hair, looking at Selah, who didn't open her eyes. The dog had settled in as if she'd lived here her whole life. "Should I ask them if I can stay until I find a job? They'll want to know more. And I can't exactly tell them, 'Oh yeah, by the way, I'm an accomplice to a murder.'"

She shook her head. Maybe it really would be best to walk back up to the road and hitch a ride with someone else. In another town there had to be someone willing to give her a job.

"Let's go, girl."

Selah flew off the bed and was at the door before Roxi. She took one last look around the room, her eyes drawn to the photo on the desk in the corner. It had to be their son. She moved a few steps closer and examined the snapshot of a young guy with blond hair and the beginnings of a scraggly beard. He was grinning from ear to ear, his arms resting on the shoulders of Jan and Keith, framing him on each side. They looked like they were laughing from some joke he'd just cracked. It had probably been taken shortly before he died because he looked like he was seventeen or eighteen.

Roxi wondered what it would have been like to grow up with Jan and Keith. Had their son ever made them mad? disappointed?

Quickly she made her way out the door before she had time to envy him more. Selah bolted past her and took off down the stairs, but not before Roxi noticed her still favoring that front leg. She hitched her backpack over her shoulder, then saw a small note on the floor that read, *Help yourself to anything you want in the fridge. There's some oatmeal in a bowl on the counter. Find me outside whenever you're done. I'll probably be in the barn. Jan.*

Roxi pocketed the note and followed Selah into the kitchen, thankful she was alone in the house. A few minutes later they were both full of microwaved oatmeal, and it was with a heavy heart that Roxi attached Selah's leash to her collar. She wouldn't be finding Jan. Things would be better that way.

Outside in the bright sunlight her legs felt like concrete pillars, and she could barely bring herself to move them. Roxi lingered beside one of the pickups, breathing in the fresh, clean air. She hadn't realized the size of this place in the dark. The barn, horse trailers, tractor, outbuildings . . . they even had their own rusty gas tank raised up on stilts. And the mountains . . . Yesterday she woke to a view of trash and weeds; today it was a view that could've been on a postcard she'd seen on a rack at the Flying J truck stop.

At the sound of a car engine, Roxi glanced down the driveway, surprised to see a Chevy Blazer pulling into the yard.

Selah barked for the first time.

The driver parked the Blazer next to one of the pickups, and a woman who looked to be in her thirties got out and came around. She wore reinforced canvas pants with a rip in the knee, hiking boots, and a short-sleeved safari shirt. Roxi could picture her munching on trail mix.

"Hi," the woman said, pulling off silver sunglasses and attaching them to her belt loop. "Jan or Keith around?"

Selah pulled against her leash, and Roxi gave her slack. The woman immediately crouched down and patted her leg for Selah to come closer.

"I think Jan's in the barn. I don't know where Keith is," Roxi said.

The dog slowly inched toward the woman, her tail swooshing from side to side, the same way she'd responded to Roxi that first night by the Dumpster. It seemed to be her I-want-to-come-but-I'm-not-sure-about-you walk.

"She yours?" the woman asked, cooing at the dog.

Roxi nodded.

Selah crept up to the woman and let her rub her ears.

"Oh, hey, sorry." The woman, still crouching beside Selah, extended her hand to Roxi. "My name's Beth. I'm here to check on one of Keith's horses."

Roxi shook Beth's hand carefully because of her scrapes, glancing at the Chevy. The name *Eckert Veterinary* was stenciled on the door in dark blue. "Are you a vet?"

"No, I'm a mortician."

Roxi glanced back at the truck.

Beth smiled. "Just ignore me. I'm known for my stupid jokes. Yes, I'm a vet."

Kneeling across from her beside Selah, Roxi stroked the dog's back. "She's been limping, and I haven't been able to take her any-where yet."

"Limping? Which leg?"

"Front left. She fell on it the other day. You can see the scrape. I'm hoping she didn't injure it seriously."

Beth gently examined Selah's paw and leg. She checked the scrape and moved the leg around, pushing up against the paw with the palm of her hand. "Well, I don't think anything's broken. It's possible she only bruised a muscle or maybe pulled a tendon."

"She'll be okay?"

"Just look at her." Beth chuckled as Selah melted to the ground, rolling onto her back. "Does that look like an injured dog to you?"

"I was worried."

"Keep that cut clean, and she'll be fine. How old is she?"

"I . . ." Roxi thought about making something up but decided if anyone could call her bluff, a vet could. "I don't know. I haven't had her long. Some guy threw her out of a car."

"What?"

"In a parking lot. He didn't know I was watching."

"I hope you got his license plate number."

She hadn't thought of that and fingered the leash, remembering his cruelty. She'd had Selah such a short time, but she already thought of the dog as her own.

Beth gave Selah's belly one final scratch, then stood.

"How old do you think she is?" Roxi asked.

"Under a year."

"This'll sound like a stupid question, but what is she? A grey-hound?"

"That's a good guess, but they're usually much bigger." Beth stared at Selah. "More likely you've got a whippet on your hands, with prob-ably some terrier thrown in there for good measure."

"A whippet?"

"They look a lot like greyhounds, but they're smaller. I don't meet many out here. We've mostly got border collies and heelers."

Beth glanced behind her, and Roxi turned to see Keith coming around the house. He looked the part of the Marlboro man. Lanky, gray whiskers, battered white cowboy hat. He waved at them.

"Hey, Keith," Beth said. "I hear old Martin's not doing too well."

"Yeah, thanks for comin' by. I've got him in a stall. He got into the feed bin, and I'm hoping it's not founder." Keith pulled off his leather work gloves, nodding at Roxi. "Jan wanted to talk to you. She's in the barn too."

Roxi reluctantly tagged behind the pair to the huge, weatherworn structure. It would've been easier with no good-byes.

The smell of hay and horse met her as she stepped inside. It trans-ported her right back to a day when she was probably four or five and rode a pony at the fair. It had been just a few circles around a muddy corral on the back of a fat little pony who tooted gas as he walked, but it was the only other time she'd been around horses. She couldn't remem-ber who had taken her, but she'd always imagined it was Mom.

Keith and Beth headed toward one of the stalls at the opposite end of the barn, seeming to forget she was there. A wheelbarrow and pitchfork sat nearby, and an old halter lay across the half door of the nearest stall. To her right a door stood slightly ajar, and through the crack she saw Jan sitting on a bale of straw, holding a saddle between her knees and rubbing a rag into it. Her denim shirt was rolled to her elbows, and she wore dusty chaps over her jeans.

Roxi opened the door, and Jan looked up.

"You must've needed that sleep," Jan said, her face glowing with a warm smile. She squeezed some white goo onto her rag from a plastic bottle.

"I saw your note," Roxi said, still in the doorway.

"Here, have a seat." Jan moved her cleaning supplies off the bale beside her.

"Actually, I kinda should be going. I just wanted to thank you for last night."

"But I thought you didn't have anywhere to go."

Roxi shifted her pack to her other shoulder. "I'll hitch a ride with someone. Head into town or something."

Jan's smile quickly disappeared. "So you *do* have somewhere to go?"

"It's pretty complicated."

"I talked to Keith," Jan said, rubbing the smooth leather seat of the saddle with her rag. "We've been looking to hire someone to help out around here, but we haven't found anyone. You look like you could use a job."

She felt her face stretch into an incredulous expression. "You're offering me a job?"

"You do need one, right?"

Roxi glanced at the ceiling, unsure how to respond. She could lie again. It was starting to become habit. But something about Jan made Roxi want to tell the truth—at least part of it.

"Yeah, I need a job, but I don't know a thing about ranching."

"Don't worry. You'll learn."

Was this woman serious? You didn't hire people you caught shoplifting.

Jan dropped her rag onto the bale and got to her feet, hands on her hips. "Can we level with each other here? I want to help you, Roxi. But I can't unless you let me."

"I don't understand. What's in this for you?"

"An extra set of hands."

"What?"

"Can you work hard?"

She stared at Jan for a moment. The woman was a wiry thing, like her husband, with sinewy forearm muscles popping up with each twist of her wrist.

"Sure," Roxi said.

"'Cause ranching ain't easy." Jan hefted the saddle onto a sawhorse. "The way I see it, you need a job, and we need the help."

Apparently finished with her chore, Jan scooted the hay bale up against a wall and stowed her supplies on a wooden shelf. "Why don't you try it out for a couple days? See if you can stand me."

Roxi stared at Selah, her resolve to leave melting in Jan's presence like Selah's fear had. She met the woman's mischievous eyes and let herself smile back. "I could do that."

❧

"This whole idea makes me nervous," Christy said, climbing back into the car and handing Abby her grande red eye. They'd stopped at a rest area to caffeine and sugar up at Starbucks. Brownies and coffee. Dinner was served.

Abby slurped her drink. "Yeah, me too, but we've gotta do this."

"Technically no, we don't, but I'm beyond arguing with you."

"Finally."

"But if he's home, you are flooring it, you hear me?"

Abby smiled, lifting her red eye in a toasting motion. Christy lifted her own coffee and they touched cups.

"To Hunter," Abby said.

"To Hunter."

They slurped in silence for a minute; then Abby started up the car and pulled back onto the road. They were still a couple of hours from home, and it was another hour and fifteen to Cheyenne. She glanced at Christy. She knew it was going against everything in this woman to do this, and yet she was doing it anyway for Abby. A twinge of guilt crept up inside her when she thought about how she'd deceived the clerk—and Christy—back at the bookstore. Christy didn't deserve that. As far as Abby knew, she'd been nothing but forthright with her, and it surely hadn't been easy admitting to that DUI.

Abby took a big bite from her brownie, driving with one hand. Might as well bring everything out in the open. "A couple days ago, I was suspended from my department."

She waited for the words to sink in and was surprised when Christy said nothing.

"Aren't you gonna ask me why?"

Christy leaned back into her seat. "I figure you'll tell me if you want to."

She sighed, surprised she was glad for the chance to share the news with someone. "I got this call from Michael telling me Kat was being released from the hospital. She'd collapsed at school, and I didn't hear about it until after the fact. All the old anger just took over, and the next person I arrested paid for it. I didn't know she was the mayor's wife, and I certainly didn't intend to sprain her wrist, but it happened. If she hadn't been drunk, it would've been all over the papers by now, and I wouldn't even have a job to go back to."

"How long?"

"Two weeks." Abby felt her voice going scratchy. The stress of the last couple days was finally catching up with her. "I messed up being a wife, a mother, a sister . . . and now I'm messing up being a cop. What's next?"

"You're too hard on yourself."

"I wish I could talk to Hunter about it." Abby's throat tightened. "I've kept the last e-mail he sent me in my in-box, the one where he told me about your coffee shop idea."

"It was the last thing we talked about."

Abby let a few miles of silence pass. Unlike her, Hunter had never stopped dreaming. Nothing was impossible. And somehow, no matter how she was feeling, after a phone call with Hunter everything seemed brighter. She didn't feel like a failure when she talked to her brother.

Even if she was one.

24

It was starting to get dark when they approached the house.

"You look; I'll drive," Abby said, but she still craned to get a view out Christy's window. The neighborhood consisted of drab, matchbox homes sporting metal siding, fake shutters, and ugly colors. Diego Tonelli's house looked no different from all the rest, except its driveway stretched all the way around the house to a detached garage.

"No one's home."

"Doesn't look like it, does it?"

The windows were black with no lights anywhere.

"So normal," Christy said.

Abby drove to the end of the street, then doubled back for a second look. She wasn't letting this lead go. Real answers might be within her grasp. Was this a wild-goose chase? She would never know if she drove off now.

They pulled up again, but this time instead of continuing down the road, Abby stopped the car in front of the house next to the Tonelli residence. She could almost hear Christy's brain whirring.

Abby cut the engine.

"What are you doing?"

"Neighbors talk."

"You're kidding me. Tell me you're kidding me."

"If you'd rather stay here . . ."

Christy rubbed her eyes. "I knew you wouldn't be able to 'just drive by.'"

Abby looked at the dark Tonelli house, a surge of energy filling her limbs. It was a sensation she often experienced right before answering a call, and its familiarity renewed her confidence.

"Might as well get used to it," she said. "Adventure is my middle name."

Unfastening her seat belt, Christy muttered something under her breath. Abby got out of the car and met her on the sidewalk.

"I want to register right now," Christy said, pointing at the car, "that the only reason I'm *not* sitting in that car is to keep you out of trouble."

"There won't be any trouble. We're old family friends wanting to surprise our buddy Diego."

Christy zipped up her jacket and waved at the house. "Let's just get it over with."

Abby led the way up the creaking steps to the neighbors' front porch. A rusted motorcycle sat in the corner with a shredded blue tarp doing its best to protect it from the elements. A planter of dead mums sat outside the door.

Abby opened the screen door and knocked on the scratched metal one behind it. Immediately a booming bark came from somewhere beyond the flimsy door. Great. Probably a German shepherd or a rottweiler.

The heavyset woman who finally answered had hard eyes and

curly black hair straight from a bottle. A cigarette dangled from her lips. Before Abby could get a word out, the woman opened the door wider and the dog shot out, a pit bull with a watermelon-size head. It circled her, tail wagging but not in a submissive way. He sniffed her legs like he was sizing her up for dinner.

"Hi," Abby said, determined to show no fear to this woman or her dog. She hoped Christy would do the same.

"What do ya want?" The woman pulled out her cigarette and leaned against the doorframe.

"We're old friends of Diego Tonelli's."

The woman nodded.

Bingo.

"We were hoping to surprise him, but I guess he isn't home. Any idea when he'll be back?"

"Nope."

Pit Bull moved on to Christy, and Abby could hear his loud snuffling behind her back.

"It's been so long since we've seen him," Abby said.

"Why don't you just call?"

"Tried. It rang and rang."

The woman took a drag from her cigarette, blowing the smoke toward Abby's face. "Sorry; can't help you. But I don't think I'd stick around. They're gone for weeks at a time."

"How long have they lived here?"

"Longer than me." She snapped her fingers. The dog scuttled back inside, and the door slammed in their faces.

Abby thanked the door for its time. Christy raised her eyebrows, and they walked back down the crumbling walkway.

"I'll take the woman any day," Christy whispered, "but that dog was freaking me out. I felt like a raw steak."

"Tell me about it."

"She said 'they.' Catch that?"

"Maybe he's married."

Christy tilted her head toward the door. "I think she's watching us through the blinds."

"Keep walking. We'll drive away, then double back to hit the next one."

"How did I know?"

"Remember." Abby patted her on the back. "Adventure."

Christy rolled her eyes.

In the car again, Abby got a good look at the window and definitely saw the blinds move. They parked the car on a side street this time and hiked back to the house across from Diego's. The night was working to their advantage now. They'd just be two shadowy figures out for a walk. At least until they got under a porch light. Hopefully Ms. Pit Bull had lost interest in keeping the neighborhood watch.

This time when Abby knocked, she was pleased at the absence of barking. No need to announce their presence to the whole street again. She heard a shuffling sound, and a male voice called, "Coming!"

When the door opened, Abby stood face-to-face with a stooped, white-haired gentleman using a carved wooden cane.

"Good evening, ladies," he said, meeting Abby's eyes. Even in the poor light she could see his were blue. And clear. Blue eyes on an ebony face. Striking. "What can I do for you?"

She repeated the same spiel she'd given Ms. Pit Bull.

"Family friends, you say?"

"It's been years since we've seen him," Abby said.

"My name's Howard Johnson."

Christy started to chuckle.

"Yes." Johnson winked at her. "And I've had to live with it for eighty-four years. Why don't you come in?"

This guy obviously grew up in an era before house invasions. Abby glanced at Christy and gave her a nod. "Thanks."

It wasn't what she expected. Johnson ushered them into a living room full of antiques. Plush hoop-skirt chairs. Oil paintings with elaborate gold frames. Bookshelves lined with leather tomes. A beautiful white cat with eyes to match her master's lay curled in a ball on a plaid sofa, the only modern piece in the room.

"Please make yourselves at home," Johnson said.

Abby reluctantly sat down in one of the deceivingly comfortable-looking hoop-skirt chairs. Its curved back involuntarily rounded her shoulders. Christy sat beside the cat, gently petting it. The animal leaned into her touch.

"Do you know when Diego'll be back?" Abby asked. She didn't mind being in a stranger's house—she was in one almost every day. The key was to stay in control and never let down your guard. You never knew who was in the next room.

Mr. Johnson stood leaning on his cane, seeming to enjoy watching his pet being stroked. "She's Ruby."

"So soft," Christy said, her fingers sinking into the cat's thick white fur.

Turning to Abby, Mr. Johnson studied her for a moment. "Forgive me, ma'am," he said, "but how did you say you knew the Tonellis?"

Christy chimed in. "We're just friends from years ago wanting to surprise them. Guess we picked a bad time."

Nice save.

Mr. Johnson nodded thoughtfully, shifting his weight and resting both hands on the cane. "Unfortunately, I don't know much about my neighbors. I've lived in this house for thirty-five years and watched most of my friends go to their graves. These folks now are mostly new to me. I try to be friendly and neighborly, but these days people don't warm up to each other the way they used to. Take this Diego fellow. He and his mother, Irene, moved into that place last year. We might wave at each other, but not much more. And they're gone as much as they're home."

Mr. Johnson stepped over to the window and peeked out the slats of the shade. "You ladies aren't really friends of the family, are you?"

Christy and Abby exchanged glances.

Turning back around, Mr. Johnson faced them both. "Eighty-four years and you start to recognize when someone's lying to you. So why don't we start over and you tell me the truth."

For once Abby didn't know what to say.

Luckily Christy picked up the slack. "In all honesty," she said, "we can't."

"One can always tell the truth."

Abby cleared her throat. "You're right. We aren't friends of the family."

"Mm-hmm."

"But we really can't tell you much else. I can say a crime's been committed, and we think Diego Tonelli was involved in it."

"That's not much." Mr. Johnson scratched his chin with a gnarly hand.

"If you'd like us to go . . ." Abby started to stand.

"What sort of crime?"

"A bad one," Christy said.

"And what exactly can I do to help?" Mr. Johnson hobbled over to a chair and slowly eased himself into it.

"You mentioned they're often gone," Abby said. "Do you remember if they were home last Tuesday?"

"I take it that's when this 'crime' happened?"

Abby nodded.

"They left in their camper days ago." Mr. Johnson leaned forward onto his cane. "I know little more than that. They travel often; I guess Irene retired early."

"How old is Diego?" Christy asked.

"I'm not sure; perhaps eighteen."

Abby was careful to hide her surprise. No wonder Mr. Johnson hadn't believed her story.

"I will say this," Mr. Johnson said. "Even though we haven't spoken much, when he's home, he brings my trash cans up to the house every week. And he shoveled my walk last winter several times. I hope he's not in any trouble."

Neither of them responded.

"Is he?"

"I don't know, Mr. Johnson," Abby said.

"Are you private investigators?"

"Not exactly." She didn't want to advertise she was a cop and hoped Christy wouldn't blab it.

"Something happened to someone we both love," Christy said. "Some things are pointing to Diego, but that's all we know. And we hope you won't talk to anyone else about this."

Abby noted Christy said *love* instead of *loved*. "Have you noticed anything unusual about the Tonellis?"

Mr. Johnson thought for a moment. "I'm not sure if the young lady living with them is Irene's daughter or not, but she's a quiet one."

"Three people live there?" Abby scooted forward on her own chair.

"Yes," Mr. Johnson said. "Diego, Irene, and I don't know the girl's name."

"Is she young?"

"Teenager."

"And she travels with them?"

"They all go together."

Abby wasn't sure if this bit of information was helpful or not, but in any investigation, nothing could be discounted.

"Anything else?"

Mr. Johnson looked off into space for a moment, hands still resting on his cane. Ruby the cat jumped off Christy's chair and rubbed against his legs, purring. He reached down to stroke her, and the cat butted her head against his twisted, arthritic hand. "One time I spoke with this girl. It was right before they left this last time. I was out getting my mail, and she was sitting on their porch step. When she glanced up at me, I remember her face looking so sad. I crossed the street and introduced myself. She didn't talk much, but one thing she asked me."

He stopped, looking off into space again. For a second Abby wondered if he'd lost his train of thought. But his eyes met hers again.

"She said, 'Have you ever wished you were someone else?'"

"A lot of teenagers wish they were someone else," Abby said, thinking of Kat. Did her daughter ever wish that?

"It was the way she said it."

The silence grew between them and Abby let it. During any kind of interview, when someone was talking, it was best to let them go on until they were done. Lousy interviewers filled the pauses.

"Such a serious thing to say for someone so young," Mr. Johnson said. "It stuck with me."

"Is that all?"

"Can't think of anything else," he said, leaning all his weight on the cane to stand up again.

Abby and Christy stood with him.

"Thanks for your time," Abby said.

Christy shook the old man's hand. "You've been very helpful."

"I hope you ladies find what you're looking for." Mr. Johnson walked them to the door, seeming more stooped than when they entered.

"Me too," Abby said.

When they were outside again, she didn't say anything for a moment. Neither did Christy. They were both no doubt soaking in the information, distilling it, trying to pull something noteworthy from the fragments.

"He's just a kid," Christy finally said.

"And none of them were here when Hunter was killed."

Standing on the sidewalk, they both stared at the shadowy Tonelli house. If only walls could speak.

Christy stuffed her hands into her pockets. "Did the police say whether there was more than one person in the Barn that night?"

Abby glanced at her. "They didn't say either way."

"You should ask them."

"I doubt they'd tell me."

"Something about this doesn't seem right."

She crossed her arms, glad to feel the bulk of the Beretta against her ribs. "Like why do they go for weeks at a time?"

"I'm thinking about what that girl said." Christy started walking down the sidewalk toward the car.

Abby stared at the house. She'd hoped they would find answers, but now all she had were more questions.

"You coming?"

All at once an idea hit Abby. She glanced from Christy to the house, then back to Christy. No way would she go for it. No way. Abby shifted her weight, calculating the risk. It was dangerous, no doubt about it. But could she let the opportunity slip through her fingers?

It was also against the law.

Yeah. A fact she couldn't exactly ignore. But it wasn't like she had much more to lose. She was already on suspension, and even if she *was* caught, she could probably talk herself out of the situation.

Abby shook her head at the way she was already justifying her actions, no doubt like half the criminals she'd locked up.

Christy walked back to her. "What's wrong?"

"Nothing."

"Then let's go."

"I have an idea."

Christy paused. "What now?"

"You're not going to like it."

25

"YOU BETTER BELIEVE I DON'T LIKE IT!"

Abby turned on the engine to get the car's heater going. "Told you."

"You're a cop, for cryin' out loud, and you want to break into their house?"

"Just a quick look."

"Oh, that makes all the difference in the world."

Abby held her hands toward the heater vents, her thoughts jumbling in her head. "Listen, I need to know about these people. I'm never gonna have a better chance than I have right now."

Christy grabbed her arm and looked her right in the face. "If you're caught, you could lose everything you've ever worked for. Think this through. Is it worth it?"

"I'm not gonna get caught."

"What if you do?"

"I was driving by and thought I saw someone in the house. The door was open, and I was just checking things out."

Christy threw herself back into her seat with a groan.

"I'm not asking you to go with me." Abby reached for the door handle. "I expect you to stay right here and call me if anyone shows up."

Christy shook her head.

She was right, really. It *would* be breaking and entering. But her brother was dead, and this house could belong to the person who killed him.

She didn't expect to find anything incriminating. There would be no way it could be admitted as evidence anyway. That wasn't what this was about. *She* had to know. Who was Diego Tonelli, and what part did he play in Hunter's death?

"I'm going in," Abby said, slipping on a pair of latex gloves. She'd take her flashlight and the lock-picking kit she kept in her trunk. She buttoned her black leather jacket over her light sweater so she would blend into the night.

"I hope you know what you're doing," Christy said.

"Don't worry." Abby opened her door. "I won't be gone long."

"What if they have an alarm?"

"I doubt it."

Christy gave her a concerned look. "Please be careful."

"You got it."

She took a moment to familiarize herself with her surroundings. No one was around. She took off at a brisk clip, passing a house with a television flashing in the window. She could always bail if something happened.

On the sidewalk in front of the Tonelli residence, she paid special attention to Ms. Pit Bull's house, watching for movement. She had a feeling that woman was sharper than she first appeared, and Abby wouldn't want to meet her in a dark alley.

She walked up the driveway, her heart pulsing in her ears. She needed to be quick. If anyone was watching out for the Tonelli house and called the police, she might have only a matter of minutes. And while she was fairly confident she'd be able to talk her way out of the situation, it wasn't something she relished doing.

Pausing outside the back door, she listened. So far the coast was clear. She pulled out her kit and started in on the lock. The piece was old and responded in moments with a welcoming click.

She twisted the knob, heard no screeching alarms, and stepped into the house. Closing the door behind herself, she swallowed hard. Okay . . . she was in. Now what? Pulling out her flashlight, she kept it at the ready, but she'd do without it for as long as possible.

The house was cold and stuffy. She found herself in the kitchen and immediately went to the fridge. A quick flick of her flashlight revealed several magnets stuck to the appliance door. One in the shape of Texas with a painted desert scene. A peach with *Georgia on my mind* written across the face. A Statue of Liberty. Another shaped like Florida and decorated with palm trees.

Interesting. Perhaps they were souvenirs from vacations.

She opened the fridge, but there wasn't much to see. Some cans of Coke and Dr Pepper. Condiments in the door. But if they traveled in a camper, they'd probably taken everything perishable with them. Which meant they planned on being gone for more than a few days. Not unusual if they were vacationing, but Ms. Pit Bull said they were gone often. The freezer was relatively bare too, with just a frozen pizza, some green beans, and a half gallon of store brand chocolate ice cream.

The counters were clean, appliances minimal: toaster, microwave, coffeepot. A lone mug sat in the sink with a moldy bag of green tea inside. So they'd been gone awhile.

In the living room she had to use the flashlight to keep from tripping, and she hoped the venetian blinds would hide the bouncing beam from the street. On the coffee table lay a poorly refolded local newspaper dated three weeks prior. The TV and stereo across from the sofa were name brands but not top-of-the-line. A DVD and CD rack housed mostly classic films like *Casablanca* and *The African Queen*. Come to think of it, Humphrey Bogart seemed to be a favorite. There was *The Maltese Falcon*, too. Musically, the selection favored Celtic with some movie sound tracks mixed in with the Enya and Clannad. Not exactly what she'd expect for a young guy. This stuff probably belonged to the mom, Irene.

Abby took in a long breath, trying to get her bearings. What exactly was she looking for? A written confession? Hopefully the bedrooms would provide something noteworthy, because so far she was coming up empty-handed.

It was right when her foot touched the carpeted steps leading to the second floor that she heard something. Instantly she clicked the flashlight off. And listened. Held her breath. Listened again.

Creak. A door.

Coming from the kitchen.

The back door.

Had she missed Christy's warning call on her cell?

Another creak, this time more like a floorboard.

Great.

Abby reached under her coat and felt the grip of the Beretta. What if this Diego guy had come back without Christy noticing? A murderer could be walking toward her this very second.

Calm down. Exhale. She was overreacting.

A dull thud came next, like someone bumped a wall with a shoe.

With her thumb, Abby flipped the snap holding the Beretta in place, her fingers tightening around the grip. Slowly she drew it out and held it at her side. Ready. Except *she* was the intruder here.

Should she announce herself?

She didn't have time to think up a plan before a dark human form appeared in the living room doorway.

Abby tensed. Not good. If she could just—

From across the room a flashlight beam hit her right in the eyes, and she instinctively dropped to the floor, temporarily blinded but determined not to be a target. Whoever this was, they could be armed, and she wasn't about to—

"Abby?"

She froze. What the . . . ?

"Are you okay?"

Christy.

Abby cursed and climbed to her feet. "What do you think you're doing?"

The room went black as Christy flicked off her flashlight. "I'm sorry. I didn't mean to scare you."

Abby's shoulders relaxed. "I could've shot you." She didn't wait to hear Christy's response. "We have to hurry," she whispered, sheathing her gun. She'd lost her lookout now, but she'd gained a second set of eyes. Another five minutes and they'd be gone anyway.

"Find anything?"

"Just normal stuff. I was about to go upstairs. What changed your mind?"

"Even cops need backup," Christy said.

"Yeah, but they usually work together."

At the top of the stairs Abby turned on her flashlight and Christy did the same. They headed to the first bedroom. The four-poster double bed was neatly made, a colorful quilt folded at the bottom. The faint scent of incense met their noses, and sure enough, on the dresser was a small incense holder with the ash of several sticks in its basin.

Christy pointed her flashlight at a framed photograph on the nightstand, and they both leaned toward it. An auburn-haired woman smiled broadly, crouching beside a small boy on the beach. He held a pail and shovel, grinning himself.

"She looks familiar," Christy whispered, and Abby blinked.

"You recognize them?"

"No, not really. It's just . . ."

"Have you seen them before?"

"I don't know." Christy reached for the photo, but Abby stopped her before she could leave prints on it.

"Think."

"I am thinking."

"At the store maybe?"

"For a second I thought so, but now I can't remember."

"What about the boy?"

"Never seen him before."

Was he Diego and the woman Irene?

They made quick work of the rest of the bedroom, finding little else interesting. The closet was unusually bare, and Abby reminded herself again that most of the clothes had probably been packed in the camper.

The next bedroom seemed like a guy's room. Dark blue walls. Twin bed with covers thrown up but still rumpled. A small desk with a computer and printer sitting in the corner. Two posters of current rock bands tacked to the wall.

On the dresser was an old silver belt buckle, some loose change, and a pocketknife with a carved ivory handle. Abby checked the closet and found two very worn pairs of size eleven men's boots, some Levis, a few long-sleeved knit shirts, but little else.

Christy was shining her flashlight on the set of bookshelves by the bed, and Abby joined her. At first glance, there was no doubt this guy liked Stephen King. The whole top shelf contained nothing but King. Before Abby could stop her, Christy pulled one of the books off the shelf. *Carrie,* said the black, seventies-era font.

"This was his first novel," Christy said, flipping the pages. "Wow."

"Wow, what?"

"This is a first edition." She turned to the last page and held the book open for Abby. "See that code?"

"No."

"In the gutter." She pointed with her finger to an almost-unnoticeable *P6* printed on the inner margin of the leaf near the spine. "That has to be there on page 199 for it to be a true first edition."

"That's crazy."

"And even though this is an ex-library copy with a card pocket, stamps, and everything, it's still worth three or four hundred."

Christy snapped the book shut, returned it to the shelf, and pulled off another. *Cujo.*

More flipping pages.

Abby let another curse word fly. "You didn't wear gloves."

Christy's expression was grim as she examined a few more books, either ignoring Abby or not hearing. Then she shook her head and backed away from the shelf.

"More first editions."

"So he's a book collector. That doesn't bode well for him, does it?"

"No."

"Let's go," Abby said.

The third bedroom was even sparser than the first two. Remembering what Mr. Johnson had said about a teen girl living here, Abby would've expected her bedroom to have more personality. But this room looked more like a hotel room. Bed, dresser, table, lamp. Everything functional but completely void of personality. A portable CD player on the dresser was the only hint of someone's touch.

Abby held her light on the dresser and carefully pulled open the drawers. They found some fashionable Gap jeans, a red hoodie, pastel blue pajamas decorated with sheep—normal teen girl attire.

Abby glanced at her watch. They'd been in ten minutes. Too long. "Hurry."

In the top drawer, Abby's flashlight landed on a few pairs of socks and a stray bra. Christy pushed them aside, then suddenly stopped, staring into the drawer.

"What?"

Slowly Christy pulled out an unframed four-by-six photograph, shining her own light on it. Whatever she saw stopped her cold.

"What is it?"

"Oh, my word."

Christy handed the photo to Abby. She took it and saw an older version of the woman in the beach photo. Standing beside her with his arm around her shoulders was a handsome young man of maybe seventeen or eighteen.

"I saw them." Christy's voice came out almost inaudible.

"You did? When?"

Christy took the photograph from her and stared at it again. "In the bookstore. The day Hunter died."

26

Whenever Jan Mercer needed to think, she mucked stalls. They had to be cleaned every day anyway, and the simple monotony of pushing a pitchfork under dirty straw, sifting manure, and dumping the pieces into the wheelbarrow freed her mind. She barely even smelled the ammonia from the urine anymore.

Push, sift, dump.

Something wasn't right here.

Push, sift, dump.

If only she could get Roxi to open up.

The barn door creaked, and Keith walked toward her under the bare lightbulb. At almost six-five and still lean as beef jerky, he was the quintessential cowboy she'd fallen in love with over thirty years ago.

He strolled across the wooden barn floor, pushing his white Stetson farther up his head. "Thought I'd find you out here."

"Lot to think about," she said, leaning on her pitchfork.

Keith jabbed his thumb toward the house. "She's in Trae's room now. Out like a light."

"Think I worked her too hard?" Often she forgot some folks weren't used to their rugged, outdoor lifestyle. She'd worn out many a guest without even realizing it. Last Thanksgiving Keith's sister and brother-in-law brought their entire motley crew over for the weekend, and they'd all ended up on horseback. Keith told her later his sister hadn't exactly appreciated them enlisting her children as ranch hands, but Jan saw it as a chance to teach the kids there was more to life than iPods and video games.

"A little sweat's good for everyone," Keith said. "Especially a girl her age."

"We hauled a bunch of manure up to the top pasture and repaired that fence down by the creek."

"How'd she do?"

"Good. Didn't complain at all."

Keith leaned against the stall door, picking at the wood with his chipped fingernail. "Find out anything?"

Jan shook her head. "She's not from around here. Said something about Wyoming, but I didn't grill her."

"Maybe you should."

"Hon, I can't."

He nodded reluctantly. "Still wish we knew more."

"Me too."

"Though I suppose if I were in trouble, I wouldn't go blabbin' to some old couple like us anyway."

"Oh, stop. We're not old."

"Yeah, I know. Just seasoned, right?" He smiled, tilting his head toward the house. "Why don't you come on in and I'll make you a cup of tea."

"This is the last stall." Jan grabbed hold of the wheelbarrow. She was pleased that Roxi *had* worked hard, and the girl wasn't afraid to get dirty. What she didn't know—which was a lot—they could teach her. But soon they'd need to find out the truth about her situation, whatever it might be. And Jan had thought of all sorts of possible scenarios. She could be a runaway with a worried family searching for her even now.

But when Jan looked closely at the girl and gazed into her fearful eyes, all those concerns vanished. Maybe she *had* run away. Maybe she *was* a juvenile offender. It didn't matter. Obviously the people who were supposed to look out for her hadn't, and Jan was nothing if she wasn't a mother hen.

"Something you're not telling me?"

She pushed the wheelbarrow out the double door. The sun had been down now for hours, but the yard light illuminated her way. "It's nothing, really."

Keith followed and watched her dump the manure in the designated pile. Over the spring and summer it grew to be quite a mound they would spread strategically around the ranch in the fall. Some made it to the hay fields. Some reinforced the dirt driveway. But it was all eventually recycled.

"What do you mean?"

"I'm not sure." Jan returned the wheelbarrow to the barn and flicked the lights off. She and Keith slowly walked up to the house side by side. "For the last couple days I've felt like God's been trying to prepare me for something."

"Roxi?"

She shrugged. "All I know for sure is I couldn't leave her out there on her own like that."

Keith rested his arm around her shoulders, giving her a gentle squeeze. "I'm glad you didn't."

"There's so much trouble behind her eyes."

"I noticed."

"She sure *seems* like she's running away from something."

"Guess we won't know until she tells us."

Jan nodded. "Yeah, I guess."

❧

The knock barely registered in the back of Roxi's sleeping mind, so when someone shook her shoulder, her eyes flew open, and she struggled to sit up in the bed.

"Hey, hey, take it easy. It's just me."

The bedroom door was open, the light from the hall pouring in. Roxi squinted to see Jan standing beside her, fully dressed and wearing her blue down vest. Selah wasn't in bed with her anymore. She'd probably bolted out the door as soon as Jan opened it.

Roxi fell back onto her pillow, groaning. "What time is it?"

"Five."

She groaned again, covering her eyes with her arm.

"Up and at 'em, girl."

Forcing herself up, she sat bleary-eyed on the edge of the bed. She didn't tell Jan that muscles she hadn't even known existed ached from their work yesterday. The thought of doing it all again was less than invigorating when she could barely crack open her eyelids.

"Be downstairs in ten minutes," Jan said, grinning. "If you can. Got something I want to show you."

Roxi lifted her hand in acknowledgment, steeling herself to stand in the freezing room. She was gonna have to get used to this if she expected them to keep her on. They were hiring her to work, not sleep. And as hard as the chores were yesterday, she'd put her all into it.

She quickly slipped into her newly washed T-shirt and hoodie, surprised at how good it felt to put on clean clothes again. Right before bed yesterday, she'd taken a long, hot, glorious shower, and Jan had washed her meager wardrobe. She'd been embarrassed about how little she owned, but Jan hadn't said anything. When they paid her whatever they were going to pay, she would buy some more clothes. She'd just make do for now.

By the time Roxi was dressed, her grogginess had mostly worn off and she could make better sense of her thoughts. Taking her backpack over to the bed, she carefully pulled out the two stolen books and swallowed hard at the sight of them. It was impossible to push the image of that manager's dying face from her mind. And no matter how hard she worked here, it would shadow her, reminding her she would always be running from something. What would happen if Jan and Keith found out? Her job would no doubt go flying out the window. Or worse.

Stuffing the backpack under the bed, she snatched her jean jacket off the chair and headed downstairs. She found Jan and Keith sitting at the kitchen table nursing mugs of something hot. They both looked up and smiled when she entered. Selah flew off her makeshift bed of old horse blankets in the corner of the room and threw herself at Roxi, tail swooshing from side to side like a crazed metronome.

"Hey there, girl." Roxi dropped to her knees, rubbing the dog's ears and neck. Was this the same animal she'd met behind the Safeway? The dog seemed to have come into her element, fear and trembling replaced with excitement and energy. Food and a warm bed had done wonders—for both of them.

"You ready?" Jan scraped her chair backward across the linoleum, rising to her feet.

Roxi slowly stood too, her hand still resting on Selah's head. She eyed the back door. It wasn't even light out. "What are we doing?"

"You'll see."

Grabbing a silver thermos and a paper bag sitting on the counter, Jan gestured for her to follow.

Keith winked at her. "Selah and I'll hold down the fort. She's warming up to me."

"You sure?"

He nodded. "Go on."

Jan tossed the thermos to her and led the way to one of the pickups. "Breakfast," she said, holding up the paper bag. "You've got the coffee."

"I could sure use some." Roxi yawned, eyeing the fence posts and roll of barbed wire in the truck bed. "Fixing fences again?" Her arms and shoulders hadn't appreciated learning to use the posthole digger.

"Later, but first I want you to see something."

"What?"

Jan jumped in the driver's seat, and Roxi envied her spunk at an hour like this. "Have to wait and see."

Climbing in beside her, she couldn't help but notice the stark contrast. When she'd climbed into this truck two days ago, she'd been scared and unsure of what Jan was going to do next. She half suspected Jan would drive her straight to the cops for shoplifting. Now she still didn't know what Jan was up to, but she wasn't afraid. Jan almost seemed to care about her.

Jan maneuvered the truck through the yard, driving right up to the gate leading to the main field. She got out to open the gate for the truck, drove through, then got out again and closed the gate behind them.

"You can do it on the way back," Jan said as she returned to the truck. "How'd you sleep?"

"Okay." *Except for the nightmares.* Jan didn't need to know about them.

"You did good work yesterday."

She leaned against the door and tried to keep her eyes open. "Thanks."

For the next few bumpy minutes, Roxi watched the headlights illuminate the field. It was already lighter than when they'd first come out, midnight's black replaced with predawn's gray, but there was still only enough light to make out the forms of things. She could've sworn she saw glowing eyes staring back at her from behind one of the scrubs and decided she didn't want to know what kind of animals roamed these hills at night.

Apparently they were making their own road. To the right a pine forest jutted up against the fence they were following. The mountains in the distance were dark, hulking monsters stretching almost halfway up the sky.

She hugged herself, glad for the truck's heater and thankful she wasn't wandering around looking for somewhere to sleep. What would Mom or Irene think of her being a ranch hand?

"Where in the world are we?"

"Still our ranch."

"How far are we going?"

"Not much farther."

As the truck crested another ridge, its headlights caught a small cabin nestled at the edge of the forest. Jan parked the truck in front of it, pocketed her keys, then pulled another down vest, a red one, from behind the seats. She handed it to Roxi.

"Might need this, at least until the sun comes up."

Roxi slipped it on over her jean jacket, and they both walked up to the cabin's small porch. Built out of logs, it couldn't have more than one room. Two rustic chairs sat on opposite ends of the porch. Jan scooted them together, facing the direction they'd come.

"What is this place?"

"The original homestead cabin my granddaddy built." Jan rested her hand on the back of one of the chairs and stared eastward like she was imagining what it must've been like all those years ago. "He sawed and hewed the logs entirely by himself. My parents spent their honeymoon up here. Before Momma died, she made Keith and me promise never to tear it down. You've got to see the sunrise from this porch."

Roxi wasn't sure if she should sit, say something, or just stare at the horizon with her. She didn't have any trouble picturing Jan as a pioneer woman. Another time, another set of clothes, and Jan herself could've been felling those trees.

"This place means a lot to me," Jan said softly. "Our Trae's dream was to turn it into base camp for the outfitter business he wanted to start. He was even going to add on a room."

Jan sighed. "Hard not to think about him up here, but that's not why I brought you. I figure if you're gonna work for us, you need to know some of this ranch's history. This is about as historic as we get. Have a seat. Let me get some cups."

Roxi did as she was told, watching Jan unlock the cabin with a key she drew from a crack in the wall. She appeared again with two mugs sporting the logo of Walker's Feed Store, and soon they were both resting in the chairs, sipping hot coffee.

"Biscuits and bacon," Jan said, pulling two tinfoil packages from the paper bag. When she opened them, little puffs of steam floated into the air. She took a few strips and one biscuit for herself, then handed the rest to Roxi. "Good cold, hot, or in-between."

The first bite of the still-warm biscuit made Roxi's stomach growl for more, and she followed it with a huge bite of bacon. Not too crispy but not limp either, the salty meat melted on her tongue. As they munched on the food, Roxi found herself wondering more about Jan and Keith.

"Did you ever want to be anything other than a rancher?" She imitated Jan and rested both feet on the porch railing. Holding her mug right under her chin, she breathed in the warm steam of her coffee.

"I was born here. It's in my blood."

"Keith's too?"

"His family ranched about fifty miles away. Tough times forced his daddy to sell off their spread when he was a teenager."

"You been married a long time?"

"Twenty-eight years, but we've known each other almost thirty-five. He worked for my parents. That's how we met. Then after we got married, Daddy gradually handed Keith and me the reins. We all lived together in the house we're in now."

"Was that weird?"

"You'd be surprised how many ranch families are multigenerational."

"Like the Waltons."

Jan smiled. "Exactly."

"Must've been nice having both your parents around."

"It was. I learned so much from them."

"I never knew my dad," Roxi said, surprising herself for saying it.

"Divorce?"

"They weren't married."

Jan took a sip of her coffee.

"I don't even know his name," Roxi said.

"You never asked your mom?"

"Once I did, but she got all bent out of shape and told me he wasn't worth knowing."

"Well, I guess sometimes no father's better than a bad one."

"I wasn't supposed to happen."

Jan cradled her mug with both hands. "How do you know that?"

"Doesn't take a genius."

Leaning back in her chair, Jan let out a long breath. "You know, years ago they told me I could never have children."

"They did?"

Jan nodded. "I'd gotten used to it being just Keith and me. I started liking it that way too. I didn't envy gals tied down by a kid. But lo and behold, Trae showed up. Even though he wasn't expected, I was honored to have him. I bet your parents didn't regret you. You were probably just an unexpected gift, like Trae."

Roxi pulled her feet off the railing and crossed her ankles. A memory she'd long tried to forget was surfacing. It was before her accident, so she'd probably been six or seven. Mom had brought a new boyfriend home. All Roxi remembered about him was he wore flip-flops—in winter. He stuck around for a couple of months, then disappeared like the rest.

Suddenly the story came spilling out of her.

She'd woken up in the middle of the night to go to the bathroom and heard voices in the kitchen. Creeping to her bedroom door, she listened. Mom and the guy were arguing.

"You didn't tell me you had a kid!"

"She won't bother us."

The guy yelled words Roxi had never heard before.

"Shh. You'll wake her."

Heavy footsteps paced across the floor, and she pictured him in his dirty white undershirt, jeans, and flip-flops, sucking on a cigarette.

"Forget about her," Mom said, her voice dreamy and relaxed.

The pacing stopped, and she heard someone thunk down into a chair. "Why'd you go have a stupid kid anyway?"

The room got quiet; then Mom had laughed. "Didn't have money for an abortion."

Roxi gulped down the last of her coffee and reached for the thermos to refill her mug. Her hands were shaking, and she needed to keep them busy. Mom had probably been high, but it didn't make the words sting any less.

"I'm sure she didn't mean it," Jan said.

"You don't say stuff like that unless it's true." Roxi squeezed the mug's handle the way the anger was squeezing her stomach. "She still wants nothing to do with me."

"She doesn't?"

With a sinking feeling, Roxi realized she'd said too much, and she couldn't take it back.

"Is that why you don't have anywhere to go?"

She got up and walked to the end of the porch, her back to Jan. The sky was now washed in pink. "When does the sun rise around here anyway?" *Just drop it. Please.*

"Sweetheart."

Roxi heard Jan's chair creak.

"God doesn't make mistakes," Jan said, a little softer. "No matter what anyone says. He loves you exactly like you are."

Stupid, stupid, stupid. Roxi held her eyes closed. How could she have let herself bring this up?

"Whether your mom meant to have you or not doesn't change that."

It might not change it, but it sure didn't make it any easier a pill to swallow. She could look at it through rose-colored glasses all she wanted, but it didn't change the truth.

Roxi opened her eyes.

The sunrise saved her from further conversation. Right then it peeked over the horizon, the first rays of dawn shooting through the air like brilliant lasers. Roxi gazed across the rolling, golden hills. She was letting herself get too comfortable. A mistake every time. Hadn't she learned her lesson with Irene?

In a moment Jan was standing beside her. "Beautiful, isn't it?"

She blinked back unwanted tears.

"I want you to know you're welcome here." Jan rested her hand gently on Roxi's shoulder.

Her throat tightened. No. She was *not* going to lose it in front of this woman.

"And if you want to talk about anything, I'll be here."

She sidled out from under Jan's touch and walked toward the pickup. It was time to lose herself in whatever work Jan had planned for the day. The harder, the better. Maybe a little physical pain would help her forget about Mom.

27

By eight o'clock that evening Abby found herself in the corner of her father's living room trying to be civil to a crowd full of partying strangers and relatives. Apparently by mutual consent—but without asking her—the whole town had descended on her dad's place after the funeral. The shriveled old lady barking orders from her wheel-chair was Aunt Clarisse. Cousin John, who'd made millions invest-ing in real estate, was loudly giving money advice to another cousin whose name Abby couldn't remember. If this went on much longer, she'd be throwing them out of the house herself.

Everyone had a glass of either wine or beer in hand, and she took a sip from her own goblet, wishing for a moment she was the type to get smashed. Getting drunk would allow her to escape, if only for a few hours. But besides that one time in college when she and some clueless girlfriends drank a few too many mudslides, she hadn't touched anything stronger than a glass of good merlot with dinner, and even that was rare. She'd taken some flak for it over the years from the guys in the department who loved to wind down at the local bar, but the problem with alcohol was that it *did* dull your senses. The bad ones and the good ones.

The only amusement of the evening was trying to pick the book dealers out of the crowd. It wasn't hard. Most of them wore outdated sport coats or gaudy dresses and were yukking it up in exclusive gaggles. They were throwing around words like *incunabula*, *fore edge*, and *endpapers*. She had a feeling most were here for the free food, glad Hunter was gone. If the Book Barn closed, their biggest competitor in the region would be out of the picture.

Abby spotted the detective working Hunter's case. He was the bored-looking guy built like an Army sergeant popping olives and crackers like candy. Often a killer attended the funeral of his victim, so she knew the detective would be checking the guest list for suspects and listening in on more than one conversation. She made her way toward him. He hadn't returned her calls yesterday or this morning, and she'd been hoping to catch him here.

"Detective Stephens?"

He looked up as he stuffed an olive in his mouth. She put him at thirty-five, a blond crew cut completing the Army image.

"I'm Abby Dawson."

He shook her hand with an iron grip, swallowing the olive. "I'm very sorry about your brother."

"I need to talk to you . . . in private."

Stephens glanced around the room. He wiped his mouth with a napkin. "Where would you suggest?"

Abby led the way through the house to Dad's study. When the door was closed, she offered Stephens her father's leather office chair. He shook his head, crossing his arms. A power move if she ever saw one.

"What did you want to talk to me about?"

"Let me first thank you for coming."

He gave an almost-imperceptible nod.

"Any new leads?"

"Your father's been cleared."

She waited for Stephens to offer more, but he went tight-lipped, arms still crossed. Even if he had information, she knew he wouldn't share it. No good detective would.

"I knew that would happen," she said.

"You can understand why we had to investigate him."

Stephens knew she was a cop, which was why what she had to share would no doubt make him bristle. Cops could have egos the size of Alaska. Nothing would rub him the wrong way more than thinking another cop from another jurisdiction was trying to do his job for him. But there wasn't anything she could do about that. She had to get him in on this.

"I found one of the stolen books," she said.

His eyebrow twitched.

"Listen, Detective, I don't want you to think I'm trying to interfere. But since I knew my brother better than anyone, I took the liberty of doing some searching."

Stephens was a statue with piercing eyes.

Abby decided to lay it down straight. If he took it the wrong way, that was his choice. "Two days ago I visited a bookstore called Pages Past in Santa Fe. They were listing a book on the Internet that seemed to match one stolen from the Barn."

She walked over to Dad's desk and picked up the copy of *Farmer Giles of Ham*, still safely sealed in the evidence bag. She handed it to Stephens.

"All the points match. It's a first edition, with its dust jacket, and it has the bookstore's mark, a small penciled *D*."

"I'm aware of the store's mark, Miss Dawson."

She leaned against the edge of the desk and crossed her own arms. "My brother's murderer held that book."

"Maybe."

"No maybe, Detective. It's one of the stolen books. And I got the name and address of the person who sold it to the store. You'd be wise to check it out."

She immediately regretted her choice of words when she saw Stephens's jaw muscle flex.

He held up the book. "You've gotta be kidding me. I can't use this as evidence."

"I know. What you really need is this." She produced a piece of paper with Diego's name, address, and license number written in bold blue ink.

Stephens sighed.

"Why didn't your people find this book?"

It was the wrong approach, but she couldn't help it. Stephens stared at her for a moment, his eyes cold and unrelenting. She'd hate to be a suspect he interrogated.

"We are doing everything we can to find your brother's killers, Miss Dawson."

She noticed he used the plural form of the word. "Then you won't mind following up on this name and address."

"You shouldn't have done this."

"Detective—" she didn't break eye contact and pointed at the book in his hand—"this guy needs to be found, brought in, and questioned."

"I'll make that call." Stephens held up his hand when she started to respond. "Don't think I don't know where you're coming from, but—"

"You have no idea where I'm coming from, Detective."

Stephens shrugged. "I'm sorry you feel that way." He tucked the paper with Diego's address into his shirt pocket and let himself out the study door.

⚜

Abby found Christy hiding out in the kitchen with her sister, May, amid the greasy chip bowls and bottles of flat soda. They both looked up when she entered, their genuine smiles of sympathy the first she'd seen all evening.

"How you doing?" Christy asked. She set down her blue plastic cup.

Abby shook her head, wondering for one brief moment what Christy was drinking. "I hate these things."

"Me too," May said.

If Christy hadn't introduced her younger sister in the receiving line, Abby might not have guessed they were related. She probably would've thought May was ten years Christy's junior instead of three. Her complexion still held a youthful shine, and her eyes didn't tell stories like Christy's.

"We were just talking about you," Christy said.

A sliver of envy snuck into Abby. Christy had lost her fiancé, but she still had family to love. Close family. Abby went to the fridge and found a chilled Diet Coke in the very back. Her conversation with Detective Stephens still rang in her ears.

She popped open her can. "Were you now?"

"I'm going back with May tomorrow to her ranch in Elk Valley."

"No worries. I'll move to a hotel."

Christy and May exchanged a glance. "I'm wondering if you'd like to come with me."

Abby paused, the Diet Coke halfway to her mouth. "What?"

"It would be good for both of us to get away from—" Christy gestured toward the living room—"all this."

"Whoa, whoa. I can't just pick up and *leave*."

"Why not?"

"You know why not."

Christy took a step toward her, meeting her eyes. "Abby, consider it. You could use the break. I know I could."

She glanced at Christy's sister. "But—"

"It was my idea," May said.

"We'd love to have you," Christy said. "You can still work on all your leads from there."

She took a big sip of soda. Now was not the time for mushiness, but for some reason it meant more than she could say for them to ask. Abby wouldn't have held it against either of them to cling to each other and forget about anyone else, but instead they were reaching out to her. And what Christy said was true. With her laptop and cell phone she *could* do everything remotely.

"I'll think about it."

❧

At some point Abby realized she hadn't seen Dad for hours. She poked her head in the living room. Lynn was sitting in a chair by the fireplace, still managing to converse politely with the lingering guests. Dressed in a tailored navy blue suit with a strand of pearls gracing her neck, she had an aura of elegance Abby hadn't noticed before. She bet Lynn could have tea with the Queen of England and hold her own.

"Have you seen Dad?" Abby asked.

Lynn shook her head.

Fifteen minutes later, Abby had changed into jeans and a sweatshirt. She slipped into her leather jacket and somehow managed to sneak out the back door into the night without anyone noticing. If Dad's car was still here and he wasn't in the house, he could be in only one place.

She stuffed her hands into her pockets and slowly walked down the driveway. Cricket songs pierced the night, and she drew in the faint scent of wood smoke. She'd surprised herself by not crying during the service. Part of her had wanted to let it all out, but nothing had come. Maybe it was her training. She'd fought hard to gain respect in the male-dominated police field, avoiding tears at any cost. You didn't cry on the job or show weakness of any kind, especially not to your peers. Unfortunately it had seeped over into her personal life, and Michael and Kat had taken the brunt of it. She knew better a few years too late that she could seem cold and unfeeling.

Abby's sneakers crunched on the gravel driveway. How many times had she bottled up her emotions rather than talk to her own husband? Too many times to count. *And they say guys are the ones who do that.*

Stopping for a moment, Abby lifted her eyes to the starry sky. Someone who created all this . . . why would He care what went on down here? She took a deep breath, turned in a complete circle, and took in the whole sky. Faith in God was something she'd abandoned a long time ago. God had probably given up on her by now too.

She picked out the constellation Orion like Hunter had taught her. Christy chose to believe in something she couldn't see, even when she was just as sad and broken. She wasn't perfect, and she admitted it. She didn't wave a Bible around and spout off about hell and damnation. She just believed.

And that was fine. For Christy.

Abby started walking again down the lane to the back door of the Barn. Sure enough, it was unlocked.

"Dad?"

She stepped inside, making her way to the front room, where she and Christy had examined the shelves that first day they'd met. The lights were on, but she saw no sign of her father. She paused, listening. Only the hum of the fluorescent bulbs met her ears.

"You in here, Dad?"

She thought about returning to the house. Maybe her father just needed to be alone. But she needed to understand, to know. Did he really plan to sell the store? She tried not to look down as she walked over the spot where Hunter died.

She pushed open the door to the kitchen area. She hadn't been back here in over twenty years, and like the rest of the place, it hadn't changed much. The refrigerator was probably new, and some of the furniture had been replaced, but being in this store was almost like walking back in time for Abby.

Dad wasn't in any of the rooms, including his smaller bookstore office. There was only one more place to check, and it was the place Abby least wanted to see. Hunter's apartment would speak of him louder than anything else.

She glanced toward the stairs leading up to the apartment. For some reason her brother had come down here that night. What had he heard? When did he realize he was going to die?

Abby walked up the stairs, remembering the odd layout of the apartment. The kitchen and offices made up the first floor, but the second held the living room, bedroom, and bathroom. There was an outside entrance to the second floor too. But Hunter had rarely used it. He chose to walk through the store most days.

When Abby walked into the living room, she was surprised to see it was empty. The bookcases Hunter had crafted and stained himself no longer held the precious volumes he'd collected over the years and sent her pictures of. In fact, she didn't see a book any . . .

Then she saw the stacks of sealed brown boxes beside the door.

Rustling came from the bedroom, and Abby almost ran into the room. On Hunter's bed were more boxes, only these weren't sealed.

They were stuffed with his clothes. And standing at the closet, his arms full of Hunter's flannel shirts still on their hangers, was her father.

"What are you *doing*?"

Dad barely acknowledged her as he stuffed the shirts into one of the boxes.

"Dad." She walked right up to her father, resting her hand on his arm.

Without meeting her eyes, he pulled away. His voice was low. "Please go back to the house."

"What's going on?"

"Please leave me alone."

"What are you—?"

"What does it look like I'm doing?" He jerked more shirts from the closet, his tone rising.

"Dad, stop."

"I'm packing—" he slammed the shirts into the box—"my dead son's things."

"But you can't. Not yet."

"I said go back to the house!"

Only then did their eyes meet. His were puffy and bloodshot. He was still wearing his black suit pants from the funeral, except now they were rumpled and dusty. Sweaty half-moons stained the underarms of his dress shirt. And there was anger in his eyes—directed at her.

"I came to see if you were okay," she said, her voice almost catching. Even during all the arguments in her teens and the silence in between them, Abby had always somehow believed her father loved her. They just clashed sometimes. But staring into her father's eyes right then, she wasn't sure anymore.

"It always has to be an argument," he said, cutting the air with his hand karate-chop style. "You'll never just do what I ask."

She went to the bed and grabbed a handful of clothes. "What gives you the right to come out here without anyone knowing and . . . do this?"

"He was my son."

"And my brother! And Christy's fiancé and Lynn's stepson! Did it even cross your mind that maybe we would want to have the chance to go through his things too? Or are you still so selfish?"

"Still?"

"Yeah, Dad. Still."

He shook his head. "And you're *still* not listening to a word I say."

She fingered a green chamois shirt, looking away from her father. She could face down crazed drug addicts or fighting drunks, but she'd never been able to face her father. She'd end up either yelling like this or running away. One day it dawned on her why. On the streets her badge and gun gave her respect. But no matter how much she accomplished or how hard she worked, in her father's eyes she would always be that clueless teenager.

"Christy told me you'd changed." She briefly met his eyes again. "But this is just like it's always been."

Her father went to the closet again.

"Dad, I want things to be better between us."

He jerked hangers off the silver rod, returning to the bed with an armful of jeans. He threw them into the closest box. When he met her eyes again, there was less anger.

"Why didn't you ever tell me—" he glanced away—"what Vince did to you?"

"And why didn't you ever notice? Hunter was just a kid, and he knew."

"I would've fired him on the—"

She held up her hand. "It's done. It doesn't matter anymore."

"It does to me!" He ran his fingers through his messy hair. "You never even gave me a chance to help you."

"You knew about him and Christy and you didn't do anything about that."

"She wasn't my daughter. I couldn't just—"

"Sure you could. But you turned a blind eye, just like you did with me, and let Vince abuse someone else. He almost killed her."

Her father deflated at the words, and Abby sighed. "Listen, I'm not saying I wasn't to blame too. I was stupid."

"I could've helped you," Dad whispered.

Abby decided to let it go. The fact was, she didn't know *what* her father would've done. Vince had deceived everyone into thinking he was a cultured gentleman who wanted nothing but the best for the bookstore and for Abby, and he'd taken her father in more than anyone else.

"I never meant to hurt you," Abby finally said. "But I couldn't admit to myself what was happening. I wish you'd understand that." She felt a lump forming in her throat. "I can't pretend to imagine what you're going through right now, Dad. Hunter was . . . It feels like something was ripped out of me too."

"I . . ." Dad blinked quickly. "I really need to be alone."

She glanced at the boxes full of her brother's possessions. Even when she tried to reach out, Dad pushed her away. What was she doing wrong?

The silence became thick.

"You're selling the store anyway, aren't you?"

"Ab, please."

"I need to know."

"We talked about this."

"And you haven't changed your mind?"

A pause. "No."

"Then I'll leave you alone."

In a moment she was walking back up the driveway to the house. This time she didn't notice the stars, and she realized her presence here was pouring salt into her father's wounds.

28

"Ever ridden a horse?" Jan handed Roxi the reins to Sally, a gentle mare she'd raised from birth. She could put a three-year-old on her back and know the child would be safe.

"Sure," Roxi said.

Jan led her own mare into the pasture, and Roxi followed, leading Sally. It was only an hour after dawn, and they would be searching for a stray bull that had managed to elude both Jan and Keith for the past two weeks. It would be easy riding, and she hoped Roxi would open up to her at some point along the way.

"Need a leg up?"

"No, I'm good."

Out of the corner of her eye, Jan watched the girl struggle to get her foot in the stirrup. When she hoisted herself into the saddle and almost fell over the other side, Jan fought to hold back a smile.

It looks like it, sweetheart.

Jan effortlessly swung into her own saddle. Riding a horse was like riding a bike. Once you learned, you never really forgot. Roxi's inexperience was obvious, but it disappointed her that the girl felt the need to lie.

She nodded toward Roxi. "Relax your fingers and give her some rein. She'll lead for you."

They rode for a few minutes in silence, and Jan kept thinking about what Roxi had told her up at the cabin yesterday. Maybe she'd lied about other things, but not the story about her mother. Jan's heart ached for the girl. Every child should know they were loved by someone, especially her mother. Had anyone ever loved Roxi?

She glanced over at her young face. A few freckles dotted her nose, and her brown hair glowed in the sunlight. If anyone had, it was a long time ago, which made Jan just plain mad. This girl had been alone and afraid when Jan had picked her up on that road. She'd probably slept more than one night on the street. No one should have to do that, especially a kid.

Had her family written her off as some sort of teenage rebel? Roxi's standoffish ways might cause someone to do that. But when Jan looked Roxi in the eyes, she didn't see a rebel. She saw a scared kid who needed somebody to look out for her. What would've happened if she hadn't picked her up that night?

Please give me wisdom, Lord. Jan lifted her eyes to the sky. On a whim she'd hired a girl who knew nothing about ranching just to keep her from running away. Was she crazy?

"I don't know if I can do this."

Roxi's shaky voice pulled Jan out of her thoughts, and she realized her mare had pulled several feet ahead of Roxi's. Jan twisted around to see Roxi clinging to the saddle horn with both hands.

"Just sit back and loosen those fingers," Jan coaxed. "She's gonna take care of you; don't worry."

Slowly Roxi let go of the horn, but her death grip on the reins was throwing even patient Sally into an uneven step.

"Take a deep breath and let it out long and slow. It'll relax both of you."

"I can't do this."

"Yes, you can."

The girl looked like she was about to cry.

"You're doing fine."

Suddenly Roxi jerked back on Sally's reins, and the mare came to an abrupt stop.

"Easy, easy," Jan said. "She'll respond to the lightest tug."

Terror flooded Roxi's eyes, and Jan doubled back. No, she wasn't crazy. Somehow she and this girl had been flung together for a reason.

"What's goin' on?"

Roxi's shoulders were taut, her knuckles white. "The only time I ever rode a horse was when I was four. And it was a pony at the fair."

Jan tried again to hold back a smile but couldn't. "I kinda figured that."

"But I can learn. I *want* to learn."

"Okay." Jan gave her a nod. "Good enough for me."

She could tell Roxi was surprised she wasn't making a big deal of her deception. It looked like a two-ton weight had just lifted from her back.

"You could've told me right away, you know."

"I thought you might . . ."

"First of all," Jan said, "I meant it when I said I'd teach you what you needed to know. That includes riding. Second, the truth never hurt anybody."

She thought she saw something flash on the girl's face, but Roxi looked away before Jan could decide if it had been her imagination. Gently she urged her mare forward by lifting her reins and squeezing with her thighs, explaining to Roxi how to do the same.

"Listen, I know there's a lot of stuff you don't want to talk about," Jan said.

Roxi was looking at the back of the horse's head like most beginning riders.

"And that's okay. You don't know me any more than I know you. But I hope someday you'll trust me enough to be honest with me."

No response. Jan decided she'd pushed the girl far enough. Time to change the subject.

"We've got about three thousand acres out here. Lease about a thousand more."

The rhythmic beat of their horses' hooves and the creaking of saddle leather became the only sounds. Jan rested her hands on her own saddle horn, eyes peeled for that bull. Daddy used to say he'd had her in the saddle the day she was born. It might've been true. Her earliest memories were sitting in front of her father in the saddle while he worked cattle. She could still remember the way he'd let her rest her little hands on his huge ones and guide the horse. She never felt more content and at peace than when she was riding.

She glanced at Roxi again, for a moment imagining what it would be like to teach her about horses and cattle the way her father had taught her and she and Keith had taught Trae. Something just felt right about having Roxi around. If only she could break through some of her walls.

"So . . . all this—" Roxi waved her hand out in front of her—"is yours?"

"Over six square miles of it."

"Wow."

"It's really not that big compared to some. Guy north of us has a spread that stretches across almost fifteen."

"What about those mountains over there? What are they?"

Jan stared at the beautiful Spanish Peaks, like she had every day for over fifty years. They'd had an early dusting of snow last week, and it hadn't melted off the upper elevations. From here, on the edge of their eastern pasture, you could see both peaks and several of the monstrous dike walls jutting from the mountains. She told Roxi how as a little girl, she used to daydream she was an eagle who could soar to the very top of one of those summits.

"How tall are they?"

"Highest is the West Peak. Clocks in at almost fourteen thousand feet. The East Peak is about a thousand feet lower." Jan rested her hands on the saddle horn. "My dad always used to say a week in Colorado would cure any atheist."

"What do you mean?"

Jan tipped her hat farther up her forehead. "Who can see that kind of beauty and not believe in God?"

Roxi went quiet on her again, and Jan wondered if she'd made a mistake in bringing up her faith. So many people these days bristled at the mention of God, and yet they were the ones who needed Him most. Jan would never purposely rile someone by talking about her beliefs, but she couldn't hide the most important aspect of her life either. She wasn't ashamed of it, but she didn't want to turn Roxi off. Something inside told her to take things slow and gentle with this girl.

"A lot of people," Roxi finally responded softly.

Jan hesitated to ask the question on the tip of her tongue, but it would be good to know where Roxi stood. "Are you one of those people?"

Keeping her eyes on the mountains, Roxi brushed away strands of hair that had fallen out of her ponytail. "I'm not sure."

"It'd take an awfully big coincidence for these mountains to just materialize on their own."

Roxi turned toward her. "If He does exist, then why can't He, just for once, cut me a break? Is that too much to ask?"

Jan just smiled. "Maybe He did. You're here, aren't you?"

Roxi's forehead wrinkled like she was trying to figure out if that made sense. So when she finally met Jan's eyes and smiled back, Jan realized it was the first time she'd seen any kind of happiness on the girl's face. She determined it wouldn't be the last.

Silence fell around them again, and Jan prayed for the right words. Nothing came, so she held her tongue. Maybe all she was meant to do was plant seeds in this girl's heart.

"I'm really sixteen," Roxi said quietly.

She didn't mention she'd already guessed as much. "I appreciate your telling me."

And apparently it was *all* Roxi would be telling her because the girl buttoned up after that. They spent the next hour searching for the bull. Any further talk was limited to Jan's riding tips, but that was okay with her. In time she'd learn what she needed to know to help this girl with whatever troubled her so much.

❧

After the confrontation with Dad last night, Abby had decided Christy was right. She did need to get away. So early the next morning she'd thrown her suitcase into the trunk of the car and took off following Christy's Honda and May's pickup. They formed a small caravan.

A few hours later, the outskirts of Elk Valley came into view. Not that there was a whole lot to see. They passed a garage with silver hubcaps hanging on its fence that looked like it had been servicing cars since the Depression. A shack selling "Rocky Mountain Treasures" was clearly targeting the tourists Christy said flocked here for the skiing up in Cuchara.

Abby leaned forward to see better out of the windshield. She had to admit those mountains were breathtaking. Probably only a couple of miles away, their serrated peaks cut at the blue sky. No wonder Christy came out here most weekends.

They drove through the small but civilized downtown section. The lampposts all sported blue flaglike banners that read, *Elk Valley: Celebrating 125 years.* Abby noted one older-model police cruiser in front of the station beside the post office. In a town this size, she bet they had only two full-time officers at most.

Her cell phone rocked out on the passenger seat. Abby scooped it up and flipped it open without checking caller ID. She and Christy had been talking back and forth the whole way.

"Yeah?"

"Want some coffee?" Christy asked.

"Do you even know me?"

"I told May you'd be sweeter with a little caffeine in you."

"Ha-ha."

"There's a nice coffee shop coming up. May's pulling in right now."

Ahead, Abby saw May's truck pull into a parking space on the street. "I see her."

She snapped the phone shut and managed to park a few cars down. Stepping out of her car, she stretched and took in a deep breath of the fresh, dry air. She met May and Christy on the sidewalk in front of The Perfect Blend coffee shop.

After the tension of last night, it felt good to relax in the sisters' company. At first Abby had wondered how the dynamics would work. After all, she *was* an outsider here. But the sisters made her feel comfortable and free to be herself. She didn't have to prove anything to these women, which was refreshing. They seemed to accept her for who she was. Caffeine addiction and all.

Inside, the guy behind the counter greeted May like they were old friends. May introduced him as the owner, Stan Barlowe.

"Welcome," he said. "What can I get you today?"

May ordered a medium house blend coffee and a plain egg bagel, Christy went for a large vanilla latte and a chicken salad sandwich, and Abby got her beloved red eye and a brownie. She quickly sidled past Christy to the register. "My treat," she said, plunking down her Visa.

They sat outside in the warm sun at one of the cast-iron tables with the big blue umbrellas.

"Think they have a twelve-step program for caffeine addicts?" Abby joked, then remembered Christy had mentioned going to meetings.

"If you need a sponsor, I'm your girl." Christy grinned.

May leaned back in her chair, and Abby noticed she was watching them both, probably assessing how they were dealing with their grief but not wanting to ask questions.

They spent a few minutes chatting, munching their treats and sipping their drinks. No one brought up Hunter, but Abby knew they were all thinking of him. Late at night lying in bed, she allowed herself to dwell on the fact that he was really gone. She'd never see her brother again. It was a realization that had almost broken her last night, and another reason she'd agreed to come down here with Christy. She certainly couldn't talk to Dad about it. He was too absorbed in his own loss to notice hers.

Walking back to the cars, Abby took in the street. She could see how some would call it charming. She was more of a city girl herself, needing a little more stimulation than beautiful scenery, but it was certainly a place she'd enjoy visiting.

She punched the unlock button on her key remote just as she noticed a man walk out of a shop close by, a stack of books reaching all the way to his chin.

"Is there a bookstore up there?" She pointed.

May threw her empty coffee cup inside the covered trash can. "That's Aaron's Book Exchange. He's been here for as long as I have."

"Used books?"

"And rare."

"He makes a living in this . . . ?" She was about to say "hick town" but caught herself.

"I know," Christy chimed in. "I wondered the same thing. Most of his stuff is general stock, but he does travel around. You wouldn't believe some of the stories I could tell you about book sales. I was at this one where a guy poured a box of books on top of another dealer's head because he took a book he wanted."

"That's why his hours are so crazy," May said.

"It's only him in there," Christy said. "A tough row to hoe, let me tell you. Probably wouldn't be here if it weren't for the Internet. Half his business comes in that way."

Abby opened the passenger door, reaching inside her glove compartment. She pulled out one of the flyers she'd made up and e-mailed to every bookstore within two hundred miles of the Barn. "I'll be right back. Gonna give him one of these." The flyer included a list of the most valuable titles stolen, a blurb about the store and Hunter, as well as all her contact information.

It couldn't hurt to get it in as many hands as possible.

29

THE STORM CAUGHT THEM BOTH BY SURPRISE. One minute Roxi was riding along beside Jan trying to follow all the riding tips she'd given her, like looking in the direction she wanted the horse to go and holding the reins as she would a baby bird. The next minute the sky above them was filled with dark gray, swirling clouds, the wind wrapping around them and pushing against their backs.

"We're gonna get wet," Roxi said, tilting her head up and feeling a drop of cold rain tap her chin. They'd ridden for so long she had no idea how far they'd traveled from the ranch house. She saw nothing but wilderness in every direction. Not a human being or house in sight. A field stretched before them, and massive evergreens stood guard on its edge at least a half mile away.

Jan's brow furrowed. "Think you're up for a lope?"

A lope? Roxi couldn't think of a suitable response. She wasn't really sure what a lope was but guessed it was something faster than what she would be comfortable with. Even though she'd started to relax over the miles they'd covered, she was still way out of her comfort zone. But of course she couldn't admit that to Jan.

"You just follow me."

Three more drops hit the top of Roxi's head. She took a deep breath.

"Wanna give it a try?" Jan's smile deepened the wrinkles around her eyes, and Roxi realized she'd do just about anything to win this woman's approval.

"I . . . guess."

She barely got the words out before the downpour hit, and the beat of a million raindrops hitting the hard ground overtook them. The rain became so heavy so fast, it snatched away the ounce of confidence she'd managed to muster up for Jan. All she wanted was to dismount and huddle under her horse.

"Let's go!" Jan yelled, and without any further discussion, she set her eyes forward, gave the horse a little kissing sound, and took off across the field.

Roxi wasn't sure which would be worse—racing after her or being left behind in the middle of nowhere. After several moments of hesitation, she gathered the nerve to urge Sally with a light touch of her heels. That's all it took. The mare shot forward, and Roxi held on to the horn for dear life, barely able to see through the rain pelting her face.

Somehow she made it to the edge of the field, still in the saddle. Jan was waiting for her with a proud smile. That's when Roxi realized where they were. Nestled in the trees was the old homestead cabin they'd visited yesterday. She hadn't even noticed it from across the field.

Jan dismounted and ran her horse to the small corral and lean-to shelter beside the cabin. With deft fingers she swiftly undid the buckles and clasps, then with one smooth motion slid the saddle and blanket from the horse's back. Leading the animal into the corral, she removed the bridle just as quickly.

By the time Roxi clumsily slid off Sally and Jan unsaddled and led Sally to the corral, they were both completely soaked. Grabbing their tack, they raced to the cabin. Jan unlocked the door and swung it open.

At first all Roxi saw was darkness. But as her eyes adjusted, a one-room cabin came into view. It was furnished with a table, stove, two cots, and a gas lantern sitting in the middle of the table.

"Saddle can go over here," Jan said, dropping hers in the corner of the room. Roxi placed her own next to Jan's. It was surprising how heavy they were, yet Jan had hoisted hers across her back and shoulder with practiced ease—an ease she exhibited in everything, it seemed.

Roxi wondered what she'd have to do to upset Jan's calm. With Irene she never knew when something she said or did would send the woman into silent-treatment mode with anger bubbling just below the surface, churning and twisting Roxi's stomach into knots. Jan seemed so steady.

"We've got some extra clothes in here," Jan said, striking a match and lighting the lantern as the rain continued to drum on the tin roof. "Let me just get the fire going in the stove, and then we'll change out of these wet things."

"What can I do?"

"There's some newspaper on that shelf there. Start wadding up a few pages."

Once a fire was burning and Jan was satisfied with its progress, she went to a chest in the corner and started pulling out shirts and pants. She held up a pair of jeans that were obviously sized for Keith. "We could both fit in these," she said with a grin and threw a different pair in Roxi's direction. "Here's some of mine. They'll be too big for you, but at least they'll be dry."

Roxi kicked off her boots and peeled away her own wet jeans. Jan's Wranglers were at least four inches too long in the legs and baggy everywhere else, but she was right. They were dry, and the only warmth to be found until the woodstove heated up.

"Take this, too." Jan handed her a flannel shirt.

Roxi pulled her soaked hoodie over her head, warding off a shiver. Exposing her arm, she knew Jan would see her scar again. It had turned an ugly purple, like it did whenever she got cold. Catching Jan's quick glance, Roxi said under her breath, "I fell out of a window."

A pause. "That's terrible."

She furiously buttoned up the flannel. "I was eight."

Roxi rubbed her hand up and down her sleeve. Even after so many years, this stupid scar always zoomed her right back to the awful memories of Mom's abandonment. She'd debated getting a tattoo to cover it up, but the thought of a needle piercing the tender scar had stopped her.

"People usually ask me about it the second they see it."

"I wouldn't like that." Jan rummaged through the two cabinets above the stove, producing a stove-top coffee percolator. In a few minutes they were both huddled around the fire sipping Jan's brew of Folgers from their mugs, just like they had yesterday morning outside on the cabin's porch.

For some reason, Roxi wouldn't have minded if Jan had asked her about the scar, even though she would have with anyone else. When she was with Jan, she felt oddly safe. Was this what having a mother was supposed to feel like? Before she realized what she was doing, she was telling Jan more than she'd ever told anyone.

"Mom wasn't home, and I was trying to close the blinds. I got up on this chair, and the next thing I knew I fell through the window. The glass cut my arm. I've got other scars too, but they're not as noticeable."

Her throat tightened, and she could barely get any more words out. At the hospital she'd been so frightened by the pain and all the masked doctors and nurses poking, washing, and asking a million questions. Then after they'd x-rayed and stitched her up, some woman had grilled her about Mom. Roxi had answered truthfully, only later realizing the woman had probably been with social services. If she'd lied that night, would she and Mom still be together?

The worst part was being alone in that dark hospital room, listening to the endless beeping of monitors. She'd silently cried until her sobs became pathetic whimpers.

"Mom never even visited me in the hospital."

"Oh, sweetheart, I'm so sorry."

"Not once."

"I can't even imagine what you must have gone through."

"They put me in a foster home after that."

And she still remembered that first one. The couple wasn't mean or anything, but they had four of their own children, always screaming for their attention. She had kept to herself and tried to stay out of trouble, but every time one of the other kids did something bad, they'd told the parents it was her. The couple always believed them. When the lady got pregnant with her fifth child, they'd sent Roxi back, ripping out a piece of her heart. It was like that with each new family. Nine in all. She didn't know how much of her heart she had left.

But the group homes were always the worst. The staff couldn't possibly keep track of everyone at all hours, and the kids knew it. If it was only one bully, Roxi was usually okay. She was tough and could defend herself. But when they ganged up on her . . .

"You never went back to your mother?"

She shook her head, pushing her chair away from the stove and standing. She'd already said too much. If she didn't stop blabbing now, she'd end up telling Jan everything.

Thankfully Jan didn't ask any more questions and got up herself. "I'll try and give Keith a call and let him know we're up here." She pulled out her cell phone. "Reception's spotty, but it might work."

"Shouldn't we be getting back?"

Jan opened the cabin door. The rain had stopped, and Roxi was surprised at how dark it had become.

"Not sure if that's happening tonight. I should've realized how late it was getting." Jan waved her hand toward the stove. "But that's why this place is stocked. We won't starve, we'll stay warm, and tomorrow we can head back bright and early."

"What about Keith?" *And Selah,* she almost added.

"He'll understand." Jan fooled around with the cell phone, walking out onto the porch. A minute later, Roxi could hear her talking to someone, so she must've gotten through. Unable to make out the conversation, she sat down again, running her fingers through her wet hair. What was she thinking, telling all that to Jan? Once Jan knew the truth, she'd probably be no different from Mom or Irene.

Roxi swallowed back the lump forming in her throat again. No matter what she did, she always ended up alone. And now she was more than alone. She was running from the law, a man was dead, and she felt as if her own finger had pulled the trigger. Would she ever be able to forget his pleading face? How could she keep this cancerous secret to herself?

She glanced outside at Jan, still on the phone. She wanted to tell her the truth so badly—which she could never do, right? She couldn't tell anyone. Juvie was ten times worse than any of the group homes.

Jan walked back inside a minute later. She held up the cell phone. "It took a few tries, but I finally got through. He said to tell you Selah was fine and eating like a horse."

Roxi smiled.

"And the bull we were looking for?" Jan shook her head. "Believe it or not, this evening he wandered back on his own. Keith caught him right near the house. Don't know what he was doing the past two weeks."

"So we're spending the night here."

"Is that okay with you?" Jan pulled a pot from the cabinet. "We can use flashlights to see our way back tonight if you'd rather, but that'd be tricky. I think it might be better to stay. We can hightail it at dawn and not lose more than an hour or two."

She was still shaken from her babbling, so Roxi pasted on a fake smile and offered to help make dinner. That turned out to be corned beef, baked beans, and corn bread. Within a half hour the little cabin was filled with the delicious aroma, and by the time dinner was ready, Roxi was starving.

Jan mixed the beef into the beans like a goulash, and with a piece of corn bread Roxi was surprised at how good it tasted. For dessert they drizzled maple syrup over more corn bread. After cleaning up and feeding the horses, they were both tired enough for bed. Scooting their cots closer to the stove, they climbed into the olive green Army surplus sleeping bags Jan said Keith had bought at an auction.

Maybe to some a cot would be uncomfortable. But after sleeping on the pavement, Roxi was still thankful for a roof over her head. She snuggled down into the bag, pulling the fabric to her chin.

The only light came from the glowing embers in the stove, and for a brief moment Roxi was scared. Even when she'd gone camping with Irene and Diego, there were usually other campers nearby. Out here there was no one. Just the horses, Jan, and who knew what else. Cougars and bears probably roamed these mountains. Jan would know what to do to keep them safe, wouldn't she?

Roxi closed her eyes, then quickly opened them again, preferring the minuscule light from the stove to the complete darkness of sleep just yet. She'd been having more nightmares about the manager, and she wasn't ready to face them.

From across the room a flashlight clicked on, and Jan played with her fingers in front of the light until they formed shadowy figures on the wall.

Roxi pulled herself up onto her elbow. "What are you doing?"

"Haven't you ever tried this?"

A bird appeared on the wall, flapping its wings.

"Yeah, like when I was four." Roxi couldn't help but laugh at the sight of Jan acting like a schoolgirl. "Only I could never even do a rabbit."

"Oh, that's easy." With a few twists of her fingers, Jan created a perfectly formed bunny and made it hop across the wall.

"Show-off."

Jan laughed, and Roxi decided she liked the sound of it. Not high-pitched or cackly like some women. It was a laugh that came easily, like she'd had practice perfecting it.

"Back when Trae was small, we'd bring him up here as often as we could," Jan said. "When you ranch, you can't take many vacations, so it was our way to get away for an evening."

Roxi rolled onto her back again. She let her arm hang over the cot's edge, her fingers grazing the rough-hewn wood floor. "What was Trae like?"

"People used to say he looked like me, but he acted like Keith." Jan flicked the flashlight off, and the cabin went silent again for a moment. "His dream was to start this outfitter business and guide people through parts of the ranch and even up into the national forest. They'd camp, fish, and ride. It would've been a way to make ends meet when cattle prices aren't what they should be."

"He was seventeen when he . . . ?"

Jan sighed. "Yeah."

She wanted to know more but realized Jan might not want to talk about it. "I'm sorry; I shouldn't have brought it up."

"No, it's good for me to talk about him. It's how I keep his memory alive."

"Did he ever make you mad?"

"Any mother will tell you children are a gift from God, but they can sometimes act like the spawn of Satan." Jan chuckled. "I'm kidding. Trae was a good boy. But when he was sixteen, he bought a motorcycle behind my back. Keith knew about it, but neither of them bothered to tell me. When I found out, I was livid, and I don't get mad easily."

"About a motorcycle?"

"That's what *he* said." Roxi couldn't see Jan's face anymore, but she could hear a smile in her voice. "Mothers and motorcycles just don't mix well."

"They are kinda cool."

"Not you, too!" Jan laughed again. "I did let him keep it, but I made him swear not to take it anywhere but the back roads, and never above the speed limit."

"When he died, how did you . . . you know . . . ?"

"Cope?"

"I'd have wanted to die," Roxi said.

"I never thought *anything* would ever make me think like that, but I went through that phase. There's really nothing that can prepare you for the news that your only child is dead. Really, I didn't handle it well those first few weeks. I lost like thirty pounds and could barely make myself get out of bed. But then one day while I was out riding, I had this, I guess you could say, *experience*."

Jan was quiet for a moment. When she continued, her voice was softer. "It was like in a flash I actually saw into heaven. I saw Trae up there strong and full of life, smiling his goofy smile and having the time of his life. And the most amazing thing is that I really think I saw Jesus. He was walking with Trae, laughing and clapping him on the back like a big brother."

Roxi stayed still on her cot, staring at the ceiling. What Jan was saying sounded crazy, and yet there was something about the awe in the woman's voice that made Roxi realize this wasn't some silly story here. Jan really had experienced . . . something.

"It was the quickest of flashes, but it made me realize my grief wasn't doing me or Keith—or anyone—one lick of good. Trae was in heaven. Even if he *could* come back, he wouldn't. In fact, if anything, I should've been envious he'd gotten there before me. I realized Trae isn't in my past. He's in my future.

"After that I got closer to God than I'd been my whole life," Jan said. "It's like I saw Him in a whole new light. As my friend. My Father. The only One who could bring me through something as terrible as losing Trae."

Roxi tucked her arms into the sleeping bag. Was God really like that?

"Mind if I read a little from the Bible before we go to bed?" Jan shone her flashlight on a small black book in her hand. "Helps me get to sleep."

Roxi didn't mind, which surprised her. "No, that's fine." She closed her eyes then, the only sound the crinkling of pages.

"'He who dwells in the shelter of the Most High,'" Jan softly read, "'will rest in the shadow of the Almighty. I will say of the Lord, "He is my refuge and my fortress, my God, in whom I trust." Surely he will save you from the fowler's snare and from the deadly pestilence.'"

Roxi felt her body relax as she listened. The words didn't make a lot of sense, like the psalm Gordon had told her about. But there was something strangely calming about them. As Jan read, she felt herself drift toward sleep.

"'You will not fear the terror of night, nor the arrow that flies by day, nor the pestilence that stalks in the darkness, nor the plague that destroys at midday.'"

"You will not fear."

Was that even possible?

Jan quietly read on for a few more minutes. Then Roxi heard the flashlight click off and a light thump—Jan's setting the book on the floor. As she floated between awake and asleep, she heard Jan whispering. She must've thought Roxi had already fallen asleep. Barely able to make out the words, one sentence followed Roxi into the land of dreams:

"Lord, help me show her how much You love her. . . ."

❦

Diego turned off the steaming shower water and quickly toweled himself off. It had been nice to enjoy the warmth. With these cooler nights and Ma keeping the poorly insulated RV at frigid temperatures to save on propane, he was glad for the days they stayed at a campground with hookups. Forget dry camping. He'd take an unlimited supply of hot water and electricity any day.

As he quickly slipped into his jeans and knit pullover, another stab of worry hit him about Roxi. Had she found somewhere to stay? He rubbed the back of his neck. She was stupid to run off with nothing but her pack. Why hadn't she told him? He could've at least slipped her some cash.

Diego hung his towel over the top of the shower. He stood there staring at himself in the bathroom mirror, disgusted with the guy looking back. She'd left so suddenly. Without even talking to him.

After what he'd done, no doubt Roxi couldn't stand to look at him any more than he could stand to look at himself.

He rested his hand on the closed door separating the bathroom and back bedroom from the kitchen and living area. Ma was out there on her computer mapping their next route. Was this how it was going to be for the rest of his life? Every time he saw a police car, would he think they were coming for him? Diego studied the dark circles under his eyes. He hadn't slept for more than an hour straight since it happened. He hadn't told Ma, but now he kept the gun beside him under the extra pillow. When he'd wake from his nightmares, he'd sometimes lie there imagining what a bullet to his head would feel like. Maybe that would be better than life in prison.

With a deep breath, Diego slid open the door and put on his best game face. No way would he let on what he'd been thinking. He had to stay strong. If not for himself, then for Ma. She'd given up everything to support him, and he couldn't just abandon her.

Ma held up her hand when he walked over to the dinette, where she sat with her laptop open on the table. Her cell phone was pressed to her ear. He couldn't make out the words, but he could hear the tone of a woman's voice on the other end.

"Thanks for letting me know," Ma finally said after a moment. "I have no idea why they were there. Did they leave a card or something? Okay, I'll give them a call as soon as I get off with you and see what this is all about. Let me just find a pen."

Diego grabbed a pencil from the cabinet above the sofa and handed it to her. She took it without looking at him.

"I'm ready." Ma scribbled on the scrap of paper. She thanked the voice, then flipped the cell phone shut.

Diego marched to the fridge and pulled out a bottle of spring water. "Who was that?"

"Sheryl Landon."

"What's she calling for? Everything okay?" Sheryl was their next-door neighbor, and when they were away, she kept an eye on the house.

His mother twisted around in her seat. "A police car was in our driveway today."

Diego tried to keep his voice steady, but it cracked anyway. "Does she know why?"

"The cop was asking for you." Ma's piercing green eyes met his. "By *name*."

Cold fear spread across his chest. How did they know his name?

"Did she . . . say why they were there?"

"They didn't tell her," Ma snapped.

Diego took a deep breath and set his water on the counter unopened. "What are we going to do?"

"You know why this is happening, don't you?"

He opened his mouth to speak, but Ma cut him off.

"It's *her*." Ma paced to the front of the RV, all of six feet away, and then came back to him, pointing at his chest. "She told someone."

"Ma, I don't—"

"She betrayed us. There's no other explanation."

Diego found himself defending Roxi. "She wouldn't do that."

His mother didn't answer. She set herself down at the dinette table again and started tapping at the laptop.

Grabbing the water bottle with a shaking hand, he didn't wait to hear her response. He bounded out of the RV, slamming the door behind himself, half-expecting to see a police cruiser's lights flashing through the campground and coming straight for him. He couldn't deal with this. No way.

Outside he unscrewed the lid and chugged down half of it in one shot. He couldn't let Ma see how this whole thing was just about killing him. What would happen if the cops tracked them down? Guys like him had been tried as adults before. Would he end up behind some steel door, never to see the light of day again? If only he could go back and relive that night. He'd never have brought the gun. Or tried to steal from the store in the first place. He would've stood up to Ma and refused.

How could he have *done* it? He'd never intended to hurt anybody, just scare the guy enough to stay put so they could leave.

Diego balled up his fist, wanting to hit something. He felt like a mouse in a room full of cats. He could run for only so long before one of them would catch him.

30

Shortly after dawn, Jan and Roxi returned to the main house. Jan set the girl right to work chopping wood. The supply had been dwindling and needed to be replenished before winter. It was a job Dad used to give Jan—one that built endurance, character, and calluses. She smiled to herself. Roxi would sleep well tonight.

After a quick stop inside to get a pot roast started in the slow cooker, Jan found Keith repairing stalls in the calving shed. Holding two nails between his lips like tiny metal cigarettes, he still managed a smile when he saw her.

"Everything go okay?" Jan asked.

Keith plucked the nails from his mouth and gave her a hug. "Yep. How 'bout you?"

She took a second to respond. Even though she was glad Roxi had opened up to her, she hadn't enjoyed hearing how much the girl had suffered in her young life. Jan wouldn't exactly call her own life sheltered, but out here in ranch country, family was everything. Many farm and ranch families still clung to the last vestiges of a time gone by, honoring the traditions of loyalty and respect everyone else had thrown to the wind. That's the way Jan had grown up and the way they'd raised Trae. Family stuck by each other. Parents didn't dump their kids when the going got tough, and the kids didn't dump their parents when they got old.

"The more time I spend with that girl," Jan finally said, "the more I think God's placed her with us for a reason."

"Why? What happened?"

She took a deep breath, then let it out slowly. "First of all, she's sixteen, not eighteen."

Keith stopped, hammer in hand. Jan knew what he was thinking because she'd been pondering the same thing. If Roxi was a minor, someone must be responsible for her. How obligated were they to find that person?

"We could call around," he said.

"And send her back to what?" Jan paced up and down the walkway between the stalls. In a flurry of words she told Keith everything she'd found out about Roxi, from her childhood accident to her mother's abandonment. When she finished, Keith could only shake his head.

"That'd mess up any kid," he said.

"If half of what she said is true, then she's better off *without* her mother. And I just can't imagine turning her over to some stranger. Who knows where she'd end up."

"A lot of foster parents really care about their kids."

"I know. But moving around like that . . . you said it yourself: it's gotta mess a kid up."

Keith rested his forearm on the top edge of a stall, still holding the hammer. "We've gotta find the truth."

"How could anyone just leave their little girl alone like that?"

"Sounds like she could've been strung out. Maybe she didn't know what she was doing."

"She should have."

Keith looked away from her, pounding in another nail. "I've got a confession to make."

Jan raised an eyebrow.

"While you were gone, I . . . went through her things."

"What?"

"Not before thinking about it for a long time."

Jan sighed. "Hon, you shouldn't have done that."

"I know." His brow furrowed. "But we gotta get to the bottom of this."

"She trusted us, Keith."

"Which is why I've been feeling horrible all morning." He stepped away from his work, slipping the hammer into his tool belt. "But she might need help. You know how kids are—they wait to ask for it until it's too late. And she's here in our house."

"Do I want to know what you found?"

"Actually, I'm not sure what to make of it."

Outside, Jan could hear Roxi's ax chopping away, but still she lowered her voice. "What did you find?"

"Two old books. And a Bible."

"A Bible?"

"Looked like a Gideon."

Maybe Roxi was searching more than Jan had first realized. She was glad she'd taken the time to share with her a little about God.

"Here's the thing," Keith said. "Those other books. They have *first edition* written on the inside of 'em with pencil, like what you'd find in a bookstore."

"She bought them maybe?"

"With what money? You said she had nothing. And I just have a feeling they aren't school copies, you know? They look like original classics, and usually those are worth something, right?"

Jan shrugged. Sometimes she and Keith watched *Antiques Roadshow*. A couple of episodes had featured old books, but neither of them knew much about that sort of thing. She couldn't remember the titles they'd shown.

Keith pulled a piece of paper from his pocket and handed it to her. "There was also a business card from a used and rare bookstore in her wallet. I copied down the info."

Jan studied the card. *Christy Williams. Wasn't that the name of May Williams's sister?*

Lifting his Stetson, Keith wiped his forehead with the back of his arm. "I'm going into town to pick up our order at Walker's. Maybe I can talk her into coming with me and you can try the numbers while we're gone."

"I guess we should."

"Either that or sit her down and make her give us some real answers."

Suddenly Jan felt uneasy. What if she'd been wrong about Roxi? What if she really had stolen those books? What else would she steal? "We don't even know her last name, do we?"

"There's a lot we don't know about her."

❧

Roxi hadn't spent much time alone with Keith, so when he asked her to come with him into town, she hesitated. She'd finally gotten comfortable being with Jan, but her husband was still an enigma. He didn't talk as much as his wife, making it hard for Roxi to get a good read on him. She agreed to go anyway and ran upstairs to clean up.

After all, she was living under the same roof with the guy. If she was going to do this job well so they'd keep her around, she needed to know what he expected of her.

That's when she got the idea. Closing the bedroom door behind herself, she quickly crossed the floor and dug her backpack out from under the bed. Aaron's Book Exchange had been closed before, but maybe it would be open today.

A couple of minutes and a quick shower later, she burst into the kitchen.

Keith was washing his hands in the sink, dirty suds dripping off his fingers. "Ready to go?"

"Yeah." She hoped he wouldn't ask why she was bringing her backpack with her.

Roxi let Selah outside to do her business, then sat down with her on the porch stoop waiting for Keith. She rubbed the dog's ears and neck, Selah's goofy expression cracking her up. When she scratched a certain spot right behind her ears, Selah's back leg thumped involuntarily like she was scratching it herself.

A minute later Keith met them outside, and Selah actually wagged her tail when she saw him.

"Told you she was warming up to me." He petted the pup gently on the head.

Roxi had always been told dogs were good judges of character. If Selah liked this guy, then she could give him a shot too. After closing her in the house, much to Selah's disappointment, Roxi followed Keith to his green truck.

"What are we picking up?" she asked once they were heading down the long, winding driveway. How in the world had she slept through all these bumps when Jan first brought her here?

"Feed, fence posts, some salt blocks. Should load us down."

She decided the best way to ask her next question was to keep it as low-key as possible. "Would it be all right if you dropped me off at the coffee shop in town?"

"You one of those four-dollar-latte kind of girls?"

"Not really. I like plain coffee."

Keith laughed. "I think we can swing that."

They spent most of the drive in silence, and Roxi couldn't help wondering what Keith was thinking about her. Jan chose to pick her up off the highway, but Keith hadn't been given a choice. As he kept his eyes on the road, she tried to study him. Graying stubble dotted his chin, and leathery skin crinkled around his eyes and mouth. Wearing that soiled Stetson and maroon bandanna tied loosely around his Adam's apple made him look like he could've walked out of a John Wayne movie.

Then Roxi found herself staring at his beefy hands wrapped around the steering wheel. With surprise she realized he was missing a finger. Where the ring finger on his right hand should have been was a short, half-inch stump. She quickly looked away.

"Got it tangled in a rope," Keith said. "Cow took off, and so did my finger."

She winced.

"Good one to lose, though. Doesn't affect me much."

"Guess I don't have to ask if it hurt."

"Not as much as you'd think, right away. But it hurt like the dickens within about sixty seconds. Real messy, too."

Roxi couldn't help a grimace, and Keith laughed.

"Can't wait to see you deliver a calf," he said. "Talk about messy."

"Deliver a calf?"

"Next spring."

Was he implying what she thought he was? He actually expected her to be around in a couple of months?

"Nothing like holding a life in your hands," Keith said.

"I can barely chop wood," she muttered. *And my legs are so sore from riding, I can hardly walk.*

"You're doing just fine."

"You really think so?" The question came out before she could stop it, and she wished she could pull it back. She didn't need to put any doubts in this guy's head.

But Keith just nodded. "You're not afraid of hard work. That's half the battle right there."

Roxi leaned back in her seat, staring at the fence zipping by outside the truck window. Was Jan right? Could God have brought her to this ranch? She hadn't considered the possibility until Jan brought it up. One thing she did know: if Jan hadn't helped her, she probably would've ended up in even more trouble.

Glancing at Keith, she tried to imagine what it would've been like to have him as her father. It was hard to picture. The only men she'd known growing up were Mom's various boyfriends. Some were worse than others, but she never would've wanted to call any of them Dad. What had it been like for Trae to have these parents? Had he known how lucky he was?

Before she knew it, they were driving into Elk Valley, and Roxi pulled her backpack onto her lap. The last time she'd seen these streets, she was drowning in desperation. Had it been only four days?

Keith pulled up in front of The Perfect Blend coffee shop. "I'll pick you up in a half hour, okay?"

"I'll be here."

"Oh, almost forgot." Keith dug into his pocket and pulled out his wallet. He peeled out a five and handed it to her with a wink. "For that coffee. You've earned it this morning."

She smiled, then walked inside the shop, waving at Keith over her shoulder. She intended to walk out again the second he pulled away from the curb, but as she was about to make her exit, someone called her name.

"Roxi?"

She spun around.

The guy behind the counter broke into a huge grin, quickly walking toward her. Oh, terrific. It was the owner, Stan What's-His-Name, the only other person in this town who suspected she was a runaway. Before she could turn to leave, he grabbed her hand and started pumping it, that grin still plastered on his face.

"It's great to see you again," he said. "How are you?"

"Okay."

"You find a job?"

"I'm working on a ranch nearby." She felt like rubbing his nose in the fact that she *could* get a job without his dumb references and permanent address, but she knew he hadn't meant anything personal by refusing to hire her—even though it had felt like it.

"That's terrific. Which one?"

"Lonely River Ranch."

"Keith and Jan Mercer's place?"

She nodded.

"Great people," Stan said. "Come in about once a month. Usually order large French roast drips with room for cream."

"You actually remember what they order?"

"And you like my house blend." He was already reaching for a cup. "Black."

"Pretty good."

He tapped his head. "A gift."

Roxi edged up to the counter. She hadn't planned on ordering anything, but who could refuse a good cup of coffee? This time she had money to pay for it, and buying something would keep her from having to lie to Keith.

"Sorry it didn't work out for you here," Stan said. "No hard feelings, I hope."

"It's okay." Roxi glanced at the drink menu, leaving it at that. Everything was handwritten with colored chalk, little drawings of coffee cups decorating the corners.

Stan slid her coffee toward her, lifting his hand when she tried to give him the five. "This one's on me."

"The last one was on you."

"Hey, don't look a gift horse in the mouth. You can pay next time."

She took the coffee. Keith would be picking her up again soon, and she needed to get moving.

"I'm real glad things are going well," Stan said.

"Is that bookstore up the street open today?"

He wiped the counter with a wet cloth. "I think so."

"Thanks," Roxi said, and before he could ask her any questions, she was out the door and walking up the street toward Aaron's Book Exchange, sipping her coffee as she went.

That storm last night had brought cooler weather, and she was glad for her jean jacket. The warm coffee cup felt good in her hands. When she got to the bookstore and saw the orange Yes, We're Open sign, she breathed a sigh of relief. Surely this guy would know enough to give her an idea of these books' value. She didn't need to sell them right now since she had a job, but it couldn't hurt to have a security blanket. If this thing with Jan and Keith didn't work out, at least she'd have something to fall back on.

When she stepped inside the bookstore, a bell above her head jingled, and she was met with the musty book smell she might've enjoyed in a different life. All it did today was remind her of all the rare books she'd stolen with Irene and Diego.

She spotted who she guessed was Aaron standing on one of those rolling ladders that librarians or museum curators used—the ones that reached to the very top of the ceiling. He reminded her more of an old professor than a book dealer with his white hair, spectacles, and tweed coat with leather patches on the elbows.

Roxi carefully watched him for a moment. He took the dust jacket off a book and examined the blue boards beneath. His glasses sitting on the very edge of his beaklike nose, he was the type they could've easily scammed. She'd probably get the job of distracting him, asking about a book way in the back, something he couldn't answer without coming to see for himself. Then when he wasn't looking, Irene and Diego would slip something from the front display or a shelf near the door. The guy wouldn't know what hit him.

"May I help you, miss?"

Snapping out of her thoughts, Roxi rubbed on her practiced teen-girl-needing-help smile as Professor climbed down from his ladder.

She cleared her throat. "My grandmother died recently, and I found these books in her attic. I was hoping to find out if they're worth anything."

Professor came to the front of the store and planted himself in a rickety old desk chair behind the three-foot bookshelves he'd boxed around himself to form a makeshift cubicle. It seemed to double as a crude checkout counter, allowing books to be displayed on the outside for customers to see, with more stacked on top. A computer sat on a small table beside him, and the cash register found its place on top of one of the bookshelves.

"Let's see what you have," Professor said in a bored tone, leaning back in his chair and surveying her over his glasses.

She removed the books from her backpack, carefully peeling away the plastic bags she'd been using as protection. Handing them both to Professor Aaron, she watched his face for a reaction. He slid his glasses even farther down his nose, first studying the C. S. Lewis title.

Roxi knew little about rare books in comparison to Diego and

Irene, but she could usually pick out titles worth taking. *The Lion, the Witch and the Wardrobe* she guessed would be worth at least two hundred. A bookstore would be able to offer only a third of that, at most. She might be able to pocket fifty—one night in a decent hotel room.

It was a good sign when Aaron slid his chair to the computer and started tapping at the keyboard. He pulled up the home page of AbeBooks.com, a popular book search site, but she couldn't see his search results.

Sliding back over to her, he studied *The Great Gatsby*. She wasn't sure, but she thought she saw his eyebrows rise when he looked at the copyright page and checked under the dust jacket. He was obviously looking for the various points that the clerk had told her determined a first edition.

Aaron took another slide across the floor to his computer, this time taking the book with him. In typical book dealer fashion, he was handling the volume like it was made of glass, only opening the binding a crack, peeking in, and cradling it in his hands. That's another thing Diego had taught her. If real estate agents chanted, "Location, location, location," book dealers chanted, "Condition, condition, condition." A book could be slashed in value from something as little as tears in the dust jacket or if the hinges were cracked.

"These were your grandmother's books, you say?" Aaron asked, still staring at the computer.

"She loved to read," Roxi said. The grandmother thing was a good spiel she'd heard Diego use when he'd sold some of their finds.

Swiveling around to a shelf beside the computer that was accessible only to him, Aaron pulled a well-worn book with yellow Post-it notes sticking out of the top. She couldn't see what it was, but she guessed it was one of the reference books dealers usually kept close at hand. Author bibliographies sometimes had this information too, and Irene had told her these pricey books could pay for themselves with one rare find. Aaron thumbed through the book. When he found the page he was looking for, he ran his finger under the words as he read and reread the page, checking back with the *Gatsby* repeatedly.

Roxi desperately wanted to know what he was finding, but she didn't dare ask and appear too anxious.

After an eternity, Aaron scooted his chair back to where she stood, setting her books on the counter between them. "Well," he said.

She waited. His eyes were definitely brighter than when she'd first come in.

"Your grandmother had good taste," he said, finally pushing his glasses up on his nose.

"Really?"

"As far as I can tell here, these are both first editions." Aaron leaned back in his chair again, crossing his legs and picking up a pencil. He twirled it between his fingers. "I'm going to be honest with you here. These are both extremely rare."

Roxi did her best to keep her face expressionless. If she acted too eager or stupid, he would offer less. There were a lot of sharks in this business.

"The Lewis here—" he picked it up and glanced at the copyright page again—"even without the dust jacket is worth anywhere from five to six hundred, with the right buyer of course. But that's not the best news." A hint of a smile played at the edge of Aaron's mouth. "I had to do a little research, but first editions of *The Great Gatsby* are *extremely* rare. And with the dust jacket . . ." He leaned forward. "We're talking at least twenty-five grand, possibly thirty or forty."

Suddenly she felt both elated and nauseous. No wonder Irene had insisted they go back to the store.

"Now, needless to say, I can't buy these from you outright," Aaron went on. "What would you say about consigning them?"

This was *not* what she'd expected. Books that valuable would get people talking. Now she knew why the *Gatsby* had made the news.

"I was thinking sixty-forty," Aaron said.

She swallowed down the lump of fear forming in her throat. Not to mention the fact that she'd probably have to show him ID she didn't have.

"Does that sound reasonable?"

"I . . . don't know if I want to sell them."

He blinked away the dollar signs in his eyes. "Oh."

"They were my grandmother's, after all."

"Think of it this way: you could buy something really special with that money to remember her by."

What had she been thinking? Roxi reached for the books.

"Eighty-twenty?" Aaron picked up the *Gatsby*, reverently turning it over in his hands. "I can't believe I'm actually holding this."

"Please give it back."

"Are you sure you don't want to sell them?"

"Yes." She quickly rewrapped the Lewis in her plastic grocery bag.

Aaron looked like she was walking away with his winning lottery ticket. She had to give him credit for not trying to rip her off. He could've just offered her a hundred bucks and been done with it. A clueless teen would've left the store screaming with joy at the huge payoff.

"Here's my business card." Aaron flipped one out of his shirt pocket and practically glued it to her hand. "If you change your mind, you know where to find me. What a pleasure to have seen this. If I'm not open, you can call this number or e-mail me anytime. I'll remember you."

Great.

Roxi stuffed both novels into her pack, nodded her thanks, then practically ran out of the store. When Keith picked her up at the curb five minutes later, she was still shaken.

"Are you okay?"

On went the fake smile. "Yeah, sure."

"You look upset."

"I'm fine."

Keith didn't seem to buy it, but he dropped the subject. "Hop in."

She did, stuffing her backpack under the seat. It felt ten times heavier now.

31

With Selah at her feet, Jan double-clicked the Firefox browser icon on her computer. She was online in seconds. They'd only recently gotten high-speed Internet access, so it still surprised her to see what used to take minutes now happen in the blink of an eye.

Her fingers hesitated over the keyboard. Did she really want to do this? It would be a lot easier to believe what she wanted to about Roxi. But that wouldn't exactly help the girl, would it? If there was something going on, Jan needed to know.

Without letting herself think anymore, she punched in the Web site Keith had copied from the bookstore's business card. It loaded in seconds. In the center of the home page was a picture of the store—a huge, four-story stone barn. There was a one-story addition with a porch on the side where its main doors were. Smoke curled from a chimney. A few stray patches of snow sat on the porch steps. She could imagine bibliophiles flocking to this place.

Jan read a little about the store's history, how it had been founded forty years ago by a man named Robert Dawson. Then she pulled up Google to see what other people were saying. She typed *Dawson's Book Barn* in the text box and hit Search.

The first result stopped her cold:

Booked to Die? Manager of Famous Book Barn Found Dead in Store

The link took her to a national newspaper's Web site. Dated last Thursday, the article reported how Hunter Dawson, the store manager and son of the owner, had been shot to death in his own store. The authorities suspected a robbery gone bad, and over fifty thousand dollars' worth of inventory was missing. Jan sat on the edge of her chair as the piece went on about the rare books stolen, mentioning one book in particular:

Among the missing books is a rare first edition of F. Scott Fitzgerald's *The Great Gatsby*. Highly collectible, the book made national news earlier this month when Dawson's Book Barn came into possession of the title. Found in a forgotten box of books donated by a local gentleman cleaning his attic, the *Gatsby*, worth anywhere from $30,000 to $45,000, sports the especially rare first state dust jacket in which Jay Gatsby's name was accidentally misprinted with a lowercase *j*.

Jan leaned closer to the computer monitor. Wasn't one of Roxi's . . . ? She grabbed Keith's paper again. He'd written both titles at the very top, and something twisted in the pit of her stomach when she read: *The Great Gatsby, The Lion, the Witch and the Wardrobe.*

How had . . . ?

What were the chances of Roxi, a scrawny teen girl for crying out loud, being involved in this crime? Even if she did have one of these stolen books, it didn't mean she had been involved. She could've gotten it from someone else. But why did the girl have the business card from Dawson's Book Barn? There had to be an explanation. Jan truly hoped there was.

She picked up the phone and punched in the bookstore's number. Maybe Christy knew Roxi and could explain everything.

On the sixth ring a man answered.

"Dawson's Book Barn," he said, sounding out of breath.

"Is Christy Williams available?"

"She isn't here. We're closed."

"Is there any way I can contact her?"

"Listen, we've talked to enough reporters."

"I'm not a reporter; I just . . ." She faltered for a moment, unsure how much she should say. "It's important."

"Try her cell phone." He rattled off a number, and Jan scrambled for a pen.

"Thanks, I really—"

The line clicked before she could finish, but Jan didn't care. She punched in the cell phone number without skipping a beat. It immediately rolled into voice mail, and she decided not to leave a message. It would be hard enough to explain why she was calling in person. She wasn't risking saying the wrong thing on someone's voice mail.

Jan returned the phone to its cradle, letting out a long breath. *Oh, Roxi, what have you done?*

❦

When Abby and Christy walked into the ranch house kitchen, May met them with Abby's cell phone. She held it out to her like it was a dirty sock.

"This thing has been shrieking and beeping for the past twenty minutes."

Abby playfully punched Christy's shoulder. "I knew I should've brought it with me." It had been Christy's idea for them to leave their technology behind for a few hours and enjoy the peace and tranquility of the mountain air. Christy had wanted to show her around the ranch, and they'd spent the better part of the afternoon walking the property.

Abby glanced at her cell phone, and sure enough, the tiny envelope indicating she had a voice mail sat on the screen. She dialed in.

"You have one new message. To play your—"

She jabbed the 1 key. The message she heard rocked her to the core.

Immediately she tried to return the call, but the phone on the other end just rang. She let out a curse, and May and Christy looked at her.

"Was it important?" Christy asked.

She stuffed the phone into her pocket and dove for her coat and car keys. "That was the guy from the bookstore here in town I gave the flyer to." She bolted for the door. "Someone just tried to sell him a first edition of *The Great Gatsby*."

❧

"Hey, wait!" Abby slammed her car door and ran across the street. They'd caught the bookstore owner outside the shop right as he was closing up.

When he heard her yell, he pivoted, eyes wide, still clutching his keys.

"We have to talk to you!" She was on the sidewalk in three more strides, Christy right behind her. "You left me a voice mail. I'm Abby Dawson. I tried to call you back, but no one answered."

Aaron's shoulders relaxed. "Yes, yes."

"Who was it? Where are they?"

Pocketing his keys, Aaron zipped up his blue nylon jacket. "Unfortunately, I didn't remember your flyer until *after* she left."

"She?"

"A young girl. Probably in her teens."

Abby and Christy exchanged looks. The age of the girl Christy saw with Irene and Diego Tonelli the day Hunter died.

"Where is she now?"

The guy shook his head. "I don't know. I'm sorry."

"Please tell us exactly what happened," Christy said. "Are you sure it was a first edition *with* the dust jacket?"

"Oh, most certainly." Aaron's eyes lit up. "It was a wonderful copy too. Only a few small chips. Beautiful."

Christy shook her head, glancing at Abby. "Sounds like ours."

"This girl—what did she say?"

"Her grandmother died." Aaron nodded while he spoke as if to help himself remember. "And she wanted to know how much her books were worth. Had another one as well. *The Lion, the Witch and the Wardrobe* by C. S. Lewis. Also a first. I offered to sell them on consignment, but she didn't go for it. Seemed a little flustered, but who wouldn't be after finding out they held a small fortune in their hands."

Abby turned toward Christy, racking her brain for what other titles had been stolen. "Did we have that second title?"

"I think so."

They could check the list later, but right now she needed every bit of information this guy could remember. Whoever this girl was, she couldn't be far. This wasn't a big town. Someone else had to have seen something.

"Did she give you her name?"

"No."

"Have you ever seen her before?"

Aaron shook his head just as a shrill cell phone ring cut through the air.

"It's mine," Christy said, fishing out her phone and checking the display. Abby saw her brow furrow as she reluctantly stepped away to take the call.

Abby didn't miss a beat with Aaron. She was so close to a breakthrough in this case she could feel it. "What did she look like?"

"Brownish hair, a few freckles."

"When did she leave?"

"An hour or two ago." He shifted his weight. "I heard about the murder on the news. You really think these books were stolen from that store?"

"You didn't see a car by any chance?"

The guy gave her another head shake. "Wish I did."

Christy was still talking on the phone behind them, and when Abby caught the words *books* and *Gatsby*, she approached her.

"Who is it?" Abby mouthed, but Christy held up her hand, listening intently to whoever was on the other end. By the look on her face, Abby knew something was definitely brewing.

"I think that would be a good idea," Christy finally said into the phone. "We'll be right over."

"What's up?" Abby asked the second she hung up. She wasn't sure what she saw in Christy's expression. Disappointment? Worry?

Even Aaron was leaning forward, waiting to hear her response.

"The girl who tried to sell you those books?" Christy sighed. "I know where she is."

32

ROXI STARTED IN AGAIN on the wood pile as soon as she and Keith got back. She was finally getting the hang of how to set the wood up and let loose with the ax. At first she had to concentrate on not chopping into her own leg if she swung wrong, but after a while she got into the rhythm.

The wood was dry, and it sometimes split in half with her first swing. Most of the time she got the ax stuck in the log and had to bang the wood down onto the stump they used as a base to break the ax through.

After an hour of chopping, she was really feeling it in her shoulders. In a way she was glad for the monotony and the physical pain. It took her mind off the books. Somehow she'd managed to calm down on the ride home, but worry was weaving back into her thoughts.

Roxi wiped her sweaty forehead with the back of her sleeve. She glanced out at the fields where some cattle and horses were grazing. Back when she was little, she used to think every new foster family was going to adopt her. At night she'd lie awake imagining calling her foster parents "Mom" and "Dad." By the time she was twelve and in her fifth placement, she'd stopped the game. *Home* became just another word for *house*. A place to eat and sleep. That's it.

She took a swing at the log before her and split it right through the middle. Would *home* ever mean more than that? Keith talked like she'd be here next spring. It was hard to picture staying for that long, but she had to admit the idea was growing on her. Jan and Keith made her feel like she actually belonged somewhere. Was that what it was like to have a family?

She split another log, then set the ax down and stacked the pieces on the pile like Jan had instructed her. She couldn't let herself start to think like that. This was a job. Jan and Keith were hiring her to work on their ranch. It wasn't any more than that. Thinking it was would be foolish. Hadn't she learned her lesson with Irene?

Roxi was still lost in her thoughts when Keith stuck his head out the back door, waving at her. She waved back.

"Could you come inside for a minute?" Keith didn't look happy.

Roxi sank the ax blade into the stump, peeling off her gloves as she walked toward him. She could definitely use the break.

He held the door open for her. She thanked him, but he didn't respond. Selah met her at the door and Roxi stooped to pet the twirling dog. If it had been up to Selah, she would've been at Roxi's side as she chopped, but she'd been so worried about the flying wood chips hurting the dog—not to mention her inexperienced ax—that she'd shut her inside while she worked.

"Come in the living room," Keith said in a brusque tone.

She followed him, Selah at her side. As they entered the room,

Jan stood from the sofa. When Roxi saw her serious face, she knew something was definitely up.

"What's goin' on?"

"Sit down," Jan said.

Roxi didn't obey her and remained standing. She glanced back and forth between Jan and Keith, a familiar feeling rushing through her body. They were going to get rid of her. Like everyone else had. She knew life here was too good to be true.

"Please sit down, Roxi," Jan repeated, pointing at the sofa.

She finally went to the sofa and eased onto its very edge. Selah jumped up beside her. "Did I do something wrong?"

Keith crossed his arms. "That's a good question."

Suddenly Roxi knew everything she'd feared was about to come crashing down on her. She was standing outside of herself watching the wave roll in, but she couldn't run or even speak.

Jan sat beside her, hands in her lap, staring straight ahead at her husband. Keith took the chair across from them. A pregnant silence spread through the room. They knew. She didn't know how, but somehow they knew.

"I went through your things," Keith finally said.

She started to protest, but Jan stopped her with a firm grip to her arm. "Let us do the talking for a minute."

"I found your books," Keith continued. "And a bookstore's business card."

Roxi felt her hands start to tremble. Her gaze drifted to the floor, unable to meet Jan's or Keith's eyes. All her thoughts of home dissolved. It was over. What was going to happen to her?

"I called the store," Jan said, "and spoke with Christy Williams. She said the books we found in your backpack were stolen. And that you were seen with the people they suspected of a burglary and murder that happened at their store a week ago."

They suspected Irene and Diego? She'd actually talked to the clerk? Roxi felt sick. She swallowed the acid pushing up the back of her throat. There was nothing she could say. They knew. The cops would show up next, handcuff her, and she'd never see Jan or Keith again.

"I think it's time you tell us the truth," Jan said.

Keith eyed her from across the room. "And let's begin with your name. Your real one."

"Roxi *is* my name," she muttered.

"Did you steal those books?"

She leaned her elbows on her knees, burying her face in her hands. It was over.

"We're waiting," Keith said.

"Sweetheart, the only way we can help you is if we know the truth."

She was fighting tears. This was how it always ended up. She'd get her hopes up only to have them dashed to pieces. Jan and Keith would send her back to the state, she'd do time in juvie or prison, and she'd never trust anyone again.

"Roxi." Jan took hold of her shoulder and forced her to look up. "We might be able to help you. But only if you talk to us. We need to know what happened."

She squeezed her eyes shut, shaking her head. "You can't help me."

"Did you take those books?"

She slowly nodded.

Neither Jan nor Keith spoke for a moment, and Roxi realized what they must be thinking. "But I didn't kill that guy! I didn't!"

Keith shook his head as he looked at Jan.

"You have to believe me," Roxi said, her words coming out as a whimper. She was crying now, the emotions she'd kept bottled up for so long coming in a torrent. She pulled in jerky breaths, barely able to talk. "It wasn't my idea to go back."

"But you were there with these people?" Keith said.

For the thousandth time, Roxi relived the moment in her head. Diego's gun going off, the blood, the man's gurgling breaths.

"He d-d-d-died in . . . front of me." Sobs shook her shoulders, and she held her arms around her knees. She'd never be able to forget it. That man's face would haunt her for the rest of her life. How could she expect Jan and Keith to believe her? They'd be no different from any of the foster parents she'd lived with. As soon as she got in trouble, she'd be shipped off somewhere else. A new town, new people, no friends. Only this time it was worse than that. She'd actually witnessed a man's murder. Played a part in it.

Jan surprised her when she reached over and wrapped her arms around her. Without thinking, Roxi clung to the older woman, crying into her shoulder. And Jan just held her.

"I wanted to tell you," Roxi sobbed.

"Oh, sweetheart, why didn't you?"

"Because I knew you'd send me away."

"Send you away?"

"They'll . . . they'll put me in jail, won't they?"

"Now wait a minute." Jan pulled back, looking her right in the face. "Who said anything about that?"

"I stole those books."

Keith sat beside Jan on the sofa. He squeezed his wife's hand. Then they both turned toward her.

"Why don't you tell us everything," Keith said.

That's when Roxi realized there was no anger on their faces. They weren't yelling and swearing at her for making such stupid choices. They were actually listening and waiting for her to tell her side of the story.

Roxi swiped at her eyes with her sleeves. "I don't know where to start."

"Do you live with your mother?" Jan asked.

She shook her head. "What I told you about her is true. I hadn't seen her since I was eight, but a week ago I found her. She has a new family—a little girl, even." Roxi fought to keep from crying again when she thought about how Mom had treated Erin. "She didn't want to see me and told me to leave."

"Is that why you ended up here in Elk Valley?"

Roxi ran her shaky hands through her hair. "I bummed a ride with a trucker."

She could tell Keith didn't like that, and it almost made her feel better. Like he was looking out for her.

"What happened at that bookstore?" Keith asked.

She leaned back in the sofa. How could she possibly tell them? She could barely think about it. What would they say if she told them about the other stores? What if she told them about Diego?

"I didn't want to go back that night," she said. "Honest, it wasn't my idea. But Irene, she made—"

"Who's Irene?" Jan asked.

Roxi suddenly wasn't sure if she should've mentioned Irene's name, but Keith caught her gaze and held it. "You need to tell us everything, Roxi," he said.

She swallowed back the emotion in her throat. "She's my mom's cousin. They found her after I got in trouble at the group home. Some kids were beating me up when the counselors weren't around. It got so bad she agreed to take me in."

"Why didn't she take you in at the beginning?"

"I don't know," Roxi said.

Jan seemed to be thinking. After a moment she said, "She *made* you steal these books?"

"I . . . guess I could've said no. But I thought she—"

"Did she threaten you?"

"No, it wasn't like that. I didn't want to let her down. I wanted . . ." Roxi glanced at her feet. "I wanted to make her proud of me."

Keith and Jan exchanged looks again, but Roxi didn't understand why.

"If I'd done a better job in the first place, we never would've gone back. But that day, when we first went to the bookstore, I didn't keep the clerk busy long enough." She was gushing more than she'd intended, but it was like a dam had broken inside her and she couldn't help the words spilling from her mouth. She wiped her eyes as they teared up again. "That was my only job, and I blew it. We went back later that night because of me!"

The living room got deathly quiet, and Roxi wished one of them would say something. Selah seemed to sense her distress and rested her head on Roxi's leg.

Jan took a deep breath. "We believe you when you say you didn't kill this guy. But you *were* there. You were stealing their books. We're going to help you, but we need to know what really happened. Who *did* kill him?"

She looked away. If she told them Diego did it, would he go to prison? He was a minor like her, but they could try kids as adults, right? She didn't want him to spend the rest of his life in prison.

Before she could answer, a knock came at the front door. Roxi jumped, but Jan and Keith acted like they were expecting it.

"Am I going to jail?"

Jan leaned over and squeezed her forearm. Her eyes were clear and firm. "All you're going to do is talk to these people."

"The cops?" Roxi jumped up from the sofa. "Jan, please—"

"It's not the police," Jan said.

Keith got up to answer the door.

"The lady whose business card you had—I asked her to come over."

Roxi was shaking her head. "I can't. I just can't."

"You don't have a choice on this, honey," Jan said.

"But she won't believe me!"

Keith was opening the door, and as Roxi heard the voices on the other side, her instinct to run kicked in. She bolted through the kitchen and out the back door. She couldn't face the clerk she'd deceived that day in the store. The woman had been nice to her, but because of Roxi, her fiancé was dead. Maybe Jan and Keith wouldn't call the cops, but the clerk surely would.

Out in the yard, Roxi hesitated long enough for Jan to spot her from the back door. She heard the door creak open and *whap* shut but took off before Jan could catch up.

She couldn't do this.

"Roxi, please come back!"

Sprinting for the corral fence, she reached it and tried to vault over the top board. But instead of making it over, she slipped and ended up in a heap, holding her side as it throbbed with pain from slamming into the ground. By the time she clambered to her feet, Jan was beside her.

"You okay?"

She nodded, wincing.

"Now listen to me." Jan had her by the arm. "All you're going to do is go in there and talk to this lady like you talked to Keith and me."

"I lied to her. I took her books."

"Then that's exactly what you'll say."

"How do you know she won't call the cops?"

"We're gonna have to talk to the police at some point. But you won't be doing anything alone. Keith and I will be right with you."

"Why would you do that? I lied to you, too."

Jan didn't immediately respond, as if she were trying to find the right answer. For a second Roxi wondered if she was about to take everything back, if all her words had been empty promises.

"I didn't tell you this," Jan said, "but for days before I ever picked you up, I felt like God was telling me to get ready for something."

"He did?"

"I didn't know what, but now I do." Jan smiled at her. "It was you."

Roxi didn't understand. "Me? Why would God do that?"

"Because He loves you." Jan reached out and cupped Roxi's chin with her fingers. "And so do I."

She looked away, trying to keep herself from crying again. "I've done so many bad things you don't even know about."

The setting sun caught Jan's face in a way that made Roxi think of a painting she'd seen in a book once about cowboys and cowgirls. All the wrinkles on Jan's face were glowing, but they didn't make her look old. Her eyes were as clear and bright as if she were twenty. "Sweetheart, if real love was based on perfection, none of us would have a chance."

"Then why doesn't my mom want anything to do with me?" She scrunched up her face to keep from completely losing it. "What did I do wrong?"

"You didn't do anything wrong." Jan pulled her into a hug as she had in the living room, and for a second time, Roxi found herself crying in the woman's embrace. Her shirt smelled faintly of hay and leather, and her strong arms folded around Roxi's back.

"People mess up," Jan said. "And your mom doesn't know what she's missing."

Roxi didn't know how long she stood there with Jan holding her, but only when she finally stopped crying did she let go and try to smile at Jan. She didn't want the moment to end.

"You ready?" Jan cocked her head toward the back door. "I know it won't be easy, but we have to do this."

Roxi glanced at Jan one last time. She wouldn't have wanted anyone else standing beside her right then. "You won't leave me?"

"I'll be right here," Jan said.

Together they walked back to the house. As they stepped inside, somehow Roxi knew nothing would ever be the same.

33

On the sofa, Roxi hugged her ribs, her side still throbbing from her tumble outside. She instantly recognized the clerk named Christy sitting across from her, and she could tell the woman recognized her too. But Roxi had never seen the woman beside Christy. Keith introduced her as Abby, and the way she stared made Roxi afraid to look at her.

"You weren't researching for a school paper, were you?" Christy asked in a low, tired tone.

She dared to glance into the woman's face and was surprised to see no anger. Just a deep, tangible sadness.

Christy seemed to be struggling for her next words. She turned her focus to Keith and Jan. "I'd like to see those books please."

"I'll get them," Keith said, running up the stairs.

Roxi covered her face with her sore hands, completely exhausted. If she'd only hidden the books better—thrown them away, even—none of this would be happening. She'd still be out there chopping wood and thinking about where this new life would take her. But that was never the way things happened for her. She should've learned that by now.

She rubbed her eyes, thankful for Jan's presence. How could Jan say she loved her? Was that even possible?

Keith returned with the books still wrapped in the plastic grocery bags she'd been using to protect them. He handed them to Christy, and Roxi stared at the bundle. The *Gatsby* was on top with its blue illustrated dust jacket, and the sight of it made her stomach turn.

In silence Christy deftly examined the books like the guy at the bookstore had, flipping around to certain pages, probably checking for the same points.

"We mark all our valuable books," Christy said, standing. She showed something in the *Gatsby* first to Keith and Jan, then brought the book over to Roxi, pointing at a small penciled *D* on the last page. Roxi couldn't take her eyes off the woman's diamond engagement ring.

"Most people would never know to look for it." Christy sat back down, the books cradled in her lap. "How did you get these books?"

It was all she could do to keep from jumping up and running outside again. The only thing keeping her here was the sliver of hope that Jan and Keith believed her, that their words hadn't just been empty promises. She knew she was grasping at straws, but should she trust them?

Her answer came out a whisper. "I took them."

"When?"

"The same day you took me up to the science section. After the store closed."

Roxi saw the other woman, Abby, clench her jaw.

"The three of you came back?" Christy asked.

She nodded.

"My fiancé died that night. What I want to know is . . ." Christy took a deep breath, her voice catching. "Who killed him?"

Roxi clasped her fingers together to keep them still. Her whole body was jittery and weak, like she'd downed ten shots of espresso. How could she betray Diego and tell them he pulled the trigger? They'd show him no mercy. She knew it.

She glanced at Jan.

"Go ahead and answer her, sweetheart."

"It's okay," Keith said.

Roxi swallowed. Hard. Maybe they really did believe she hadn't done it.

"Was it you?"

Abby's accusation made Roxi snap her head up. "No! I would never . . . I didn't kill him. It wasn't me, I promise. I—"

"Who was it then?"

Jan reached for her hand and squeezed it. "Just tell us the whole story."

"We went back," she said. "I didn't want to, but Irene . . . she has this way of making you do what she wants. Diego and I, we did whatever she said."

"Diego is Irene's teenage son," Abby said, nodding at Keith and Jan.

Roxi couldn't keep her eyes from widening. "How do you know that?"

"Never mind. Keep talking."

What else did this woman know? Roxi felt heat creeping up her neck, and she had to force herself to continue. "We broke in and started filling our bags. We were almost done." She shook her head as the scene replayed in her mind's eye. If only she could pinch herself and wake up. "That's when the guy turned on the lights."

The woman named Abby leaned forward, her black leather coat hanging open. Roxi blinked. For a split second she saw something under the woman's coat. A gun.

Her words caught in her throat, and she felt herself shrink back.

"What happened next?"

Roxi stared at the floor. "We froze, not knowing what to do. Then Diego pulled out a gun." She was almost whispering now, and a tear leaked down her cheek. "I couldn't believe he brought it."

"You knew he had a gun?"

"I didn't know he had it with him."

Abby rolled her eyes.

"It's the truth! You have to believe me."

Jan rested her hand on Roxi's back. "Just keep going with what happened."

"Diego told him to stay where he was, but he didn't listen. Then this book fell behind us. Diego swung around, and the guy jumped him." She pleaded with her eyes for Abby to believe her. "I swear, he didn't mean to shoot him. The gun just went off, and the next thing I knew . . ."

"So you left him there." Abby was clenching her right hand, her knuckles white and bulging through the skin.

"I didn't want to—honest, I didn't—but Irene . . ."

"How 'bout calling 911?"

"I tried, but—"

"But what?" Abby stood up, glaring at her.

"Irene . . . she wouldn't let me."

"You could've stayed to help him. But you ran away instead."

Roxi was crying now. She couldn't help it. Even if Jan and Keith did believe her, she was guilty to these people.

Abby came toward her like she wanted to punch her. Almost at the same time, Jan jumped to her feet.

"Enough," Jan said, placing herself between Roxi and Abby. She glared at the woman. "I said you could talk to her, not harass her."

"She could've done something to help him," Abby growled.

"I think it's time you left."

Abby pointed at Roxi. "She admitted she was there. Don't you get it? It doesn't matter who pulled the trigger. She's just as guilty of murder."

Jan took a step in Abby's direction, squaring her shoulders as Keith got up and stood with his wife. "I don't care what you think. We believe her."

"So do I."

All eyes focused on Christy. She also got to her feet, grabbing Abby by the arm. Roxi was the only one left sitting. She wanted to curl up and die right there on the sofa.

There was an intensity in Christy's voice. "Listen to me, Abby. It wasn't that long ago *I* was falsely accused of a crime." She was giving Abby a look Roxi couldn't read. "Now sit down and give the girl a chance to talk."

Like a switch turning from on to off, something in Abby changed at Christy's words. She squeezed the bridge of her nose and closed her eyes. "I'm sorry."

Christy and Abby returned to the sofa.

It took Jan longer to sit down. When she slowly took her seat next to Roxi, she never took her eyes off Abby. And her hand never left Roxi's arm.

Christy continued the questions. "Why aren't you with Irene and Diego now?"

Roxi hugged her sides again. Did this woman really believe her? "I ran away. I couldn't stay and be a part of it anymore."

"Do you know where they are?"

Roxi shook her head, not looking at any of them. "I left them in Albuquerque." It wasn't a complete lie—she really didn't know where they were—but the one thing she did know, and certainly wasn't telling this Abby lady, was that she knew how to find them. She knew Diego and Irene's cell phone numbers by heart.

Abby interjected, "Why were you with Irene in the first place?"

That's when Jan spoke up and told them how Irene was her mom's cousin and how she'd been placed in her care after the group home experience. She went into detail about the way she'd been mistreated, and Roxi wasn't sure, but she thought she saw Abby's face soften just a bit. When Abby spoke again, her words weren't quite as harsh.

"I take it this isn't the only store you've stolen from."

Again, Roxi kept her gaze on the floor as she nodded. She didn't want to see the disappointment on Jan's face or Keith's.

"Okay, listen," Abby said. She rested her elbows on her knees. "I'm not gonna lie to you here. I've been investigating on my own. We've been to Irene's house, and it doesn't look like anyone's been there for quite some time."

"You've been to the house?"

"Yeah, and here's something else you probably didn't know." Abby paused. "I'm a cop."

Roxi's gaze flashed to Jan, but she could see that Jan was as surprised as she was at this revelation.

"I'm not here officially. But you need to know you're in some serious trouble."

Keith crossed his arms. "She does know that."

"No, I don't think she does. Because she was there committing a felony, she's just as guilty as this Diego guy. It's called felony murder, and she could receive the exact same punishment he does."

Roxi tried to swallow, but her mouth suddenly went dry. "Prison?"

"Possibly. Depends on whether you're tried as a juvenile or an adult, and on a host of other things."

"But she didn't do it," Jan said.

"Doesn't matter."

Fear gripped Roxi. What had she done?

"Surely you can see the only reason she was there in the first place was because of this Irene woman."

"So she says." Abby lifted her hand when Jan started to respond. "Whether you and I believe her makes no difference. The DA is going to look at this from all angles."

Roxi's voice came out a whimper. "I'm sorry."

"You'll need to get a lawyer."

Jan and Keith were nodding, but all Roxi could think about was Diego. She couldn't believe she'd ratted on him. Would he have done that to her?

"What about Diego?" she asked.

Abby gave her an incredulous look. "I would stick to worrying about yourself at this point."

"He's not a bad guy."

The woman's jaw clenched again, and Roxi realized how that must've sounded to her.

"I didn't mean—"

"I know what you meant."

"He might be tough on the outside, but he's got a good heart. He helped me find my mom, and he's . . . he's the only friend I've ever had."

"You know where he is?"

"No."

"Then there's not much we can do for him."

"What if he turned himself in? Would that help?"

"Let me put it this way." Abby met Roxi's eyes. "Cooperation is always a good thing."

❧

And just like that the conversation was over. Abby exchanged contact information with Jan and Keith Mercer, the couple assured them Roxi wasn't going anywhere, and she and Christy left. They weren't out of the driveway before Abby was leaving a message for Detective

Stephens to call her immediately. Tomorrow morning they'd probably arrest the girl.

Abby snapped her phone shut. Everything in her wanted to hate Roxi, probably the last person to see Hunter alive. She had left him to die. But no matter how much Abby wanted to, she couldn't. Every time she tried, she thought of Kat. The girl was no older than her daughter. Sitting before them hadn't been a murderer but a scared, impressionable kid this Irene woman had taken advantage of. She'd looked into the eyes of enough criminals to realize Roxi was no more a murderer than Kat was.

"I'm sorry for the way I acted in there," she said.

Christy took in a deep breath and just nodded.

And Abby surprised herself by not really hating Diego either. If what Roxi said was true—and she had a feeling it was—he was apparently an impulsive, hotheaded boy who'd gotten his hands on a gun and thought it would make him a man. The one who should've known better, the one who'd manipulated the teens into robbing the store in the first place, was Irene. If she hated anyone, Abby realized, it was her.

"We actually have some answers," Christy finally said. "I should be relieved."

"But you're not."

"No, it's almost worse this way. Those kids . . ."

"She's holding something back."

Christy glanced at her. "What?"

"The girl. She's not telling us everything."

"Why do you say that?"

Abby turned the car onto the main road back to May's ranch. "Gut feeling. I think she knows where they are."

34

Roxi stayed on the sofa, her limbs weak. A part of her was relieved she didn't have to hold everything inside anymore, but mostly she was numb. If she tried to stand up right now, she didn't know if she could.

Jan and Keith were talking about how they had to find a lawyer. Keith said he knew a guy who was considered the best criminal defense attorney in the state. They'd call him and make an appointment tomorrow morning. He'd be able to advise her of her rights and . . .

What if they didn't believe her? What if she was tried as an adult?

"Sweetheart?" Jan reached her arm around Roxi, and she let herself melt into the woman's embrace. "I know that wasn't easy."

"She's right," Roxi said. "I was there. I'm just as guilty as if I pulled the trigger."

Keith crouched in front of her. He rested his hand on her knee, and Roxi wished more than anything he were her father and Jan her mother. How different her life would've been if she'd grown up here on this ranch.

"I don't know a lot about this legal stuff," Keith said gently, "but one thing I do know. We're going to get you the very best help we can."

"Don't they give you lawyers?"

"They can, but sometimes it's better to hire your own."

"I don't have any money. And I don't want—"

He held up his hand. "You're not to worry about any of that."

She started to protest again.

"I'm serious," Keith said. "Okay?"

The tender look on his face did her in. Only a couple hours ago she hadn't known where he stood about her being here. But he was telling her now without saying a word. Roxi didn't think she had any more tears left to cry, but a few pushed to her eyes. "I . . . I don't want to go to jail."

"I know, kid." He patted her knee. "I know."

❧

Later that night Roxi lay awake in her bed. She'd spent hours staring at the ceiling and stroking Selah's ears. Rolling onto her side, she closed her eyes, longing for the relief of unconsciousness. But it didn't come. She kept thinking about Diego. In her heart she knew he hadn't meant to kill that guy, but accident or not, it was still a murder.

Where was he?

Sooner or later he wouldn't be able to live with what he'd done. Eventually guilt would eat him alive, just like it was eating her.

Roxi threw back her covers and cracked the bedroom door. This would be her fourth visit to the bathroom. She started to creep past Jan and Keith's room to keep from waking them, but then she saw the light still oozing from under their door. She could hear them talking softly.

She froze, straining to discern the words, but all she could hear were mumbles. She stepped closer until she was right outside the door.

"He said three hundred an hour, not even counting the retainer."

"How can we afford that?"

"I've already talked with Grant. He still wants to buy the cabin."

"Could you get him to come up a little?"

"Maybe."

Silence.

"Hon, we can't let her go to jail."

"He's the best lawyer in the state."

Sheets rustled like someone was getting out of the bed, and Roxi flew back down the hall to her own bedroom. She quietly closed the door. Leaning her forehead against its hard wood surface, she made up her mind.

❧

Diego was almost asleep when his cell phone vibrated madly right beside his head. He usually remembered to turn it off, but he'd been forgetting a lot of things lately. Ma even had to grab the wheel of the RV today when he'd drifted into oncoming traffic.

He groggily felt for the phone. When he finally got it in his hand, he didn't recognize the blurry numbers flashing on the screen. Who in the . . . ? It was three o'clock in the morning. He jabbed at the Send key.

"Hello?"

Nothing.

"If this is some kind of—"

"Diego?"

Three seconds and he was instantly awake. It had been a week since he'd heard that voice, and he recognized it instantly. "Rox? Is that you?"

"It's me."

She sounded as tired as he felt. Diego flipped over onto his stomach and crawled on his elbows up to the very corner of his bed in the RV. By the window. Somehow he had to keep Ma from hearing. "Where *are* you?"

"I . . ."

"Are you okay?"

"Yeah. I'm okay."

It was like a twenty-five-ton semi lifted from his shoulders.

"Diego."

"What were you thinking? Where'd you go?"

Roxi paused. "I'm gonna turn myself in."

"What?" The word slipped out louder than it should've. He lowered his voice. "You can't do that."

"They told me I'm guilty too, just for being there."

"Whoa, whoa, whoa." He squeezed his head with his hand. This was not what he'd expected. "Who's 'they'? What are you talking about?"

"I told the people I'm staying with what happened."

He pressed the phone harder against his ear. So Ma was right. She *had* ratted on them.

"I didn't mean to, but I couldn't help it."

"What did they say?"

"We could . . . we could all go to prison."

"You didn't do anything."

"I was taking the books just as much as you, and I was with you when—"

"But I'm the—"

"It doesn't matter who did what."

"That's crazy!" He took a deep breath. "I shot him, Rox. Not you."

They both paused. It was the first time he'd verbally admitted what he'd done, and it was actually a relief to hear himself say it. He couldn't keep pretending everything was gonna be okay. He knew it wasn't.

"Every night I relive it." Diego cursed under his breath. "I wish I could go back. You don't know how much."

"If you tell them it was an accident . . ."

"I still killed a man. Nothing's changing that."

Diego could tell Roxi was doing her best to keep from crying. And she was whispering too, like she was hiding the call from someone herself.

"I don't know what to do," Roxi said. "This couple who took me in wants to hire me a lawyer, but they don't have any money."

Something changed in Diego right then. Maybe it was hearing Roxi's voice. Maybe it was his conscience finally winning. He didn't know for sure, but he suddenly made a decision.

"Where are you?" he asked.

"Elk Valley, Colorado."

"We're in Santa Fe."

"Do you hate me?"

Diego rubbed his forehead. If she'd kept her mouth shut, there was a chance no one would've ever found out. He could've gone on living this life of freedom Ma had built for them, adventure at his beck and call. But how free would he really have been? The walls of his conscience had been closing in on him more each day.

"You did what you thought was right."

She sniffed. "I just wish we really could go back."

"But we can't." Diego hesitated. His next question would essentially seal his fate. "Where would be a good place to meet you?"

The line hushed. All he could hear was her breathing.

"Are you serious?"

"Don't try to talk me out of it now."

"But what are—?"

"I'm going with you. We can both turn ourselves in."

More silence.

"What about your mom?"

"Just tell me where to meet you."

"There's a coffee shop in town. The Perfect Blend."

He muttered the location under his breath to commit it to memory. He could ask for directions at a gas station. "The Perfect Blend. Elk Valley."

"It's the only coffee shop in town."

"Are you gonna be alone?"

"Yeah," she said softly. "When can you be here?"

He did a few quick calculations in his head. Ma would have to be asleep when he left, and she was waking up earlier these days. They'd already unhitched the van, so he wouldn't have to worry about making noise that way. Not like he'd be needing to take much, either. His gun would stay behind. He never wanted to see that thing again.

"Seven. Maybe."

He felt a connection travel between them. It was like they were both taking in these last seconds before their lives would change forever. A calm settled over him. They could finally stop running.

"Diego?"

"Yeah?"

"I'm scared."

He thought about lying to her and putting a brave face on the whole thing. But this was Roxi.

"Me too," he said, and despite his best efforts, his voice cracked.

❧

The Mercer house was quiet and dark, and Roxi stood in the middle of the shadowy kitchen, fully dressed. Selah sat patiently beside her, looking up at her every few seconds as if to ask what they were doing awake at this hour.

Roxi glanced around the simple room, remembering the first night she'd stayed here. Jan had bandaged her cut right over at that sink. She'd fed them that delicious stew at that table. Roxi reached out and touched its rough wood surface. Everything had been strange and unfamiliar, but the moment she'd walked into this place, she'd felt something. It had taken all this time to realize what it was, but tonight she knew.

Peace. There was a peace in this house she'd never experienced before. Even on the good days with Mom, she'd never felt anything close to what she felt here. It didn't make sense. Jan and Keith's life hadn't exactly been a bed of roses. They should be bitter and angry, but they weren't. Despite their tragedy they'd found a way to go on and still have room in their hearts for her, a hopeless girl who'd lied to their faces. She *really* didn't understand that. They were even willing to sell their beloved cabin to help her.

Roxi swallowed the lump in her throat. That cabin meant everything to them, and it was the last tangible reminder they had of their son's dreams. No matter what happened, she couldn't let them sell it. She'd rather go straight to jail.

Squaring her shoulders, she glanced at Selah and almost lost it. She'd debated whether to keep the dog closed up in the bedroom but eventually decided to give her the run of the house. Without thinking, Roxi dropped to her knees and buried her face in Selah's neck.

"You be good now."

The dog wiggled in her grasp, trying to lick her face.

"They'll take care of you."

Roxi kissed her one last time on the top of the head, then quickly stood and grabbed her backpack. If she put it off any longer, she wouldn't go through with it. She hoped Selah wouldn't think she was abandoning her, even if she was.

Unlocking the kitchen door, Roxi tried not to look back. But she couldn't help it. Selah's eager face stared at her, and she burst into tears.

"I love you, girl," she said, shutting the door.

She could hear Selah's pitiful whines from the other side, and it was all Roxi could do to walk down the porch steps. But she had to. There was no choice. She covered her mouth to muffle her sobs and ran into the night.

35

Sleep had been fitful at best for Jan. After that detective had called and told them he'd be coming this morning to question Roxi, she'd spent most of the night awake staring at the ceiling. Thinking, praying.

In those horrible months after Trae's accident, everything had reminded her she would never hug him again. His bedroom was a tomb of memories. The sight of his gelding made her cry. She and Keith both walked around like zombies, doing chores by rote and lying awake at night. In the first few weeks she'd often forget, and in those brief, wonderful moments, Trae was just working in the barn or out with some friends.

Jan crossed her arms over her chest. Even after that experience God had given her, she didn't think she could ever love a child again. Her wounds were too raw, her emotions worn out. But in the five years since, God had healed her, restoring what had been ripped away. She was living life again. Laughing. She'd never forget her son, but now she could go on. People needed her. This ranch needed her.

She closed her eyes, thinking about what she'd told Roxi outside. She couldn't deny God's hand in this. Somehow He'd orchestrated her being in that Safeway right when Roxi was trying to steal those protein bars. He'd made sure she drove right past the girl on the road later that night. It didn't make sense that He'd drop Roxi in their laps if they weren't supposed to help her, but she never dreamed she'd have to sell the cabin.

Carefully slipping out from under the covers, Jan wrapped her soft flannel bathrobe around herself. Might as well get up. She wouldn't be sleeping again tonight. Tiptoeing down the hallway, she stopped outside Roxi's door. The cabin was just a thing. It would hurt if it were no longer in the family, but this poor girl's life was more important.

Jan rested her hand on the door, picturing Roxi the way she usually found her in the mornings, sprawled on her back, covers askew. When she was asleep, all the hurt and pain disappeared from her face, and she was just a girl who needed someone to guide her and show her how to become the woman God intended her to be. More than once Jan found herself pausing and staring down at the young life that had been placed in her care. Was she that someone? Roxi had awakened something inside her she thought had died with Trae, and Jan couldn't deny how good it felt to actually feel like a mother again. Was that what the Lord wanted? She and Keith to take this girl in . . . forever?

Slowly Jan walked down the stairs. It was a question without an answer, at least for the moment. They would do everything they could to protect Roxi. If it meant selling the cabin, then so be it. Trae would understand.

She shuffled into the kitchen to start the coffeemaker and found Selah sitting by the door. As soon as the dog saw her, she bolted toward her and jumped on Jan's thighs, knocking her off-balance. Then in a flash of black fur she was at the door again begging to be let outside.

"What are you doing in here?" Roxi had been keeping Selah up in the bedroom with her every night.

The dog let out a plaintive whine, and suddenly Jan knew. Even from here she could see the dead bolt was unlocked.

Oh, dear Lord . . .

Running back upstairs, Jan didn't bother knocking on Roxi's door. She flung it open, her heart sinking when she saw the empty mattress and rumpled bedcovers. One frantic check under the bed where Roxi liked to keep her backpack revealed nothing but dust bunnies. Was there any chance she was just up early and already busy outside? They'd check, but somehow Jan knew the truth.

Prayers for the girl's protection came to her lips even as she ran to the bedroom to wake Keith.

❧

Roxi walked for over an hour before she hitched a ride into Elk Valley with some gal in a beat-up Suburban who sang along to the oldies station for the entire drive. Fine with her. She didn't feel like talking. At six thirty she walked into The Perfect Blend, hoping Stan wouldn't notice her.

"You're up early."

He waved at her from the espresso machine. Dumping a shot into a cup of coffee, he handed it to a guy in a postal service uniform who thanked him and left.

Roxi tried to paint on a smile, but she knew it fell flat. "Just running some errands."

He pulled a large paper coffee cup from the tower beside the counter. "Same as before?"

She nodded.

"Bagel too?"

"Not this time." She wasn't sure she'd be able to keep it down.

"You've got a long face. Everything okay?"

Was she that transparent? "Yeah."

"Heard there was a pack of coyotes up near your place." Stan handed her the cup, now filled with steaming house blend. "You heard 'em?"

She placed two crumpled dollars on the counter. He'd called the ranch her place. Right. In her dreams.

"No, I haven't yet."

"You will. Those critters can make quite a ruckus."

"I'll just—" she gestured toward a table—"sit and drink for a little bit."

"Oh, sure, sure." Stan smiled at her again, and she did her best to return it.

There were only two other patrons in the place. A guy wearing a backward baseball cap tapping at a laptop and some white-haired lady flipping through a *USA Today*. Slumping into a chair, Roxi dropped her backpack on the floor and checked her watch: 6:37.

She took the white plastic lid off her coffee and took a sip, wincing as it burned the roof of her mouth.

What if Diego didn't show?

❦

"You've gotta be kidding me."

Abby was already out of bed and pulling on her jeans with one hand, holding the cell phone to her ear with the other.

"We looked everywhere," Jan Mercer said, her voice higher than normal.

"When do you think she left?"

"Before five."

The girl had at least an hour-and-a-half head start.

"Any ideas?" Abby cradled the phone in her neck as she pulled on her sneakers.

"We've gone up and down the local roads, and I'm heading into town now."

"Christy and I'll meet you there."

Abby stuffed the phone into her pocket and grabbed her gun.

⚜

Roxi had finished half her coffee when she felt the caffeine. And not in a good way. Her mind began to spin, and questions zipped around in her head like wild, frantic animals desperate for freedom. How could she go through with this?

Holding her head in her hands, she sucked in a deep breath. Please. She couldn't lose it. Not now. But she'd be spending tonight in jail, wouldn't she? Would they stuff her in a holding cell with a bunch of creepy women? Or would she go straight to juvie while they figured out her case? What then? They wouldn't believe her, would they? She couldn't expect everyone to be like Jan and Keith.

Roxi almost started bawling right there in the coffee shop. Why had Jan and Keith treated her the way they did? Even after they knew everything, they were still willing to stand by her and sell their beloved cabin just so she could get a good lawyer.

"Hey."

Roxi jumped, ripping her hands from her face. Diego stood right in front of her, and she hadn't even heard him walk up. When she saw him, she did cry. Not a sound escaped her, but the tears just dripped down her cheeks. She tried to wipe them away, but they kept coming.

Diego pulled out one of the black, cast-iron chairs and sat across

333

from her. He didn't say anything, just reached out and touched her hand. It was the tenderest gesture he'd ever shown toward her, and she appreciated it more than she could tell him.

"I'm sorry," she said, finally getting hold of herself.

"It's okay, Rox."

Their eyes met, and she realized the cocky guy she used to know was gone. In his place was a Diego she'd never expected to see—a broken one.

"Can we really do this?" she whispered.

"They're gonna find us sooner or later."

She stared at her hands. A man was dead. Turning themselves in wouldn't change that, but for once they'd both be telling the truth. And maybe, years from now, they could start over again knowing they'd done the right thing.

They looked at each other without a word. Diego went up to the counter and ordered his own black coffee, and they spent a few silent minutes sipping their drinks. There was nothing left to say; it was as if they both needed the time to fully digest what they were about to do.

Roxi finally broke the calm. "Where should we go?"

"I figure the state police. If we go somewhere around here, they'd probably just have to transport us."

She swallowed the wad in her throat, determined not to cry again. This *was* the right thing to do. Whether it felt like it or not. She blew her nose into a napkin, realizing it might be the last time she . . .

Her gaze drifted toward the front door of the coffee shop, and adrenaline flashed through her chest. Diego swung around in his chair and cursed. Walking through the door was the last person either of them wanted to see.

36

Irene smiled as she sat down at their table. "Did you think I'd let you do this all by yourselves?"

It was all Roxi could do to keep from completely freaking in front of everyone. She threw a frantic glance at Diego, and by his deer-caught-in-the-headlights look, Roxi knew he was as shocked as she.

"Did you follow me?" Diego glared at his mother.

Irene hesitated, then lowered her voice. "I overheard you."

"We've made up our minds. You're not talking us out of this."

"I don't plan to." Irene rested her hand on her son's arm.

He jerked away. "We're turning ourselves in, Ma. I can't live like this anymore."

Irene just nodded like she understood completely. It didn't make sense.

D

"He's serious," Roxi said. Wasn't Irene the one who had chewed her out when she dared to question her in that Flying J restaurant?

"I know he is."

"And you're okay with that?" Diego crossed his arms.

Fingering a napkin, Irene nodded again. "Listen. I'm just as upset as both of you." She leaned toward her son, and their eyes connected. "But, honey, you're almost a man now. You need to do what you think is right."

"I don't understand," Roxi said. "You're just gonna . . . *let* us do it?"

Irene reached across the table and wrapped her freckled hand around Roxi's. It hadn't been a minute, and she could already feel herself falling under Irene's spell. She couldn't quite bring herself to pull her hand away.

"We got in this together," Irene whispered. "We get out together."

"I don't . . . What are you saying?"

"Both of you—" Irene briefly met her eyes, then reached for Diego's hand as well—"are my family. And family sticks together."

She squeezed their fingers, and Roxi noticed Diego didn't pull away either.

"We'll get through this," Irene said. "I'll tell them everything that happened. How it was my idea. Everything."

"I'll do time, Ma. I know it."

Roxi wasn't sure, but she thought she saw something flare behind Irene's eyes at those words, but it vanished just as quickly.

"Let's wait and see," Irene said. "There's a lot about this process we don't know."

"We were going to the state police," Roxi said.

"Then we better get moving."

Irene stood, and Roxi looked at Diego again. Was he buying this change in his mother? Time froze as Roxi tried to make sense of the whole exchange. Irene couldn't really be okay with this, could she? It didn't fit. But then again, Diego had changed more than she would have ever thought possible. If he could change, then maybe his mother could too?

"The RV's parked up the street." Irene pulled out her keys. The fob was a real rabbit's foot she'd picked up in some gift shop. "We can drive out of town and hitch up the van. I passed a good place on the way in."

Roxi's head ached from the lack of sleep, caffeine on an empty stomach, and now Irene. She'd never wanted to see this woman again. Ever. She still recoiled from her presence. Irene had used her. Plain and simple. She was nothing like Jan, and Roxi could see that clearly now.

But as much as she hated the idea, it did make sense. Irene was a part of this crime too. The sooner they got this whole thing over with, the better. Reluctantly, Roxi and Diego followed Irene out the door of The Perfect Blend coffee shop.

❧

Jan slammed the truck's brakes at the stop sign, and her cell phone went airborne, clunking to the floor. She and Keith had taken separate trucks to cover more area. Jan would meet Abby and Christy in Elk Valley. Keith was on his way to Walsenburg. It was a long shot, but if Roxi wanted to disappear, she might've headed that way.

Gunning the engine, Jan had the truck zooming again before the count of three. How could she have been so dense? She knew running was generally Roxi's first reaction. She'd seen the girl do it twice, and Jan could hardly blame her, knowing all she'd been through. But she'd hoped Roxi had seen that she and Keith were different from the other adults in her life. Was she so damaged that she couldn't trust them?

Then a troubling thought came. Once they went to the police, they would take Roxi into custody, wouldn't they? What if the girl really did end up in prison? How could she explain that to Roxi when she was the one who made her tell the truth?

Jan jumped when her cell phone vibrated and rang at the same time, scuttling across the truck's metal floorboard. She stretched to reach it while she was driving, but it had already slid to the passenger side. Why was she so worried Roxi was in danger? Was the Lord trying to tell her something?

Checking the road to make sure no cars were coming, Jan slammed on the brakes once more and lunged for the phone. She had the truck going again and the cell to her ear before the third ring.

"Yeah?"

"Jan Mercer?"

She pulled the phone away and glanced at the display. She didn't recognize the number or the man's voice.

"This is Jan."

"I'm Stan Barlowe from The Perfect Blend coffee shop."

It took her a second to put a face to the name, but then she remembered the friendly guy with the glasses who'd usually taken her order. His name could've been Stan.

"I got your number off Google," he said. "I wanted to ask you something about the girl who's working for you. Roxi."

Jan's heart jumped. "Have you seen her?"

"Uh . . . yeah."

"When? Where?" Her foot punched the gas pedal harder.

"In here. She just left."

"Where is she now?"

"I don't know."

"Where was she headed?"

Stan cleared his throat. "Is she okay?"

"No, she's not. Please, Stan, did she say anything?"

"A guy her age came in here a little after seven. Shortly after that, a woman came to their table. They both seemed to know her, so I didn't think much of it."

Jan's fingers tightened around the cell and the steering wheel. "Did she leave with them?"

"About five minutes ago."

"You didn't by any chance notice which way they went?"

"Actually, yes," Stan said. "Something didn't seem right. That's why I thought I should call. She applied for a job here first, you know."

"Which way, Stan?"

"Toward Cuchara. The woman was driving an RV, if that helps."

Oh, Lord . . . she's so young. Please spare her life.

⁂

It wasn't much of a turnoff. Diego and Roxi followed the RV in the van, and a mile or two out of town, Irene maneuvered the rig to the side of the road. There was just enough space to hitch the van up to the RV without its rear sticking out in the two-lane road.

"You okay?" Diego asked, turning off the engine.

Roxi shook her head. "No."

"Yeah, me neither."

He started to get out, but Roxi caught his arm. "Shouldn't we have gone the other way back there?"

"We'll turn around after we hitch up."

"Think she'll really go with us?"

Diego looked up through the RV's back window. Irene was moving around in there, but all they could see was her shadow.

"Seems like."

"I would've thought she'd be mad."

"Weird, huh?"

"What are we going to say to the cops?"

Leaning against the van's headrest, Diego sighed. "The truth. It's not as overrated as I thought."

She knew they should be getting out, but neither of them moved.

"So where did you go when you left?" Diego asked.

"I saw my mom."

"You did?"

"She practically slammed the door in my face."

"Aw, man. I'm sorry, Rox."

"Has a new family and everything." The ache of that experience was still raw, and she wondered how long it would take before it healed. "I hitched a ride with a trucker who brought me here."

"But you said someone took you in?"

"Yeah." Jan's and Keith's faces projected across her mind, and she took a deep breath. "A nice couple."

"They know you're gone?"

"Probably by now. But I didn't tell them where I was going."

He nodded. "Guess we better get a move on."

They both got out of the van just as Irene stepped out of the RV.

Irene waved for Roxi to come over. "Let's go for a walk while he's hooking up."

Diego was already concentrating on the tow hitch. "I'm not gonna be long, Ma," he muttered without looking up.

"I know, but it'll be good for us."

A week ago Roxi would've been thrilled Irene wanted her company on one of her walks. She usually didn't let anyone join her. But today Roxi just wanted to stick with Diego.

"We need to talk," Irene said.

"I think I'll stay here."

"Heart-to-heart."

She rolled her eyes.

"Come on, honey. It's important."

"I don't feel like it."

Irene glanced away for a second, and when she looked back, Roxi thought she saw tears in her eyes. "I know I haven't done right by you. And I couldn't possibly make it up to you in a five-minute walk, but I want to try."

Roxi looked to Diego for help one last time, but his back was to her.

"Please?"

Fine. She had a few things to say to Irene too. What better time than the day they all went to jail? She raised her hands to indicate the woods. "Where?"

Irene smiled, resting her arm on Roxi's back and guiding her into the forest. "Thank you."

She resisted the urge to slip out from under the woman's touch. She didn't like how chummy Irene was being.

"Make it snappy!" Diego called from behind them.

"Don't worry," Irene said over her shoulder. "I'll be back in a couple minutes."

37

ABBY WAS GOING WELL OVER THE SPEED LIMIT, and on these back roads she and Christy were feeling every pothole. She should've known this would happen. Hadn't she seen the desperate look in that girl's eyes?

Her cell phone vibrated on her belt, and she snatched it up.

"Did you find her?"

"*Cómo estás* to you too, Abby." The male voice chuckled. "I've got some info on that guy you called me about, Diego Tonelli."

"What?" She'd almost forgotten about asking her PI friend Cesar Martinez for the favor back in that hotel room with Christy. "Sure, sure. Right. I need to know anything you've got. Especially now."

"Well, he doesn't bring up a whole lot. One speeding ticket six months ago."

"That's it?"

343

"For him, yeah." Some papers rustled. "I checked around about his family, though, just to get some history."

Abby glanced at Christy and mouthed, "It's about Diego."

"His father died when he was four years old," Cesar said.

"Okay."

"Reports say someone broke into the guy's house one night and shot him in the head. Sounds like he didn't even know what hit him. Never found who did it." Cesar cleared his throat. "Here's where it gets interesting. I tracked down the detective who handled it. He's doing security for a company downtown now. Crypto Technologies. You know it?"

"Rings a bell."

"Anyway, we chatted a little. He warmed up to me after a bit, so I asked him about it. Took him a second, but he remembered the case."

"And?"

"Confirmed what I told you and then some. There'd been little to no evidence linking anybody, so the case went cold fast. Your Diego grew up without a father, raised by his single mom. I'm about to get off with the detective—already said good-bye, even—and then he blurts out, 'I still think his ex knocked him off.'"

Abby switched her phone to the other ear and checked her mirrors. "Diego's mother?"

"She'd divorced him a couple months before the incident, and she was their first suspect. But like I said, there wasn't much evidence. Guy was a lowlife too. Beat the kid, apparently."

Now this was interesting. "What else do we know about this woman?"

"Nothing seemed fishy at first, but I've got a half-dozen different addresses for her in the past four years alone. All rentals. And I got her employment history."

"Anything stand out?"

"Nothing. Worked for a couple bookstores. That's it."

Abby pressed her phone tighter against her ear.

"Help you at all?"

"Certainly explains some things."

"Let me know if you need anything else," Cesar said.

Abby thanked him, and they said their good-byes. She quickly gave Christy the rundown of the conversation. Then the cell phone rang again. Abby glanced at the display and this time threw the phone at Christy. "It's Jan."

They were still several miles from town. Abby gripped the steering wheel with both hands, concentrating on the road and easing up a little on the gas. They didn't need an accident now.

Had Irene really killed her ex-husband? From everything Abby was learning, it was plausible, and that detective still thought so, even after all these years.

Abby concentrated on the road. It was because of this woman's greed that Hunter was dead, wasn't it? Roxi had been telling them the truth. Irene thought up this heist, and the kids had gone along with it to please her. Did that mean Roxi really was just an innocent victim in this? And what about Diego? It was his finger on the trigger.

"Are you sure?" Christy massaged her temple, looking out the windshield as she talked into the phone. "No, we haven't seen anything, but we'll keep looking."

Christy ended the call and kept the phone cradled in her hand. When she didn't speak right away, Abby knew it couldn't be good news.

"Tell me they found her."

"Jan just got a call from the owner of that coffee shop we visited, and Roxi apparently met a guy about her age in there this morning. Shortly after that, a woman came in too. How much you wanna bet that was Diego and Irene Tonelli?"

"Is she still there?"

"She left with them about ten minutes ago."

Abby cursed under her breath.

"They're in a big RV and a minivan."

"Headed which way?"

"Ours."

Abby pointed at the cell phone in Christy's hand. "Call 911. This woman could be dangerous."

❧

Roxi stepped over a decomposing pine log, already regretting that she'd agreed to this. Her head still ached, and a verbal sparring match with Irene wasn't going to help. "Diego's probably done."

"He can wait."

Irene was taking huge strides, and Roxi was already out of breath trying to keep up. "I thought you'd be angry with us."

"This was your idea, wasn't it?"

A burst of heat rushed up her neck. "We . . . we both decided."

"You called him."

"I . . ."

"He would never turn himself in if you hadn't talked him into it." Irene glanced at her, and Roxi instinctively drew away. For a minute back there, she'd thought things might be different, that Irene had genuinely changed. But this was the Irene she knew, and Roxi wished with all her heart Jan was walking beside her instead.

"He's smarter than that," Irene muttered, still walking.

"Irene, he killed a man! And we helped."

The older woman stopped, slowly turning to face her. She pointed at Roxi with a long finger. "This is what I mean. You're not going to do this to him. To us."

"What are you talking about?"

"You're not ruining Diego's life."

"I wouldn't . . ."

Irene shook her head. "I'm sorry, Roxi."

The older woman's piercing eyes met hers, and the hate she saw in them sent a chill up her spine.

❧

Diego crossed his arms and leaned against the outside of the RV. He knew this would happen. And now he had to wait while they had their stupid heart-to-heart talk. What could Ma possibly have to say to Roxi anyway? She'd admitted to his face she never really cared about her.

It was all too strange. He just wanted to get this over with while he still had the guts. Seeing his mother again had put a million doubts in his head. Was this really the right thing to do? He'd thought it was when he was with Roxi. Now he didn't know what to believe. Would his mother go to jail too?

Diego ripped out his keys, unlocked the RV, and climbed inside. They'd left five minutes ago. Did they expect him to just wait around?

He took in what had been his home for the past month. Yeah, it got cramped and he'd often complained about the lack of personal space, but he had to admit he loved traveling. There was nothing like hitting the road. In this thing he could go anywhere, anytime. No worries about hotel reservations, plane tickets, car rentals, or luggage.

Diego shook his head. Anywhere in North America had been within his grasp, and there were still so many wild and unexplored places. He'd dreamed about visiting Alaska someday and seeing all that rugged, untouched land.

He sank into the sofa, rubbing his sore eyes. None of his dreams were gonna happen now, were they? Even if he got off easy, he'd be doing some serious time. And he deserved it. That was something he'd finally come to grips with. He was a murderer. A judge couldn't ignore that. A man had died because he'd been stupid enough to threaten someone with a gun.

Glancing at his loft, he thought about the weapon stuffed in between the wall and the mattress up by the front windows. The police would want it, wouldn't they? If he gave it to them, would they cut him a break?

Diego stood on the front seats and reached for where he'd stashed it. If there was any chance at leniency, he was going for it. Expecting to feel the metal against his fingers, he was surprised when all he felt was dead space. And a few dead bugs. Maybe it had slid around when Ma was driving. The roads out here needed some serious work. Jumping onto the bed, he checked the entire crack.

The gun wasn't there.

❧

Irene closed the space between them, her face inches away. Roxi could see the red, spidery veins in the woman's eyes.

"I won't let you turn him in," Irene said.

"I'm not—"

"My son is a good boy."

Roxi backed up. "I know he is."

"He is *not* a killer."

"But he—"

"You will not do this to him."

"Irene, what are—?"

"My son is not going to jail."

Roxi took another step backward. What happened to the woman in the coffee shop who wanted to turn herself in too? the woman who'd agreed to tell the whole truth? Wherever she was, Roxi wanted her back because *this* Irene was scaring her.

"But you said you'd go with us."

Irene lifted her gaze to the canopy of white pines above them, shaking her head like Roxi had said the stupidest thing in the world. "You just don't get it, do you?"

"You're . . . you're not making sense." Roxi was suddenly aware of how utterly alone they were. It was desolate out here. In every direction, all she saw were trees. The RV was nowhere in sight, and the only sound was some magpie squawking.

"Nothing but trouble," Irene said, "everywhere you go."

Even after all that had happened, the words still stung. Roxi had longed for this woman's affection so badly, but no matter how hard she tried, Irene had kept her at arm's length. She had only ever been kind when she wanted something.

"Trouble for your mother, trouble for me."

Tears were coming, and Roxi couldn't hold them back. "But I tried. I always tried."

Irene raised her hands in frustration. "Fat lot of good it did you. You almost sent your mother to jail."

Her words came out a sob. "That wasn't my fault. I—"

"And now you want to turn in my son."

"He shot a man! What do you expect him to—?"

Without warning, Irene slapped her. "My son is *not* going to prison."

Roxi held her fingers to her throbbing cheek. Diego had to be done by now. And even if he wasn't, she had to escape this madwoman. "We should go back."

Irene shook her head, taking a step toward Roxi. "I'm sorry. I really am. But I have to do this. You don't leave me any choice."

"Stop it, okay? It's time to go back." Roxi felt her pulse quicken. Except she didn't know which way back was. She hadn't been paying attention as they walked.

Something changed on Irene's face. Her resolve reminded Roxi of the way she got before hitting a bookstore—like she was invincible and nothing could stand in her way.

"Irene, please. You're scaring me."

Instead of responding, Irene reached under her shirt and pulled out a silver handgun.

She aimed it at Roxi's head.

38

"THERE IT IS!"

Christy pointed at the large RV parked on the side of the road, and Abby made a sharp U-turn to pull up behind it on the shoulder. The minivan hitched behind it also matched what Jan had told them. Abby put the car in park and Christy called 911 again. She described where they were as Abby craned to see movement inside the vehicle. The RV's rear window was covered in dust, making it next to impossible to see anything. Which gave anyone inside the advantage. They could see her, but she couldn't see them.

She flipped on the hazard lights, opened her door, and carefully stepped out. The Acura was now partially blocking traffic. If she'd learned anything in the past twenty years, it was to trust her gut. And her gut was telling her something was off here. She slammed the car door hoping the sound would stir up some activity inside. It wasn't always good to surprise people.

"They're sending someone out," Christy whispered, ending her call.

Abby glanced at the passenger side of the rig, where its main door would be, debating whether to wait. But what if something really was wrong? What if they didn't get a guy out here for another thirty minutes? Could they afford to wait that long?

Abby led the way around the side of the vehicle. She'd rest a whole lot easier if she knew Roxi was inside this thing. The girl was going to have a lot of explaining to do. Abby reached to knock on the side door, but before she could, it flew open, almost catching her in the head. Abby jumped back, right hand instantly on the Beretta. Staring at them from inside the RV was the teen guy she recognized from the photograph they'd found in Roxi's drawer. He was dressed in faded jeans and a gray T-shirt. The patchy stubble on his face was probably at least three days' worth.

"Are you Diego Tonelli?"

By the sudden wild look in his eyes, Abby knew the answer, and it hit her like a punch. She was staring at Hunter's murderer, a kid who looked barely eighteen. She'd imagined him being different. Hunter's killer would be some ugly, mean, tattooed ex-con.

Diego jumped out of the RV without putting down the steps and stood right in front of her. She had a couple of inches on him and plenty of tricks up her sleeve if it came to anything physical, but she could tell he wasn't looking for a fight. He seemed worried and distracted more than anything.

"Is Roxi in there?" Abby demanded.

Diego's eyes darted, and she knew she'd hit pay dirt. He knew the girl.

"Who are you?" he asked.

"Where is she?"

"Who the—?"

Abby grabbed the front of his shirt and shoved him up against the RV. His back thudded into the fiberglass. She needed answers, and she needed them now. Jerking out her wallet badge, she waved it in his face, and his eyes widened.

"We know she was with you. You have five seconds to start talking."

He shook his head. "She and my mom left on a walk ten minutes ago, but they should've been back by now. I gotta find them!"

"Abby, let go of him."

She'd imagined the killer's eyes full of evil and cruelty. Diego's weren't like that at all. She loosened her grip on his shirt, letting him jerk out of her grasp. But when he tried to bolt into the woods, Abby caught him by the arm.

"Hold it. You're not going anywhere."

⁂

Roxi stared into the pale face of the woman she'd tried so hard to please. The woman who now held a gun on her.

"I have to do this for my son." Irene's voice was eerily calm.

Roxi backed up. "This isn't funny. Please put that away."

"You betrayed us." Irene jabbed the gun at Roxi's forehead. "After we trusted you and gave you a home. How could you do that?"

"I'm sorry; I—"

Irene stepped toward her, but she shrank away even more, holding her hands up in surrender. "Please. I'll do anything you want."

"What kind of mother would I be if I let you turn him in?"

"Diego's like a brother to me. I would never—"

Irene lowered the gun to Roxi's chest.

If she yelled, would Diego hear? Roxi frantically glanced around.

Forest everywhere. She had to run. If Irene pulled the trigger now, she couldn't miss. They were too close to each other. But if Roxi could put some distance between them . . .

She stared into Irene's face one last time, searching for a hint that this was one big, sick joke. But Irene was a mother bear ready to tear her apart to protect her cub, and Roxi couldn't help but wish for one brief moment that someone cared about her enough to protect her like that.

"All I wanted was for you to love me," Roxi whispered, tears pooling in her eyes even as she formulated a meager plan. *Move!* She couldn't stay here waiting for Irene to muster the nerve to shoot.

Irene lifted her other hand to the gun, her brow wrinkling. She was shifting her feet, shaking her head. "Nothing but trouble. That's all you—"

"Look out!"

As she'd hoped, the older woman's eyes briefly diverted, giving Roxi a split second to do the only thing she could—run. She bolted from Irene like a track star on speed.

Twigs snapped. Her smooth-soled boots slipped on pine needles. She sucked in desperate breaths of oxygen and pushed off the rough, sticky trunk of the first tree that came into her path. She vaulted over logs. Tripped on a rock. Ducked under sagging branches that stung her face and clawed at her arms. She propelled herself through the bracken.

She could hear Irene crashing through the woods somewhere behind her, and she risked a frantic glance over her shoulder. Before she could figure out where the sounds were coming from, a gunshot blasted through the forest and blowtorch pain exploded above her right ear.

Roxi stumbled, fell to one knee, clutching her head with both hands. When she pulled her fingers away, they were coated in blood.

❧

Abby's head snapped toward the gunshot pop.

"Oh, man, man." Diego ran his fingers through his greasy black hair. "We have to find Roxi!"

"Which way did they go?"

He pointed at the edge of the woods. "You don't understand. My gun is missing. The only one who—"

"What do you mean your gun is missing?" Christy asked.

"It's gone! I hid it in the RV, and now it's gone. My mom is the only one who could've taken it, and now she and Roxi . . . Oh, man. We gotta find her!"

He took off before Abby could stop him again.

"Try to stay with him," Abby ordered Christy, and pulling out her Beretta, she ran into the woods in a different direction.

❧

Roxi struggled to stand, but the forest spun around her in a kaleidoscope of greens and browns.

Get up! Run! She's gonna kill you!

The beat of Irene's feet pounded closer, and Roxi heard herself scream. She bolstered her legs underneath herself and managed to run a few more feet before collapsing to the ground again. Her face hit the dirt, and dead pine needles stuck to her bloody hands. She curled into a fetal position, holding her head.

Run. She had to keep running.

Roxi rolled onto her stomach with a moan, willing herself up. The bullet might've just grazed her. If she could get to the RV, she'd be safe. Diego would help her.

She gritted her teeth and struggled to her knees.

Footsteps crunched in front of her, and she lifted her eyes to see Irene standing thirty feet away, gun raised and aimed at her chest.

"Please," was all Roxi could whisper before Irene fired again.

39

ABBY RAN. She would not let Hunter's killer get away. Not as long as she had breath in her body. She zigzagged through the trees, scanning the forest for human life. A low branch almost took out her eye. Her side throbbed, but she ignored it. She could hear Diego yelling Roxi's name somewhere faintly off to her left, but she was pretty sure those gunshots had come from this direction. Had she heard a scream?

Think. She had to think. Stopping behind the trunk of a huge white pine, she heaved in air and listened. The only sounds were the soft whisper of the wind whooshing through its boughs and her own heart thumping like a DJ club mix.

Irene had the gun, and Roxi was missing. There was no reason for her to be firing that thing out here in the middle of nowhere. Abby stared at the Beretta clutched between her fingers, calling on every ounce of her training to stay calm and rational. How far could they have gone?

"Now would be a good time to help me out here, God."

She held her breath so she could hear better, turning her head in the direction she thought the shots came from. More wind. A squirrel chattering. A bird answering.

Abby pressed farther into the woods in a half jog trying to listen and run at the same time. What was she going to find? Was it really Irene firing Diego's gun, or was that an excuse he used so he could get away? She didn't think so. A woman who would kill her ex-husband and coerce her own son into robbery was capable of just about anything.

Then she saw it. A flash of color far ahead through the trees.

❧

Jan held the steering wheel with both hands, trying to keep her emotions under control. She was thinking about the day she'd gotten the phone call about Trae. Keith had been out working cattle, and she had no way to get ahold of him. She'd spent three hours alone and in shock at the news of their son's death.

Lord, please protect Roxi. Wherever she is. Help us find her. And whatever You want me to do for her, I'll do it. Just give me wisdom.

She jammed her foot on the gas, and the truck zoomed toward Elk Valley.

❧

Abby broke into a run, approaching the color. She could almost make out a human form ahead, and she forced herself to breathe. She had to be smart. Who knew what could be happening up there? The rage was building in her chest. Hunter was dead. He was never coming back. Because of this woman.

Not wanting to make herself a target, Abby slowed to a fast walk and crept from tree to tree like a special ops soldier, gun brandished, nerves on edge—prepared for anything. What she finally saw brought a curse to her lips.

Her eyes locked on the woman, the same one she'd seen in that photograph, standing in the middle of a small clearing. Her hands were laced around a silver handgun aimed toward a heap on the ground.

A heap shaped like the girl, Roxi. Who wasn't moving.

Abby clenched her jaw and lifted her own gun, aiming right for Irene's heart.

⚹

A mile outside Elk Valley, Jan got stuck behind a cattle truck going thirty-five. She laid on her horn and blinked her lights. The double yellow line warned her not to pass, but she tried anyway. How could she help Roxi if she couldn't get to her?

As she crossed into the other lane, an oncoming truck sent an adrenaline rush through her body, and she swung back, barely escaping being sideswiped by an 18-wheeler.

Jan took a deep breath and tried to calm herself as she rode the other driver's bumper.

⚹

Abby's finger twitched on the trigger. It was a clear shot. This woman was the one who'd really killed her brother. Diego was just a hotheaded boy she had manipulated. She might've already killed Roxi. If Abby pulled the trigger, the world would be better off. Hunter's death would be avenged. Wasn't that what she wanted? To make his killer pay?

Yes.

She had prayed for help, and the chance to serve justice was now in her grasp. She thought of every police call where she'd arrived too late to save anyone. Irene was all the perps she hated.

She killed Hunter.

Tears pushed into Abby's eyes. She couldn't risk this woman getting off through the court system. How many criminals had she seen hire hotshot lawyers like Michael and get away with an insanity plea or some other kind of loophole? Someone once told her it was better to let ten guilty men go free than to lock up one who was innocent. She wasn't so sure anymore.

Sweat trickled into her eyebrows. If this woman got away, she'd never forgive herself. Justice was too important. Justice for Hunter.

Abby cursed under her breath again. What was she waiting for? If she were ever to do anything meaningful as a cop, let it be this! People would understand. It was self-defense. Irene shot the girl, then turned on Abby. No one would blame her, and maybe Kat would finally look up to her real mother.

She was squeezing the Beretta so hard, she could feel her pulse in her fingertips. She saw herself doing it, actually shooting this woman and watching her fall. She saw herself standing over Irene's body, saw the bullet hole in her shirt, the blood. But what then? Would the rage disappear? the grief that cut at her every time she thought about her brother?

Her tears fell, and she couldn't stop them. No. Hunter would still be dead. Abby's heart cried for justice, but when she pictured him looking down on her from somewhere up in heaven, his image stopped her.

Self-defense was one thing, and if it came to that, Abby wouldn't hesitate to take Irene down. But could she ever expect to teach her daughter right from wrong if she shot this woman in cold blood? If she killed Irene, how could she ever look Kat in the eye again?

Despite all the gray areas that seemed to prevail for criminals and cops alike, black-and-white still existed somewhere inside her. And she knew exactly which color this act would be. She would always know.

Abby stepped out from behind the tree. "Police! Drop your gun! *Now!*"

Irene's head jerked toward her.

"Drop it, or I *will* shoot!"

❧

As soon as the double yellow line became broken, Jan passed the cattle truck at seventy-five without hesitation. Only a few days ago she'd picked Roxi up on this same road. If she'd known all that would happen, would she still have stopped? There was no doubt in her mind that she would have.

Jan barely slowed as she crossed the railroad tracks. *Father, give me another chance to help her. And show her how much You love her, Lord. No matter what she's done, I ask You to protect her.*

❧

Facing off against someone with a loaded gun was something they taught about at the academy, but nothing could really prepare an officer for it. One wrong move and she'd be dead.

It was all Abby could do to keep her focus on Irene and not look down at Roxi for signs of life. Was she still breathing? *If You really care, God, don't let this girl die. She's just a kid.*

"Drop the gun!"

Suddenly Diego and Christy were beside her. Diego took one look at Roxi lying on the ground and charged toward his mother screaming, "What did you *do?*"

He lunged for Irene's arm, threw it up in the air, and twisted the gun out of her hands. He flung it into the woods, and Abby heard the metal *clack!* when it hit rock.

She holstered her own gun and rushed into the clearing after him. She was on Irene in seconds. The woman's eyes widened in shock as Abby punched her in the stomach as hard as she could. Air whooshed from Irene's lungs, and she doubled over.

"That's for my brother," Abby said.

She kneed the woman in the face and felt something crunch. "That's for Roxi."

Grabbing Irene by the nylon fabric of her coat, Abby threw her face-first to the ground, wrenching both of the woman's arms behind her back. She twisted them much harder than necessary. Irene groaned, and Abby felt Christy's hand squeeze her shoulder.

She forced herself to relax her grip on Irene ever so slightly. She nodded at Christy. "Check the girl."

Christy rushed over to where Roxi lay on the ground, but Diego was already holding her in his arms.

"I'm sorry, Rox. I didn't know she'd ever . . ." His face contorted in anguish. "I didn't know."

"Is she okay?" Abby craned to see, holding her knee firmly in Irene's back. "Where's she hit?"

Diego didn't answer. He was crying openly, and Abby saw him again as he really was—a scared boy who'd had a stupid lapse in judgment. He hadn't meant to shoot Hunter. It really had been an accident, like Roxi said.

Christy stood. "We gotta get her to a hospital fast."

Abby finally got a good look at Roxi. The girl's eyelids flickered open. Lines of blood dripped down the side of her ashen face, and her hoodie was soaked at the shoulder area. Abby twisted Irene's arms behind her back tighter than ever. The woman groaned again, but this time Abby didn't loosen her grip.

❧

Jan arrived at the turnoff and skidded her truck to a stop. When she saw the cluster of people marching out of the woods, she rushed to meet them.

Abby was leading the way, firmly holding a woman who had to be Irene Tonelli by the arm. The woman's hands were tied behind her back. A shirtless young man carried Roxi. Someone had wrapped strips of what was probably his shirt around Roxi's head, and bright red blood had already soaked through it. Christy held another blood-soaked cloth to Roxi's shoulder.

Dear Lord, am I too late?

As they walked, Abby threw a bunch of keys at Christy. "Use my car. I'll stay here till the police come."

Jan went into autopilot. She ran to the vehicle and swiped the backseat clear. The young man lowered Roxi into the car, and Jan slipped in, cradling her.

"Hurry," he whispered, then closed the door.

Christy dove into the driver's seat and tires squealed as she swung the car out onto the road and raced them to the hospital, an agonizing forty minutes away.

Roxi whimpered, her face strained with pain.

"It's okay, sweetheart. Everything's gonna be okay. We're gonna get you help as fast as we can." Jan held Roxi's head in her lap, helplessness washing over her. If only she'd heard the girl leave this morning, this might never have happened. But she hadn't been able to protect Roxi any more than she'd protected Trae.

Jan peeled the rag off Roxi's shoulder, and the fabric surrounding the hole in the hoodie instantly glistened. She reached around and felt the girl's back but didn't find an exit wound. Could the bullet have hit an artery? Was it still inside? Jan gently pressed the cloth back onto the wound and held it firmly in place.

God had brought them together for a reason. This girl deserved a chance at a life with people who loved her and who would teach her right from wrong—people who would teach her about Jesus and His perfect love.

Oh, Lord, please let her live.

40

ABBY DIDN'T GET TO THE HOSPITAL until six o'clock. Her cell phone battery had died, and she'd had no contact with anyone since late this morning. The last she heard, Roxi was getting a CT scan.

She walked through the automatic doors and found Christy in the waiting room with Keith Mercer. Both of them held Styrofoam cups and were laughing about something. A good sign.

"How is she?" Abby asked.

Christy gave her a hug. "She's gonna be okay. The bullet just grazed her head, and the one in her shoulder missed everything important. She lost a lot of blood, but she'll survive."

Abby sighed. "That's the best news I've heard all week."

"She's a tough kid," Keith said, and there was pride in his voice.

Dropping into one of the hospital's orange vinyl chairs, Abby slid down and rested her head on the back of the seat as exhaustion washed over her.

It was over.

The cops had questioned her for hours, and she'd told them everything she knew. After hearing Abby's story, the first responding officer had taken Irene, cuffed her, and put her in the back of his patrol car. She'd refused to answer his questions.

Abby had stood with a shivering Diego by the RV while the officer radioed for backup. They didn't speak, but Abby took off her jacket and gave it to him. He'd hesitated to accept it, but she'd held it out until he did.

"Is she awake?" Abby asked.

"Not yet. Jan's in with her now."

Christy sat beside Abby. "You okay?"

"I will be. Eventually."

"You did the right thing," Christy said. "You saved her life. If you hadn't been there, Irene would've shot her again."

At least that was one thing to be thankful for. Irene wouldn't hurt Roxi anymore. Between the felony murder charge, attempted murder, and maybe even the reopening of her ex's case in light of this one, the woman probably would spend the rest of her life behind bars.

Abby wasn't so sure about Diego. He would do time too—no DA in his right mind would let him walk for something like this—but if he was tried as a juvenile and a case was made that he was coerced, he might experience freedom again someday.

But how would the authorities deal with Roxi? Abby had told Jan and Keith the truth yesterday. In the law's eyes, Roxi was just as guilty of the felony murder as Irene. But the DA also had some wiggle room. Chances were she'd have to pay somehow, but maybe not like Diego and Irene.

"The cops are gonna want to talk to her," Abby said, noticing an officer loitering in the hallway.

"Will they let us take her home?" Keith was looking the part of a worried parent, and Abby found herself glad Roxi would have this couple on her side.

"I really don't know."

"She's just a girl," Keith said.

Abby got up and asked the receptionist for a piece of paper and pencil. She scratched a name and number on it and gave it to Keith. "That's the best defense lawyer I know. He's out of state, but he can get licensed here to help you."

Keith stared at the paper longer than needed. When he finally met her eyes, she knew what he was thinking. She'd seen it before on more than one desperate face.

"Don't worry," she said. "I wouldn't be surprised if he does this pro bono."

Keith's expression relaxed. "Old friend?"

Abby smiled. "Ex-husband." And despite their differences, Abby knew that deep down, he was a good man.

❧

Roxi woke up to the pungent smell of disinfectant and bandage tape. It was an odor she'd never forgotten. Eight years ago as a scared little girl, it had been branded on her senses.

She reached up and touched the side of her head, covered with soft gauze. For a second she couldn't remember what had happened, but then it all came pouring back. The last thing she remembered was running from Irene. How did she get here?

Jan was sitting beside her in a molded plastic chair, an open book in her lap. Her head was bowed. Roxi watched her for a moment. When she faced Irene back in those woods, she'd wished Jan was with her. But now Roxi felt ashamed. This woman had tried to help her, and what had she done? She'd run away.

Roxi shifted in the bed. "What . . . happened?" Her voice came out raspy, and it hurt to swallow.

Jan was immediately out of the chair and standing beside her. Roxi licked her parched lips, and Jan helped her sit up and take a few sips of water from a clear plastic cup, then gently eased her back onto the pillow.

Roxi winced. It felt like someone had clobbered her in the head with a baseball bat, and she couldn't move her left arm without a zap of pain. "It hurts."

Tucking a stray chunk of Roxi's hair behind her ear, Jan smiled at her. "You're gonna be okay. The bullet didn't make it past your hard head, my dear. They operated and took out another one in your shoulder. It barely missed a major artery. You'll need therapy to get all the range of motion back, but they might release you as early as this weekend."

"How did you find me?"

"Stan Barlowe called me. He thought something might be wrong when he saw you leave in that van with the RV. Abby and Christy were coming into town from the other direction to look for you, and they saw the RV on the side of the road. It was actually Abby who kept Irene from . . ." Jan paused, blinking fast a couple of times. "We're all really glad you're okay."

An awkward moment passed between them, and Roxi couldn't meet Jan's eyes. She knew she'd hurt the woman with her disappearing act. "I didn't want to leave this morning. I really didn't," she finally said. "But I couldn't let you sell your cabin. Not for me."

A puzzled expression flashed across Jan's face.

"I . . . I overheard you and Keith talking."

Jan shook her head, placing a hand on Roxi's. "Oh, honey. Is that why you left?"

"I know how much it means to you."

"Sweetheart—" the older woman gently squeezed her fingers— "you mean more than any old cabin."

"But you don't even know me, not really."

"I know all I need to know. Maybe someday, when you're ready, Keith and I will earn your trust. If you want that."

She closed her eyes for a second, then opened them again. Was it even possible? "I'm not a good kid, Jan. No matter how hard I try, I always get in trouble. I always mess things up. I'm not worth your time. I'll just disappoint you."

"Listen," Jan said softly, "I want you to understand something. I've known you weren't telling me everything from the moment I picked you up. I knew you weren't eighteen. I knew you had nowhere to go. But that didn't matter. I saw a young girl who needed someone to help her. That's what I still see."

"I don't—"

"No, wait. Let me finish. I know there may be things you still haven't told me. But I also know you have a good heart. Don't let anyone, including yourself, tell you otherwise."

"How can you say that?"

Jan looked her right in the eye. "Because I love you."

Roxi felt her throat constrict. Ever since Jan had said it outside at the corral last night, she'd wanted to believe it. But she couldn't let herself. If she did, it would only deepen the wound when she lost Jan like she'd lost everyone else. But the woman was still here, wasn't she? She'd had the chance to give up on her, and she hadn't.

A tear dripped down Roxi's cheek. She'd tried so hard to be strong and independent, to not need anyone or anything. But for as long as she could remember, there'd been this void inside her—a longing for something or someone she couldn't explain.

Jan wiped the tear away with her fingers.

"How can you love me? After what I've done?"

Jan took a deep breath, then let it out slowly. "Let me tell you a story, Roxi. I think it might help. When I was growing up, I knew this girl who grew up in a loving family. She had everything going for her. Nothing to worry about. Everyone thought she was perfect. She got good grades, was popular at school, did everything people expected of her. She went to church and even helped out in Sunday school. But when she turned sixteen, your age, she was tired of playing things safe and started questioning everything. She thought she had all the answers."

Looking off into space, Jan turned grim. "She started hanging out with kids at school who encouraged her to do things she never would've tried before. She smoked her first joint that year, had her first of many beers. Her parents guessed something was wrong, but they didn't realize all that she was doing. When they tried to talk to her, she would tell them what they wanted to hear, brushing off their concerns. They were just parents. What did they know? Her new friends were the ones she listened to. They had the answers."

Roxi wondered how a girl with a loving family could do that. She would've shaved years off her life to have parents who cared.

"One night after her mom and dad went to bed, she snuck out of the house," Jan continued. "Her friends picked her up at the end of her driveway, and when she got in the car, she could smell they'd been drinking. Most of them were already drunk. For a moment the girl hesitated, but she quickly shrugged it off as the leftover influence of her controlling parents." Jan's voice got quiet. "If only she'd listened. She went with them to their usual hangout, and soon she was drunk too. Someone asked her to drive the car home, and she did. She didn't see the deer that jumped in front of the car before it was too late."

Roxi suddenly looked up at Jan, realizing what that meant.

The woman nodded. "The car rolled several times, and when

it stopped, two of her friends were hurt so badly, they each spent a month in the hospital. The third friend almost lost his leg, and to this day it's an inch shorter. The fourth friend . . . she was dead."

"Dead?"

"At the scene. And you know the irony? The girl, the one who was driving, she walked away with nothing but a few scrapes."

The tragedy of the story shrouded both of them, and Roxi didn't know what to say. She understood what that girl must've gone through, the guilt she must've endured. To be the one at the wheel . . .

"What happened to her?" she asked quietly.

Jan squeezed her hand again. "The girl was me."

Roxi felt her mouth open in surprise.

"Sweetheart, I know what it's like to mess up." Jan smiled sadly. "But my parents never stopped loving me. It was the only thing that helped me go on. If you want us to, we'll fight with everything we have to keep you here with us."

Jan leaned down and kissed her on the forehead. It was then Roxi remembered the fantasy she used to have, about waking up and finding her life had been a bad dream and she really did have a mom and dad who cared about her.

Maybe it wasn't a fantasy anymore.

41

"I ALMOST FROZE TO DEATH UP THERE," Christy said, pointing at the hill in the distance. "It's called Squatter's Mountain."

The setting sun painted the mountain a beautiful shade of red, and Abby stared at it with Christy and May. She wondered what the view would be like from up there. It faced the larger, rockier Spanish Peaks, and she imagined it was something you'd have a hard time forgetting.

When they got back from the hospital, there was only an hour of daylight left, and all Abby had wanted to do was crash. The three of them sat in wooden chairs on the front porch with Diet Cokes and their feet propped up on old feed buckets.

Abby knew a little bit about Christy's accident from what she'd told her during their drive to the bookstore. A year and a half ago the woman had been riding a horse on that mountain in dangerous weather conditions, trying to escape Vince. The horse slipped and fell, knocking her unconscious and severely injuring her ankle.

"I was so scared I'd lost her," May said. "By the time we found her, she was hypothermic and in shock."

"It was the most pain I've ever experienced," Christy went on. "I still limp a little."

"Haven't noticed," Abby said.

Christy chuckled. "Good."

"So I hear you and God had a little heart-to-heart up there."

"When you realize you're gonna die, you take stock real fast. I just assumed God didn't want anything to do with me. I realized later I'd been trying to fill a God-shaped hole in my life with everything *but* God."

Christy's gaze drifted toward Squatter's Mountain again. Shadows were now engulfing the hill in an inky embrace. "I didn't know for sure He was what I needed until I actually broke down and accepted what Jesus did as something for *me*. It was hard because of all the stuff I'd done. May had told me He loved me, but I didn't understand how it was possible."

"What changed your mind?"

"Her, mostly." Christy reached over and patted her sister's arm. "She treated me like a prodigal, giving me nothing but love and acceptance."

Abby smiled at both of them. Their sisterly affection for each other was touching. "You know, you two are the only Christians I've ever known who haven't tried to shove God down my throat. I appreciate that. I've thought more about God in the last week than I have in twenty years."

She leaned back in her chair and took in a breath of the clear mountain air. Had she ever grasped the real concept of faith? If someone had asked her, she would've said yes. But it would've been based more on knowing the right answers than truly believing in something. She wasn't sure whom she trusted more—herself or God.

"Sometimes we make things way too complicated," May said.

"Life *is* complicated." Abby lifted her hands in the air. "I wish I could be like you guys and have your childlike faith. I really do. But it's hard for me to believe in something I can't see."

Christy nodded. "This is all still new to me too. I don't understand why God set it up the way He did. But, Abby, it took nearly dying for me to realize I couldn't do it on my own anymore. Don't wait until something like that happens. Trust me, it's not worth it."

"Mountaintop experiences aren't all they're cracked up to be?"

Christy laughed. "I'm serious."

"I know you are. I'll think about it."

"Good enough for me."

May went inside and came back with three oversize sweatshirts. Abby slipped one on over her T-shirt, glad for the warmth. When the sun dropped in this dry climate, no matter how hot it was during the day, evening would always bring coolness. Squatter's Mountain had disappeared into the darkness, and a few stars sparkled like flecks of silver glitter.

Abby tilted her head back and finished off her Diet Coke. She still felt shell-shocked over all that happened. She was glad Roxi was going to be okay, but this wasn't exactly the ending she'd expected. It was all so messy, but at least Hunter's killer was caught.

Now she had to face returning home to an empty house. She knew what would happen soon enough. She'd throw herself back into her job, be the sport who took the overtime and worked holidays for the guys with families. It was an empty life, and she knew it.

She was the first to spot headlights bobbing their way down the ranch's long driveway.

"Think that's the Mercers?" Abby asked.

"I doubt it," Christy said. "I'm sure they're still with Roxi."

All three women relaxed in their chairs, watching the vehicle approach. Only when it drove under the yard light did Abby realize the car was a white Ford Expedition. She almost cursed. "Did you tell my dad I was here?"

Christy glanced at May, then met Abby's glare. "I called him about the arrest."

Abby shoved herself out of her chair. She was sick and tired of trying to make things right with her father. There was nothing to say to him anymore.

The Expedition eased to a stop. Her father got out and slowly walked toward the porch. His shoulders seemed to be permanently slumped these days, but when he saw Abby, she thought he smiled.

Abby stood at the top of the porch steps and shoved her hands into her jeans pockets. "What are you doing here, Dad?"

He took off his tweed touring cap. "I came to talk to you."

"Did you call? I didn't get any messages if you—"

"No, I didn't call. I needed to see you in person, Ab. Could we . . . ?" He gestured toward the porch.

She didn't have the energy for an argument with her father—and certainly not in front of her new friends. "Dad, I'm awfully tired."

Her father's shoulders deflated a little more; then with a nod he reached into his coat and pulled out a wad of papers. He tried to hand them up to her. "I found a buyer for the store."

She shook her head.

"Just take a look."

"I'd rather not." Abby glanced back at Christy and May. They had both stood and were edging toward the door to the house. This wasn't the time or the place to air the family's dirty laundry. She was a guest here, for crying out loud.

"Listen, I think you'll—"

"Hunter's killer hasn't spent a night in jail and you pick *now*?"

He opened his mouth to respond, but she held up her hand. "I'm telling you, this isn't a good idea."

Christy and May slipped inside, and Dad came up onto the porch and sat in the chair Christy had just vacated. Abby crossed her arms. Of all the . . . Was her father *that* insensitive?

"I understand you're upset with me," Dad said.

She held back the response she wanted to say and forced herself to count to ten. This man was her father. She should be thankful they were at least talking. But how could he do this on tonight of all nights? Was this how it was always going to be between them?

"I'm sorry," Dad said. He was still holding the papers. "For everything."

"I'm really not interested in who bought the store, okay?"

"I think you might be."

The way he said it made her try to meet his eyes, but his expression was hidden in a shadow.

Abby slowly sat down in the chair beside him, rubbing her eyes. "Do you have any idea how much that place meant to Hunter?"

Her father set the papers in her lap. Shaking her head, Abby finally glanced at them. And there, illuminated by the dim light coming through the living room window, she saw her own name.

Dad was grinning. "I'm selling it to you. For a dollar. You just need to sign right here."

She had to reread her name three times before his words started to sink in. "I . . . I don't understand."

"Remember when you talked about finding someone to run it who would honor Hunter's dreams? I know of no one better to do that than you."

"Dad, I . . ." She swallowed back the emotion gushing up her throat, suddenly embarrassed about how she'd reacted. "I'm sorry too. I haven't treated you the way I should."

He let out a long sigh. "I'd love the chance for us to start over."

Abby couldn't speak. She tried, but nothing seemed adequate. How many years had she longed for something like this? for just a hint of understanding between her and her father?

"I could do that," she finally said.

The reality of what he'd done for her suddenly became overwhelming. Run a bookstore? She knew nothing about the business anymore, lived hundreds of miles away. . . . She had a job and a daughter she was not giving up on. She started to voice her worries, but Dad just chuckled.

"What?" Abby smiled.

"You'll do fine," he said. "You've got a good head on your shoulders. And you can do whatever you want with the place. Hire somebody to run it for you, whatever. I know it's what Hunter would've wanted."

Abby let a long moment pass. She stood, and so did Dad. Side by side they stared out into the darkness, and Abby realized how much she'd missed having this man in her life. She also realized for the first time how much she was like him, and she hesitated to voice the question on the tip of her tongue.

"But is this what *you* want?" she finally whispered.

Without a word her father reached out and gave her a sideways hug.

Epilogue

ROXI SAT ON HORSEBACK between Jan's and Keith's mares, taking in the view of the Spanish Peaks as she had during her first ride here on this ranch. There was more snow on them than before, and she wondered what it would be like around here during the coming winter. She still couldn't believe she might actually have the chance to find out.

A cool wind played with her hair, and the hint of dry grass and warm horse met her nose. So much had changed. It had been two weeks since they released her from the hospital, and she'd surprised herself by feeling comfortable enough today to ride with her arm in a sling.

Roxi stared at the West Peak. It looked so mighty and proud with its rocky crags standing out against the clear blue sky. What Jan said about seeing natural beauty and believing in God made a little more sense now.

Thankfully, the court had granted Jan and Keith temporary custody of her while the legal proceedings ran their course. Her lawyer, Michael Cantrell, seemed hopeful the DA would take into account the special circumstances of her case, but he'd warned her there was still the possibility of her doing time at the Youth Authority. Sitting on a horse between Jan and Keith, she knew somehow it would be all right. No matter what happened.

"Here's a good place," Keith said, dismounting from his horse. He helped Roxi do the same. She still needed help getting off and on, and she winced as she hit the ground.

Keith gently rested his hand on her back. "You okay?"

She nodded and patted her leg for Selah to join her. The dog was having the time of her life running alongside the horses, sometimes darting ahead of them after a jackrabbit or ground squirrel that dared to cross her path. Roxi had been worried about her accidentally getting kicked, but she seemed to sense the danger of the horses' hooves and kept well out of their way.

Keith spread a colorful Native American blanket on the ground, and Jan dismounted and brought over her leather saddlebag stuffed with a picnic lunch of roast beef sandwiches and homemade potato salad. They sat on the blanket, and Keith reached for her and Jan's hands. He closed his eyes.

"Father, thank You for protecting Roxi and bringing her back here safely to us. We appreciate that more than we can ever say." He squeezed her hand, and she felt a warmth travel through her that had nothing to do with the temperature. "We know there are still things we have to deal with down the road, but we choose to trust You to help us."

Keith paused, and Jan took up the prayer. "We ask You for wisdom, Lord," she said. "Help the three of us each step of the way. Show us what to do in everything. And thank You for this great food."

"Amen," Keith said.

Roxi just smiled. *The three of us.* Had a nice ring to it.

❧

Not only has renowned used bookstore Dawson's Book Barn changed ownership, but it's also changed names. At its grand reopening ceremony on Saturday, new owner Abby Dawson and freshly appointed store manager Christy Williams unveiled a new sign for the store, created by local craftsman Jared Morgan. The historic landmark, which made headlines earlier last month when the owner's son and former store manager Hunter Dawson was tragically killed in a robbery gone bad, will now be called Hunter's Book Barn in honor of the deceased. Ms. Dawson explained to a crowd of book-loving patrons, "Hunter was the best brother anyone could ask for. This store was his dream. And while the Barn won't ever be the same without him, I hope to make him proud."

Dawson and Williams also revealed plans to partner with local coffee shop The Daily Grind to open a full-service franchise inside the bookstore. "It was Hunter's latest dream," Williams said with a smile before ceremonially unlocking the front door for the first eager customers.

CLIPPING FROM THE *LONGMONT TIMES-CALL*

A Note from the Author

ON SEPTEMBER 3, 1999, a young man was arrested for a series of rare book thefts in California. He had stolen the books from used bookstores and sold them to other stores. According to police, the man usually posed as a customer and often returned to the bookstores five, six, or even seven times. He'd also managed to get into locked display cases. Sometimes he purchased an inexpensive book while hiding a stolen book under his shirt. He hit bookstores all over the country, and because of his all-American good looks, quiet manner, and knowledge about antiquarian books, he didn't arouse suspicion from owners.

And thus Irene and Diego Tonelli's little family business was born in my imagination. Unfortunately this isn't a far-fetched scenario. I've been involved in the used and rare book field for over twelve years, and I've seen just how far book dealers will go to get their hands on one rare title.

Most people picture used booksellers as highly educated, scholarly folk who puff on pipes and engage in long, literary conversations. I've certainly met some very intellectual people in the antiquarian book world, but I've also met dealers who have no qualms about doing whatever it takes, even stealing, to survive. And that's what it's all about for so many of them—survival. Many book dealers live hand to mouth. One rare book could put gas in their car and food on their table for months.

A couple of years ago, the renowned used bookstore Baldwin's Book Barn in West Chester, Pennsylvania, made national news when they discovered a rare first edition of *The Great Gatsby* in a box of books someone had donated to their store. It was valued at anywhere from thirty to one hundred thousand dollars. I thought it was the perfect book to feature in this story. In fact, all of the rare book facts and values in my novels are real.

Something else I didn't make up is Roxi's broken heart and her search for love. It saddens me that so many teens today find themselves in her situation. If you take away one thing from *Bound by Guilt*, may it be the challenge to look past outward appearances and reach out to a hurting teen in your life. Teenagers, even those with tattoos and nose rings, need people like you and me to love them for who they are. I hope we can be Jesus' hands and feet and love this generation unconditionally.

About the Author

C.J. began writing the story that would become her first novel, *Thicker than Blood*, when she was a fifteen-year-old homeschool student. Later it won the 2008 Jerry B. Jenkins Christian Writers Guild Operation First Novel contest. She has been in the antiquarian bookselling business for over twelve years, scouting for stores similar to the ones described in her novels before cofounding her own online bookstore. In 2006 C.J. started the Christian entertainment Web site www.TitleTrakk.com with her sister, Tracy, and has been actively promoting Christian fiction through book reviews and author interviews. She makes her home in Pennsylvania with her family and their menagerie of dogs and cats. Visit her Web site at www.cjdarlington.com.

Bound by Guilt
Q & A

Where did the idea for *Bound by Guilt* come from?
I read a news article about a young man who'd been arrested in
California for stealing rare books from various bookstores and
selling them to other stores for a profit. I wondered what kind
of story I could build around that idea. For many years I'd also
wanted to write about someone who suddenly found herself with
nowhere to go and nothing but the clothes on her back. What
would she do? How would she survive? These two ideas propelled
the story.

Why did you choose to deal with guilt in your book?
When I started writing this novel, I didn't have a specific theme
in mind. I had a few elements of the plot and several characters
I wanted to include. But most of the story came about organically

as I wrote. My working title actually wasn't *Bound by Guilt*. What's really cool is that when my editor suggested that title, I stepped back and looked at the story and realized how perfectly it fit. Even the first line, which was written long before we had the title, is about guilt! However, this story is also about forgiveness in a big way. How do you become free from guilt? By being forgiven. There are characters in the story who desperately need to forgive, and there are those who desperately need to receive forgiveness. The wonderful thing, as we see in the Scripture Gordon shares with Roxi, is that not only can God forgive our sins, but He can forgive the guilt of our sins too.

Did you have a sequel in mind when you finished your first book, *Thicker than Blood*, or did you write the sequel because of reader interest?
I wrote most of this novel before *Thicker than Blood* was ever contracted. I didn't set out to write a sequel, but I loved the settings I'd introduced in my first novel and wanted to know what happened next to the characters.

Do you form emotional attachments to your characters?
My characters are real people to me. I might see someone walking down the street and think, "Wow, she really looks like Roxi." It can be hard to finish a book because it's like saying good-bye to close friends. I sometimes have to remind myself they're imaginary!

Which character is your favorite in *Bound by Guilt*?
Roxi. Wounded characters like her touch my heart. But I also really like Jan Mercer. The scenes with Roxi and Jan together were my absolute favorites to write.

Your stories focus on the world of antiquarian books. How did you research this?
I've been involved in the rare book industry since I was seventeen. My sister and I began book scouting for local stores, and within a year or so, we started our own online bookstore selling directly to consumers. Much of what I write regarding rare books comes from personal experience or from something I've heard in my travels. I've been to book sales all across the country, from California to Connecticut, and I'll tell you: book dealers are a colorful group!

During your travels to scout books, what was the most intriguing situation you've experienced?
What sticks out in my mind is the book that got away. Every book dealer has a story like this, and they're painful to hear. Mine was when we found a first edition copy of *The Velveteen Rabbit* that even had its very rare dust jacket. Unfortunately we didn't know how rare it was. We listed that book at an online auction site for three hundred dollars, and we were thrilled when it sold. Years later I realized we could've gotten ten times that—or more.

How do you "get into the heads" of difficult characters such as Vince in *Thicker than Blood* and Irene in *Bound by Guilt*?
I actually find writing the bad guys easier in some ways than writing the good guys. But I almost never get them right the first time. In the rough draft of this story, for example, Irene was very one-dimensional. We didn't understand why she was doing what she was doing. I had to dig deep into her character and ask myself to really think about her motivations. Much about their characters comes from asking myself what-if questions. And letting my imagination run wild.

Your writing reveals a deep affection for and an understanding of animals. Have you always felt this?

I love animals. I grew up with dogs and cats, and at one time we had a pony and a miniature donkey too. Selah was actually inspired by my whippet mix, Story, whom we rescued. Did you catch how Selah's story actually parallels Roxi's? They were both thrown away and forgotten, had trust issues, and needed someone to love them. One of my favorite quotes is: "Dogs are not our whole life, but they make our lives whole." That applies to all the animals we love.

What do you hope readers take away from this book?

I hope they'll be challenged to look past outward appearances and see people, especially teens, the way God sees them. Love them for who they are with no strings attached. Love them even when they make mistakes. Love truly does cover over a multitude of wrongs.

If God gave an endorsement of this novel, what do you hope He would say?

My biggest hope would be that He would say, "I can use this book to stir people's hearts."

Will there be a sequel to *Bound by Guilt*?

I'm currently writing a third book that is closely connected to both *Bound by Guilt* and my first novel, *Thicker than Blood*. We'll see what happens!

Discussion Questions

If your book club reads *Bound by Guilt* and is interested in talking with me via Skype video or speakerphone, please feel free to contact me by e-mail at cj@cjdarlington.com, and I'll do my best to arrange something with you. Thanks for reading, and you can always visit my Web site, www.cjdarlington.com, for more info, including several fun freebies especially for book clubs.

1. Who feels bound by guilt in this story and why?

2. Which character was your favorite, and which one did you relate to the most? Why?

3. What is Roxi searching for? How do her needs change throughout the book?

4. Talk about your first impression of Irene. Do you think she genuinely cared for Roxi when she took her in? What motivates her, and do you agree with her motivations?

5. What events in Abby's life have changed her the most? How could she have handled them differently? What events in your own life have deeply affected you, and how has God used them to change you?

6. All the characters respond to the tragedy in chapter 6 in different ways. What do you learn from how they react? Do you wish any of them had responded differently?

7. When Gordon gives Roxi his Bible, he shares with her Psalm 32. What does this passage, especially the line about God forgiving the guilt of our sins, mean to you?

8. Abby needs to forgive several people in her life. Who are they, and what's holding her back from doing so? Whom do you need to forgive, and what has been holding you back?

9. How does Roxi's story parallel Selah's? What are the similarities in their journeys?

10. What book-collecting fact sticks out in your mind as the most surprising? What interesting points did you learn about that can make a book more valuable?

11. Different characters show Roxi the love of God throughout the story. Name them and tell how each one affected her. Who in your life needs the love of God? Can you think of a way

to show them God's love with your actions rather than your words?

12. What were your thoughts about Diego throughout the novel? Did they change at all as the story progressed? Does he deserve what happened to him?

13. Should Roxi face any punishment for what she did? What would you most like to see happen to her? Why?